PRAISE FOR *AFTER IMAGE*

"Thrilling and seductive, *After Image* sucks you in with irresistible twists and holds you with its wrenching portrait of difficult love. Years after the disappearance of her wild party-girl stepsister, Natasha can't let go, and her search for the truth leads her straight into Allie's dangerous world of drugs, Hollywood parties, and reckless privilege. With gripping, confident prose, Jaime deBlanc offers readers a powerful vision of sisterhood, found families, and the lies that protect our deepest secrets. A must-read debut."

—Amy Gentry, bestselling author of *Good as Gone* and *Bad Habits*

"A cold case comes calling in Jaime deBlanc's debut novel about the ties that bind and shatter. Four years ago, Natasha's stepsister, a member of a Hollywood power family, vanished. Now clues as to what really happened to Allie—or what Allie might've done—start to surface, and Tash is the one to hunt them down. Because, as deBlanc's suspense novel proves, there is something stronger than money or fame: the unyielding force of sisterly love."

—Jenny Milchman, Mary Higgins Clark Award–winning author of *Cover of Snow* and *The Usual Silence*

"The notoriously troubled child of a Hollywood star disappears and her stepsister struggles to uncover what really happened in Jaime deBlanc's sharp and propulsive debut. *After Image* kept me riveted from the first page to the last, deftly exploring distorted perception, the weight of secrets, and the dark side of fame."

—Allison Buccola, author of *The Ascent* and *Catch Her When She Falls*

AFTER IMAGE

AFTER IMAGE

JAIME DEBLANC

This is a work of fiction. Names, characters, organizations, places, events, and incidents are either products of the author's imagination or are used fictitiously. Otherwise, any resemblance to actual persons, living or dead, is purely coincidental.

Published by Thomas & Mercer, Seattle

www.apub.com

Amazon, the Amazon logo, and Thomas & Mercer are trademarks of Amazon.com, Inc., or its affiliates.

ISBN-13: 9781662520945 (paperback)
ISBN-13: 9781662520938 (digital)

Cover design by David Drummond
Cover image: © Klaus Vedfelt / Getty

Printed in the United States of America

afterimage (n): an optical illusion in which an image persists in the eyes after the original stimulus is gone

CHAPTER 1

January 2017

They've found a woman's body in Turnbull Canyon. Yesterday, on New Year's Eve, a hiker strayed from the trail while chasing after his dog and stumbled across the remains.

I sit on the sofa in my shoebox of an apartment, watching the TV coverage and clutching my phone in my hands. On-screen, a grim-faced police officer speaks to the crowd of reporters gathered at the entrance to the preserve. "From what we can tell, the remains have been there for some time. Years, probably."

A reporter pushes her microphone closer to his face, her manicured fingernails glistening in the sunlight. "Do you think this could be the body of Allie Andersen?"

Allie Andersen. Her name has been spoken so often that it no longer feels private, personal to me. Allie. Al. Als. My sister.

The officer frowns, then glances over his shoulder at the scene behind him. Some policemen are making their way up the trail; others are trudging down. "It's really too early to speculate."

Too early for him. But not too early for the reporters who are swarming, hungry for scraps of a story. Four years ago, the Allie Andersen investigation dominated the news cycle for a solid two months. And if this really is her body—well, that spells higher ratings, doesn't it? The story of the year.

The reporter persists: "The hiker who discovered the body described long, dark hair—"

Against my will, a picture materializes in my mind. Allie's body. Allie's face. What it must look like now.

"We really can't say anything else at this time," the officer says sharply. He shifts restlessly on his feet. It's clear he wants to get back to work. "We'll need results from the lab before we can make any formal identification."

Something about the way he says it—a slight emphasis on the word *formal*—makes me think he knows what they've found. He knows the body is Allie's. He just can't say it out loud.

The reporter turns to talk directly to the camera, her eyes alight. "Four years ago, Allie Andersen—the daughter of acclaimed actress Isabel Andersen—vanished without a trace. At the time, police investigated several people close to Ms. Andersen, including her best friend, Greg Novak, and her college professor James Macnamara. But no charges were ever filed."

Now they're showing footage from the days right after Allie's disappearance. Police cruisers parked outside the yellow stucco apartment building where we lived in college. Me, being walked up the front steps of the building by Detective Ruiz. And of course, no montage of the case would be complete without that clip of Isabel, the interview where Diane Sawyer asks her, "And what would you say to Allie if you could see her now?" As if on cue, Isabel's face crumples, and she covers her face with her hands.

On the TV screen, the reporter chatters on: "The Andersen investigation stirred public interest in a way we hadn't seen in this state since the Laci Peterson case in 2002. In the years since Allie's disappearance, her case has inspired a made-for-TV movie, two podcasts, and several popular online forums."

Images continue to flash across the screen, photos they've pulled from the archives. Allie at fourteen, walking down the red carpet with Isabel at the Golden Globes. Allie in our freshman year at the LA

College of Science and Arts, sitting on Greg's lap at a table outside Café Bijou. Allie at twenty-one, leaning up against the brick wall of the school's theater department. This is the iconic photo, the one featured on the cover of *People* when they ran a story about the investigation. In it, Allie stands with one foot propped up against the wall behind her, a cigarette resting between the middle and ring fingers of her left hand. A wisp of smoke leaks from between her lips. She's looking directly at the camera with an expression that's angry—or is it flirtatious? It's hard to tell.

It's one of the better photos I've ever taken.

The reporter yammers on: "After four years of heartache and unanswered questions, the family of Allie Andersen still has no closure. Is it possible, with the discovery of a body in a lonely canyon, that we may now finally—"

I mute the TV, then force myself to loosen my grip on my phone. I've been holding it so tightly that red lines have become etched into the palms of my hands. Shakily, I press a finger to the phone's screen. I already have Detective Ruiz's number pulled up; I did that as soon as the news clip started playing.

More than anyone, it's Ruiz I want to talk to, Ruiz who will be able to tell me what's going on. He'll be calm but straightforward. He'll tell me what I need to know.

My finger hovers over his number. All I have to do is press it, and I'll hear his voice on the other end of the line. Instead, I find myself glancing down at our call history. My last call to him more than two years ago. Ruiz doesn't want to hear from me, not anymore. And I'm not sure, after everything that's happened, that I can bear to reach out to him.

I stare at his number for a full minute before I set the phone down on the coffee table and let the screen go dark.

CHAPTER 2

January 2013

In the interview room, Detective Ruiz slid a Styrofoam cup across the table to me. Coffee, watery and weak. It was hot, though, and I wrapped my hands around the cup, hoping it might stop my shivering.

His partner settled into the seat beside him, a pair of green-rimmed spectacles perched on top of his bald head. Detective Golanski was in his late fifties and built like a prizefighter. The expression on his face said that nothing had ever surprised him. Ruiz, on the other hand, looked like someone who might sit next to me in classes at LACSA. He looked too young to be a cop, let alone a detective. His button-down shirt was a size too large, and his wrist bones jutted out from under his skin.

"So," Golanski said, sliding his spectacles down over his forehead and settling them on the bridge of his nose. "Let's get a few things clarified. When was the last time you saw your stepsister?"

Sister, I wanted to say. *Stepsister* sounded so . . . distant. I thought of the night, a few months before, when Allie had come home drunk and wanted me to stay up with her, talking on the couch, even though I had an exam in the morning and really needed to sleep. Settling her head in my lap, she'd clutched my hand, her rings pinching my skin. "Don't go," she'd said. "I'll feel so much better if you stay." So I'd stayed that way until she fell asleep, her breath warm against my legs.

"Four days ago," I told Golanski. My voice echoed against the walls of the room, sounding small and thin.

He looked at me, then clicked the top of his Bic pen four times. "And the two of you live together?"

Ruiz had a notepad and pen, too, but he wasn't taking notes, just observing me.

"Yes. We share an apartment," I said.

The interview room we were in now wasn't as nice as the first room I'd been ushered into when I came to make my report. That room had been decorated with cheerful posters, couches with yellow cushions. This one contained only one scratched-up table and three metal chairs.

"And you two are close?" Golanski asked.

When I managed to speak, my voice was strained. "She's my best friend."

He frowned. "And you've only just noticed she's gone?"

"No. I noticed before."

Golanski lifted his head from his notebook. "So, when exactly was the last time you saw her?"

"Thursday night," I said. "Around ten thirty."

Another scribble on his notepad. "And where was this?"

"At our apartment." My mind skittered back to that moment, when Allie and I stood in the kitchen, and then I forced myself to pull my focus back into the room. "I thought she was just going out to a friend's house or something."

"A friend? Anyone in particular?"

"Um. Greg, probably," I said.

"Greg Novak?" Ruiz asked. This was the second time he'd heard this story from me. The first time we'd spoken, just the two of us, in the nicer room, his tone had been gentler, more concerned.

I nodded. "He lives about ten minutes away from us."

"Anyone else she could've gone to see?" Golanski asked.

I didn't want to say Macnamara's name aloud. I didn't want to get anyone in trouble. On the other hand, Allie had been gone for four days. "Um, James Macnamara, maybe?"

"Who's that?" Ruiz asked.

"Her English professor."

That got Golanski's attention. "You're saying she went to his house?"

I shrugged, warmth rushing to my cheeks. "I mean, she might have."

"They're close, are they?"

I rubbed my thumb along the edge of the table. When they heard the word *professor*, they probably thought of some old man with a beard. Not someone whose RateMyProfessor profile read like a fan page for a boy band. *Go for the lectures; stay for the baby blue eyes.*

"Yeah, I guess."

Golanski frowned, deep wrinkles appearing on his forehead. "They seeing each other?"

"I mean . . ." I shrugged again. "I don't know." It was a flimsy lie, and I could tell that neither of the detectives bought it.

On his notepad, Golanski made a sharp mark by Macnamara's name. "And you first noticed something was amiss . . . when?"

I took a sip of the terrible coffee, hoping it would ease the tightness in my throat. "The next morning."

"So, Friday?"

I nodded.

"And you looked for her then? Texted her? Called around to friends and family?"

I shook my head. Despite my shivering, I could feel my shirt starting to stick to the small of my back.

"Why not?" Ruiz asked.

"I just . . . didn't."

"Was she in the habit of staying away all night?"

"I mean, sometimes she did," I said.

"And the next day?" Ruiz persisted. "You didn't start calling around then?"

"No."

"Saturday, then?" he asked. "When you saw she was still gone?"

I flushed. It was like he wanted to believe in a better version of me than the one that existed. "No."

"Why not?"

I lifted my hands, a helpless gesture. How could I explain to them the way Allie had left the apartment? The things she'd said? They wouldn't understand. "Allie isn't the most reliable person in the world," I said. "I thought she was just . . . doing her thing."

Golanski raised his eyebrows. "For *four days*?"

I blinked rapidly, then stared up at the ceiling.

"Has she ever gone missing like this before?" Ruiz asked gently. "Have there been previous incidents like this?"

I wiped at my face, embarrassed by my tears. "No. No."

Golanski's gaze felt like a laser on my skin. "So, let me get this straight. Allie goes missing, and you wait four days to report her missing." He paused, resting his pen against his lower lip. "Your best friend."

CHAPTER 3

The images on my TV are still moving silently, people mouthing words I don't want to understand. I slump back against the couch cushions, a familiar sense of nausea washing over me. That day at the police station, I didn't need Detective Golanski to tell me how badly I'd failed Allie. I knew. I knew. That was the reason I couldn't sleep through the night those first six months after I'd reported her missing. As the investigation dragged on, I'd lived with the knowledge that I could have helped the police find her, if only I'd acted sooner. If only I hadn't assumed, that week, that Allie was just being Allie.

That Friday morning, when I'd gotten out of bed, I'd seen Allie's closed door at the end of the hall and figured she was holed up in her bedroom, sleeping off a hangover. At noon, I'd ventured down and cracked open the door, leaning my head inside. It was the usual mess in there, but Allie wasn't in her bed. Her rumpled comforter and a pile of pillows had been pushed against her headboard. Quietly, I closed the door and walked away.

She'd probably gone to Luxe the night before, to blow off steam, to join the mash of bodies on the dance floor. And after that, she'd gone home with some guy. Or maybe she'd crashed at Greg's. She and Greg had been fighting recently, but maybe they'd made up. They had that kind of friendship—one minute they were mortal enemies, and the next they were laughing hysterically over margaritas.

A third possibility: she was at Macnamara's. Allie and Macnamara had broken up a few days before, but that wouldn't mean much to Allie, not if she felt like rekindling things. She could be extremely persuasive when she wanted to be.

Since there were a lot of options for where Allie could be—and none of them seemed particularly worrisome—I did nothing.

By Saturday, her absence had become more striking, but I still didn't mention it to anyone. Instead, I went for a long hike in Runyon Canyon. To be honest, I was pissed at her. Staying away from the apartment so long was a cheap stunt. I knew she'd expect me to freak out. She'd anticipate that I'd call around to her friends, maybe even reach out to my mom, or—God forbid—hers. And once Allie returned home and found me worried sick, she'd laugh at how uptight I was being. After all, she was an adult, wasn't she? Couldn't she take off for a few days if she felt like it?

When I got back on Saturday evening and she still wasn't there, I felt a flicker of concern. But I quickly squashed it. *It'll do her good, this time, not to get a reaction. Let her realize, for once, that she's not the center of the universe. That she's just like everyone else.*

It wasn't until Sunday, when I heard a faint buzzing sound coming from down the hall, that I walked back into her bedroom. The room was the same mess it'd been on Friday, but now the disorder seemed unsettling. Without the scent of her perfume and her ever-present cups of coffee, the room smelled stale, abandoned.

With a start, I realized that the edge of her pillowcase was vibrating. For a moment, that seemed impossible, and then I realized that the vibration was also the source of the buzzing noise. After walking over to the bed, I pulled aside the pillow and saw a flash of gold amid the sheets: Allie's iPhone.

Allie never went anywhere without her phone.

I picked it up, pressed the Home button, and saw the incoming call that had just gone to voicemail: Greg. On an impulse, I typed in her passcode and saw a list of missed calls over the past few days. Greg, James, Isabel, Marisol, Giles, Matthew, Greg, Greg, Greg.

It was only then that I started to feel afraid.

⁓

When I can no longer bear watching the talking heads on the TV, I stand up and wander into my cramped kitchen. A small window over the sink looks out onto my neighborhood. North Hollywood, faded apartment complexes interspersed with red bottlebrush and anemic palm trees.

I remember the early days of the investigation, when I'd been racked with guilt, seeing the ripples of Allie's absence spreading through her family. Isabel barely slept. And Isabel's brother, Matthew, lived in a frenetic state, glued to his phone as he spoke to either the media or the police or the private investigator the family had hired. He'd even started calling me, wanting to talk about Allie, about the case.

Matthew had been like a father to Allie when she was young, in the years after Isabel's divorce from Allie's dad. In a magazine profile on Matthew, I'd seen pictures from those days. Photos of Matthew walking through the streets of Rome, carrying a four-year-old Allie on his shoulders. Matthew and Allie sitting under a table at some awards ceremony, sipping orange juice out of champagne flutes. Matthew and Allie wading in sunlit water near a lakeside cabin.

The two of them were so alike. They shared the same dark good looks, the same spiky sense of humor. The same dimple that flashed at the camera when they smiled.

But in the years before Allie went missing, they had barely spoken.

You don't know how terribly I regret that, he told me once. And his voice had broken. *I shouldn't have given up on her like that.*

He meant: Allie's drinking. Her erratic behavior. Both of us, in our own ways, had lost patience with her. And so, had failed her.

Back then, I'd found these conversations with Matthew dizzying. He was a film director, part of Isabel's world, one of those glamorous people who appeared in the pages of magazines. But suddenly he was at the top of my Recent Calls list; he was the one who understood what I was going through. We were both juggling various prescriptions for anxiety and depression, both teetering on the edge of functionality. And together, we began to pick apart every new development in the case with a dedication other people found troubling.

We talked on the phone almost daily. He gave me updates after he'd met with the private investigators, debriefs after gatherings of the Lost and the Missing, a support group for family members of people who'd disappeared. On Fridays, we'd have dinner at his house overlooking the canals in Venice Beach so we could pore over the new evidence in person and I could fill him in on what I'd been reading on the forums.

In the wake of Allie's disappearance, some amateur journalist from San Diego had set up WhereIsAllieAndersen.com, an outgrowth of the hit podcast *She Never Came Back*. Its forums were flooded with comments: people claiming they'd seen Allie, that she'd been kidnapped, that she'd joined a cult.

"That site is completely ridiculous," Matthew told me.

"I know." But I knew he read it, too, despite his disgust. It was hard to stay away. Because occasionally, just occasionally, a snippet of information surfaced that we knew to be real. Facts only someone close to Allie would know. For example: the fact that she'd been sober for months at the time she went missing, or the fact that she'd ruined her phone that October by accidentally dropping it into the toilet at Luxe. One of the commenters, I was fairly sure, had been in Macnamara's writing workshop with Allie—because who else would know what she had worn on the first day of class, a shirt that slid off one shoulder and revealed an expanse of tanned arm?

Even if the forums weren't that helpful, they were at least an antidote to the sluggishness of the police investigation, which was dragging to a standstill. The detectives had nothing new to share with us, but the forums churned with information—mostly gossip and innuendo, but at least it gave me the feeling that *something* was happening. Could happen. At times the forums made me feel like I could—if I really dedicated myself—solve Allie's disappearance all on my own.

I pour myself a glass of water and drink it standing in the kitchen, feeling its coolness trace a path through my insides. Then I set down the glass and run my hands over my face. I should call Matthew now, tell him about the news story. But I can't. He's on his honeymoon in Saint Lucia. With any luck, he's far, far away from a TV screen, enjoying his new life with Chloe.

I close my eyes. Who else can I call? My mother is on a school camping trip with her high school seniors in Joshua Tree. Isabel's filming a movie in Hungary. Allie's father, Giles, is in London. And the friends I've made in law school—well, it's a stretch to call them *friends*. They don't even know my real identity. After the investigation, I started using my mom's maiden name, Barias, tired of the recognition attached to my old name. Natasha Rossi's Delayed Reporting Hobbles Andersen Investigation. Rossi Questioned a Third Time. The picture in the initial newspaper story showed me at my worst—a tall, gawky girl, face devoid of makeup, with a cloud of curly hair in dire need of brushing.

I bite my lip, shutting out the image.

Then my phone buzzes, and my eyes jolt open. I walk over to the coffee table, then lean forward to see the name illuminated on the screen.

Ruiz.

My stomach drops like I've just taken a step off a high dive. If Ruiz is calling, then there's news about the body.

I don't touch the phone. If I don't allow Ruiz to tell me what he knows, then Allie can't be dead. For a few more hours, if only in my mind, she will still be alive.

Coward, Allie says.

Ever since she went missing, I often hear her voice in my head, as clear and real as if she's standing right beside me. A coping mechanism, my psychiatrist says, a way for me to still feel close to her. If that's true, though, why do I so often want to tell her to shut up?

Just get it over with, Tash, she says. *For God's sake.*

Allie never hesitated about anything.

Slowly, I pick up the phone and answer. "Hello?" I'm surprised by how normal my voice sounds.

"Natasha? It's Detective Ruiz." His voice is deeper than I remember.

My eyes sting. He sounds so formal. Every month, he used to meet me at a diner in Santa Monica so he could keep me updated about the case. He kept up that kindness long after there were any new leads to tell me about.

He clears his throat. "I'm guessing you've seen the news."

"Yes." I stare down at the beige carpet, at the shadow cast by the squat coffee table.

"Okay," he says, drawing in a breath. "So. I just want to let you know where things stand. We've taken DNA samples from the body, but it'll take two weeks, maybe more, to get the results."

"What about dental records?" I'm trying to keep my voice steady. There was another body, three years ago, up in Modesto, and from the dental records they'd been able to tell right away that it wasn't Allie.

There's a pause on his end of the line. "Unfortunately, that's not an option in this case."

I don't want to ask him what that means. Already, unwanted images have started to bubble up in my head.

"So that's it? We just have to wait?" Two weeks is unthinkable. I know I won't sleep until the results come in.

He lets out a breath. "I'm sorry. We've got a backlog over here. Everything's taking longer these days. Believe me—I wish it wasn't like this. But . . ." He hesitates.

"But what?"

"There is something that we may be able to do sooner."

"What?"

I hear him shuffling some papers around on his desk. "We've recovered some personal items from the body. It might be helpful if someone who knew Allie could come down and view them. Let us know if anything looks like Allie's." Another pause. "I'm only reaching out because no one else in the family is available right now."

I can't seem to find the words that should come so easily. *Of course I'll come.*

"Natasha, look," he says hurriedly. "You are in no way obligated to do this. I only ask because . . . well, I thought the less time you have to sit and wonder about this, the better."

He knows how this feels. I remember him telling me, once, the reason he got into police work. *When I was a kid, one of my family members was killed. They never caught the guy who did it.*

I gnaw on the edge of my thumbnail. The last thing I want to do is go down to the station, a place where I was treated, at best, like a fool, at worst, like a suspect. But the alternative—sitting and waiting and not knowing—is worse.

"Okay," I say. "I'll do it."

"You sure?" he asks. "Giles said he can; he just won't be able to until—"

"Yes, I'm sure," I answer quickly. And I feel myself getting stronger as I say it. The faster this happens, the less time I'll have to think about having to do it.

I'm already standing up, rifling through the mess on the coffee table for my house keys. I don't feel scared anymore, or sad. This is the part of me that takes over sometimes, the part of me that refuses to feel anything until what has to be done is done.

CHAPTER 4

As I approach the entrance of the police station—a modern asymmetrical building that seems ill suited to its purpose—I catch sight of my reflection in the glass doors. A tall glimmer. Stylish clothes and sleek hair. I look nothing like the girl who walked in here four years ago, frizzy haired and panicked, wearing ripped jeans and an oversize cardigan. The me that was captured so unforgettably by the news cameras. What was the phrase *Entertainment Weekly* used? *Allie's ugly duckling sister.*

In the last few years, I've tried to erase all traces of that Natasha. I've even started wearing makeup, the way Allie taught me. When we were teenagers, Allie used to pester me to pay more attention to my appearance. But I never cared about that stuff. To me, her obsession with looks always seemed shallow. It was only after she disappeared that I realized what Allie had known her whole life: that your looks are your armor, the shield you hold up between yourself and the world.

It's funny—in Allie's absence, I find that I understand her more. I know now what it's like to have a camera shoved in your face, to have your private moments spread across the pages of a magazine. When that's your reality, what you look like is the one thing you can control.

I push open the doors of the police station and take in a steadying breath as I step inside. The smell in here—disinfectant, barely masking body odor—hasn't changed. The woman at the front desk is deep in conversation with a disgruntled man wearing a sleeveless leather vest, so I take a seat in the row of blue plastic chairs against the wall, then text Ruiz that I've arrived.

Be right out, he replies.

I shift in my chair. On the Uber ride down here, I didn't allow myself to think about what it would be like to see him again. But now I feel myself getting jittery. I adjust my shirt, taking comfort in the slide of the expensive fabric against my skin. The shirt is one of the things I bought with the money Matthew gave me for Christmas. I imagine it makes me look older, more sophisticated.

A woman sitting across from me stares intently at me, and I tense. Does she recognize me? It's been a long time since my face was featured on the news, but occasionally, as I'm going about my day, someone will study me as if trying to remember how they know me.

I pretend to be absorbed in my phone.

"Natasha?"

A tall, bearded man has emerged from the double doors next to the reception desk. At first, I think Ruiz has sent someone down to fetch me. And then, as I stand up, I realize that this *is* Ruiz. Those are his gray eyes; those are his broad shoulders.

"Oh," I say, feeling off-balance as I stand up. The beard makes him look older. And he's filled out since I last saw him. He looks like he's been going to the gym, lifting weights.

We don't quite know how to greet each other. A hug is too familiar, but a handshake doesn't feel right either. He settles for a solemn nod, then shoves his hands in his pockets.

"You've changed your hair," he observes.

"Oh. Yeah." Without thinking, I reach up to touch my head. I straightened my hair carefully this morning, transforming the tight blonde curls into straight lines. "A while ago."

There's an awkward silence.

"So . . . ," I begin.

"Well, thanks for coming," he says at the same time.

The man at the front desk starts arguing with the receptionist, and Ruiz catches her eye with a silent inquiry: *Need help?* But she waves him away; she has it covered.

He returns his attention to me. "Shall we head back?"

I nod. And then we walk to the double doors that lead back into the station, Ruiz holding one door open as I walk through it. As he does, I remember the day, maybe a week after Allie went missing, when he drove me back to my apartment after another long interview at the station. When we'd pulled up to a throng of reporters huddled around the apartment entrance, he'd gotten out of the car and walked me up the front steps, one hand on the middle of my back, the other pushing away the reporters' cameras.

That seems like a very long time ago.

"Okay," he says, as we walk down a long corridor, the walls studded with bulletin boards featuring recruitment posters and community notices. "We've got the belongings set out in a room for you. Everything's bagged in plastic. We just need you to look and see if you recognize anything. It'll only take a few minutes."

Ruiz used to wear slacks and a button-down shirt with a tie, but today he's wearing jeans and a flannel shirt with the sleeves rolled up. Of course, it's a Sunday, and New Year's Day. Has he come down to the station just for this?

When we reach the elevators, he punches the Down button, and we stand in silence facing the doors. Just when it seems the quiet will become unbearable, the elevator arrives and we step inside. As the doors close, he says suddenly, "I'm glad it's you who came to do this."

A sudden warmth blooms in my chest.

"You're the person who'll be the most familiar with her clothes, her jewelry," he continues. "Since you were living with her at the time."

Oh. The elevator lurches as we begin our downward descent.

"Yeah, I guess so," I say, focusing on the changing lights on the button panel. Back at the apartment, I convinced myself I was strong enough to come here, to do this, but now I'm wondering if I've made a mistake.

The elevator shudders as we reach the basement level, and then the doors sigh open. This hallway is starker than the one we've just walked through. No bulletin boards or cheery recruitment posters here. This is not a hallway for the general public.

As we walk out under the glare of the fluorescent lights, I focus on details to keep my anxiety at bay. There are six doors on either side of the hall, and two bathrooms—a women's and a men's—at the end of the corridor. In the middle of the floor, there's one long scrape where something sharp has dragged against the linoleum.

The farther we go along the hall, the dizzier I feel. When Ruiz stops in front of the last door on the left, all I can think is: I'm not ready. *I thought I was, Allie, but I'm not.*

Ruiz turns to me. "You sure you're up to this?" he asks.

I nod, not meeting his gaze. "Yup."

Putting a hand on the doorknob, he pauses. "They're not the clothes you reported her going missing in," he says. "But since we aren't sure if she took any clothes with her that night, they could still be hers."

I nod again.

Clothes were Allie's thing. Buying them. Designing them. Making them. The first time I ever saw Allie in a magazine, before I ever knew her, she'd been captured by the cameras at some film premiere she'd attended with Isabel. The caption had read: Isabel Andersen, in Oscar de la Renta, and her daughter, Alastriana, in a dress of her own design. Those words had struck me. In a dress of her own design. What, I wondered, would it be like to have that kind of confidence? Later, when we lived together, I'd sit on her bed as she rifled through her clogged closet, and occasionally, she'd toss an item over her shoulder at me. *Here. You take this.* It would inevitably be something expensive, designer, something I never could've afforded to buy for myself.

Ruiz still hasn't opened the door to the room.

"I'm ready," I say, trying to convince myself as much as him.

He opens the door, and I step past him, bracing myself for what I'm about to see.

In the small, airless room, there's nothing but a stainless steel table with a few plastic bags laid out on its surface. Ruiz stands back, waiting for me to approach the items and look more closely.

I clench my fists, digging my fingernails into my palms. All of a sudden, it occurs to me: I'm twenty-five years old, and it's New Year's Day. In another life, I'm sleeping off a hangover from a party the night before. No plans except for brunch later in the day. But in this life, here I am, standing in a basement, about to look at clothes that have been pulled off my dead sister.

Wow, Allie murmurs. *So sorry my death has thrown a wrench in your weekend.*

I grit my teeth, willing her to be quiet. But she's right. This is no time to wallow in self-pity.

Taking a deep breath, I step up to the table. This should be the easiest thing in the world. All I have to do is look. But it takes a long moment before I can make myself reach out and pick up one of the bags. I start with the smallest. There's a ring inside, with a stone in the setting that might've once been blue but is now caked with something black. Dirt. Or blood.

Allie loved rings; she used to wear three or four at a time, a mix of designer pieces and thrift-store finds.

Something sour rises up in the back of my throat. I swallow it down and force myself to look at the next bag. This one contains a set of copper bangles, bent out of shape. The third bag holds a necklace with a broken clasp.

I feel lightheaded. The room seems to be expanding and contracting around me. But there are still two more bags to go.

In the next one, a red shirt. In the last, a pair of jeans. Both are filthy and slightly charred. Bits of ash gather in the corners of the plastic bags. The body they found in the canyon . . . it must have been burned.

My vision flickers.

I back away from the table, knocking into Ruiz as I turn and push my way out of the room. I make it to the women's bathroom just in time to throw up into the small metal sink. Nothing comes out but a thin trail of liquid, but my stomach still clenches, trying to rid itself of something that isn't there.

Once the spasms stop, I spit a few times and then reach out to turn on the faucet. But I can't see it; I can only find it by fumbling with my hands. Everything in the bathroom has gone black. As I rushed in here, I'd been vaguely aware of beige bathroom stalls, a checkered tile floor. But I can no longer remember the layout of the room, where exactly the door is in relation to the sink.

Fuck. Not now. These episodes began about a month after Allie went missing. The first time it happened, I was at the vigil for Allie on the LACSA campus, in the middle of the quad. One moment, I was standing next to Isabel as she spoke into the microphone; the next, the crowds of people had vanished, as if a black curtain had descended and separated me from them.

Conversion disorder, Dr. Rajmani explained to me later. A psychosomatic response to stress. They used to call it hysterical blindness, before that became an outdated term.

"Natasha?"

It's Ruiz, his voice muffled behind the door.

I manage to turn the faucet on and cup water to my mouth, the cold liquid sliding over my lips.

I hear the door creak open and then his voice again, louder now. "Can I come in?"

I straighten, blinking rapidly, but there's no difference between my eyes shut and my eyes open. I hear Ruiz step into the bathroom, and then the door clicks shut behind him.

"It's not her," I say. "It's not Allie."

There's a long pause. Then he says, "Okay. You're sure?"

Hot tears gather at the edges of my eyes. "The clothes, the necklace—she would've never worn things like that." Department-store stuff. Cheap, generic jewelry. If Allie wore something, it had to be special. It had to stand out.

I feel Ruiz's hand on my shoulder, the sudden contact jarring me.

"It's okay," he says.

"No. It's not." I shake my head, unable to hold back the tears. "You don't understand. I wanted it to be her. I wanted her to be dead."

"You want closure," he says, his voice reverberating against the walls. "Anyone would want that."

I put a hand over my eyes. It isn't just that. Yes, I want closure. But I also want Allie to stop taking over my life. Since the beginning, she did that. And she's still doing it, even when she's not here.

"Hey. Look at me," Ruiz says.

I pull my hands away from my face and turn my head in the direction I imagine his face to be.

"What's going on? Do you need to sit down?"

I can smell the soap he uses, cedar and something else I can't quite place. I feel the warmth of his body as he steps closer to me.

"C'mon, let's get you out of here." He puts a hand on my elbow and tries to guide me toward the door, but I resist.

"I can't."

"What do you mean, you can't?"

My shoulders tense. There are only three people in my life who know about my episodes: my mother, Matthew, and Dr. Rajmani. I'd like to keep it that way. But I can't walk out of the bathroom like this.

"I can't see," I say, my ears turning hot.

"What are you talking about?" he says sharply.

"My vision, it's—" It would take too long to explain, so I just shrug. "I can't see anything right now."

There's a long silence. "You're serious."

I press my lips together. What I'd wanted, today, was to not seem like a train wreck. To seem like a new Natasha.

"It happens sometimes," I say, going for a casual tone. "It'll pass in a few minutes."

"This has happened before?" he says, his voice rising.

"It's not a big deal."

"Jesus. When did this start?"

I close my eyes. The blackness feels less disorienting when my eyes aren't open. "A few weeks after she went missing." In the months after the vigil, I'd be going about my day—washing dishes, making toast—when suddenly the world would simply vanish. Like I'd dropped into some other reality. Which didn't even seem that strange to me, at that point. After all, Allie had vanished, so why not everything else too?

"The episodes hardly ever happen anymore," I say. "Just when . . ." I lean back against the sink, its metal edge pinching my lower back. "The doctor says it's stress related."

Ruiz steps back, and my sense of the room changes. I'm adrift in space.

"Jesus, Natasha. If I'd known about this, I would've never called you down here."

"It's nothing. Really."

I want so badly for that to be true. And I don't want him to be angry with me. So I don't tell him what else Dr. Rajmani has told me. That if I want to get well, I need to stop obsessing about Allie. I need to put as much distance as possible between myself and the investigation.

CHAPTER 5

Ruiz walks me back to the reception area, one hand on my elbow as he guides me down the hall. I hate the way the blindness makes me feel—like, at any moment, I could be sideswiped by something unseen. When we pass people in the hall, I flinch at the sound of their voices.

Finally, we walk through the double doors that lead back into the lobby, and Ruiz eases me down into one of the plastic chairs. "Wait here, okay? I'll be back in a minute."

I settle into the chair, grateful to sit still, and listen to Ruiz's footsteps retreating across the room. There's a TV on the wall in one corner of the lobby. I hadn't paid much attention to it when I came in earlier, but now its noise seems deafening. After a brief mention of the cold front expected to roll in tonight, the newscaster launches into the story of the body found in Turnbull Canyon.

"Although investigators have not yet released much information, we do know that it is the body of a Caucasian female in her twenties, approximately five feet six inches tall—a description that has prompted locals to wonder whether this may be the long-missing Allie Andersen. You remember the Andersen investigation, don't you, Jill?"

"Yes, I do, Darren. What a disturbing case."

"For those who don't remember, Allie Andersen went missing on January 10, 2013." Now they're replaying an old segment I recognize, recorded the same year Allie went missing. Dramatic music plays as a deep voice proclaims: "Allie Andersen, the daughter of acclaimed actress Isabel Andersen, was last seen in a coffee shop on Pacific Coast Highway. She was twenty-one years old at the time of her disappearance, finishing out her junior year at LACSA, where she'd been majoring in costume design . . ."

They're running through the last-known movements of Allie Andersen. But I don't need this refresher. I know the details by heart.

It was ten thirty when Allie left our apartment in West LA that night, wearing vintage jeans, a green silk shirt, and Greg Novak's battered leather jacket.

Thirty minutes later, her image was captured on an ATM camera at the Wells Fargo near Olympic and Bundy. At 11:02 p.m., she withdrew $300, the maximum amount allowed, leaving just $23.17 in her account.

At 11:23, she entered Barclay's, a doughnut shop on PCH near Washington Boulevard, where CCTV cameras showed her ordering a coffee and taking a seat near one of the windows facing the street.

Barclay's wasn't a place you'd expect to see someone like Allie Andersen. The place had stained linoleum floors and scratched windows, and it charged a dollar for a cup of coffee. Allie's order at her usual coffee shop, Café Bijou, was an almond milk latte with extra foam. But at Barclay's, the camera showed her holding a Styrofoam cup of drip coffee, which she clasped between her hands for sixteen and a half minutes, during which time she took exactly two sips.

On three separate occasions, she opened a flip phone she held in her right hand, then closed it again. Eventually she set the phone down next to her key ring, which held a chaotic assortment of keys, her LACSA ID card, and a panda-bear key chain.

At 11:35, two truckers—Roy Tucker and Miguel Hernandez—came in and bought extra-large coffees and a dozen doughnuts. At 11:37, Tucker glanced over his shoulder at Allie and then did a double take. Because he recognized her from the tabloids? Or maybe because—even under fluorescent lights, wearing hardly any makeup—Allie drew attention like a magnet. As the two men left the shop, Tucker took one last look at her before stepping outside into the darkness.

Allie continued sitting at the table until 11:39 p.m., when a call came through on the little black flip phone. She answered the call, listened briefly, said one word—"Okay"—and then walked out of Barclay's, leaving behind an almost-full cup of coffee.

The newscaster's voice continues: "But no one knows who was calling her. Or where she went next."

Cue more dramatic music.

"Where was Allie Andersen going that night? And why? Four years after her disappearance, no one has been able to discover the answers to these questions. And Andersen's fate remains a mystery."

Not for lack of trying, I think.

I tried, Allie, for so many years. But where has it gotten me?

CHAPTER 6

February 2014

In my mother's living room, I typed the WhereIsAllieAndersen address into my browser, then glanced over my shoulder to make sure the house was still quiet. It was three in the morning, so there was very little chance Mom would discover me out here. But if she did, and she saw I was back on the forums, she'd have a fit.

I couldn't stay away from them, though. Allie's disappearance was a mystery that should have been solvable. I thought of all the information, all the technology, at the cops' disposal. But still, they hadn't come up with anything. At this point, it was up to me to keep searching for new clues, new information.

As the WhereIsAllieAndersen website loaded, familiar snapshots of Allie appeared at the top of the page. Allie and me at Carbon Beach, sticking our tongues out at the camera; Allie and Greg and me taking a moody selfie in front of Angels Flight; Allie dancing at Luxe, her eyes glassy and her makeup smudged. Hurriedly, I navigated away from the home page, not wanting to linger too long on Allie's face. It hurt to see how beautiful she looked. How alive.

The main forum page was more soothing—no photographs here, just neatly listed categories: *Overview*, *Suspects*, *New Developments*, *Lingering Questions*. The bluish glow of my computer screen cast an eerie light in the darkened room.

I knew I should stop, go back to bed. Dr. Rajmani had advised me to stay off the forums, especially at night. He felt they were a key factor in my insomnia.

After clicking on the *Suspects* page, I ran my cursor over the names listed in bright-blue font: *Greg Novak. James Macnamara. Natasha Rossi.*

Greg first, I decided. After Allie's disappearance, the police had arrested him. And although they'd later released him—they hadn't had enough evidence to bring charges—he remained the leading person of interest in the case.

Greg's subheading read: *The Best Friend.* The label still rankled. *I* was Allie's best friend—or at least I had been until Greg strolled into her life. The first time he showed up at our apartment, he'd been wearing a worn Psychedelic Furs T-shirt, electric-blue nail polish, and jeans so torn it was a wonder they stayed on his body. He had a line of piercings down each ear and a permanent sulky expression on his face. But nothing could disguise the delicate beauty of his features.

At the top of the page, a paragraph summarizes the relevant facts about Greg.

> Greg Novak argued with Allie the night she disappeared, possibly about money, or Novak's drug dealing, or both. Novak's car—a vintage Porsche 356—went missing that same night and has never been located. (Novak claims the car was stolen, perhaps by Allie herself, along with $200 he had lying around his apartment.) Police questioned Novak extensively during the investigation but were never able to shake his alibi. He attended a party in West Hollywood that night, and four separate eyewitnesses confirmed he didn't leave until dawn.

I scrolled down to the newest comments:

ChrisT: People get sentimental about his friendship with Allie, but c'mon. You're an idiot if you don't think he killed her. HIS CAR WENT MISSING THE SAME NIGHT SHE DISAPPEARED, PEOPLE.

Here's my theory: I think Greg was hanging around Allie for the reasons most people were: she was famous and she had connections. Don't forget that Greg was trying to break into acting. He was totally using their friendship as an "in." When Allie started causing trouble for him, threatening to expose his drug dealing, he killed her. Maybe not on purpose—I think it could have been an accident—but he definitely did it.

Vero88: So tell me how he's supposed to have killed her and disposed of her body while he's also at a party in West Hollywood. Also, the cops went through his apartment and there was no sign of a struggle taking place there.

ChrisT: Uh, except for his blood on the wall!

In Greg's statement to the cops, he'd said that he and Allie had argued the night she went missing, and, in a moment of frustration, he'd punched the wall. Which might have been true. But the blood and his bruised knuckles didn't sit well with the cops.

Beryl85: And those witnesses who saw him at the party? They were all his friends. Or his clients. Greg was selling to practically everyone at LACSA. He could have easily gotten people to lie for him. As for his apartment, let's say he kills her and it's not,

> **like, a blood-spatter type of thing. Like, maybe he strangles her. It's quiet and leaves no trace.**

I worked my jaw back and forth. The people on the forums had no trouble imagining Allie's death in a thousand vivid variations.

I skimmed through the commenters rehashing a variety of theories about that night. The first and most popular: Greg killed Allie in his Porsche and then disposed of the car. The second, he and Allie had a fight; then she stole his car and ran off the road somewhere remote. Least popular, the car just happened to be stolen on the same night that Allie went missing, and the car going missing was a total red herring. That option was treated with some contempt.

> **ChrisT:** That's asking us to believe in a hell of a coincidence. And I'm not a big believer in coincidence. My bet is that the car was covered in Allie's blood, which is why Greg got rid of it.

I swallowed, trying not to imagine Greg's immaculate Porsche stained with blood.

That was the last post in the thread. I knew I should stop reading, but I couldn't seem to help myself. As if propelled by some outside force, I clicked on the *Macnamara* thread.

> **PI-Leo:** Look, he was sleeping with her and she was his student. That gives him the most motive out of anyone. He wanted to break things off, but she could've made a lot of trouble for him if she went public about their relationship. And he was in a boatload of debt. He needed that job.

> **Abraham437:** Well, neighbors definitely overheard their breakup at his apartment on Wednesday

evening—it wasn't quiet. But she left his place at least 24 hours before she went missing.

AJBaltimore: **so? maybe he tracked her down later and the argument continued. imagine: she threatens to tell the administration about their relationship. they argue. he pushes her, she falls and hits her head and is killed by accident. he panics, drives her body out of the city, and dumps it somewhere.**

This was a popular theory, but it was easy to poke holes in it. How had Macnamara gotten rid of all the forensic evidence? Plus, he'd been visiting a friend in San Diego that week, had been with the friend that night. Would it even have been possible for him to drive back to LA, kill Allie, dispose of the evidence, and return for breakfast with his friend the next day?

A headache began to pulse at the base of my skull. Dr. Rajmani was right; my mother was right. I had to stop doing this to myself. I needed to put down the laptop and go to bed. Try to get some sleep. But, as I clicked out of the *Macnamara* thread, I found my cursor hovering over the last name on the *Suspects* list.

Natasha Rossi.

I didn't need Dr. Rajmani to tell me it was a bad idea to read this thread. Still, I only paused a few seconds before clicking on the link. I scrolled quickly down to the most recent comments, avoiding the picture at the top of the page. I'd seen it too many times already: a snapshot of Allie and me at a college party our freshman year. In it, Allie wore a green dress with an asymmetrical neckline and could easily have passed for twenty-one or older. Standing beside her, dressed in jeans and a black tank top, I looked exactly like what I was: a recent refugee from high school. I stood like I wasn't sure what to do with my arms, and my eyes glowed orange in the camera's flash.

At the bottom of the page, I found the newest comments, the ones I hadn't pored over already.

> **ShaunaRose:** I always thought there was something weird about this girl. She had, like, no reaction to Allie's disappearance.

I flushed, as if I were standing in a crowded room rather than sitting alone with only my laptop for company. I'd never known what to do when I was interviewed on camera. It paralyzed me, made me forget the words I meant to say. But that didn't mean I was guilty of anything.

> **Vero88:** The cops thought something was off about her too. I mean, how many times did they interview her?

> **ChandlerEsq:** Because she was Allie's roommate. It makes sense they'd want to talk to her the most.

> **ShaunaRose:** But I still haven't heard a good explanation of why she didn't report Allie missing for 72 hours. That's 72 hours when the cops might've had an actual chance of finding her.

I fought back a wave of nausea, a feeling I experienced so persistently these days that I had difficulty eating. Food just didn't taste good anymore; my body didn't seem to want it.

> **DNAmy:** I think Natasha was jealous as shit of Allie. Allie was everything Natasha wasn't: rich, beautiful, popular. I think she got sick of Allie getting all the attention.

Chazzer: Disagree. I know people who went to LACSA when they were there, and they said they were really close.

ShaunaRose: I heard they weren't that close that last semester. Like, it seemed like something happened between them.

ChandlerEsq: What are you suggesting? Natasha couldn't have killed Allie in their apartment. The cops went over that place with a fine-tooth comb. Also, Allie had like twenty pounds on Natasha. I don't see Natasha overpowering her.

ShaunaRose: Yeah, I don't see Natasha getting violent in that way. But she's scary smart, right? Perfect SAT scores, top of her class. If she wanted to get rid of Allie, she wouldn't be obvious about it. She'd be subtle.

I leaned forward, heat prickling over my skin. These people didn't know me, I told myself. They didn't know anything about me.

ShaunaRose: Look, Natasha knew Allie's weak spots. Her addiction issues. Her history of depression. Maybe it's like the cops initially thought: Allie killed herself. But maybe she got a little push from Natasha first.

The light from the computer screen was too bright, stinging my eyes. Slowly, I lifted my hands from the keyboard and pressed them over my face. And when I took them away, the room had disappeared. The familiar black curtain had descended.

CHAPTER 7

As I sit in reception, listening to the blaring commercials on the TV, my vision begins to return. I can make out shapes and colors now: the blue squares of the chairs across from me, the dark huddle of a man sitting in the far corner of the room. And then the double doors on the other side of the room swing open, and someone walks toward me. I blink as his details begin to solidify.

Ruiz.

I stand up, gathering my purse against my stomach. When he reaches me, I say, "I'm feeling better now." The room is still fuzzy and indistinct, but I could walk through it on my own if I wanted to.

He frowns. "How did you get here today?"

"I took an Uber." I can't drive, not with my condition. Not until I've gone a full year without an episode. Before today, I'd been a month away from that mark. Counting down the days.

He nods, then seems to come to a decision. "I'll drive you home."

"You don't have—"

"I know I don't," he snaps. Then, he tries again, softening his tone. "I'd like to, okay? I'm headed home anyway. I'll drop you off on my way."

He feels guilty, I think, for bringing me down here. For putting me through this.

I follow him out into the parking lot. It's chilly out here, but the sun is bright, reflecting off the tops of the cars. I take in the colors, the textures, absurdly grateful for this simplest of things: my sight. My episodes never last longer than a few minutes. But while they're happening, all I can think is: What if the darkness doesn't end? What if, this time, it stays for good?

When we reach a Jeep—a newer model, glistening black—Ruiz unlocks it with a press of a button.

I hesitate. "What happened to your old car?" He used to drive a battered old Nissan with rips in the seats.

"That thing? It finally bit the dust."

When I get in, I'm enveloped in new-car smell. I run a hand across the upholstery. I don't know why I find it so jarring that he drives a different car, one that doesn't seem to match up with my mental picture of him.

Ruiz opens the driver's-side door and slides behind the wheel but doesn't start the car right away. Instead, he stares straight ahead, through the windshield. "So, these episodes," he says. "Is that why you stopped driving?"

I fiddle with my seat belt strap. Ruiz had noticed, years back, that I wasn't driving anymore, but when he asked about it, I'd told him my Civic had broken down and I couldn't afford to fix it.

"Yes."

He shakes his head slightly, as if irritated. "So what is it, exactly, with this—you called them 'episodes'?"

I buckle the seat belt around me. "My doctor calls it conversion disorder. It's not that uncommon, apparently," I say lightly, as if the episodes don't bother me that much. As if they don't make me feel like I'm losing my grasp on my sanity. "I take pills," I say, marveling at my steady voice. "That stops them, mostly."

"But it didn't today."

"No. Not today." I haven't been taking the Inderal lately. It hasn't seemed necessary. I've been doing so much better.

I wait for Ruiz to say something more. But he just sighs, then turns the key in the ignition and puts the car in reverse. He drives out of the parking lot and onto the street. For a few minutes, it's totally silent in the car.

Finally, when we're stopped at a red light, he says, "So I hear you're in law school now."

I glance over at him. "Where'd you hear that?"

"Matthew."

Of course. Matthew is the one who fields calls from the detectives, acting as a buffer for Isabel, who tends to get emotional whenever new information arises.

"How far in are you?" Ruiz asks.

"This is my first year."

After dropping out of LACSA, I'd had no desire to go back to school. I couldn't see the point. But eventually, with considerable prodding from Mom, I finished my degree through online classes and then worked up the nerve to apply to Loyola Marymount.

"Well, that's great." The light turns green, and he accelerates through the intersection. "I know that's what you always wanted."

Was it? I honestly can't remember. "Thanks," I say quietly.

Now that I'm in law school, I'm not sure I really like it. In my head, it always held a kind of glamour, but the reality involves reading through pages and pages of dry text until my eyes hurt. Still, I've always done well with that kind of thing—logic, memorization, standardized tests—and people expect you to do something worthwhile with skills like that. My mother is elated about this chapter in my life. Some days I think that's reason enough to keep going.

I change the subject before Ruiz can ask anything more. "How's your sister doing?" He has three younger sisters, but it was the youngest he was always worried about: Raquel, with the unpaid parking tickets and the loser boyfriend.

"Oh, she got married," he says, and it's the first time today that I've seen him smile.

"Oh wow." I'd always thought of Raquel as a teenager, but I suppose she's in her early twenties now. "To the loser boyfriend?"

He shakes his head. "No, a new guy. A good guy. She's got a baby now. A little girl."

This, too, feels like the ground shifting from beneath my feet. I don't know how to find my balance with Ruiz anymore. It seems strange that we once talked so easily to each other.

Finally, Ruiz pulls up to the curb outside my apartment building. It occurs to me now that I never told him where I lived. But of course, my address must be on file somewhere.

"Well, thanks for the ride," I say as I unbuckle my seat belt.

"No problem." He turns to me, and for a minute I think he's going to say something else, something that matters. But he just waits a moment, then says, "Take care, Natasha."

As I walk up to the door of my apartment building, I keep my head high, my shoulders straight. The important thing is to hold on to my pride, or what's left of it after my breakdown at the station. I can't allow myself to feel the rest—the horror of those evidence bags, the knowledge that Allie is still missing—until later. Until I know I'm alone.

CHAPTER 8

The elevator stops on the third floor, and I step off into the hallway that leads to my apartment. Gray carpeting stretches from one end of the corridor to the next, and the place smells like cheap air freshener.

Personality-free, Allie observes. *Couldn't you have at least chosen a place with character?*

I wrinkle my nose. Allie never understood what it was to have a budget. Or career concerns. Her grand plans for what our lives would look like after LACSA involved us traveling through Southeast Asia or renting a picturesque apartment in New Orleans. It sounded great, but Allie was ignoring one crucial reality: there was no way I could have afforded to accompany her. My mother and her father had divorced in our senior year of high school, so I was back to living an ordinary person's life, with an ordinary person's budget. My mother expected me to get a job after college, not jet-set around the world, partying with Allie and her friends. Still, I let Allie continue dreaming up ideas. In her mind, I knew, my ability to come along was not an issue. She'd just pay for me. Wasn't that what trust funds were for?

I turn the corner at the end of the hallway, squinting under the overhead lights that make everything look dull, institutional. This apartment complex is decidedly not the future Allie once imagined for me. It's not even the future *I* imagined for me. I don't know what I expected my early twenties to look like, but it definitely wasn't this.

My neighbor Abby emerges from her apartment, her wire-haired Chihuahua clutched in her arms. "Oh, hi," she says when she sees me approach.

"Hi," I say, creasing my face in an imitation of a smile. As soon as she moves past me, I let the friendly expression drop. I'm exhausted, and all I want is to get back inside my apartment, where I can curl up in bed and watch old movies on TCM until my brain goes numb.

But when I near my front door, my footsteps slow. There's something lying across the doormat, a lumpy, dark shape. My breath hitches in my throat, and I remember the early days of the investigation, when I'd come home to find strange pieces of mail on the doorstep, packages from true-crime fans that I had to hand over to the police to inspect. But that was years ago. No one should know where I live now. The name on my mailbox downstairs just says N. BARIAS.

As I get closer, I see that the huddle on the doormat is just a piece of clothing that has fallen in a loose heap. Looking closer, I see the familiar curve of a collar and realize it's my blue coat. Relief floods through my bloodstream. In my rush to get to the police station, I must have dropped it on my way out. I hadn't even noticed I'd left it behind.

I bend down to scoop it up, then let myself into my apartment and toss the coat over the back of a dining chair. I walk down the narrow hallway to the bathroom and open the medicine cabinet. Inside, I find the bottle of Inderal and shake it gently. Only one pill left.

Shit. If I want to refill it, I'll have to make another appointment with Dr. Rajmani. I stopped seeing him months ago, which had felt like a reprieve. I'd gotten so tired of rehashing my thoughts and feelings for his benefit. These last few months, I've come to think another approach is better. Don't stir things up; just let them settle, like sand on the ocean floor. It had been working really well, until today.

I push my hands through my hair, pulling it loose from its neat ponytail. If the episodes are back, I need those pills again. But if I call for an appointment, Dr. Rajmani will want to talk about why the episodes have returned. And I can only imagine the expression on his face if I tell him about today, about going into the police station.

If only there was an easier way to get the pills—no talking about feelings required. If this was four years ago, I'd know exactly how to get my hands on what I wanted. Greg Novak. Back then at LACSA, if you wanted anything prescription—Xanax, Vicodin, Ritalin, you name it—you called Greg.

Greg and Allie met halfway through our freshman year, in a theater class. I'd seen him around on campus, of course—he was hard to miss—but suddenly he was always in our apartment: rummaging in our kitchen cupboards or flopped across Allie's bed, swiping through Grindr profiles on his phone.

One day, during the second semester of our freshman year, Greg walked into our apartment and tossed a little baggie to Allie with a cheerful "Delivery for you!" before heading into our kitchen and pouring himself a drink. Allie opened the little velvet pouch, the kind that jewelry comes in, and peered inside. "Ooh la la. Thanks, Greggie." Then she blew him a kiss before tucking the baggie in her jeans pocket.

Greg's delivery service. Everyone knew about it.

I close the medicine cabinet and stare at my pale reflection in the mirror. Well, Greg's hardly an option now. We haven't spoken since his arrest. After the police named him their prime suspect, his picture was splashed all over the tabloids. The *National Enquirer* ran a front-page story with the headline DID HE DO IT? emblazoned above a picture of his face.

But Greg had never been charged with Allie's murder. He never even faced charges for the pile of pharmaceuticals the cops found in his apartment. His family hired some big-name lawyer, and before you knew it, it wasn't Greg in the headlines anymore; it was the LAPD under the microscope, facing allegations of mishandling evidence and putting undue pressure on Greg during their interrogations.

Still, Greg didn't get off scot-free. His name would forever be associated with Allie's disappearance. And his friends—that crowd of people who'd surrounded him at wild parties—they all melted away. After his arrest, an in-depth investigative piece by the *LA Times* shone a light on LACSA's robust prescription drug economy, and a string of expulsions followed. Then Greg's parents shipped him off to rehab in Wyoming. That was the last I'd heard of him—from the people in our circle of friends, at least.

The commenters, of course, stayed on top of his movements. Some said Greg had followed up his stint in rehab with a year in an ashram outside Mumbai. Others said he'd moved to the Caribbean, where he finished up his degree at some obscure university.

About a year ago, one of the most obsessive commenters, MayBee634, had spotted Greg walking past the coffee shop where she worked in Silver Lake. **Holy fucking shit, guess who just rolled past me?** she wrote. She hadn't gotten a photo—**He was moving fast, like he didn't want to give anyone time to recognize him**—but the sighting set off a ripple of interest on the forums. **Greggie's back!** The commenters who lived in LA were determined to track him down. And they were surprisingly resourceful.

One of them found Greg's new residence and posted a picture: a sleek, modern house, lots of sharp angles and massive panes of glass. **Some people always fall on their feet, I guess**, MayBee634 said.

It wasn't long after her post that someone spray-painted across Greg's garage doors, in large red letters: WHERE IS SHE?

I'd watched this drama play out with mixed feelings. On the one hand, Greg did seem like the most likely person to have been involved in Allie's disappearance. On the other, I could never quite make myself believe that he'd hurt her. As much as he irritated me, I knew that Greg worshipped Allie. Once, when they'd been standing in line for coffee at Café Bijou, holding hands, I'd watched him lift up her hand and casually kiss her knuckles, as if he was hardly aware he was doing it.

And if their relationship was complicated—love mixed with resentment, admiration crossed with fear—I could understand that. Perhaps better than anyone.

CHAPTER 9

May 2007

The first day Allie came over to the apartment where Mom and I lived, I'd been caught off guard. Mom had mentioned Giles was coming over for an early dinner, but she hadn't said anything about him bringing his daughter. When I answered the door, though, there she was, standing next to Giles in skintight jeans and a shirt so sheer that I could see the outline of her lace bra underneath. Gold geometric earrings glinted at her ears. She looked a lot like her mom, whose face was currently featured on several billboards overlooking the 405. But while Isabel's beauty was ethereal, Allie's was definitely of this world. She had full lips and a smattering of freckles across her cheeks. Big black eyes that dared you to keep staring at her.

"Natasha, this is my daughter, Allie," Giles said, his eyes hidden by a pair of expensive sunglasses.

"Hi." I wiped traces of peanut butter from the edge of my mouth. My clothes were rumpled from lounging on the couch, my hair frizzy after having been let loose from its ponytail.

Allie glanced over her shoulder at our apartment courtyard, where the neighbor's kids had scattered their toys. Our complex was one of the nicer ones in the neighborhood, despite being located in what the kids at school laughingly called the "Slums of Palos Verdes." The joke being that Palos Verdes was so ritzy that the "slums" consisted of white stucco apartments with red tile roofs and pink bougainvillea climbing the walls.

Giles nudged his daughter. "Allie, this is Natasha," he prompted.

Allie turned her attention back to me. After a pause long enough to make me wonder if she was going to say anything at all, she finally said, "Hello." Then her lips curved upward in what might've been—but didn't feel like—a smile.

When she stepped into the apartment, I felt the place shrink somehow. The cheery living room I'd known my whole life suddenly seemed dingy and cheap. The mustard-colored throw on top of the couch couldn't mask the sunken cushions underneath it. And the potted plants, I noticed, were covered in a thin film of dust.

Allie turned, doing a 360-degree assessment of the room.

"Is Elena here?" Giles asked, his fingers toying with the earpieces of his sunglasses, which he'd slipped off as he walked inside.

He was nervous, I realized with surprise. I'd never seen him nervous before. When my mother first introduced us, he'd talked to me for a long time about books. And when he discovered I didn't have any strong opinions on the novels I was reading for school, he'd told me that was something I needed to develop. *You don't want to be a passive consumer of things,* he'd said. *You've got to have a point of view.*

But now he seemed fidgety, like he couldn't quite find the right way to guide the situation forward. It was Allie, I realized, who was setting him on edge. He kept his eyes on her as she moved around the living room, examining the bookshelves, running her fingers across the seashells on the windowsill.

"She's upstairs," I said, wondering why Mom hadn't come down yet. "I'll go get her."

Allie didn't look over when I spoke. And I realized then—it wasn't her clothes or her jewelry or even her beautiful features that made her so striking. No, it was something about the way she held herself. Like she knew you were staring at her, and she did not give a shit.

From upstairs, Mom called, "I'm coming! Sorry, sorry—I was on the phone." And then she was hurrying down the stairs, her long legs threatening to trip her up. She'd changed out of her teaching clothes and was wearing jeans and a men's button-down shirt with the sleeves rolled up.

"Giles!" Her face lit up when she saw him. "You're early." She was about to embrace him when she saw Allie and pulled up short. "Oh!"

Allie stood by the maidenhair fern, one frond pinched between her fingers.

"Well, you must be Allie," Mom said, smiling in that way that transformed her face from plain to beautiful.

But Allie's face remained stony. "In the flesh," she said.

I thought of the photos I'd seen of Allie in magazines. Pictures of her partying at nightclubs she should have been too young to get into, sweat glittering on her skin.

"Sorry to surprise you like this," Giles murmured to Mom. "At the last minute, Allie decided she wanted to come along." Something in his tone made me think this was not an idea he'd been pleased with. But he smiled expansively at me, then put one hand on the small of Mom's back. "Allie moved in with me last month," he explained. "We're just getting settled in."

My mother turned to Allie, her face flushed with pleasure. "I'm so glad to finally meet you."

"Let me guess," Allie said, one corner of her mouth twisting. "You've 'heard so much' about me."

Mom glanced at Giles and pushed a lock of hair behind her ear. "Actually, not enough," she said. "I'd love to know more." She reached out a hand, and after a moment's hesitation, Allie reached out hers and let Mom grasp it. "We'll have to get to know each other better."

For the first time, Allie hesitated, scanning Mom's face with a puzzled expression. "Sure," she said. She took in Mom's makeup-free face, her bare feet, then turned to Giles. "*How* did you two meet?"

He pulled Mom closer to him, curving an arm around her waist. "She came to my reading at Skylight Books. Elena's a real lover of literature."

"Well, what's she doing reading your books, then?"

Giles laughed, a little too loudly. "Ah, you see," he said to Mom, "Allie likes to give me a hard time."

"Oh, your books sell, all right," Allie said casually, walking along our bookshelf and running her fingers along the spines of the books.

Giles laughed again. "And thank God they do. How else could I afford to keep you in the style to which you're accustomed?"

She turned and raised an eyebrow. "Oh, *you* do that? All this time, I thought it was Isabel."

I shifted uncomfortably. They were tossing off the words lightly, as if this was familiar banter. But there was a distinct electric current between them that left the room feeling charged. And I couldn't figure out why she didn't call her mother "Mom," like any other teenager would, but "Isabel," as if the two of them were the same age.

Mom glanced at Giles. "Well, *I* think he's an amazing writer."

Allie's eyes met mine, and her mouth twitched. Then she smiled at Mom. "Hey, why don't we leave you two to yourselves for a bit? Natasha and I can hang out upstairs while you guys . . . catch up."

Mom looked startled. "Oh . . ." She was used to directing teenagers, not being directed by them. She reached out and squeezed my arm. "Well, Natasha? What do you think?"

What could I say? *For God's sake, please don't leave me alone with her.* "Oh. Uh, sure," I said, trying to sound easygoing.

But as I led Allie upstairs to my bedroom, I felt a flicker of panic. Maybe there was still time to change course, to bring her somewhere else—anywhere but my bedroom, which still had glow-in-the-dark stars stuck to the ceiling, remnants of my eleven-year-old-self.

I paused on the landing.

"Everything okay?" Allie asked.

"Yeah."

Laughter floated up from the living room. My mom sounded different when she was around Giles. Younger. It hadn't occurred to me, before Giles entered our lives, that Mom was still a young woman. That, despite the stress of single-motherhood, she was someone men took notice of.

Another peal of laughter echoed from downstairs.

I frowned. I was still adjusting to this new version of my mother. Was this what she'd been like, before my dad died? Had she blushed when she answered the phone? Had she tried on five different outfits before leaving for a date?

"Well, Giles is smitten," Allie said as we started walking up the stairs again. "And not in his usual way either."

Usual way? Before I could ask what she meant by that, we'd reached my bedroom and she'd walked in ahead of me. Just like she'd done downstairs, she circled the room, examining my belongings with interest, like they were an exhibit in a museum. Nothing escaped her notice—not the patchwork quilt on the bed, not the line of battered books on the bookshelf. When she plucked a novel off the shelf, I felt myself redden. Out of all my books, why had she chosen that one? It was a kid's book, the first in the Mia's Shoes series, which I'd been obsessed with when I was nine.

"Oh my God, you read these?" She plopped down on my bed, flipping through the pages of the book. "I used to be crazy about them. Still am, really." She smiled at me, a real smile this time. The effect on her face was startling. She looked like an entirely different person.

"Seriously?" I said.

She pulled her legs up beneath her to sit cross-legged. "Oh, fuck yeah. At one point, I even tried to convince Isabel to legally change my name to Mia. But no dice."

I laughed.

"I still might," she said contemplatively, turning the book over in her hands. "Change my name. Mia is better than Alastriana, anyway." She rolled her eyes. "Seriously, what were my parents thinking?"

Then she let the book fall out of her hands and onto the bedspread. She pushed herself off the bed and walked over to peer more closely at the calendar on the wall over my desk. I'd marked the days when I had upcoming tests with a neon highlighter.

"Giles said you were smart," she said quietly.

I winced. "I don't know about that." I wasn't like those kids at school who were naturally brilliant. I just worked really hard. All my life, I'd known I'd need a scholarship for college; my mom had drummed that fact into me early on. And the only reason I could attend a school like Palos Verdes Prep was because my mom worked there, and I had a faculty scholarship. Most of the other students drove brand-new BMWs and went skiing in Aspen over winter break.

I expected Allie to make fun of my calendar, but her attention had already jumped elsewhere, to a smattering of black-and-white photos I'd taped to the wall, portraits I'd done for last semester's photography class. "What's this?"

God, I never would've taken her up here if I'd realized she was going to examine every single thing I owned.

"Just some photos," I muttered. She stared at one I'd taken while standing on the soccer fields on a misty morning, aiming my camera at the janitor sitting in his golf cart. The photography teacher had let me borrow the camera with the Canon zoom lens, and the shot had captured every crease in the janitor's lined face.

She turned to look at me. "You took these?"

"Yeah," I said, folding my arms across my stomach.

She examined the pictures for a long moment, and then made a face, like she was mentally upgrading her opinion of me. "They're good." Then she turned and sat down on my bed again, bouncing up and down a little as if testing out the mattress. "So, you go to Palos Verdes Prep?"

"Yeah."

She nodded. "Cool."

So, we were going to talk. A normal conversation. I sat down in the swivel chair by my desk, searching desperately for some common ground. "Where do you go?"

"Where do I *go*?" She looked at me as if I'd posed a trick question. This was the Allie I'd seen on the doorstep earlier, the one whose face was unreadable, dangerous.

Had I said something wrong? "To school, I mean."

"Oh." She studied me. "I thought Giles would've told you."

I shrugged. "He doesn't really talk to me that much."

Allie snorted. "Of course he doesn't." Then she leaned back, propping herself up on her elbows. "I'm not in school. Well, I was. But I got expelled. I just got out of rehab."

"Oh." I flushed. I didn't know anyone who'd been to rehab. It was probably bad taste to ask about it, what it was like. Even if I did want to know.

"But I got kicked out of there too."

"Oh." God, I sounded like a robot. "I didn't know you could get kicked out of rehab."

She grinned. "Oh, it's tough. But it's possible. If you put in the effort." Appearing bored by the conversation, she got up off the bed and went over to the window that looked down into the courtyard, where a stone fountain was surrounded by wilting geraniums. "I like your place."

I laughed.

"No, seriously. I do." She turned and brushed her hand over the curtains, which my mom had sewn herself. "What's so funny?"

"Nothing. It's just—you must live in a place that's, like, a million times nicer."

She wrinkled her nose. "Giles's place? Sure. But he throws a fit if I even leave a *towel* on the floor. Your house is more . . . real." She examined the stitching on the curtains. "What's your dad like?"

I braced myself. When I told people my father was dead, their reactions veered between embarrassment and pity. Both of which were hard to respond to, because I didn't remember my father, and I couldn't pretend to feel the sadness I saw in other people's faces.

"He died," I said.

"How long ago?" She picked at a loose thread on the curtain, as casually as if we were discussing the weather.

"I was two."

"No shit."

Now she would ask me how he'd died. *A car crash,* I'd say.

Allie released the curtains, letting them swing back against the wall. "Your mom's really pretty, you know."

I let out a surprised sound. "*My* mom?" This was coming from the daughter of Isabel Andersen. The face of Dior perfume. "You're kidding."

"No. She really is. But not in, like, an artificial way." She scuffed the heels of her boots against the carpet. "She really doesn't know anything about me, does she?"

"Like what?"

"Like, the stuff in the tabloids."

I shook my head. "My mom doesn't really follow any of that stuff." She didn't even flip through the magazines at the grocery checkout, like I did. She was too busy watching the checkout girl scan the items, mentally calculating the bill.

"And you?"

"Not really," I said. But of course, I did. I'd read all about Isabel. And Allie. But with the stress of my upcoming exams, I must've missed the story about Allie's stay in rehab. "I mean, I read some stuff," I amended. For some reason, I felt she'd be able to sniff out if I was lying. "I've seen you in some pictures before."

"Occupational hazard, I guess," she said lightly. "When your mom's Isabel Andersen." Then she walked over to the dresser and stared at herself in the mirror, a line appearing between her eyebrows. What she found to be dissatisfied with, I couldn't imagine. She toyed with her hair, pulling it up into a mass on the top of her head.

"How come you don't live with her?" I asked—then instantly regretted it. That was a nosy question.

But Allie only laughed. "You mean, how did Giles get saddled with me? He's as surprised as anyone, believe me." She turned her head, examining her profile in the mirror. "Seabrook—the rehab place—tried to send me home to Isabel. But she said I couldn't stay with her anymore. So, Giles it was."

"Why couldn't you stay at Seabrook?" I didn't usually ask so many questions, but Allie didn't seem to mind, and there was so much I wanted to know.

She made a funny face. "*Behavioral issues.* I didn't *honor the contract.*" She laughed. "They make you sign this stupid contract when you get there. To say you'll sincerely focus on your recovery, blah blah blah. Anyway, I did all that. Went to therapy, did all the group sessions, as dumb as they were. The problem was, they assigned me to this whole equine therapy thing. You know, bonding with horses. It's supposed to make you grow as a person, or some shit like that. Anyway, the guy who led that program was a total fox. Late twenties. Young Russell Crowe vibes. And, well . . ." She shrugged, as if I could guess what happened next.

"Well, what?"

She rolled her eyes at having to spell it out. "Well, we fucked." The word hung in the air, almost visible.

"Not really, though . . . ," I said slowly. She was joking, trying to see if she could shock me.

She laughed. "You should've seen the shitstorm that kicked up in group therapy. Well, they'd asked me to be forthcoming, and I was." She brushed her hair out with her fingers, then drew it forward over her shoulder. "Afterward, they told me I couldn't stay at their precious rehab anymore." She pouted at her reflection in the mirror. "Boo-hoo."

From across the room, I studied her. "Which is what you wanted all along," I said slowly. She'd planned it that way. Knowing she'd be kicked out.

She smiled, surprised and pleased. "Aw. You get me."

CHAPTER 10

In the morning, I drag myself out of bed and begin my morning routine. Shower. Apply makeup. Blow-dry hair. Every action seems to require twice as much effort as usual, but I plow through, not skipping any steps.

It's just a regular Monday, I tell myself. Nothing special about it.

But my body is already bracing for the hit. One week until the anniversary of Allie's disappearance. Each year, from New Year's onward, I feel the date bearing down on me like an oncoming train.

This year, though, I'm not going to let it affect me. This year, I won't fall apart. I'll eat, I'll sleep, I'll remember there's a world beyond the confines of my apartment.

I pull my hair into a twist at the back of my head. I have a part-time job as a receptionist at a law office, and though it doesn't pay much, it allows me to scrape up some spending money. I've taken out loans for law school, and Matthew is helping with what the loans don't cover, but I still feel flat broke most of the time.

In my bedroom, I pull on a gray skirt and a white blouse, then insert simple silver studs in my ears.

Allie sighs. *Is that really what you're wearing?* I can almost see her behind me, lying across my bed, her legs kicked up in the air.

It's a job, I say. *This is what people wear to jobs.*

Oh, please. That's not a job. You made more when you were babysitting those horrible little kids that used to live next door to us.

I pick up my bag and sling it across my shoulder. I'm already breaking one of my New Year's resolutions: stop having mental conversations with Allie.

So you're just going to work today, Allie says. *Like nothing happened. I mean, it's not like two days ago you were hoping they'd found my body.*

She's beginning to get on my nerves. *What do you want me to do, Allie?* I say. *Put my whole life on pause?*

I don't know. Maybe have a feeling *every once in a while. Maybe act like you* care.

I shake my head, as if that will get her voice to stop. I need to stop responding to her. I need to remember that she's gone. No amount of talking will bring her back. I draw in a deep breath and try to focus on the present moment.

In the living room, I pull on my coat and head out the front door, locking the door behind me. I'm glad to have work today, to have something to occupy my time. My classes don't start up again until the twenty-second, and this in-between time stretches long and formless. Without the structures of assignments and test dates, I feel it more: the yawning space in my life where Allie used to be.

While I walk to the Metro station, I pull my coat tighter around me. The promised cold front has moved in, and it's a shock to everyone's system, feeling the bite of winter in Southern California.

As I walk down Chandler Boulevard, I pass by two women chatting animatedly with each other and feel a pang. I don't have friends like that anymore. Not that I was ever a social butterfly. But I'd had Allie. And when I was with her, there were always other people around, people who felt, by extension, like my friends. After Allie's disappearance, though, those connections dissolved. Now, in my law school classes, I sit apart from the other students, listening to them chatter about concerts, parties, dating.

You don't even try to talk to them, Allie says.

It's true. Why bother? I'm not like them, not anymore. What could they possibly understand about my life?

When I step into the subway station, I pick up my pace so I won't miss my train. A man jostles me as he rushes up the stairs past me, and I have to grab on to the handrail to steady myself. I hate the crowds here in the mornings; they make me feel claustrophobic. After hurrying to the train, I find a spot near the window at the back of the car and settle into a seat. This is when I always put my headphones in, to seal myself off from the other passengers. But as I dig through my coat pockets, searching for the familiar tangle of headphone cords, my fingers brush up against something else—an object an inch or so across, round and irregular.

Puzzled, I clasp my fingers around it and pull it out.

At first, all I see is black-and-white plastic. I have to turn it over in my palm a few times before I register what it is. A panda-bear head, just like the one on the key chain Allie used to carry. Except Allie's key chain had an entire bear on it, and this is just the head.

I turn the panda head over and see that someone has written something on the flat plastic underside: *Allie.*

A low-voltage shock runs up my arms, and I drop the bear as if I've been burned.

CHAPTER 11

"Hold on," Ruiz says. "Slow down. Tell me exactly what happened."

I press my phone against my ear. My hands are still shaking. As soon as I got off the subway, I found a corner of the station where it was quiet enough for me to call him.

Ruiz is in a crowded room somewhere—I can hear the chatter of voices and the clatter of typing—and then the sound is suddenly muffled, as if he's closed a door behind him. "Her key chain, you said?"

"In my jacket pocket. Just now."

"Are you sure that's what it is?"

I turn the panda head over in my hand and look at the writing I've read over and over again since getting off the subway. In looping cursive, on the base of the panda head, the word *Allie*. "Yes. It has her name on it. And there's something else."

I run my finger over the rectangular cutout right next to Allie's name. "The key chain—it was a flash drive. The head is the cap, but the bottom must have the drive."

"And the bottom? Was that in your pocket too?"

"No." I'd rifled through my pockets after getting off the subway. "No, just the top half. But it's Allie's. I'm sure of it." It's battered in exactly the same way hers had been, the paint wearing off the plastic of the bear's nose.

"Okay, where are you?" he says. "I'll come to you."

I tell him I'm at the Westwood station, and he says he'll be here in twenty minutes.

While I wait, I call the office and tell them I've been delayed by a traffic accident. They don't question it—they don't think I'm the type of person to lie. As I wait for Ruiz to arrive, I realize I've been clasping the key chain so tightly that my palm has begun to sweat. I loosen my fingers, suddenly afraid my grip has wiped off the ink that spells out Allie's name. It hasn't. The letters are still there, the ink clear and bright.

How had the key chain gotten into my pocket?

Hey! Isn't that lucky? Allie says.

And suddenly, I remember, one Saturday during freshman year, after Allie and I had gone to a street fair, I'd reached my hand into the pocket of my jeans and found a bracelet I'd admired at a stall earlier that morning. Surprised, I turned it over in my fingers. I hadn't bought it, and for a moment I wondered if I'd put it in my pocket unconsciously. When I asked Allie about it, she just widened her eyes, but in such a way that I knew she'd bought it for me when I wasn't looking. Bought it, and then slipped it into my pocket for me to find. All she would say, though, was, *Hey! Isn't that lucky?* As if the bracelet had just appeared like magic.

In the noise of the morning crowd, I look down at the panda head in my palm. Is this another of her gifts? Who else would have this key chain? Who else would leave it for me like this?

I feel dizzy. The air in the subway station is warm and close, rich with the scent of coffee. I lean my back against the wall and focus on the breathing exercises Dr. Rajmani taught me. *Breathe in for three counts, and then out for four.*

By the time Ruiz arrives, I've progressed to seven counts in and eight counts out. It's helped a little; my hands aren't shaking anymore. Ruiz jogs across the station, his cheeks flushed. When he reaches me, he says, "Hey," a little breathless.

Without a word, I extend my hand, the key chain resting in my palm. But instead of grabbing it, he reaches into his jacket pocket, pulls out a plastic evidence bag, and tilts my hand to one side so that the panda head drops inside.

Only after he's carefully sealed the bag does he take a closer look at the panda head. Then he glances up at me. "Someone put this in your pocket?"

I nod.

"When? Can you think when they might have done that?"

I scour my memory. I wore the coat on Friday. I remember emptying my pockets after work that day: headphones, lip balm, my key card from the office. The key chain wasn't there then.

"Sunday," I said. "It had to be yesterday." I tell him how I'd accidentally dropped my coat on my doorstep on my way to the station.

Ruiz pulls the knitted cap off his head and balls it up in his hands. "What's the security like in your building?"

"There's a key card swipe to get in the front door," I say. "And then another for the stairs and elevator."

"Okay," he says. "But it'd be pretty easy for someone to piggyback through those doors after someone else swiped their card." He rubs his knuckles across his chin, thinking. "I don't like this," he says eventually. "Whoever left this for you, they know where you live. They've figured out your new name."

I open my mouth to tell him about Allie, about her "lucky" gifts.

But Ruiz hasn't stopped talking. "You need to get some added security. You have an alarm system in your apartment? A doorbell camera? Anything like that?"

I shake my head.

He pulls out his phone and starts typing. "When I get back to the station, I'll send you some info on systems you can get. At the very least, you should get a camera installed—that way, if someone tries a stunt like this again, you'll be able to see who it is."

A stunt. My lips feel numb. "But the key chain . . ." *She left it for me,* I want to say, but I can't quite get the words out. I know it will sound crazy. "It's hers. *Look* at it."

He looks up from his phone, his fingers hovering over the screen. "I have looked at it."

"And?"

He puts his phone back in his pocket. "Look, Natasha—I know how this must feel."

Of course he doesn't. How could he?

"But the writing on this thing, it's not Allie's. We took handwriting samples back then, and Allie never wrote in cursive."

I feel like I've turned a corner and run into a wall. Why didn't that occur to me? He's right. Allie had a distinctive print: bold downstrokes, cramped lowercase letters. I know its style as well as I know my own.

"Look, most likely scenario—this is someone wanting to mess with you."

"What if it was someone who was with her, on the night she . . . disappeared?"

He rubs at his eyes. "That seems unlikely. If the person who took Allie had this, why would they give it to you?"

He's right. It doesn't make sense. Still, I feel the wheels spinning in my mind, searching for possibilities that might make the key chain more than a cheap stunt. "Maybe, I don't know—maybe that person is sorry for what they did, and they want to give this to me, to . . ."

"To what?"

I force myself to think logically. "The key chain was attached to a flash drive. So maybe there was something important on that. Something they want me to see."

He chews that over for a second. "Then why not give you the flash drive itself? This, just the top half—this tells us nothing." He sounds frustrated. "Look, there's nothing I want more than for this to be the break in the case that we need."

He looks tired. And I remember what he went through in the aftermath of the *LA Times* piece about the mishandling of Allie's case. His partner, Golanski, had already been a heavy drinker; after the article was published, Golanski went into a downward spiral and had to leave the force. Ruiz was left to answer for the shortcomings of the initial investigation all by himself. He, for his own reasons, wants to solve this case as much as I do.

"It *could* be hers," I insist. Ruiz must think so too. Why else come all the way down here to meet me?

His eyes rove the station. It's a habit he has, assessing the scene. But he's thinking things over. "Look, I just don't want you to get your hopes up. This is probably a hoax. I mean, you remember how things were right after Allie went missing."

I close my eyes. I remember. The envelope with a lock of dark hair in it. The YouTube video showing the silhouette of a woman locked in a basement. Both of which turned out to be pranks.

"But what if Allie—" My voice gets hoarse. "What if it's her? What if she left it?" I hear the desperation in my voice. I know how unlikely it is that Allie is still alive. After all this time, the odds are slim to none.

Someone jostles me as they walk by, and Ruiz pulls me to one side, out of the path of commuters. "Listen, I'm going to look into this. If Allie left this for you—well, then this is the first solid lead we'll have had in years." He sighs. "But, Natasha, think about it. Allie leaving it for you makes even less sense than her killer leaving it. If Allie's alive, why not send you a letter? Or just knock on your door?"

My chest deflates. I know he's right. But I'm not ready to let go of hope, not yet.

"Hey, if this thing is legit, I promise we'll pursue it with everything we've got," he says. "I just want to prepare you, okay? It might be nothing."

He's worried. Maybe he remembers the last time, right after the YouTube prank, when I stopped sleeping, stopped eating.

He takes one last look at the key chain and hesitates. After a moment, he passes the bag back to me. "Did you see this other marking here?"

Below Allie's name is a little drawing, just a few millimeters wide. A circle with two vertical lines and a smaller circle inside it. I'd thought it was a stamp, part of the branding, but I can see now that it's hand drawn, in the same ink that was used to write Allie's name.

"Do you recognize that?" he asks.

It looks like an emoji—two lines for eyes and a small round mouth. "No."

He frowns. "Okay. We'll look into that too." He slides the evidence bag into an inner pocket of his jacket. "Look, I have to get back to the station. But I'll be in touch."

"Okay," I say, stomping down the urge to ask him to stay just a little longer. In a moment, I'll have to gather myself and walk into the office as if this is any other morning.

"In the meantime, be careful, okay?" he says. "Keep an eye on people in your apartment building. If anyone looks suspicious—anyone at all—give me a call."

"Okay," I repeat.

And then he turns to go. Just like that. As I watch, he weaves his way past a group of businessmen, his steps purposeful. And when he reaches the sliding glass doors, even when he has to slow down and wait for them to open, he doesn't turn and look back.

CHAPTER 12

When I reach the office, I take the elevator to the twentieth floor, trying to focus on the shine of the elevator doors, the jazz music piped in through the sound system. Normal life.

My hand still feels the shape of the key chain against my palm. And when I close my eyes, images of Allie flash against my eyelids. Allie in the CCTV footage at the coffee shop. Allie walking out of our apartment door for the last time.

When I get to my desk, I go through my usual morning duties—making coffee, checking voicemail messages, typing up the notes from last week's staff meeting—but I can hardly concentrate. My usually perfect typing is pockmarked with errors, and the sentences I read seem strange, as if they're written in a foreign language.

After an hour or so, when I've run through all the pressing tasks, I pull my phone out of my bag and check my email. As promised, Ruiz has sent me some information on security systems. In his email, he says I should install a doorbell camera right away. He's underlined the words *right away*. He says I should probably look into a more comprehensive security system too.

After glancing up to see that no one is watching, I click on the links he's sent over. The price makes me wince, but I order the doorbell camera immediately, paying the extra fee for same-day delivery.

As soon as the purchase is confirmed, I feel a growing sense of relief. If whoever left me the key chain comes by the apartment again, I'll be able to see their face. See if it's someone I recognize. Against my will, I picture Allie standing in front of my door, kneeling down to tuck the key chain into my coat pocket, her hair falling across her face.

Once I've allowed that image to appear, others flood in.

Allie tossing her keys on the kitchen counter in our apartment and reaching for a bottle of wine. *You would not believe the bullshit Isabel pulled today.* Allie drifting off to sleep as we watched TV on our living room couch, her hair spreading like ink over the couch cushions. Allie sitting at one of the kitchen stools in our apartment, typing away on her laptop, her key chain lying on the counter next to her coffee mug.

I blink and sit up straighter.

One night that winter, maybe a month before she went missing, I'd woken up to hear Allie typing on her computer in the kitchen. Rolling over in bed, I pulled my comforter over my head to block out the sound of her fingers clacking on the laptop keyboard.

At the time, I'd thought she was online shopping, or maybe writing an email. But now that I think about it, that wouldn't account for the amount of time she'd been typing.

At some point, after the sound of clicking laptop keys continued, I'd rolled over in bed, fumbled for my phone, and checked the time: 3:04 a.m. "Fuck," I muttered. Groaning, I got up, shuffled down the hall, and wandered into the kitchen. Allie sat on one of the kitchen island stools, her face illuminated by the laptop's glow.

I wandered over to the cupboards to find a water glass. "What are you doing?"

She had her hair pulled up into a tangled topknot, and one of her feather earrings was coming loose from her ear. "Just feeling a little wired."

I yawned. "Hot tip: Don't drink coffee at three in the morning. Then you won't feel so wired."

She grinned and gave me the finger. Then she got up off the stool to stretch her arms over her head. As she turned away, working out a crick in her neck, I leaned over and tilted her laptop toward me, trying to see what was on the screen. But I only caught a glimpse of bright white before Allie turned and slapped the laptop closed with the palm of her hand.

"Jesus," I said, startled.

For a moment, her face was fierce. Then she laughed. "Sorry. Must be more wired than I thought."

She was trying to lighten the moment, but it didn't quite work.

I went to the sink and poured myself a glass of water, a strange buzzing sensation running over my skin. "Like I care what kind of porn you're watching," I said lightly. If she wanted to joke, I'd joke too.

Allie laughed. "Believe me—you couldn't handle the kind of porn I'm watching."

But when I turned, I noticed her hand was still on the laptop, like she needed to stay in contact with it.

"Huh," I said. I knew she hadn't been looking at porn. If she was, I'd be the first person she'd show it to. I was easily shocked, and one of Allie's chief forms of entertainment was proving to me how repressed I was.

Now, I lean back in my office chair and swivel around to look out the floor-to-ceiling window. Below, the city stretches out gray and cold. The ocean is a faint line in the distance.

That moment in the kitchen with Allie had been strange—but no stranger, I guess, than anything else she'd done in those last few months. She'd been unpredictable that winter. Hard to pin down. Half the time, I didn't know where she was. She'd say she was going to the gym or the coffee shop, but for some reason, I'd be convinced she was lying.

On the night Allie was up late typing, I'd left her there in the kitchen with her computer. But the whole interaction left me feeling unsettled.

Eventually, I'd brushed off her behavior as just another annoyance. But now, I wonder: What had she been so touchy about?

My phone buzzes, and I see a text has come through from Matthew.

Dinner tonight? Chloe and I flew back today.

I sigh. Matthew must've heard the news about the body. Why else would he come home early from his honeymoon? Still, even as I'm sad for him, a selfish part of me is relieved.

Sure, I type back. Which house?

Usually, we meet at his place in Venice Beach. But just before the wedding, he'd bought a bigger house in Beverly Hills, a place with room enough for him and Chloe and Chloe's eleven-year-old daughter, Sara. He's put the place in Venice on the market; it'll sell soon.

Venice, he types. Chloe wants some one-on-one time with Sara.

I feel my shoulders relax. I like Chloe a lot, but when she's around, Matthew and I don't talk in the way we used to. In front of her, Matthew and I pretend to be functional human beings. We talk about the weather, politics, movies. We don't dwell on the case.

See you at 7, he types, and I send back a thumbs-up emoji.

Almost immediately, I feel better. It hits me now how much I've been wanting to talk to Matthew. I need to tell him about the key chain. He won't dismiss me out of hand, like Ruiz did, when I say Allie might have left it. He'll want that theory to be true just as much as I do.

CHAPTER 13

At the end of the day, my boss leaves, but I linger at my desk, looking out the window. From this height, the city looks like a circuit board. As the sky darkens and the streetlights flicker on, I imagine the cars are little electrical impulses, flickering from place to place.

Turning in my chair, I face my computer screen again. I have some time to kill before traffic dies down enough for me to take an Uber over to Matthew's place. And I know what I want to do with that time. After checking to see that no one is watching, I open a private browser window and type in the address for the forums.

As the page loads, it's hard not to feel guilty. Dr. Rajmani would not approve of this backsliding. I've been so good recently. I haven't logged on in almost four months—a personal record. As I navigate to the forums, I feel a twist of anticipation in my gut. Four months is a long time. What if, in that time, some new piece of information has surfaced, something crucial I've ignored because I've been so busy "taking care of myself"?

I click on the *New Developments* thread, then feel a swift thud of disappointment as soon as I see the most recent entries. Only two new posts in the last four months.

After all this time, the only people who've stuck around the forums are the die-hards—the obsessives, the retired PIs, the morbidly preoccupied housewives. Just the kind of people who might leave a look-alike key chain on my doorstep. People who've pored over paparazzi photos of Allie long enough to spot a panda-bear key chain clutched in her hands.

Quickly, I scan the first new post: a long, rambling paragraph from a woman who is sure she spotted Allie in Oaxaca. These types of posts are a dime a dozen. So many people have had "Allie sightings." Sometimes people even upload fuzzy snapshots—girls with dark hair and dark eyes who bear only a passing resemblance to Allie.

The second post is about Matthew's wedding, and the commenter has just copied and pasted the text from a recent news article.

> Writer and director Matthew Andersen tied the knot with Chloe Navarro this Thursday in a small ceremony in Wayfarer's Chapel in Palos Verdes. The two met through their charitable work for the nonprofit The Lost and the Missing, which provides aid to the family members of missing persons. Andersen's niece, Allie Andersen, went missing in 2013. Chloe's brother, José Navarro, vanished during a rafting trip in the Grand Canyon in 2009.

Then there's a picture of Matthew and Chloe outside Wayfarer's Chapel. Chloe wears a sleek, simple dress, her dark hair falling in loose curls around her shoulders. Matthew has one arm around Chloe's waist and the other around her daughter, Sara, as she laughs at the camera.

Below the article, AceDetective33 has commented: **Nice to see a bit of good news for this family.**

I exit the page and click through the other forum links, looking for new entries since the last time I logged on. In Greg's thread, there's just a smattering of conversation from the past few months.

> **AceDetective33:** And let's not forget that detail about Allie's laptop. The cops tried to go through

it, but it had been water-damaged. The hard drive was fried.

That November, Allie had bought herself a brand-new rose-gold laptop, although she didn't really need one. It was for her work in Macnamara's class, she said. But I suspected she just wanted a new toy to carry around, something that would pair well with her outfits.

Vero88: What's that got to do with Greg?

AceDetective33: Simple. Greg was dealing a shit-ton of drugs, which Allie knew about. Some people even say she was helping him. So let's say she had some information on her computer about that. After Greg gets rid of her, he has to get rid of that incriminating evidence.

The muscles in my neck tighten. Is that what was on the flash drive? Information about Greg's dealing? I've never paid much attention to these theories about something of importance being on Allie's laptop, but now that the key chain's turned up, I'm beginning to wonder what I may have overlooked.

I skim through the rest of the Greg comments, but there are no more mentions of the laptop.

Marciex3: Personally, I can't see Greg hurting her. By all accounts, Greg loved Allie. I think he knew she planned to leave town, and he helped her escape.

AceDetective33: But why would she need to leave town?

Marciex3: She was depressed, and her parents had cut off her allowance. They were pissed about those TMZ photos.

The TMZ photos. At the beginning of junior year, photographers had caught Allie leaving Luxe, propped up by Greg on one side and her theater buddy Christie on another. In the photos, her head lolled to one side, and she looked like she was one step away from collapse.

AceDetective33: Check your dates, Marciex3. The TMZ photos came out months before she disappeared. If they bothered her so much, why didn't she skip town right after the scandal?

Marciex3: Maybe it just built up over time—her getting sick of it all. I think she wanted a fresh start somewhere. Greg helped her, and he's kept quiet all these years to protect her. They're probably still in contact.

ChrisB: Oh, Jesus—another FFer.

Marciex3's theory is so popular that it's acquired its own nickname: "Friends Forever." The FFers are a sentimental group who like to post photos of Greg and Allie with their arms around each other. Greg and Allie were a photogenic pair, and it was easy to imagine, looking at them, that their friendship was something deep and real—if you didn't actually know them. If you didn't know that Greg was instrumental in getting Allie shit-faced on a regular basis. If you didn't see that, as much as he loved her, he was dragging her down.

Or maybe I'm being cynical. Maybe I don't want to believe the FF theory because, if it's true, it means Allie loved Greg more than she loved me.

AceDetective33: Look, that's a sweet thought, but I think Allie's ending was darker than that. She was behaving really erratically those last few days, right? That kind of behavior isn't uncommon among people who are about to commit suicide. I mean, think about it: the day she goes missing, she drives to her stepmom's house in Reseda, stays there for, like, just a couple of minutes, and then drives away. The stepmom says she has no clue what Allie was doing there. Her behavior doesn't make sense because her mind wasn't right.

I sit back in my chair, the mention of suicide settling like a weight on my chest.

The Thursday Allie went missing, the CCTV camera at the end of Mom's block had caught an image of her driving into Mom's neighborhood, then, fifteen minutes later, driving out again. Mom was at work that afternoon, so there wouldn't have been much point in Allie going to her house. It's one of the many details of the case that has never made sense.

I blow out a frustrated breath. None of this information is new. Or enlightening. Still, now that I've started, I might as well finish. As the sky behind me darkens, I click on James Macnamara's thread. The picture at the top of the page loads slowly, revealing Macnamara standing in a bar, holding a glass of wine and smiling at the camera. He's wearing a button-down shirt with the sleeves rolled up, looking a shade too young and good looking to be a literature professor.

The first time Allie saw Macnamara, we'd been standing in line at the coffee shop at the edge of campus, waiting for the barista to slide our coffees across the counter. Suddenly, Allie turned, doing a complete one-eighty as she looked out toward the sun-drenched sidewalk. "Damn. Who is that?"

"Who?"

She pointed at the man lingering on the corner, digging through his laptop bag. I recognized his slender build, the curly hair that had grown long enough to touch the back of his shirt collar.

"Like, the Daniel Day Lewis look-alike," Allie said, pulling off her Bialucci sunglasses.

"That's Professor Macnamara," I said.

Allie's head snapped around. "Excuse me?"

I handed her the coffee she'd just ordered and grabbed my own. "C'mon. Greg's waiting for us."

"*That's* Professor Macnamara? The guy whose class you're taking?"

"Yeah."

She pointed a finger in my face. "You . . . you've been holding out on me."

I dragged her away from the counter—we were late to class already—but the whole walk to campus, she pestered me about him. *You never told me he looked like* that. *This whole time, I thought you had, like, an* intellectual *crush on him.*

I brushed her off, trying to move off the subject as quickly as possible. *He's just a good teacher, that's all.*

Why didn't I just tell her the truth? I could've told her about the number of times Macnamara had asked me to stay after class to talk about something I'd said during class discussion. Or the way he'd tried to recruit me for his creative writing seminar: *It'll be challenging, but I think you'd really thrive there.*

It was just the kind of story Allie loved to hear. She would have hung on my every word, and then she'd have offered advice: *Here's what you say the next time you see him. Here's what you do.*

But that's exactly why I didn't tell her. I wanted my feelings about Macnamara to belong to me only. To Allie, the whole thing would've been entertainment, a chance to play matchmaker—or puppet master. And that was the last thing I wanted. The way I felt when Macnamara talked to me . . . that felt serious. That felt real. Every day in his class, I waited for his blue eyes to scan the room and come to rest on me.

The office phone rings, jolting me out of my memories. I let the call go to voicemail and pull my attention back to the Macnamara thread. There are only a few new comments since the last time I checked in.

AJBaltimore: personally, I can't picture that guy committing murder. i mean, look at him.

DNAmy: Oh yeah, because no handsome, upper-middle-class guy has ever killed someone.

AJBaltimore: that's not what I'm saying. he had no history of violence, none of that, his past girlfriends all said he was a great guy. And you've seen his interviews during the investigation—the guy was a hot mess. he seems like the type to panic at a crime scene, not come up with a nifty body-disposal plan. can I see him sleeping with a student? hell yeah. but getting rid of a body? no way.

DNAmy: He's a smart guy. It's not that hard to dispose of a body if you do a little bit of research. Easy enough for him to pack her inside a suitcase, haul her out to his car. Then: dismemberment, sulfuric acid . . . take your pick.

My eyes skitter away from the post—this kind of detail will haunt my dreams—and pick up farther down the thread.

Chazzer: Have you seen the YouTube videos of his lectures? Unless he's a psychopath, he does a good impression of being a pretty great guy. Down to earth. Funny.

Dr.Sleuth: That is exactly the impression that psychopaths are skilled at conveying. Psychopaths are good at appearing completely normal to other people. They learn to reflect back the emotions they see in other people, to hide the fact that they don't feel those emotions themselves. A psychopath can be well educated, can hold down a demanding job. Sometimes even their friends and families don't realize what they're really like.

I reread that paragraph, a queasy feeling sliding over my chest. I remember sitting across from Macnamara during his office hours. How charming and personable he was, how—despite my shyness—he always managed to make me smile. To come out of my shell. Was that an indication of his warmth, or evidence that he couldn't be trusted?

One afternoon when we'd been talking, he leaned back in his office chair and said, "Sure I can't tempt you over to the dark side?" He gestured behind him at the bookshelf that was crammed, every inch, with books. "Who needs prelaw when you could have a degree in literature?" He grinned. "Look at the glamorous life this career path could lead you to."

I smiled. His office was cramped and cluttered, and the air-conditioning only worked sporadically. But in fact, there was something alluring about it.

"I can't," I told Macnamara. My mother had drummed it into my head: I needed a career path that paid. *You have to be able to support yourself, Tasha,* she'd told me. *Don't put yourself in a position where you have to rely on someone else.*

"Why not?" He had a way of holding eye contact for a very long time. I was always the one to look away first.

"I just can't."

"Hmm." He tapped his pencil on the stack of essays on his desk. "Well. Just know this." He handed me back my essay, and I saw the grade he had scrawled at the top: A+. "If you want a spot in my creative writing seminar, it's yours. Think about it."

Now, I chew on my fingernail and stare at the picture of Macnamara on the web page. He's looking at the camera like he and the photographer are in on the same joke. And I remembered how, in his writing class, he used to give me that same look. Whenever I laughed at a reference of his that no one else caught, I could feel the connection between us shimmering in the air.

During lectures, he called on me frequently, making jokes that seemed aimed specifically at me. He told me once that I was too good for LACSA. *What I can't understand is how a student like you ended up* here.

With a sharp click, I close the browser window. Clearly, I'd been wrong about Macnamara, about whatever vibes I thought I was getting from him that semester. If I thought he was flirting with me, I was delusional.

Because the next semester, when Allie took his seminar, I found out how he acted when he was *really* interested in a student.

CHAPTER 14

At six thirty, I call an Uber to take me to Matthew's house. From the back seat of the Uber, I watch the cars ahead of us, their red brake lights bleeding into the night air. We're inching down Pico, and I have plenty of time to examine the shops lining the street—coin laundries and hamburger joints and tattoo parlors. And I remember how in high school, after I got my license, Allie used to make me drive to different neighborhoods: Boyle Heights, Little Tokyo, Thai Town. *This is your education, Tash Ross,* she'd say, turning the radio up loud and singing along.

After our parents got married and we'd moved into the new house on Via Montemar, Allie and I started to spend all our time together—which had surprised me. I'd thought, after Allie enrolled at Palos Verdes Prep, that she would find her place among the popular kids. Sophie Engel, Blake Bryson, Tilly Choi—the kids who sat out in the full sun of the amphitheater, rather than the shaded courtyard by the choir room, which was where I sat with my friends. But Allie had shown absolutely no interest in joining Sophie Engel's crowd. Instead, every day, she sat in the courtyard and ate lunch with me.

One afternoon, Sophie came over to us and said to Allie, "You know you don't have to sit here, right? All of us are sitting out by the stage." She didn't even bother looking at me.

Allie chewed on a bite of her sandwich, taking her time before she swallowed. Then she took a sip of her drink. "Us?"

"Yeah. Me and Tilly and Bryce and AJ."

Allie set down her drink and gazed up at Sophie. Finally, she said, "It's Sophie, right?"

Sophie smiled, delighted to be recognized. "Yeah!"

Allie crossed her legs and leaned back against the tree behind her. "Well, no offense, Sophie, but my sister and I are trying to have a conversation here."

Sister. It was the first time she'd called me that.

Sophie looked confused.

"So maybe you could fuck off and leave us alone," Allie clarified.

That was the last time Sophie tried to approach Allie.

Later, at home, Allie told me, "Believe me, I know exactly why Sophie Engel wants to be my friend. She wants to see if I'll invite her to the house in Malibu; she wants to meet Isabel. So she can brag about it to all her weasel-faced friends." She made a gagging sound. "Thank God you're not like that."

Now, I stare out the car window at a Vietnamese restaurant where the windows are still lined with Christmas lights, green and red bulbs flashing against the glass.

Allie had been wrong about me, back then. She'd thought I was different from Sophie and her friends and all those girls who whispered behind her back at school. But the truth was, I wanted to meet Isabel just as badly as they did. I wanted to see Isabel's house in Malibu; I wanted to bask in the glow of her beauty.

But I knew it would be disastrous to let Allie see that. So when she talked about Isabel and Matthew and their movie projects, I pretended not to be starstruck.

Sometimes, at home, when the landline rang, it was Isabel Andersen, asking to speak to Allie. (Allie never answered Isabel's calls to her cell phone.) And, if it was one of the days when Allie refused to come to the phone, Isabel would talk to me, asking me questions like: *How is school? Is Allie settling in okay?* I'd find myself talking to her as if this were normal for me, as if I talked to Oscar-nominated actresses on the phone all the time. And I let myself daydream about the day I'd finally get to meet her, when I'd get to peek into that other world.

Outside the car, the Christmas lights blink frantically, persistently, and when I close my eyes, they're still there, flashing on the insides of my eyelids.

CHAPTER 15

December 2007

Isabel and Matthew came over for Christmas not long after we'd moved into the spacious midcentury house on Via Montemar. The place had a pool and a landscaped garden and a view of the ocean. It felt like a palace, although, after all my years of living in a tiny apartment, it often seemed more like a hotel than a home to me.

That Christmas Eve, I stood by the decorated tree in the living room while Isabel, the star of *Alchemy* and *Broken Bones*, chatted with my mother about mashed potato recipes. On the couch, Matthew and Giles sipped cocktails and discussed the latest film Matthew was directing. The room was bright with laughter and tasteful background music.

I watched the scene as if it were something out of a movie. *This is my family,* I told myself. And I waited for it to feel real. But none of it did, none of it except for Allie. She was curled up in one of the oversize armchairs on the other side of the room, texting someone and looking like she'd rather be anywhere else. If only she'd looked up, we could've exchanged glances, and suddenly I would've felt at home in my own skin again. But she just kept typing, her eyebrows drawn together.

So I turned to the fireplace, trying to act as if I was suddenly fascinated by the pictures on the mantelpiece. My favorite of these was a framed photo of Giles and Matthew, taken the year they were nominated for Best Adapted Screenplay at the Golden Globes. The photographer had captured them at some after-party: dress shirts rumpled, cigarettes dangling from their mouths. I often studied that picture—the way Matthew's dark hair fell over his forehead and Giles's drink had been caught in mid-slosh. They looked so young, so handsome, teetering on the edge of success.

I turned around when Giles started laughing at a joke Matthew had made. Isabel, backlit by the Christmas tree, pulled her long, dark hair over one shoulder and toyed with one of her earrings.

"I know what we should do," Mom said, clapping her hands together. "Let's take a photo in front of the tree."

I winced. You couldn't just pull out a camera in a group like this. Allie had told me stories about her family being pestered by paparazzi—on vacation, during Isabel's divorce, even on morning trips to Starbucks.

But Isabel smiled graciously. "That sounds lovely." Then she turned to me. "Natasha, would you do the honors? Giles says you're quite the photographer."

I froze, taken off guard. It was news to me that Giles thought my photographs were good. "I mean, I take photos," I said. "I'm not a photographer."

"Oh, don't be so modest," Isabel said. "Giles says you're very talented."

So I ended up getting my Nikon SLR from upstairs and coming back into the living room, where I carefully balanced the camera on a shelf and set the timer. Everyone gathered in front of the fireplace, Matthew and Isabel looking as if they were ready for a magazine shoot. Allie stood as far away from Isabel as possible. As I positioned the camera and jogged over to join the group, Giles put his hand on Allie's shoulder to draw her closer, but she shrugged it off.

"Smile," Mom said cheerfully, and then the flash went off, momentarily blinding me.

At dinner, we sat around the brand-new dining table, the low-hung chandelier casting a warm glow over everyone's faces. On the other side of the table, Allie was still sulking, so I amused myself by taking mental pictures, framing a shot and then—click—freezing it in my mind. Giles, pouring wine into my mother's glass. Matthew, eyes crinkling as he told a story about getting stranded in the middle of nowhere in Turkey during a film shoot. Isabel, politely declining the offer of cranberry sauce—*Oh, no, thank you. I'm not doing sugar right now.*

When Matthew caught me looking at him, he smiled. "So, Natasha," he said, turning to me. "When do we get to see some of your photographs?"

I felt the blood rush to my cheeks. "Um. I don't know." Giles had seen me tacking my photographs to the wall in my room as I unpacked, but he hadn't said anything about them to me, other than, "You should get these framed. So you don't have to put holes in these walls."

In all these months we'd lived together, I'd never gotten a clear read on how Giles felt about me. With Allie, he fought constantly, but he seemed to have a certain respect for her stubbornness. She was difficult, but that was evidence of her having what Giles called *spine*. I, on the other hand, kept my room clean and brought home good grades. I got the feeling that, for Giles, this indicated a lack of personality.

"Are you thinking about art school?" Matthew asked, refilling his wineglass almost to the top.

"Actually, she's interested in the law," Mom said.

Across the table, Allie locked eyes with me and made a face, waiting for me to disagree.

"Yeah," I said, folding my napkin over and over again in my lap. "If I can get a scholarship."

"Scholarship?" Matthew thumped Giles on the shoulder. "Don't you know what this guy is worth? You can take that worry off your plate."

Matthew laughed but Giles didn't, and there was an awkward pause in the conversation.

"Ignore my brother, Natasha," Isabel said smoothly. In her mouth, my name sounded foreign, exotic. "These two are always teasing each other. Like children."

"'Old Moneybags' is what I call him," Matthew said, taking a sip of his wine. "Remember when you didn't have two dimes to rub together? When we were living with Liam in that shithole apartment in Long Beach? Three writers who didn't know what the hell they were doing. And then Liam got cancer, and we nearly got evicted because we couldn't pay the rent."

Giles frowned. "Can we talk about something else?"

Liam had died, I knew, soon after his diagnosis. Giles didn't like talking about that time in their lives.

"Don't you remember?" Matthew persisted. "You borrowed money from your dad so we could stay on a few more months. And that's when we wrote the script for *Alchemy*."

Giles looks faintly irritated. "You know, I really don't recall." Allie had told me once that Giles liked to think of himself as someone who'd pulled himself up by the bootstraps. Not someone who'd taken money from his rich father.

"No, well, you were very busy after *Alchemy*, weren't you?" Matthew turned to me and lowered his voice, as if he was confiding a secret. "That was the beginning of Giles's meteoric rise. Whereas I . . ." He made a whistling sound and then made a downward arc with his hand.

Another awkward silence. I knew from my magazine reading what Matthew was referring to. The constant partying, the DUI, the scandal with that model Nico Bissett. For a time, people had become reluctant to work with him. But then, mostly through Isabel's efforts on his behalf, he'd begun to direct again. *Blockbuster films,* Giles had said to me once, dismissing them out of hand. *Not what you would call art.* But maybe Giles was just annoyed because Matthew made more money than him now, that Matthew's fame—though it would never rival Isabel's—would always overshadow his own.

"Oh, come on, folks," Matthew said to the table at large. "I'm joking." He took another sip of wine, and when he set down his glass, liquid splashed out on the white tablecloth, forming a bright-red stain.

"Jesus, will you stop?" Allie snapped.

Everyone turned to look at her. It was one of the only things she'd said that night.

"Allie," Isabel said, a warning in her voice.

"What?" A dangerous expression crept over Allie's face.

"Take it easy, all right?" Isabel said mildly. "We're having a nice dinner."

"He's drunk," Allie said.

Matthew raised his hands in the air, as if he were being held at gunpoint. "Hey, Al-ligator. It's all good. I'm just enjoying myself."

"Maybe you could try to do the same," Isabel said to Allie. There was an edge to her voice now.

"Sure. Why don't I drink a bottle of wine or two, and then maybe I could also get into the holiday spirit," she said.

"Allie, that's enough," Giles said, throwing his napkin down beside his plate.

"Oh, screw you," Allie lashed back. "You think you get an opinion now?"

My mom sucked in a breath. She reached out to put her hand on Allie's shoulder, but Allie was already standing up, and Mom's hand hovered, stranded in midair. Allie grabbed her plate of food, which she'd barely touched, and walked into the kitchen, where we heard her dump it into the sink with a crash. "I'm so sick of this," she said, her voice carrying into the dining room.

Mom half stood, as if she was about to follow Allie into the kitchen. But Isabel said, "Elena, *don't*." Then, more gently, "Please. Let her be. Getting a reaction—that's exactly what she wants."

Mom looked bewildered, but she sat down. After all, Allie wasn't her daughter; it wasn't her place to disagree. But she looked to Giles, her eyes full of questions. "Is she all right?" she asked.

"She's fine," Giles said shortly, pushing his plate away from him.

Matthew looked around the table. "What did I say?"

"Nothing." Isabel reached for the bottle of wine and topped up her glass. "That's just Allie being Allie. These days, anyway." She looked around the table, apologetic. "It's been like this ever since Seabrook. She won't forgive me for sending her there. And she blames Giles and Matthew for backing my decision." She turned to Mom. "I do hope she hasn't been causing you too much trouble."

Mom looked uncomfortable. "Oh no. She's been . . . well, to be honest, she's been a delight."

A wrinkle appeared on Isabel's forehead. "Really?" She laughed as if she had a hard time believing that.

But it was true. Ever since Allie had moved in, she'd been a perfect angel. She helped with the dishes every night. She watched whatever TV show Mom and I wanted to watch after dinner. On nights when Mom graded papers at the kitchen table, Allie offered to make her green tea, saying it was good for concentration. *And it's, like, a thousand times healthier for you than coffee.* One day I'd come home from an honor society meeting to find Allie in the laundry room, getting my mom to teach her how to work the washing machine. Later, my mom whispered to me, *She's never done a load of laundry in her life. But she wants to learn.*

I glanced over my shoulder. It didn't seem right for me to sit here while the adults talked about Allie behind her back. "I'm just going to . . ." I didn't finish my sentence—no one was paying attention to me anyway—and slipped out of the living room to find Allie.

In the kitchen, the sliding door that led into the backyard stood partially open. I peeked out and saw Allie sitting cross-legged by the pool, smoking a cigarette and dangling her fingers in the pool water. I stepped out the door and walked to the pool's edge, taking a seat beside her.

"Where'd you get that?" I asked, nodding toward the cigarette.

"Isabel's purse," she said, staring blankly at the stone wall that ran the length of the back garden.

She offered me a puff, but I shook my head. Someone could come out here at any time and catch us.

"She left her purse on the kitchen counter," Allie said, taking another drag. "She's supposed to have quit these. But she cheats all the time." She dug around in the pocket of her jeans. "This is the real find, though." She pulled out a small plastic bottle and handed it to me.

Valium. Prescribed to Isabel Andersen. The bottle was almost full.

"Allie . . . ," I said. Before she came to live with us, Giles had made her sign a contract—*An actual fucking document,* she'd told me—that outlined the terms under which she could stay with us. She had to attend all her classes at Palos Verdes Prep, to maintain at least a 2.5 GPA, and to stay away from any and all drugs.

Allie plucked the bottle out of my hands. "Oh, relax. I'm not going to *take* them." She rolled her eyes at me, then blew out a perfect smoke ring, which floated over the pool and disappeared. "But when Isabel can't find these, it will drive her out of her fucking mind." She took the pill bottle from my hand, popped open the cap, and stood up. Then she walked over to the garden wall, tapped out the bottle's contents into one palm, and flung the pills over the wall. She recapped the bottle. "C'mon."

"Where are we going?"

She didn't answer, just crushed out her cigarette against the wall, then walked back into the kitchen. As she passed Isabel's purse, she tucked the bottle back into it, a gesture so smooth that if I hadn't been watching carefully, I would have missed it.

"Allie," I hissed, following her. "She's going to freak out."

Allie turned and smiled, walking backward as she moved toward the stairway. "Um, yeah. That's the whole point." Then she turned and raced up the steps, taking them two at a time.

I hurried after her. "Why?" I didn't see why Allie had to mess with her mom like that. Allie was already in so much trouble—why invite more?

"Because," Allie said lightly. She turned into her bedroom. Once I'd stepped inside to join her, she closed the door behind us, smirking.

She wasn't worried. But I was. Allie had been with us for four months now. And I'd gotten used to having her in the house. A sister, an ally. A friend. I didn't want to think about what my life would be like if Allie got kicked out of the house. If it were just me here, living with Mom and Giles. What would I be then? The odd one out.

"Oh, relax, will you? Yes, Isabel will have a fit. When she opens her precious bottle, she'll accuse me of stealing her pills. She'll probably even get Giles to search my room. But what will she find? Fuck all, that's what." She flopped down on her bed, grinning. "And who's going to look crazy then?"

CHAPTER 16

I scramble out of the Uber onto Linnie Avenue, muttering my thanks to the driver. The car can take me only to the edges of Matthew's neighborhood, because the canals hem it in, a moat of protection for the wealthy. I have to walk over a small bridge and along the narrow walkways overlooking the water until I can reach Matthew's front door. Usually I linger on the way, enjoying the carefully cultivated gardens outside each house, the sense of peace and order that feels otherworldly after the streets of LA. But tonight it's too cold. The water, so bright and cheery in the daytime, looks brackish at night. Palm trees loom ominously against the moonlit clouds.

I pull my coat tight against the wind.

When I reach Matthew's place, I jog up his wide front steps and press the doorbell. It's a few moments before the door opens, and then he's standing there, light and warmth streaming out behind him.

"Natasha," he says. Like Isabel and Allie, he has a glamour about him, the ease of the very good looking.

After giving me a brief hug, he leads me into the large open room that forms both the kitchen and living area. The lighting, cleverly hidden in the space where the walls meet the ceiling, makes the room glow like a lit candle. The furnishings in Matthew's house are minimal but striking: a battered antique leather couch, a low coffee table with some books scattered across it. A long credenza against one wall with framed photos arranged across its surface.

My phone buzzes in my pocket, but I ignore it. It's good to be back here. This is perhaps the only place that feels like home to me right now. As I shrug off my coat, I remember how the room used to look, back in the early days of the investigation. Papers spread across every surface, coffee mugs and takeout containers wedged in among the files. I often napped on this couch while Matthew talked to the private investigator on the phone, knowing he'd fill me in on the details of their conversation later.

"Drink?" he says, gesturing to a single wineglass he's set out on the kitchen counter. His tan has deepened on his vacation. "I picked out something nice for you."

After Allie went missing, Matthew went to rehab—a decision that was long past due, he admitted—and he's been sober ever since. But he always makes sure to have a nice wine for me when I come over for dinner. *No reason for you to go without,* he always says. It seems a waste—I'll drink two glasses at most, and he'll have to toss the rest, but of course Matthew doesn't care about little things like that.

I take off my coat and throw it over the back of the couch. As I settle on one of the barstools that overlook the kitchen, I watch Matthew busy himself with the saucepans on the stove. He's put on weight since he started seeing Chloe. His body, gaunt for so long, now looks strong, athletic.

"Smells delicious," I say. The air feels bright, full of citrus and pepper. He's making shrimp and stir-fried vegetables, his movements in the kitchen practiced and easy.

He finishes slicing an onion with a gleaming knife, then slides the pieces into a hot pan. "So," he says. "How are you?" His eyes are so dark that the pupils seem to merge with the irises. "Ruiz told me about this weekend. That you went down to look at the belongings."

I shift on the stool, hoping that Ruiz didn't also mention my episode of blindness. Matthew won't lecture me about going to the station, not like my mother would, but the fact that I've had another episode would disturb him. "Yeah."

"How was it?" he says. He continues cooking, but his eyes are on my face.

"Okay," I lie. "It wasn't a big deal."

He makes a *hmm* sound.

"I was fine. Really."

He stirs the glistening onions, nodding slowly. "Ruiz called just now. To say the body isn't Allie. Definitively."

I feel the breath whoosh out of me.

"The body had old fractures on the humerus," Matthew says. "From childhood. Allie never broke a bone in her life."

Tears prick at the edge of my eyelids. Even though I'd been sure the clothes weren't Allie's, it's another thing to have that officially confirmed. At first, I feel a flood of relief. And then, exhaustion. The search isn't over. It may never be over.

In Matthew's face, I see the mirror of my own emotions. It's a sadness at odds with his overall glow of health.

Then it occurs to me to wonder: Why did Ruiz tell Matthew, and not me? I pull my phone out of my pocket and realize that the call that came through minutes before was from Ruiz. I have a voicemail waiting to be opened.

"Everything okay?" Matthew asks.

"Yes," I say, tucking my phone back into my pocket. It's time to focus on Matthew. "How was the honeymoon?"

His face softens. "Good," he says, and I catch a glimmer of a smile on his face. "Chloe loved it out there. Although she got homesick for Sara." I'd spent some time with Chloe after she and Matthew started dating, when Matthew encouraged me to come to some meetings of the Lost and the Missing. Once, she'd told me that having a daughter had made it difficult for her to date. But that was before Matthew. Matthew is great with Sara. Sometimes when Chloe watches them goofing off together, her eyes film over with tears.

Matthew finishes up the cooking and serves our meal on large white plates, which we take to the dining room table. As we sit down, he pushes aside some real estate paperwork, and I feel a sudden pinch in my chest. I've gotten used to having dinner over here, but we won't have these evenings for much longer. The Venice house will sell. And Matthew will, of course, invite me to the house in Beverly Hills—but it won't be the same. Not with Chloe and Sara there too. He has his own family now.

Matthew takes a sip of his sparkling water. "So. Isabel is throwing a little party for Chloe and me on Sunday. A kind of belated wedding reception."

I raise my eyebrows. "I thought you didn't want a reception." The less publicity, the better, he'd said. He'd had his fill of the media taking an interest in his life.

He makes a face. "Well, Izzie insists there's got to be *some* kind of party. I managed to talk her down to a small gathering at her house. Just family and close friends."

"Ah," I say, feeling strangely touched to be included in that group.

"Will you come?" he asks. "It'd mean a lot to me."

"Of course," I tell him. Matthew's always been there for me. It was Matthew who stepped in when the police wanted to question me again, months into the investigation, and made sure I had a lawyer that time around. It was Matthew who defended me to my mother when I dropped out of LACSA, insisting that I needed a break from the notoriety. "Hey, listen—" I begin. I need to tell him about the key chain. He'll want to know.

But he's talking over me. "Hey, you want to see something cool?" He pulls up a photo on his phone and tilts the screen toward me. Him and Chloe swimming with dolphins. "You have to do this sometime. I'm telling you, it was unreal."

In the pictures, he's smiling, his head tilted back, water-slicked hair catching the sun.

For some reason, this makes my heart contract. I've never seen him smile like that before. "It looks great," I say.

He scrolls through a few more images—crystalline water, a beachside bonfire, Chloe on horseback. And I realize: He's happy. Apart from that brief mention of Ruiz at the start of the night, he hasn't mentioned the investigation once. I tug at the edge of the pure-white tablecloth, remembering Ruiz's face in the subway station, his caution as he told me not to read too much into the key chain. I know Ruiz is trying to spare me the crushing disappointment I'll feel if we find out it's a fake. Can I really subject Matthew to that kind of pain, just because it would make me feel better to have someone to talk to?

Matthew is still talking. "And these mud baths, they have this direct view of the volcano . . ."

My mother thinks Matthew allows me to obsess about the case too much. But is she right? Or is it the other way around? Maybe I'm the one who keeps dragging him down, refusing to let him move on.

After Allie's disappearance, Matthew developed ulcers. His hair started going gray. But since meeting Chloe, he seems to be feeling his way back into normal life. The two of them go running on the beach in the morning. They make green smoothies and sip them on the patio overlooking the pool.

I take a deep breath, forcing myself to comment cheerfully on the photos of the mud baths. No, I can't tell Matthew about the key chain. Not yet. Not until Ruiz has something definitive to tell me.

Matthew glances over at me. "You look tired," he says. "Have you been sleeping?"

I put a hand to my face, embarrassed at what it reveals about me. "Yes."

He's not convinced. "Ruiz shouldn't have called you about that body. That wasn't right."

"Matthew—"

"No. He's got to let you get on with your life." He sets his phone firmly down on the table. "Getting dragged back into this, it's the last thing you need."

He catches the expression on my face.

"Sorry," he says. "I don't mean to sound like your mom. I just don't want you to miss out on . . . well, life. Because of what happened to Allie. At a certain point, we have to move on."

I nod, trying to look like I'm taking this in. But inside, I'm thinking: *And then there was one.* It used to be only Matthew and me who hadn't moved on. And now he's joined the ranks of the others.

"Natasha?"

I know I won't be able to speak without getting choked up. Luckily, a call comes through on Matthew's cell, and he's distracted from our conversation. As he answers, I take a large sip of my wine.

Holding the phone to his shoulder, he says, "It's Chloe. Do you mind? She wants me to say good night to Sara."

I wave to him that it's fine, and he stands up and walks into the hallway. "Hello?" he says into the phone. "Who am I speaking with? Sara? Sara who?"

I can hear Sara shouting on the other end of the line: "Sara Navaaarrro."

"Who?" he says, pretending not to recognize her voice.

I wander toward the credenza, staring at the frames arranged on it. There's a photo of a very young Matthew and Isabel, sitting on the floor of a tiny apartment and eating dinner on an overturned cardboard box that serves as their table. There are a couple of industry photos, Matthew standing beside men I don't recognize. And then, a photo of Isabel and Matthew and Allie at Lake Gregory. Allie told me they used to go up there in the summer, to Crestline, that Matthew had taught her to fish there. In the photo, Allie must be nine or ten, and she's wearing a bright-blue swimsuit. The smile spread across her face is one I never saw when I knew her: pure, uncomplicated happiness.

I look at her round cheeks, her goofy stance. She looks nothing like the Allie I knew so well.

CHAPTER 17

December 2007

After Allie and I escaped the Christmas Eve dinner, Allie lay back on her bed while I sat at her desk, sorting through the mess scattered across its surface. A half-empty perfume bottle, scraps of silver fabric, an old-fashioned lighter with flowers engraved on the sides.

Laughter floated up from downstairs.

"God, why don't they leave already?" Allie said, pulling a pillow over her face.

The dinner had continued without us. My mother tried, once, to get us to come downstairs, but when she saw Allie's belligerent face, she gave up without too much fuss.

"They're not so bad," I said mildly. I liked Isabel, who was unfailingly gracious to me. And Matthew's only crime seemed to be talking too much.

Allie yanked the pillow off her face and shot me a look that could've peeled paint off a wall. "Are you fucking kidding me?"

I fiddled with the silver lighter. "I mean . . ." All she had to do was be nice to them for the length of one dinner. It didn't seem that much to ask.

"Jesus fucking Christ, Tash, if you defend them, I will lose my mind."

"I'm not!" I had never disagreed with Allie before. I was beginning to see that it wouldn't go well if I ever decided to go that route.

"Good," she said sharply. Then she rolled over onto her stomach and pushed herself up to stand on the mattress. "God, on a night like this, I'm going to need reinforcements." She reached up to the air-conditioning vent, fiddling with the screws that held it against the wall. Once she had them loosened, she pulled the vent off, revealing a row of tiny liquor bottles, the kind you saw on airplanes, lined up on the inner ledge of the duct.

"Welcome to Café Allie," she said with a sweep of her hand. "What can I get you?"

"Allie!"

"What?" She set the vent down on the bed, grabbed a few bottles from the ledge, and then sat down on the mattress.

"You'll get in trouble," I said.

She laughed. "Only if they find out. And they won't find out." She tossed me two bottles of Baileys. "Here, you'll like that. Tastes like candy."

I turned the bottle over in my hands. Getting caught wasn't my only concern. "I thought you were sober," I said in a hesitant voice.

"I am!" Allie said cheerfully. "No pills, no coke, not even any weed. I'm practically a saint." She twisted the top off a bottle of vodka and took a long swig. "Relax, Tash Ross. Alcohol was never my problem."

Was that how it worked? Were they two separate things?

I looked at the array of bottles inside the AC duct. "Where'd you get all this?"

"Oh, I know people," she said. "Billy at the corner store likes me." She drained the last of the bottle into her mouth, then picked up her hairbrush from the bedside table and began running it through her hair. Allie had wavy hair that seemed to look artfully styled no matter how messily she arranged it.

"Why can't I have hair like yours?" I asked.

Allie stood up and walked to her dresser, where she began sorting through bottles of hair products. "Want me to show you how to do it? You just have to have the right tools."

Which is how I ended up sitting on the edge of her bed while she wielded a flat iron and a spray bottle on my hair. She drank as she worked, her mood improving with each sip. And I drank, too, appreciating the burn of the Baileys as it slid down my throat. The feel of Allie's fingers as she worked on one section of my hair and then another put me into a kind of trance.

"How long does this take?" I asked.

"As long as it takes," she said. "That's what Ray, Isabel's stylist, used to say. He always said, '*Para lucir hay que sufrir.*'"

I finished my first bottle of Baileys and twisted open the cap of the second. "What does that mean?"

"'You have to suffer to be beautiful.'"

I turned to look at her, but she yanked my head back into the position she wanted it in. "How do you know Spanish, anyway?" At school, she took French.

"Girl, Spanish is my first language. When I was little, Isabel was busy making movies. So she got Marisol to look after me."

I'd met Marisol. At Isabel's house, she often clattered around in the kitchen while the rest of us gathered in the living room. "I thought Marisol was your housekeeper."

Allie shrugged. "Now she is. But she started out as my babysitter. She used to take me to her house in the Valley sometimes, and I'd play with her kids. They taught me all the good swear words."

When she'd finished with my hair, she said "There!" and prodded me toward the mirror. As I stood up, I felt pleasantly buzzed, a warm feeling spreading throughout my body. Walking closer, I stared at my reflection. "Whoa." My hair, usually frizzy and uncontrollable, fell in soft, dark-blonde waves past my shoulders.

"Right?" Allie said, pleased with herself.

I turned my head from side to side. "Wow." Even my face looked different. Without the distraction of my wild hair, my eyes took center stage, pale and bright against my freckled skin.

Allie threw herself down on the bed, grinning. "Eat your heart out, Palos Verdes Prep." She yawned and pulled a pillow over her head.

I spent a few minutes gazing at myself in the mirror, lifting my hair up in different styles and examining my reflection. I had never thought of myself as pretty, but now I was wondering if I'd been mistaken. Maybe I could get Allie to do my makeup, too, to show me how to use all the bottles and tubes on her dresser. "Hey, Als?"

But when I turned around, I saw that her chest was rising and falling in a slow rhythm. She'd fallen asleep. It was only then that I noticed how many empty vodka bottles were strewn across the bed.

Carefully, I gathered up all the empty bottles and wrapped them in a Neiman Marcus bag I found under Allie's desk. Then I padded downstairs into the empty kitchen and shoved the bag deep into the garbage, covering it with some crumpled-up paper towels.

At the sink, I poured myself a glass of water. When I heard a sharp laugh coming from the yard, I jumped. Edging over to the sliding doors, I saw Giles and Matthew, fully dressed, floating on rafts in the steaming pool. Matthew reached out and yanked at Giles's raft, almost overturning him, and Giles let out a shout. They were both holding highball glasses as they paddled around. What was it that Isabel had said about them? *Like children.*

I was about to slip back upstairs when a voice called out from the living room: "Hello?"

Shit.

"Who's there?"

That was Isabel's voice. It was funny how familiar it sounded. I'd heard it so many times before in movies that it somehow felt like the voice of an old friend.

"It's just me," I called. "Natasha."

"Oh, Natasha! Come join me."

Slowly, I walked into the living room, where Isabel lounged on the couch, her long legs stretched out on the cushions.

She smiled at me and adjusted her position so there was room beside her. "Come sit. The boys are being very silly at the moment."

"Where's my mom?" I asked, taking a seat on the edge of the couch.

"Oh, she went to bed a while ago." Isabel had kicked off her shoes and looked completely at ease, as if this were her house, not ours. There was a fire going in the fireplace, and the flickering light played across her features. She leaned closer, and I flinched, thinking she was about to smell my breath. But she just tucked a lock of hair behind my ear. "You girls have been doing each other's hair, it seems."

I put a hand up to my hair, which didn't feel like mine anymore. "Oh. Yeah."

"Well, you look very beautiful," she said. The way she looked at me made me feel as if I were standing in a spotlight. "Oh, she blushes! I'm serious, you know. You have very lovely bone structure. And look at this skin!" She touched my cheek with one manicured finger. "If you're ever interested in modeling, I could connect you with some people."

I laughed—a loud, abrupt sound.

Isabel looked surprised, and perhaps a little offended. "Did I say something wrong?"

"Sorry, it's just . . . I'm not really model material."

"Well, of course you are! Just look at you. Like a young Nicole Kidman, that's what I thought when I first saw you." She smiled, then gazed into the fire. "You know, modeling is how I got my start when we moved out here from Ohio. Without that money, Matthew and I wouldn't have survived our first year in LA. Of course, I never had the right body type for it. Too many curves, no matter how much I dieted. But you—your height, your weight. You'd be perfect."

I glanced down at my flat chest, my bony legs. I'd never thought of either as assets.

"Anyhow," she said lightly, "if you're ever interested, just let me know."

"Oh. Thanks." Before, I'd assumed she was just being nice, but now I wondered: Was she serious? Me, a model? The thought was absurd. As was the idea of me ever picking up the phone and simply giving Isabel Andersen a call. But another part of me, the part still buzzing from alcohol, thought: Maybe I will. Maybe it's that easy. Call up Isabel, and she'll change my life.

She took a sip of her wine. "So, I hear that you and Allie have grown close."

"Yeah."

"That's nice," she said slowly, toying with the edge of her sleeve. "I know Giles was worried about . . . that aspect of having her here."

"We're great," I said. "She's great." And I felt it, in my chest, how much I loved Allie. How important she was to me.

"Mm." Isabel's long eyelashes cast shadows on her cheeks. "Just be careful, okay, Natasha?"

I paused. "Careful about what?"

"Careful about my daughter," she said quietly. She leaned forward and set her wineglass on the coffee table. "I can see you're a sweet girl. A soft girl. But Allie—she's not like you. Don't get me wrong—my daughter can be wonderful. Charming. But I don't want you to get hurt when . . ." She pulled her knees up to her chest, suddenly looking very vulnerable.

"When what?"

For a moment, she didn't say anything. "I suppose you know why we pulled her out of Seabrook," she said.

I felt my forehead wrinkle. That was an odd way of phrasing it. Allie hadn't been "pulled out" of Seabrook. She'd been kicked out. But maybe Isabel didn't want to acknowledge that.

"Yeah. She told me."

Isabel dug her toes into the leather of the couch. "She was very careful, you know, about the number of pills she took. Not enough to do herself real harm, but enough to scare the daylights out of us." She looked at me, her eyes liquid. "She wanted to punish me, you see, for sending her there. That was her way of getting back at me. Her revenge."

Outside, there was a large splash—the sound of someone falling into the pool—followed by the roar of Matthew's laughter. I squeezed the glass in my hands. What was Isabel talking about? What pills?

"Just be careful, that's all," Isabel said. She reached out a hand and placed it on my arm, the warmth of her skin radiating through my sleeve. "Allie is unpredictable. And I'd hate to see her turn on you the way she's turned on us."

CHAPTER 18

When Matthew returns from talking to Chloe, we spend the rest of the evening discussing his new house, the upcoming move. The whole time, the knowledge of the key chain digs into my chest like a splinter. But I sip my wine and smile and think of Matthew's happiness—how new it is, and how fragile.

When I leave his house, I follow the footpath along the canals, shivering in the cold. The air is icy and salt-tinged. Across the water, someone is steering a boat out of its slip, and its headlights spark against the dark water. And I think again about that moment with Isabel when we sat together on the couch at Christmas, her warm, concerned tone as she spoke.

I'd hate to see her turn on you the way she's turned on us.

At the time, I hadn't known how to take her warning. Now, though, her words seem prescient.

In the end, Allie didn't turn her anger on me the way she had with her family. But that last year, she put up a wall around herself. It happened slowly, steadily, over a period of months, and when she was done, I'd been stunned to find myself on the other side.

~

When I return home, I find a package waiting for me in the mailroom—the doorbell camera I ordered this morning. After taking the box up to my apartment, I spend the next hour figuring out how to set it up and get it to sync with my phone. The process is fiddly, but once the camera is installed, I can sit on the couch in my living room, gazing at my phone screen, and see everything that's happening outside my door.

Which isn't much. A few neighbors pass by on their way to the elevator. Abby. Mrs. Singh. No one stops or even turns their head in the direction of my apartment door. It's tempting to keep sitting here and watching, convincing myself that any minute, the person who left the key chain will show up. But that's ridiculous. The camera will send an alert to my phone if it detects activity, and I can play back the video then. There's no point in sitting here, glued to my phone.

I stuff the directions for the doorbell camera back into the box and walk to the hall closet to stash it there. When I slide the box onto the top shelf, my fingers graze against another, larger cardboard box, with the word *Photography* scrawled across the side in my mother's handwriting. Mom was the one who helped me pack up the college apartment Allie and I shared, after I decided to move out.

Gently, I pull the box off the shelf and carry it into my bedroom. Then I set it down on the bed and pry back the flaps. A familiar, dusty smell wafts out, and I have a sudden flash of our college apartment's warped hardwood floors and chintzy pink bathroom tiles. My first home away from home. On some nights, Greg came over to cook and Allie blasted music on the stereo, and the three of us would dance around the kitchen, the wine and the music smoothing out the tension between Greg and me. At those times, we almost felt like our own little family. Dysfunctional, sure, but a family nonetheless.

Methodically, I begin sifting through the contents of the box. I haven't touched any of this stuff since Allie's disappearance. At the top of the box are two SLRs—a newer Nikon and a vintage Olympus—as well as a Polaroid that Allie gave me for my twentieth birthday. Underneath those, I find plastic sleeves of negatives and stacks of prints, which have begun to warp and stick together.

Tucked up against one side of the box is an eight-by-ten manila envelope with PL STUDIOS stamped on the front. I know what's inside it, but I can't bring myself to look at those, not today. Setting the envelope to one side, I start sorting through the loose prints, wincing at the ones that rip slightly as I peel them apart.

They're mostly shots I took at LACSA. Many are of Allie, my most convenient model, my most willing subject. In some, she poses theatrically, playing to the camera. But in others, I've caught her unawares, staring out a window or absorbed in her sewing. In those moments, she looks so different from the camera-ready Allie that it's jarring. Her expression is preoccupied, her forehead furrowed as if she's worried about something just outside the camera's frame. I examine one image of her sitting in the armchair by the living room window. She's not wearing any makeup, and her face looks drawn, solemn.

I remember Detective Golanski asking me, in what must have been our third interview, "Had Allie been depressed recently?"

I'd shifted in my chair. "No," I said. "She's been doing really great. She hasn't been drinking. She's started going to her classes. She's even doing well in some of them."

Golanski frowned. "Yes, I see she got an A. In Professor Macnamara's class."

I flushed. "She earned it," I said, hearing the defensiveness in my voice. "She worked really hard in that class."

The detectives didn't understand. Allie had vowed to turn her life around a million times before. I knew, better than anyone, how empty those promises could turn out to be. But this time felt different. This time, she hadn't made any big announcement; she hadn't started some fad diet that consisted primarily of eating kale. I hadn't even noticed she wasn't drinking anymore until one night, at a party at Greg's, I reached over and took a sip of her drink. What I'd thought was her usual G&T turned out to be sparkling water with lime.

"She was doing really well," I insisted, my voice cracking on the last word.

Ruiz looked up from the folder he'd been leafing through. "But just a few months before that, she'd been in a pretty bad place, hadn't she? Failing her classes, partying hard."

"Well . . . yes." September had been a shit show—Allie and Greg had gone to Luxe constantly that month. They'd disappear into the bathroom together, and when they came out, Allie would be floating on air, her pupils dilated. *Don't leave, Tash. We have to dance!* "But that was months ago."

Fluorescent light reflected off Golanski's bald head. "Look, here's what I see. Allie had a bad year last year. She was on academic probation. Those TMZ photos caused quite a stir, and after that, her parents cut off her allowance and took away her car. Then, the week she goes missing, she has a fight with her best friend."

He meant Greg.

"Plus, her boyfriend—this Macnamara guy—breaks up with her. Finally, she leaves her phone and belongings behind and disappears." He looked at me, waiting for me to put the pieces together.

"It wasn't a good time for her," I said stubbornly. "I know that."

He sighed. "Look, given her history, Ms. Rossi, we do have to consider the strong possibility of suicide."

My stomach felt hollow. "'Given her history'?"

Ruiz found a piece of paper in his folder and slid it across the table to me. Some kind of hospital form. My eyes ran over the paper, taking in names, dates, signatures. *Seabrook. Emergency Admittance.*

"It isn't what you think," I said.

"How's that, exactly?" Golanski asked.

"Isabel told me . . . ," I said, but my words trailed off.

"Told you what?" Ruiz asked.

"She said it was a stunt," I said softly. "A way for Allie to get attention." In my head, that was how I'd filed Isabel's story away. More of Allie's dramatics. Now, though, I wondered why—how—I'd allowed myself to dismiss the event so casually.

My eyes strayed to the doctor's notes at the bottom of the page. *Continued suicidal ideation. Keep under observation.* The staff at the hospital hadn't thought the overdose was a stunt. They'd thought it was serious enough that they needed to stop her from trying again.

I closed my eyes, small details from our teenage years clicking into place in my head. Giles's need to keep tabs on Allie's movements at all times. My mother's unfailing gentleness with Allie, as if she were some kind of injured animal. All the times Allie had to go see the school counselor for no apparent reason.

They'd known. They'd all known about the suicide attempt, recognized it was serious, worried that it could happen again. But nobody had told me.

Now, in my bedroom, I spread the photographs out around me on the bed, seeing Allie in all her different modes: dramatic, silly, pissed off, sad. Was Golanski right? Suicide is the narrative that accounts for nearly all of Allie's actions the week she went missing. But still, I can't quite believe it. Not Allie. Not at that specific time.

I walk into the living room, where I find my laptop and sit down on the couch before pulling up the Barclay's footage that I have saved in a folder. Whenever I start to feel wobbly about the suicide theory, I play this video again. To reassure myself.

In the footage from the doughnut shop, Allie sits at the far table near the window, her fingers tapping against her coffee cup. She looks relaxed, but there's an underlying tension running through her that I recognize. This is the same look she used to have when we were at a party, whenever a guy she was interested in had arrived, but she was pretending not to notice him. She'd be laughing and talking as if everything was normal, but I could feel the change in her, a kind of electric energy coming off her body.

It's that intensity I see in the Barclay's video. The set of her shoulders, the look on her face. That's how I know. In this video, Allie isn't despairing. She isn't contemplating the end of her life.

She's waiting for something to *happen*.

CHAPTER 19

On my lunch break at work, I check my phone messages. It's been only a few days since I gave Ruiz the key chain: too soon, I know, for him to have found out anything. Still, I can't stop myself from texting him: Any news?

Two hours later, I get a response.

Can you meet at Gina's? 5:30?

Gina's is the diner where we used to go to talk about the case. I feel a prickle of surprise on the back of my neck. I'd been expecting him to advise me to be patient, to not expect instant results.

Sure, I type back. What could he have found out so quickly? Or does he simply want to meet to talk? I spend the rest of the afternoon jittery and distracted, and my boss has to remind me twice to locate the file he requested.

At the end of the workday, I grab my coat and bag and rush out the door. The subway ride to Gina's feels painfully slow, and I jog the short walk from the station to the diner.

Gina's is a tiny little place with orange vinyl booths and waitresses dressed in old-fashioned uniforms. It's the kind of spot with regulars, people who've been coming here for decades and have a preferred stool at the counter. The air smells of fryer grease and reverberates with a constant, low clamor.

I arrive before Ruiz and slide into the nearest empty booth as I wait for him to show. A TV mounted on the wall is tuned to a news station, and I see flashes of some celebrity news show—the latest Hollywood divorce, an actress's botched plastic surgery.

The waitress, an older woman with a limp, approaches and hands me a big plastic menu. Then she squints at me through her glasses. "Hey, I know you," she says. "Didn't you used to come in here with Adam?"

It takes a split second for me to remember that Adam is Ruiz's first name. "Um, yeah." This is the waitress who used to top up our coffees back then.

"Yeah, you've done something different with your hair," she says. "But I never forget a face." For a moment, she studies me, and I'm afraid she's about to connect me with the Allie Andersen investigation. But then she's distracted by Ruiz's arrival. "Well, hello, stranger," she says to him.

"Hey, Diane." He gives her shoulder a quick squeeze before sitting down in the booth across from me.

"Pecan pie?" Diane asks him.

He nods and tells her to add a decaf coffee. He's dressed more formally today. Suit and tie. As he settles into the booth, he loosens the top button at his neck.

When Diane turns to me, I say, "Just tea, please."

As she walks away, Ruiz blows on his hands, which have reddened from the cold.

"What is it?" I ask, too anxious to begin with niceties. "What have you found out?"

He shifts the napkin and utensils in front of him on the table. "So, the lab techs say there's no way we can pull fingerprints off the key chain—the surface is too uneven."

I close my eyes. Another dead end.

"But we've done some research, and that brand of flash drive—they only manufactured that particular design in 2012. It was a short run, so that style is actually pretty rare."

My eyelids fly open. "So it could really be hers."

"It could be," he says cautiously.

We both fall silent as Diane returns with our order, sliding mugs and a slice of pie onto the table.

After she moves away, Ruiz shrugs off his coat and resumes: "But the ink, where Allie's name is written—the lab says that's fresh. So whoever wrote that did it recently."

I straighten in my seat, picturing Allie leaning over the flash drive, painstakingly etching the letters into the plastic. "So what do you think that means?"

Ruiz cuts into his pie with the edge of his fork. "Well. The key chain could still be someone trying to mess with you. If someone was really familiar with that key chain style, it's not impossible they could've gotten a matching one on eBay. Or . . ."

"What?"

He takes a bite of the pie, chews. "Or it's genuine. And someone's trying to point us toward some information."

I think of Allie typing on her computer late at night, slapping the laptop closed before I could see what was on the screen. "What kind of information?"

Ruiz shakes his head. "I don't know. But it does suggest there's some significance to her laptop being drenched in water like it was. Maybe someone didn't want us to see what was on it."

Someone opens the diner door, letting a gust of cold air blow into the room, and I shiver. *That's not right,* I want to tell him. But I know his theory feels plausible. Was Allie killed for whatever was on her laptop, or her flash drive?

"Of course, the laptop damage could've been accidental," he says. "But it also could've been someone destroying evidence, getting rid of files they didn't want anyone else to see."

Something sour rises up in the back of my throat. "Maybe." I pause. "Files . . . like what?"

He shrugs. “My best guess? Something to do with Greg. With the drugs.”

I frown, picking at the edges of my paper napkin. “But why would Allie keep anything like that on her computer? She took pills; she didn’t sell them.”

Ruiz rolls up his sleeves, and I glimpse the edge of the tattoo on his right forearm. A twining vine, underneath which is written: *Carmen, 8-11-99.* “Look,” he says, “in those last few months, Allie didn’t have access to money, right? Her parents had cut her off. But during the investigation, what we noticed is—that didn’t seem to stop her from spending. She was still going shopping, still going to fancy restaurants, no change in her habits at all.”

“Well, yeah,” I say. “She was borrowing cash from Greg.” Greg had a trust fund too. What did he care if Allie spent some of that money?

“That’s the thing,” Ruiz says. “Greg told us he’d been loaning Allie money for weeks that fall, but then suddenly she stopped asking. But she still had money on hand. He wanted her to tell him where it was coming from.” He takes another bite of his pie. After a moment, he says, “That’s why they argued, the night she disappeared.”

“Oh.” I feel like I’ve been hit in the chest. “You never told me that.” I always thought the fight had been just some typical spat between the two of them—Greg bristling at some perceived slight, Allie flying off the handle.

Ruiz looks discomfited, as if he’s regretting telling me about it. “It was something Greg said when we interviewed him. You know I can’t share every detail of the case.”

Yes. I know that. But somehow I’ve convinced myself, over the years, that Ruiz made exceptions when it came to me.

There’s an awkward pause before he continues. “Anyway, Greg wanted to know where she was getting her money,” he says. “And she wouldn’t say. He had some idea that she was going behind his back, poaching his clients.”

I laugh. “You can’t be serious. You think Allie was selling drugs?”

Ruiz doesn't smile. "Greg thought she was."

"I mean, how would she even do that? If she wanted to sell drugs, she'd need a supplier."

He hesitates, then takes a sip of his coffee. Finally, he says, "Greg thought she'd found one."

"Are you kidding?"

"Jairo Ocampo," he says.

A face flickers in my memory. At one of Greg's parties: a stocky Hispanic guy with a shaved head lingering in a doorway. "Jairo?"

"You knew him?"

"I mean, I didn't *know* him. I saw him around, at parties. He wasn't a dealer. He bought from Greg. He didn't sell."

Ruiz rubs a hand across his face. "Yeah, that's what we heard too. Greg was adamant, though—he thought Jairo and Allie had teamed up and had gone into business together."

"That's crazy," I say.

But even as I say it, I'm remembering.

CHAPTER 20

April 2012

Allie and I stood on the balcony at Greg's apartment, next to a tabletop crowded with liquor bottles. It was some kind of theater after-party—a few people were still in costume, and the energy was high. Tequila shots had been taken. Everyone there was from LACSA—at first. Then, around one a.m., strangers started trickling in off the street. That was when I saw a group of Hispanic guys moving through the crowd. They were looking around the room, sizing up the people dancing to the pounding music. Eventually the guys gravitated toward the table on the balcony, where they started sorting through the liquor bottles and pouring themselves drinks.

Greg was nowhere to be seen, but I could hear his voice from somewhere inside, shouting at someone to change the music. The Hispanic guys were laughing and talking to each other in Spanish. Every once in a while, they'd point at someone and laugh.

The shortest one among them was also the loudest. He had a wide smile and a laugh that sounded like a machine gun. When he caught sight of Allie, who was wearing a dress that barely covered her ass, he sized her up from head to toe and then turned to his friends and made a comment under his breath.

Allie's back was to him, but suddenly she spun around and took a step in his direction, her nose level with his nose. "Say that again."

He grinned. "Hey, girlie. I'll say it to you all night long if you want."

Allie swayed a little on her feet. She'd been drinking steadily all night, and she was a little worse for wear. All of a sudden, she let loose a volley of Spanish. I couldn't make out what she was saying, but by the guy's reaction, I knew it wasn't complimentary.

I tugged at her elbow. This guy didn't look like the kind of person you wanted to mess with. But Allie didn't stop. She got more and more in his face, and as she did, his scowl deepened and his friends tightened their circle around him.

Finally, Allie ran out of breath, and the guy stared her down, his eyes narrow and fierce.

"Jairo," one of his friends said. "You gonna let her talk to you like that?"

There was a long pause; then Jairo burst out laughing. "What the fuck, man!" He turned to his friends. "I mean, what in the actual fuck? You hear that filthy mouth?" He turned and grabbed Allie by the shoulder, giving her a friendly squeeze. "Damn, *chica*. You sure as shit didn't learn that in Spanish 101."

For a moment, Allie looked furious, still hungry for a fight, and I worried she was going to hit him. Then Jairo leaned over and murmured something in her ear. Whatever he said made her start to laugh. "Oh, fuck off," she said, giving him a friendly punch in the chest.

He grinned. "So, we gonna do some shots, or what?"

By the end of the night, they'd taken over the playlist in the living room and were singing along at the top of their lungs to some rap song with Spanish lyrics.

CHAPTER 21

"What is it?" Ruiz asks.

"Nothing. I just . . . Allie did know Jairo. Not well. But I saw them talking at parties once or twice."

Ruiz leans forward, his eyes bright.

"It's not like they were friends or anything," I say hurriedly. Sometimes Allie just hit it off with someone at a party, and for an hour she'd seem to have a new best friend. Then, the next day, she wouldn't be able to remember their name.

"Huh. I wonder." He pushes his empty plate to one side. "At the time, when Greg was telling us this stuff about Jairo, it didn't seem that credible. It just seemed like he wanted us to be looking at someone else. Anyone else."

"Did you look into Jairo back then?" I ask.

"Of course." He sounds offended that I'd even ask. "We didn't get far, though. He'd been busted once for stealing a car, when he was a teenager, and he'd done a little community service time. But there was nothing that connected him to Allie. Or to dealing."

"But you could reinterview him now," I say. "You could reinterview Greg. Ask them both about the flash drive."

Ruiz runs a hand through his hair. "It's not that easy."

"Why not?"

"Listen," he sighs. "The flash drive could be important. But on its own, it doesn't give us enough cause to start reinterviewing witnesses.

If we get close to Greg again, we're going to have his lawyers down our throats." He sighs again. "And . . . I should tell you, there's been this reporter sniffing around the station. Neil Agarwal. He's doing a piece for the four-year anniversary of Allie's disappearance. He's driving my boss crazy—the original *Times* article was bad enough."

I feel a burning sensation in my chest. "So, what? You're just going to ignore this?"

"No. Of course not. But we have to be careful about how we move forward. When we do talk to these guys again, we have to be sure of what we're going after. We have to have something solid on our side. In the meantime, I'm asking you to sit tight."

"Sit tight?"

Across the room, Diane glances over at us.

"Isn't that what I've been doing for the past four years?" My hands are shaking. "You can't just take the key chain and then do nothing."

"That's not what I'm—"

"You know what? This is bullshit." I dig through my purse for my wallet and throw a twenty-dollar bill down on the table.

"Natasha—" Ruiz says.

"It's fine," I snap, grabbing my coat and bag and scooting out of the booth. I don't know why I let myself get my hopes up. Why did I think the cops could help when they never have before?

"Natasha." He's leaning forward, holding out a hand as if to get me to slow down. "I get what you're going through. I really do."

I stare down at his forearm, at the letters of the tattoo peeking out from beneath his sleeve. "Would you 'sit tight,' then? If you were me?"

There's a long silence, and he flushes uncomfortably. We both know the answer to that question.

Turning away, I brush past the other customers and hurry out into the cold night air.

When I get back to my apartment, I pace restlessly from room to room. *Sit tight,* Ruiz had said.

Screw that.

For a moment at Gina's, I'd let myself believe that the key chain was going to be the thing that broke the case open. That Ruiz would use it to actually *do* something. But clearly that's not going to happen. The police will move at their usual glacial pace, and in the meantime, whatever message I'm supposed to have gotten from Allie's key chain will drift further and further out of reach.

What I need is someone who can tell me more about Allie during the winter before she disappeared. Someone who might know something about this flash drive.

Greg.

I remember Greg lying on Allie's bed while she was getting ready for some party, complaining about her slowness as he ate Ginger-O's straight out of the packet. Eventually he got so bored of watching her try on different outfits that he grabbed her phone from the bedside table, typed in her passcode, and started flicking through her text messages. After a minute, he laughed and said, "Who the fuck is Anthony?"

Allie glanced over her shoulder. "Oh. That barista at Café Bijou." If she was annoyed by Greg going through her texts, she didn't show it. She turned to me, holding a gold top against her chest. "What about this one?" she asked.

But I wasn't looking at her. I was watching Greg type out a message on Allie's phone. "What are you doing?" I asked sharply.

He didn't look up. "Texting Anthony. On behalf of our girl."

In my living room, I halt my pacing, Greg knew Allie's passcode to her phone. What were the odds he knew the password to her laptop too? Had he scrolled through her emails the same way he'd browsed through her texts?

I sit down on the couch, open my laptop, and log in to the WhereIsAllieAndersen forums. I know exactly what I'm looking for—the picture of Greg's house that was posted two years ago. Greg's here in LA. He's within easy reach. All I have to do is find him.

After a few minutes of scrolling, I find the photo. A sleek, midcentury house set into a hillside. But there's no address. Quickly, I send a message to the poster: **Did you happen to get an address?**

MayBee634's reply appears within a few seconds. **Yeah. I posted it at the time, but then people started tagging his house and Greg sicced his lawyers on me.**

I type out a response. **Don't suppose you'd be able to share it with me—just privately?**

> **Are you nuts? His lawyers told me I could go to jail for, like, five years for spreading that info around.**

I sigh. The pic isn't much use to me if I don't have the address. Leaning forward, I study the photograph carefully. The house number isn't visible, but in the corner of the shot, partially obscured by a tree branch, I notice the edge of a street sign—the letters *rena* visible between the leaves.

Hunching over my laptop, I pull up Google Maps and scour the streets of Silver Lake, looking for a street name that ends in those letters. It's got to be Micheltorena. Switching to Street View, I painstakingly navigate my way up and down the street until I find a house that resembles the one in the picture. This has got to be it. In both images, I can see a similar view of the reservoir. But there's a different car in the driveway in the Google Maps photo. The discrepancy makes me realize: Greg may have moved since the forum post went up. Maybe the harassment drove him out of the neighborhood.

Well. There's only one way to find out.

I scrabble around in my bag for my phone, then type Greg's address into the Uber app. His place is only thirty minutes away. I stare at the phone screen. All this time, Greg's been so close, and I've never even tried to contact him. I would've, when he moved back to LA, if my mom and Dr. Rajmani hadn't been pressuring me so hard to step back from the case. If it hadn't been for the incident with Roy Tucker, one of the truckers who was in Barclay's the night Allie disappeared. He'd filed a restraining order against me after I started showing up on his street, watching him as he played with his kids in his yard.

I go into the bedroom, grab my coat and bag, and then—as an afterthought—pick up one of the cameras I've left charging on my nightstand. I'm not sure why I want it. I only know that Greg always made me feel nervous, and back in the old days, the only way I could battle that feeling was to raise a camera to my face.

CHAPTER 22

The Uber drops me off on a dark stretch of road in Silver Lake. As the car drives off and its headlights disappear around the corner, the night closes around me. Greg's house is in shadow, but a faint light is coming from the front room.

Slowly, I walk up the path to his front door. Two big agave plants flank the entryway, and their leaves scrape at my legs as I pass by. Then I'm standing in front of the heavy wooden door.

It's only now that my resolve begins to wobble. I remember my sessions with Dr. Rajmani, the way he always urged me to consider whether, in obsessing about Allie's case, I was doing more harm than good. The restraining order had been a sign, he said, that I'd lost my sense of perspective.

I draw in a deep breath. What if Greg really had hurt Allie? If so, coming here to talk to him is the absolute stupidest thing I could do.

But I can't turn back now. If I want to find out more about the flash drive, I have to blot out that fear. I have to make myself believe in the version of Greg who loved Allie, not the version who may have killed her.

I think of the night, sophomore year of college, when I'd come out of my bedroom and heard sobbing coming from the other side of the apartment. Shuffling down the hall, I hovered outside Allie's door. It was closed, but light seeped out from the gap at the bottom, casting a dull glow into the hall. After a moment, I realized: that wasn't Allie crying. It was Greg.

I had never seen Greg cry. Nothing ever seemed to pierce his shield of cool sarcasm. I couldn't imagine what could've happened to reduce him to tears.

I leaned closer to the door. Allie was murmuring, saying soothing but inaudible things. After a minute or two, she emerged from the bedroom, clutching an empty mug.

"What's going on?" I whispered, taking a step back from her.

She pulled me into the kitchen after her. "He's having a rough day," she said in a low voice. "His dad came by his apartment this afternoon."

"So?"

"So . . . his dad's the one who kicked him out of the house," Allie said. "After he came out to his family. He was only fifteen. They've, like, barely talked since."

"Oh." I watched her make another cup of tea. Chamomile. That had to be for Greg; Allie loathed herbal tea.

"Obviously, don't tell him I said anything," Allie said. "He's really private about it. He spent most of his high school years bouncing between friends' houses. I don't think he's been back to his dad's house since then."

I bit my lip, revising my mental image of Greg's high school years, in which I'd imagined him smug, spoiled, living in an opulent house with his rich parents.

"So, what's his dad coming around for now, then?" I asked.

Allie stared into the mug of tea, at the steam rising off the hot water. "He says he's willing to bring Greg back into the family again. Let bygones be bygones . . . if Greg agrees to give up his 'lifestyle.'" She let out a sharp hiss of breath. "God, I could kill that asshole."

I leaned back on the kitchen counter, feeling unsettled. I'd disliked Greg for so long that it felt strange for those feelings to suddenly waver, threaten to dissolve.

She turned to go back to the bedroom. "Anyway, back I go."

"Wait," I said, going over to the pantry. "Bring these too," I said, holding out a package of Ginger-O's.

She pulled me into a tight hug, and I was engulfed in the smell of her expensive shampoo. "You're a good friend, Tash."

But it was Allie who was the good friend. The one Greg trusted so much he'd broken down in front of her, the one he'd let see past his prickly exterior.

Now, I think: That had to mean something, didn't it? That had to mean he wouldn't have hurt her. Even if he was angry, even if he suspected she was dealing drugs behind his back.

Standing outside the front door, I know my reasoning is thin. I'm clutching at straws. As I turn and stare out at the dark street, I see a flicker in the shadows that might be a cat, or a fox. Greg loved Allie. That's why he'd been as unnerved as I was when Allie started pulling away—and why, during those last few months, his fights with Allie became more frequent. Greg had been furious with her, for her strange behavior, for the way she'd stopped showing up for him the way she used to.

I turn back to the house, knowing I'm stalling. Knowing my courage won't last much longer. Raising my hand, I knock on the door.

Nothing happens. There's not a hint of sound from inside the house.

After a long pause, I knock again. Then I peek in through one of the sidelights and catch a glimpse of the living room. Angular couches and a large sheepskin rug. The place is empty, no signs of life. Greg might not even live here anymore—in which case, I've wasted my time. Come all the way over here for nothing. With a sigh, I turn and sit down on the front step.

I slide my hand into my bag to grab my phone, but instead my fingers hit the familiar angles of my Nikon. I pull it out, balancing its weight in my hands. When I first bought it, it had seemed state of the art, a precious investment. Now, six years later, its buttons look quaint, old fashioned. I turn it on and scroll back through the most recent photos.

The pictures are blurry, full of shadows and smoke. Crowds of people in a low-lit room. Silhouettes on a balcony, the LA skyline in the background. One of Greg's famous parties. I remember this one in particular because there had been a smoke machine in the living room.

That night, I stood with my back against the wall, taking pictures of the people dancing in front of the fireplace. Playing with the focus, I framed a group of dancers in a shot, catching their silhouettes against the wisps of white smoke. Once I'd taken the photo, I paused and examined the image on the camera screen, the way the light made halos around everyone's heads.

"Hey."

Startled, I looked up. A lanky guy stood beside me, peering over my shoulder.

"Can I see?" he said, gesturing at the camera.

I hesitated but then relented. He had a nice face, and he handled the Nikon like he knew what he was doing with it. As I watched, he scrolled back through the last couple of photos.

"These are cool," he said. "Are you in Hadfield's class?"

"Hadfield?"

"Shooting After Dark," he explained. "He'd, like, go nuts over these."

I shook my head. "No, these are just for me." I wasn't in any photography class. I couldn't waste my college credits on a class like that.

"Oh, gotcha," he said, handing the camera back to me. "Well, you're really good."

He smiled at me, but I turned away when I heard Allie's laugh ring out from across the room. It was a laugh that told me she was on the verge of being very, very drunk.

"My man! Where have you been all night?" she said to someone. I craned my head to see who she was talking to, but the room was crowded, and I lost sight of her just as she disappeared down the hallway. That was the last I saw of her for hours.

Sitting on the steps of the house in Silver Lake, I keep scrolling back through the photos, seeing details of the night that have blurred in my memory. Greg wearing a gorilla mask. Some girl doing a handstand next to the fireplace.

I pause when I catch sight of Allie in the background of a group shot. In the shadows at the edge of the room, framed by the arched doorway that led into the hall, Allie stood with her shoulders turned partially away from the camera. Beside her, someone leaned close to speak in her ear. I recognize the stocky silhouette, the glint of stubble on a shaved head. Jairo. Allie's head was tilted slightly to one side. She could have been listening closely. Or pulling away in fear.

Headlights sweep across my legs, and a car pulls into the driveway. It's a sports car—silver, brand new—and the man who steps out of it wears a business suit. As he slams the door shut, I scramble to my feet, stuffing my camera in my bag, and the automatic lights snap on, bathing me in bright-white light. *Shit.* This must be the house's new owner. He does not look pleased to see me.

"Who the hell are you?" he says as he strides across the driveway.

"Sorry," I say. "I was just leaving—"

"Were you? It sure as fuck didn't look like it."

I suck in a breath. I know that voice, even if I don't recognize the person it's currently attached to.

Greg Novak.

CHAPTER 23

When he steps into the light, I see that his hair has been trimmed into a neat clipper cut, and there's not an earring stud in sight. Stripped of his piercings, his eyeliner, his outrageous clothes, he looks strangely ordinary. If I'd passed him on the street, I wouldn't have recognized him. That way he has of drumming his fingers impatiently against his thighs, though—that hasn't changed.

"Greg?" The skin on my palms is tingling.

He scowls. "I swear to God, if you're a reporter—" He steps toward me, and I stumble backward, banging my ankle against the concrete stair.

"Greg," I say, putting my hands up in front of me. "It's Tash." It feels strange to call myself that. No one calls me Tash anymore; only Allie called me that.

He stops short. "Natasha?" Then he gives me that once-over that is so familiar from our days in college—taking in my outfit, my hair—and raises his eyebrows. "Holy fucking shit," he says. "You've changed."

I try to regain my composure. My pulse is thumping in my neck. "Look who's talking."

He frowns, a dull red creeping up his neck.

"I'm just here to talk," I say, trying to sound calm, steady. This is just Greg. This is just a conversation.

"Jesus." He blows out a breath, and I catch a whiff of vodka on his breath. It's a smell I associate so closely with Greg that it might as well be his cologne. "You haven't heard of texting?" He looks around the yard, at the street. "This isn't some stunt, is it? You're not here with *Dateline* or something like that?"

I shake my head. "Of course not."

"So, you just—what? Thought you'd suddenly visit your old friend Greg?" His voice is full of bitterness.

I shift my bag on my shoulder. "Something like that."

He studies me for a long moment. "Well, isn't that interesting? You know, I've really appreciated your concern and support over the years." Sarcasm is still his weapon of choice. "When I was really in the shit. When I could've used a friend."

I can't hold his gaze. "Please. Greg. I just want to talk for a few minutes."

His jaw clenches. Now that he's standing closer, I can see the dents all up and down his ears where his piercings used to be.

"Well. Why not," he says flatly. Then he walks past me and unlocks the door with a rough twist of a key. Stepping aside, he gestures with an elaborate flourish for me to come inside. Which reminds me that Greg used to be an actor. A good one. I went with Allie to watch him in a couple of college productions, and I'd had to grudgingly acknowledge that he was good. Very good.

Slowly, I walk past him into the dark foyer, and it's only when the door closes behind us that I feel a flicker of panic. I remember the footage of Greg being escorted out of his apartment all those years ago. He'd turned his head away from the cameras, but you could see his stubble and his sweat, and—when he raised a hand to ward off the camera flashes—the yellow bruising on his knuckles.

Greg flicks on the lights and walks into a large, open kitchen. I register pale hardwood floors, a gleaming tile backsplash, then tilt my head to look up at the high ceiling, the large skylight. This place must be worth a fortune.

Greg notices me sizing up the place. "It's one of my dad's properties. He lets me use it."

"Oh." I don't know if he knows what Allie told me about his dad. "I didn't realize you two were . . ."

Greg heads to a cabinet, where he pulls down a glass and a bottle of vodka. "We mended fences, I guess you could say. After he bailed me out of the investigation mess. And now I work for him."

So. Greg's new look. His new *lifestyle*.

He gets ice out of the freezer and then glances at me. "Want some?"

I shake my head.

"Figured not." He pours himself a generous drink. "So," he says, taking a sip. "What brings you to my door?" His fingers tap impatiently on the side of his glass. "I mean, I'm assuming it's the million-dollar question." He clutches a hand to his chest. *"Did I kill Allie Andersen?"*

"No," I say slowly. "Not that."

"What, don't you think I'm guilty?" He drains his drink. "Everyone else does."

I draw in a slow breath. So he's going to be like this. It's too soon to ask about the flash drive—if he's in this kind of mood, he'll clam up completely. I decide to start with a different tack. "I wanted to ask about that last night. With Allie. What you guys argued about."

"Oh, didn't you watch the TV movie?" He yanks off his tie and throws it on the counter behind him. The vodka is making his voice sludgy. "Did you like the guy they cast as me, by the way? What a joke."

"I want to hear it from you."

He stares at me for a moment, considering, no doubt, telling me to fuck off. Finally, he says, "It was stupid. I was high. And in the mood for a fight. Allie had been keeping secrets from me."

"What kind of secrets?"

He looks at me for a long moment, his face guarded. Then he relaxes a little, perhaps deciding to trust me. Or maybe he's just bored, tired of keeping his story to himself all these years. "The end of that last year, before she . . ." He trails off. "Well, she had all this money. Wads of cash. I asked her where it was coming from."

"What'd she say?"

"What do you think? 'Fuck off,' basically." He laughs. "Classic Allie. She said it wasn't any of my business." He scrunches up his nose. "But, I mean, where would she be getting that kind of money? You didn't see her working any part-time jobs, did you? Waiting tables? Washing dishes? I don't think so."

"So you thought she was working with Jairo," I say.

He stares at me. "How the fuck—" Then he sighs. "You've been talking to that detective."

I don't say anything.

"That guy always had it out for me," he says, and I sense a rant coming on. The injustice of what happened to him. "The police—"

I try to get him to refocus. "But I don't understand the Jairo thing. Greg, she hardly knew him."

He raises one eyebrow. "Shows how much you know."

"What does that mean?" I hate that he still knows how to push my buttons.

Greg walks over to the window and opens it, letting in a cold breeze. "I saw Jairo. Outside your apartment, one time. He was driving Allie home."

The temperature in the room is dropping rapidly.

Allie in Jairo's car?

Greg returns to the kitchen island and pours himself another drink. "And I don't think it was the first time. I mean, you know what she was like back then. Whenever I texted, she'd say she was 'busy,' but she wouldn't say where she was. I don't know where she was going, but it's not a stretch to think she might've been with Jairo." He snorts. "And that was just stupid, so stupid. Jairo was just a small-time criminal, but his family—I heard they were into some serious shit. Allie had to be nuts to get mixed up with people like that. Anyway, that night—I was trying to get her to see sense."

"So you punched a hole in the wall," I say.

He raises his glass in a mock toast. "Ah, you *did* watch the TV movie. Yeah, well." He pushes away from the countertop and sets his glass down with a clang. "I wasn't in the best state of mind."

"What happened after that?"

Greg pauses, his neck muscles tensing. "Look, yes, I punched the wall. Like an idiot. Broke my fucking knuckle doing it. But then I walked out. I took a long walk around the neighborhood, trying to calm down." He draws in a deep breath. "Then I took a couple of Xanax, and I was feeling pretty damn zen by the time I got back to the apartment. That is, until I saw that Allie had taken my car—and a boatload of my money." He laughs bitterly.

"What do you mean, a 'boatload'? It was two hundred dollars." I'd seen Greg drop more than that at a happy hour.

Greg cracks his knuckles one by one. "No, it wasn't. I told the cops it was only two hundred. But I lied."

"Why?"

He grimaces. "Right after they brought me in, before I realized what a shit show the investigation was going to become, I thought Allie had just taken off for a few days. I figured she'd come back when she'd gotten over her little mood. At that point, all I wanted was the cops off my back. There's no way I was going to tell them I had ten grand lying around my apartment."

"Ten grand?" I say. "Allie stole ten grand from you?"

He shrugs. "Give or take, yeah. She was the only one who knew where I kept it."

"Jesus. You were making that kind of money?"

"Oh, for sure," he says. "I mean, I only got into dealing to make a little extra cash when my dad was being a dick about my trust fund, but when I realized how easy it was—stuff started to get out of hand."

I blow out a breath.

He stares down at his feet. "I think about that sometimes. I mean, if I'd kept going at that rate, I could've gotten myself in some real trouble."

I sit down on one of the kitchen stools, trying to fit this information into my understanding of Allie's last night. If Allie had ten grand on her when she walked into Barclay's, that changes everything. For one thing, it certainly doesn't suggest she was about to commit suicide. With that kind of money, she could've gotten a long way away from LA. She could've bought a different car, a new passport.

"But why didn't you tell the cops about the money?" I ask. "Later, I mean, after they found the drugs." It hadn't taken long, in the search of his apartment, for the police to find Greg's stash behind a panel in his bathroom wall.

He throws his hands up. "Don't you think I tried? By that point, it was too late. I'd already lied about so many things—they didn't believe a word I said. And then my dad sent his lawyer in, and that guy was crystal clear: I had to stop talking, about everything. So I did." He shakes his head. "I just wanted to keep myself out of jail, Tash. Because I didn't do anything to Allie. I'd never hurt her. You know that."

There's a long silence. From outside the window, I hear a far-off siren, its sound winding up through the hills.

"Anyway." He picks up his glass and twists it around and around in his hands. "That night, when I came back and found the money gone, I thought it was just another one of Allie's stunts." He stares out the window into the pitch-black garden. "Those next few days, I kept expecting her to show up." He laughs. "I was *still* expecting that when the cops knocked on my door."

When he turns back to me, tears have gathered at the edges of his eyes. This is the Greg I only saw glimpses of back in college. The one who relied on Allie more than he liked to admit.

It's this moment that convinces me to take the leap, to ask the question I came here to ask. "Greg, did you ever see Allie using a flash drive?"

His forehead wrinkles. "What?" Whatever he's been expecting me to say, it isn't that.

"That key chain Allie had—the little panda bear. It was a flash drive."

He looks puzzled. "So?" Then his expression changes. "What's going on, Tash? Does this have something to do with the body they found in the canyon?"

"No," I say quickly. "This is just—a lead I'm following up on. From the tip line." Will Greg believe that? "You said you thought Allie was doing deals behind your back. Is there any chance she would've been keeping information about that on the flash drive?"

He snorts. "C'mon. Allie could be reckless, but she wasn't *stupid.* If she was working with Jairo, there's no way she'd put any of that in writing."

I frown. "What could've been on it, then?"

He thinks for a minute, his head tilted to one side. "Well, if I had to guess," he says slowly, "I'd say it'd be that essay she was working on for Macnamara."

"Essay? What essay?"

Greg stares at me. "The *essay,*" he says. "Shit, Tash, don't you know anything?"

"What are you talking about?"

"Well, this Macnamara asshole—even before he started sleeping with Allie—he'd started filling her head with all this bullshit. Like, 'Oh, you're so talented, I never met a writer like you before.' Blah blah blah."

My heart constricts. "Yes, I remember."

Greg laughs. "I mean, it was textbook, wasn't it? What better way to get some undergrad into bed? Tell them they're the next Sylvia Plath or whatever." He rolls his eyes. "And then he tells her that this essay she wrote for his class—that she should try to publish it."

"What?" It's been years, but the jealousy still stings, like the sudden shock of a paper cut.

"I can't believe she never told you. She was all amped up about it. Apparently, Macnamara was friends with this editor at a big magazine. He was going to send Allie's essay there when she'd finished it."

I feel numb. Allie never told me a word about this.

Greg leans back against the kitchen counter. "I mean, this guy was blowing so much smoke up her ass. C'mon, you know Allie. She was barely passing her classes. There's no way she was some kind of literary genius."

I chew on my lip. I used to think the same thing about Allie, that she wasn't really that smart. Or maybe she had dyslexia or something, and that's why she struggled to pass even her remedial classes at Palos Verdes Prep. Then, one day, I'd come back from my Saturday SAT prep class and found Allie sitting on her bed, scribbling in a notebook she had propped on her knees.

"What's that?" I asked. I'd never seen Allie write in a journal before. Mostly when I found her alone in her bedroom, she was listening to music or doing her nails.

"Nothing," she said, flipping the notebook closed.

I jumped on the bed next to her. "Wait a sec—are you keeping a *diary*?"

"Don't be stupid," she snapped. But she looked stricken, like I'd caught her doing something heinous.

"Hey," I said. "Sorry I said it like that. I just didn't know that you . . . wrote things."

She shrugged, stuffing the notebook under her pillow. "It's nothing. It's stupid."

"I bet it's not." When she didn't respond, I nudged her shoulder. "C'mon, let me see."

But she wouldn't say anything more about the notebook, not even after I pushed a few times, so I let the subject drop. Later, though, after she'd left to go to the gym, I slipped back into her room. Feeling like a criminal, I searched through her desk drawers, even under her mattress. Finally, I found the notebook in the air-conditioning vent, tucked behind the mini bottles of liquor. Sitting down cross-legged on the bed, I opened to the first page, prepared to see a long rant about Isabel or Giles. Typical teen-angst stuff.

But it wasn't that. Allie was writing poetry. Lots of it. I read through the first few pages, my head buzzing. Silly, shallow Allie. Allie, who was in all the lowest-tier classes at school, who never spent any time on her homework—Allie could write like this? Where had she learned to do that?

I flipped rapidly through the notebook, looking at the ink spreading over the pages. The most recent poem was written in small sections, like Wallace Stevens's "Thirteen Ways of Looking at a Blackbird." Except—how would Allie know about that poem? She was in remedial English. Had she been reading my AP English textbook on the sly?

I found the notebook so unnerving that I stood up quickly, placing the notebook just as I'd found it in the AC vent. Then I screwed the panel back on with trembling fingers. This wasn't how things were supposed to be. I was supposed to be the smart one. That was the deal, the unspoken balance between us. I didn't tread on Allie's territory, and she didn't intrude on mine.

"She *was* a good writer," I say now to Greg. "Really good."

"Oh, come on," he scoffs. "We're talking about *Allie*. She copied every single one of your essays for her classes."

"Yeah, I know. But she didn't do it because she couldn't write her own. I think she had this idea that it was a mistake to let people know she was smart."

We'd had arguments about it—me trying to convince Allie that her life would be so much simpler if she'd just try to do well in school. *Oh, like your life is simpler?* she'd retorted. *I mean, look at you. You've been kicking academic ass for so long, no one even notices anymore. Now you work up a sweat if one of those A's happens to be an A minus. Whereas, I don't have to worry at all. The trick, which you have not figured out yet, is to keep expectations low.*

I told her that was the dumbest thing I'd ever heard.

No, listen: You have to disappoint them consistently—but then, every once in a while, do something halfway decent. And then they fall all over themselves telling you how great you are.

"Allie was always on the verge of failing her classes," I tell Greg. "But I think she did it on purpose."

"What, like as a fuck-you to Isabel?"

"Maybe." Who knew why Allie did the things she did? Sometimes I thought she was punishing Isabel. Other times, it seemed like she was punishing herself. "So, what happened with this essay?"

He snorts. "Well, if you can believe it, after Macnamara filled her head with all this stuff about getting published, he changed his mind. Just like that."

"Why?"

He rolls his eyes. "My guess? There never *was* any editor, any magazine. It was all part of his bullshit. Then, when Allie got serious about it, he had to backpedal. Of course, he tried to spin it so he didn't look like a total asshole. He fed Allie some line about how she should be careful about putting her name out there, like the media attention could be too much for her. It sounded like a load of crap to me. Allie thought so too. That's why she broke up with him."

I frown. That's not right. "Allie didn't break up with Macnamara. He broke up with her."

He looks at me like I've lost my mind. "Who said that?"

"Ruiz. That's what Macnamara told him."

Greg shakes his head. "Well, Macnamara's fucking lying. Allie told me all about it, and trust me, it was her kicking Macnamara to the curb. Not the other way around."

The light in the kitchen glints off the stainless steel stove. Is Greg right? Did Allie break up with Macnamara? Or was Allie just too proud to admit that she'd been dumped?

And what had she written in that essay? I thought of her notebook in the AC vent, how she'd taken care to make sure no one would discover it.

"Did you read the essay?" I ask Greg. "Did she show it to you?"

"Fuck no. She had the file passworded on her computer."

I stare at him. "How do you know that?"

He has the grace to look embarrassed. "Okay, so I tried to open it once. Sue me." He rubs his knuckles against his chin. "This one time, I showed up at the apartment. Allie and I were supposed to go out for happy hour. But then she texted, blowing me off for, like, the millionth time, saying she wasn't going to meet me after all. But I was already at the apartment and bored out of my mind, so I logged in to her computer. Just out of curiosity. But yeah, no luck."

He leans back against the counter. He doesn't seem to care whether I believe him or not. Which is what makes me think he's telling the truth.

I press my hands against the cold countertop. Allie used to let Greg log in to her phone, read her messages, even pretend to be her over text. But she'd passworded this file.

What was in it that she wouldn't show even to him?

CHAPTER 24

The next day, I'm so agitated I can barely make it through the afternoon at work. The things Greg told me are churning in my head. The night Allie left the apartment, she had $10,000 on her, and she'd written an essay she didn't want anyone to see. Ruiz needs to know all this. But after the way I stormed out of the diner last night, I'm reluctant to text him. What reason does he have to reply? Instead, I leave work early and head to the police station.

At the front desk, I ask the receptionist to let Ruiz know I'm here. She dials his extension, but after a minute, she hangs up the phone and shakes her head.

"Sorry, hon. I think he's left for the day."

My stomach sinks. I need to talk to him. If the key chain alone isn't enough to reopen the investigation, surely this other information is. Stepping away from the front desk, I pull out my phone and begin a text to Ruiz. The receptionist eyes me as she shuffles some paperwork on her desk. I wonder if she recognizes my voice from the old days, when I called the station so often that the front desk people were instructed to always put me through to Family Liaison, never to the detectives.

Just as I'm about to dial Ruiz's number, the double doors next to the front desk swing open, and he walks out with another detective beside him. Both of them carry cardboard file boxes under their arms. Ruiz's shirt is rumpled and unbuttoned at the collar. As he passes the reception desk, his eyes at first pass over me, and then he stops short as he registers my presence. "Natasha? What're you doing here?"

"I need to talk to you," I say, aware that I sound desperate.

I can see the other detective sizing me up, trying to get a read on who I am. He's tall, maybe six five, and he's holding the file box as if it weighs nothing. He raises his eyebrows at Ruiz. "See you tomorrow, I guess?"

"Yeah, see you tomorrow," Ruiz says. Then he turns back to me, frowning. "What's up? Has something happened?"

Suddenly, I find myself tongue tied. On the walk here, I'd rehearsed exactly what I was going to say, how I would lay out the details Greg told me last night. But now I can't seem to put the words together. What comes out is: "I talked to Greg."

"What?" His voice echoes across the lobby, and the receptionist looks up, startled. He lowers his voice. "Jesus Christ, Natasha, what were you thinking?"

"I was thinking no one else was going to do it," I say, an edge in my voice.

Ruiz sets down the file box on one of the reception chairs. "Natasha. You know Greg is still a serious person of interest in this case. You cannot just go talk to him."

My jaw tightens. "Well, I guess I just did." I sound like a stubborn child. "Why shouldn't I? He was my friend, too, you know." Which is not exactly true. "I talked to him, and I think you should know what he told me."

Ruiz looks furious, but he's not going to let his frustration out here, not in front of the receptionist, who's now eavesdropping with interest. "Look, can we take this outside?" He picks up the file box and gestures to the entry doors.

Silently, we walk out of the station and onto the sidewalk, where Ruiz pulls me to one side of the front steps. Tension vibrates from his body. "You didn't mention the flash drive to him, did you?"

I don't say anything, but he can see the answer in my face.

"Damn it, Natasha!"

"What?"

Across the street, four lanes of traffic away, there's an ordinary little neighborhood, squat stucco houses with sago palms dotting the front yards. People living their everyday lives.

"Don't you get it? This is exactly why I wanted you to stay away from Greg. From anyone involved in the case." I start to speak, but he interrupts me. "Just listen for a minute. What if Greg did kill Allie? What if he did, and it's got something to do with the flash drive? You've just alerted him to the fact that you know about it. Didn't you think what you might've done to our case? What might've happened to you?"

I flush, feeling stupid. He's right, and I know it. "So what should I do?" I snap. "Nothing? I'd leave it to you if I thought you were going to do anything."

At that, Ruiz flinches.

None of this is going the way I planned. "Look, if you'd just let me say what I came here to say," I continue in a softer voice. "Greg told me things last night. Things he never told the police. Don't you want to know what they are?"

Ruiz tilts his head back and looks up at the cloud-studded sky. Several people pass us on the station's front steps, their footsteps scraping against the concrete. Finally, he looks at me and says, "Yes, damn it. I do."

CHAPTER 25

At Gina's, Ruiz listens in silence as I relay what Greg told me. Methodically, he stirs sugar into his decaf coffee. Three packets. Finally, he says, "And Greg says he didn't know what the essay was about?"

"No," I say. "He never read it." I lean forward. "But at least one other person did."

He sets his mug down without taking a sip. "Nuh-uh," he says, at the same time I say, "Macnamara."

"Ruiz," I say. It's important that he listen to me. "He definitely read that essay. He knows what's on the flash drive."

Ruiz points a finger at me. "Natasha. Do not even think about going to talk to Macnamara."

Heat rushes to my face. That is exactly what I want to do. "Will you do it, then?"

He scrunches his empty sugar packets into tiny wads. "You know it's not that easy. I've got to clear it with my supervisor, make the case for why this investigation takes priority over the other cases I'm working right now." He grabs another sugar packet out of the ceramic jar and taps its edge insistently against the tabletop.

"You said yourself that finding out what's on that flash drive is important," I say. "And as far as I can see, Macnamara's our only chance of doing that."

He frowns. The fluorescent lights cast an unhealthy glow over his face. "Maybe. Yes. Let me think."

I can hardly sit still. Ever since last night, a frantic energy has been running through me, burning through the numbness of the past year. "Look, if you'd been the one to talk to Greg last night, would he have told you any of what he told me?"

Ruiz tosses the sugar packet to one side.

"He wouldn't have said one word," I say. "Not without his lawyer there. And if his lawyer *was* there, he'd just advise Greg not to talk to you. Greg would've completely shut down, just like the last time."

Ruiz folds his arms across his chest.

"He would've," I insist. "And even if you do end up getting approval from your supervisor and you talk to Macnamara, what's he going to tell you?" Macnamara, I'm sure, doesn't have any friendly feelings toward the LAPD. After his relationship with Allie came to light, he'd lost his job at LACSA. But that was only the beginning of his problems. The media attention, the #professorpredator tweets . . . Eventually, he moved out of LA altogether.

Ruiz grimaces and looks beyond me, at the other tables in the diner.

"But he doesn't have any reason not to speak to me," I continue. "I'm not a threat to him. I'm just Allie's sister." I've been thinking this over all day. "He knows me. And I think he'll talk to me. Just like Greg did."

Ruiz turns his head back to me. "It's not as simple as you're making it sound."

He hasn't shot the idea down completely, though.

After a minute, as if he's working something out in his head as he talks, he says, "Let's say you do talk to him. No information you get from him will be admissible in court. Even if he up and confessed to you that he murdered Allie—we couldn't use it."

"I know that. But whatever he tells me—it'll be information you didn't have before, right? Like what Greg told me. It could point you where to look for new evidence."

Absently, he takes a sip of his coffee and stares at the TV screen on the wall. Allie's case was his first high-profile investigation, and his first high-profile failure.

"Look," I say, knowing I'm pushing my luck, "no one would have to know anything about this. I could just drive down to San Diego—"

That snaps his attention back to me. "How the hell do you know he's in San Diego?"

The forums have kept me informed. "He moved back from Connecticut last year. He's working for some educational software company down there. Under a different name. He goes by James Macneice now."

Ruiz presses his lips together. "Okay, you've figured out that much. But you can't possibly have an address."

I look down at my lap. On the forums, there's a user—PI-Leo—who's diligently followed Macnamara's every move since the investigation went cold. Last night, I messaged him, told him I was a journalist doing an in-depth piece on the case. I may have given him the impression I was Neil Agarwal at the *LA Times*. PI-Leo, thrilled to foster a real connection to the case, was only too eager to help me out.

"You have an address, don't you?" he says.

I nod.

Ruiz slumps back in the booth. "Fuck. You're going to go no matter what I say, aren't you?"

"What if it isn't the worst idea in the world?" I ask. "What if it's actually a good idea?" I don't usually push like this. Usually, I do what I'm told.

Ruiz does his best to dissuade me, he really does. But after ten minutes of back-and-forth, he can tell he's getting nowhere. And something else has begun to creep into his expression. I notice he's rubbing his forearm, the one where the tattoo is etched into his skin. And I remember the day I first saw it, when I first found out what it meant.

CHAPTER 26

June 2015

Ruiz arrived at Gina's in a terrible mood. As soon as he walked in the door, I could tell something was wrong. He didn't smile when he saw me, and his greeting to Diane was clipped, cheerless. When he slid into the booth across from me, his face was fixed in a furious expression.

"What is it?"

"Don't ask," he said sharply. Then, when he registered my surprise, he sighed. "Sorry. It's been a hell of a day."

"Oh," I said. "I'm sorry. Do you . . . ?" If he'd been a friend, I'd have asked him if he wanted to talk about it. But he wasn't a friend, not really.

Ruiz fiddled with the plastic menu for a moment or two. Diane usually came and took our order right away, but today she was busy with a table of six on the other side of the diner. Finally, Ruiz closed his menu with a snap, saying, "Do you want to get out of here? I could really use something stronger than coffee."

"Oh—uh, okay."

He was already getting up to leave, and I scrambled to follow him. I was so used to Ruiz being polite, predictable. This new side of him made my nerves jangle.

We walked to his car, and then, hardly speaking a word, he drove us to a bar on PCH that had low ceilings and even lower lighting. As he ordered drinks at the bar, I leaned against the counter, looking at our reflections in the mirror behind the liquor bottles. We were almost the same height, but he carried himself differently—with a kind of authority that must have come from years of being a cop. Whereas I slouched, trying to make myself as inconspicuous as possible.

After we got our drinks, we settled into a table in a dim corner near the back exit. As I peeled the label off my beer bottle, Ruiz took a big sip of his whiskey.

"So, do you want to talk about it?" I ventured. "Your day."

He set his drink down, shaking his head. "You don't want to hear about that."

"Try me," I said.

The bar was empty except for us. Afternoon sunlight filtered through a dirty window and cast a golden light over the tables and chairs.

He leaned back in his chair. The tension running through his body was so strong it seemed like a visible effort for him to sit still. He took another drink of his whiskey, almost draining the glass. "Remember I told you once that someone in my family was murdered?"

I nodded.

He pushed up the shirtsleeve on his left forearm, exposing the tattoo that I'd noticed once or twice before. "Carmen. My mother. She was thirty-two when she was stabbed coming home from work. She bled out on the street, no one around to help."

8-11-99. Ruiz would've been, what, thirteen?

"Everyone knew it was her asshole ex who'd done it. He was the type of guy who'd punch her just for looking at him the wrong way. She'd just gotten up the nerve to leave him, and he wasn't happy about it."

"Did they catch him?"

He snorted. "Catch him? The guy was a fixture in the neighborhood; they could've picked him up anytime. But there was no evidence connecting him to the scene. No DNA, and they never found the knife that killed her. So no, they never caught him." He clenched his hands together.

I knew that Ruiz had joined the force at twenty-one, become a detective at twenty-seven. I was starting to understand now why he'd been so driven, so focused.

Ruiz signaled to the bartender for another round of drinks, although I'd barely made a dent in my beer.

"What happened, after . . . she was killed?" I asked. "You and your sisters, you would've been just kids."

He ran a hand over the top of his head. "Yeah. Luckily our grandma was able to take us in. Otherwise, we would've been put into foster care, separated, most likely."

"So you stayed in your neighborhood?"

"Yeah." His face was grim. "My mom's ex stuck around for a few more years. When I was sixteen, he moved away, but I kept tabs on him. Waited for him to get busted for something else. A guy like that, he doesn't stop hurting women. But there's been nothing anyone could pin on him. And today . . ."

A trickle of dread ran down the back of my neck. "He hurt someone else?"

Ruiz shook his head. "No. No, that motherfucker died. Peacefully in his bed. An aneurysm. I bet he never lost a single night's sleep over what he did to my mom." His knees shifted under the table, making the glasses in front of us rattle.

Ruiz had never talked to me like this before.

"You know what the stupidest thing is?" he said. "All this time, I thought I was going to be the one to do something about him. I was going to put that asshole in jail. And when that started to look like less and less of a possibility, I'd daydream about other ways of making him pay. I'd find him myself, in a dark alleyway. I'd bring a gun. I'd know how to do it in a way that wouldn't leave any evidence."

Maybe I should've been shocked. But all I could think was: I understand. It was a daydream I might've had myself.

He laughed suddenly, sitting back in his chair. "Christ, I sound psychotic."

Without thinking, I reached out and squeezed his hand, which rested on the table between us. He gave a start, and immediately I regretted the gesture. The invisible line between us—I'd crossed it.

I'd just begun to pull my hand away when he grasped my fingers, squeezing them tightly. For a moment, we sat like that, looking down at our clasped hands. And then the bartender arrived, sliding fresh drinks across the table. Quickly, we broke our grip, and the moment became ordinary again. But I could still feel the texture of his skin against mine. There was a cut on the edge of his hand that had only just started to scab over, and its roughness had brushed against the tips of my fingertips.

CHAPTER 27

I shift in my seat in the vinyl booth, my trousers sticking against the cheap material. I wonder if the scar on Ruiz's hand is still there, faded over time.

Ruiz drains the rest of his coffee, then signals Diane for the check. "Fuck it," he says, pulling his wallet out of his pocket. "If you're going to see Macnamara, I'm going with you."

"Are you serious?"

He frowns. "At least if I'm there, I can make sure you don't do anything too monumentally stupid. You can't go putting yourself in a situation like you did last night. And—"

Diane comes over and slides the check onto the table.

"And what?" I ask.

After Diane moves away, Ruiz says, "And, I've always had a bad feeling about Macnamara."

But it's something more than that, isn't it? I think again how different he looks from the Ruiz I knew four years ago. He doesn't yet have the look that Golanski had, that weathered lack of surprise at the world, but it's coming. Perhaps the one thing standing in the way of that detachment is his anger, which comes out only in flashes.

Ruiz slaps a few bills down on the table, then pulls on his jacket. "If Macnamara did something to your sister, there's no way in hell I'm going to let him get away with that. Let him live the rest of his life like it doesn't matter what he did."

CHAPTER 28

On Saturday, I sit on the front steps of my apartment building, waiting for Ruiz to pick me up. The morning sun slices through the buildings to the east and makes stripes of light on the street. I wrap my arms around my knees, trying to control my nerves.

At six this morning, I woke up and couldn't go back to sleep. With too much time on my hands, I spent hours painstakingly selecting my outfit, straightening my hair, doing my makeup.

What's all this for? Allie asked. *Ruiz or Macnamara?*

It's not for anybody, I told her. *It's just for me.* But I'm not sure I convinced her. Or myself.

When Ruiz's Jeep turns the corner and noses its way down the street, I stand up, shivering. As he pulls up to the curb, I walk over and open the passenger-side door. He's wearing jeans, a hoodie, and a baseball cap. As I slide into the car, I find myself noticing little details I didn't last week. The dust gathering on the dashboard. The clutter in the center console: a few charger cords, some coins, a woman's necklace. A girlfriend's necklace?

"Ready?" he says.

I nod, and he pulls out into the street, glancing behind him at the traffic. We're both quiet as he navigates his way toward the freeway. It's a restful quiet, I tell myself. But I'm beginning to fidget. We have two hours alone in a car ahead of us. What will we talk about?

"That's a pretty necklace," I say, to break the silence. Although the necklace isn't pretty, really. The round pendant is big and chunky. I run a finger over the gold chain trailing over the edge of the console.

He glances down and laughs. "That? I got that for my grandma. She's been having memory problems lately, wandering off from her house. That thing has a GPS tracker in it, some gadget they've developed for seniors."

"Oh."

"Much good it does me. I tried to give it to her, explain what it was for."

"What did she say?"

He smiles slightly. "That I could shove it up my ass."

I laugh, then tuck the trailing chain back into the console. I picture him going over to his grandma's house, taking care of her on his days off. After all these years, I still don't know much about Ruiz, not really. Even back when we used to meet at Gina's, he was careful to keep the conversation light. Funny stories about his sisters. Anecdotes about the outrageous things that happened at work. But very little about himself. He was always so professional, maintained such clear boundaries. Except, of course, for that one time.

As he merges onto the highway, I stare out the passenger window. The day is bright and clear, only a light haze of pollution resting over the city.

I clear my throat. "I've been meaning to tell you—there was something else Greg told me. The night we talked."

"Oh?" Ruiz is focused on driving, his hands at ten and two on the steering wheel.

"He said Allie broke up with Macnamara."

"Okay . . ." He shrugs, as if to say, *So?*

"Well, that's strange, isn't it? Macnamara said he broke up with her."

Ruiz glances at me. "You think that's significant?"

"I don't know. I'm just wondering why their stories would be different. Why would Macnamara say he was the one who dumped her, if he didn't?"

Ruiz taps his fingers on the steering wheel. "Pride, maybe? Or maybe he wanted to make it look like he wasn't as upset about losing the relationship. Because if he was upset . . ."

"That gives him more motive," I say.

He tilts his head, acknowledging the point.

This is how we used to talk, back when things weren't weird between us. Like a team, bouncing ideas off each other.

After another mile, he says, "He definitely wasn't up front with us when we interviewed him. In my experience, these guys—teachers who have relationships with students, bosses who sleep with their employees, whatever—it tends not to be just one girl. We do some digging and find out they have a pattern of this kind of thing, going back a while. My bet? Allie wasn't the first student Macnamara had a relationship with—she's probably just the first one we know about."

Clouds are gathering at the horizon, white and puffy.

"But you looked into Macnamara's past," I say, concentrating on the sliver of ocean I can see in the distance. "And you said you didn't find anything like that."

"Well, yeah," he says. "We didn't. But that's not the same thing as saying there wasn't anything to find."

I hesitate. Then I say, "I think you've got the wrong idea about him."

"Why's that?" he asks.

I run my fingers along the armrest. "Because Macnamara didn't go after Allie." The highway is ten lanes wide, cutting a swath through the scrubby landscape. "She was the one who went after him."

After the first evening of Macnamara's seminar, the one he'd tried to convince me to take, Allie had walked in the front door of our apartment, dumped her bag on the floor, and flopped down on the couch. "Oh my God," she groaned.

I turned from the kitchen sink, where I'd been washing dishes, and watched her through the arched doorway that led into the living room. When she'd first signed up for the class, I'd asked her: *You sure about this? It's not like your other classes—you can't just copy all my old essays.*

Yeah, no problem, she'd said, not missing a beat. *Creative writing, right? You have to admit, I'm nothing if not creative.*

Now, I figured, she must've taken one look at the syllabus, realized she wouldn't be able to skate by with minimal effort, and decided to drop it.

"That bad, huh?" I said.

She lifted her head from the couch. "No. So, so good. He's, like, seriously inspiring, isn't he? And get this: there was a total vibe between us." She propped her head up with a throw pillow. "He kept, like, looking at me. More than he looked at anyone else."

An uneasy sensation spread through my body. Why hadn't I predicted this? It was one of the rules of the universe: guys fell for Allie. But somehow I'd neglected to include Macnamara in the category of *guys.*

Now, though, I could picture him scanning the classroom, finding his gaze pulled inevitably back to Allie. He'd have noticed the shirt that slid off one of her shoulders. The way she didn't look away when he made eye contact.

I went back to rinsing out the coffee mugs, scrubbing harder than I needed to. The only surprising thing, really, was that I hadn't seen this coming. I'd actually thought that the connection I had with Macnamara was special. Had allowed myself to daydream about what it might be like if we ran into each other after I graduated.

"Seriously, though," Allie said, standing up and walking into the kitchen, "you weren't, like, smitten with him? When you were in his class?"

That was the moment I could've told her. About my visits to his office hours. How, afterward, my body fizzed with a sparkling energy that lasted for hours.

But all I said was, "No. Of course not." As if the very idea was stupid. Maybe I was afraid she'd laugh if she knew how I felt—mousy little Tash, thinking she had a vibe with James Macnamara. Or maybe I thought she'd see through me right away, spotting with her uncanny accuracy that I was lying. But she didn't do that. Not this time.

She clapped her hands together, as if the matter was now settled. "Well, okay, then."

"Allie," I said. I did not have a good feeling about her sunny expression. "What are you going to do?"

She grinned, a smile so expansive, so beautiful, that it made my heart contract. "I'm going to drop by his office hours tomorrow. Have a little chat."

There was no part of her that worried she wouldn't get what she wanted from him. She already knew she would.

In the car, Ruiz reaches down to grab his water bottle from the cup holder.

"She was the one who made the first move," I tell him. "Macnamara was the one who was hesitant." After their first kiss, the one Allie had told me about in excruciating detail, she'd been the one to suggest they go back to his apartment.

"Hmm." Ruiz takes a swig of his water. "Well, that's certainly what Macnamara wanted us to believe, when we talked to him. Still, even if he wasn't the initiator . . ."

"What?" I press.

"I don't know—I just never liked his vibe."

"Why?" I think of the forum commenters, speculating about Macnamara being a psychopath.

"You know that, about six months after Allie's disappearance, he left the country, right?" Ruiz asks. "Headed to the South of France. Stayed there for almost two years."

"Yeah. What about it?"

Someone cuts into the lane in front of Ruiz, and he swears softly under his breath. "Well, my question is: How was he paying for all that?

When we looked into him, the guy was drowning in debt, running up a balance on three different credit cards. Then he's fired from LACSA and goes to Europe, without any apparent employment."

"Maybe he has family money?" After hanging out with Greg and Allie, I'd become used to people who didn't seem to worry about income.

Ruiz shook his head. "His parents don't make that much, and besides—they don't speak to him. Some kind of rift there."

The city is behind us now, and we're passing carefully planned neighborhoods that overlook the ocean, their yards bright green from irrigation.

I hadn't known that detail about Macnamara's family. Usually, Allie told me everything about the guys she was dating. But, with Macnamara, she'd only tried that in the beginning. After that, perhaps sensing my disapproval, she'd kept things to herself. She would come home from his place, and there would be no debrief, no endless analysis of the things he'd said. She'd just go into her room and stay there for hours, listening to the Frank Ocean album on repeat.

Sunlight pours in through the windshield, highlighting every speck of dust on the dashboard. Ruiz returns his water bottle to the cup holder, and I see the faint scar that runs along the outside edge of his right hand, a reminder of the afternoon we spent in the bar on PCH.

CHAPTER 29

June 2015

We talked for a long time, until the evening regulars starting trickling in and the background noise reached a pitch where it was hard to hear each other. He cracked a joke as we stood up to leave, and I could feel the difference from all the times we'd talked before. There was an ease between us now, an understanding. Like me, Ruiz knew what it was like to lose someone he loved, to live without answers.

When we finally walked out into the parking lot, the sky was lavender, the clouds bright pink against the setting sun.

I tilted my head back and looked up at the sky. "Wow. That's gorgeous."

Ruiz watched me, amused. "The beer's gone to your head."

"Has not," I protested. Although, I realized now, I was feeling a little buzzed. Allie had always made fun of me because I couldn't hold my liquor. Ruiz had switched to sparkling water an hour ago, so he had one up on me in the sobriety department.

Ruiz laughed. He had a smile that created a deep dimple in his left cheek.

I reached for my phone to call an Uber, but he waved at me to put it away.

"I'll drive you home."

"Oh, you don't need—"

He shrugged. "No big deal. It's the least I can do after I monopolized your afternoon."

"Well, thank you kindly," I said, making a little curtsy.

He shook his head at me, chuckling.

"What?"

"Nothing. I just feel like I'm finally meeting the real Natasha."

In the car, I surprised myself by keeping up a steady stream of conversation. As we passed by a billboard for a photography exhibit at LACMA, I pointed at the sign. "That. That's what I wanted to do, in college."

"What, work at a museum?"

"Be a photographer."

He glanced over at me. "So why didn't you?"

I shrugged. "It just seemed . . . not realistic." I'd only taken one photography class at LACSA, and although I'd loved it, it was too late in my junior year to suddenly switch majors. That would have been impractical. Impulsive.

As we drove up the freeway, dusk fell and I leaned my head back against the seat, watching the stars begin to wink through the clouds. It was nice to feel this way, like there was no particular place I needed to be, nothing I needed to worry about.

When Ruiz pulled his car up to the curb outside my mom's house, the motion-sensor lights flicked on, and I blinked under their glare. Ruiz got out of the car, walked around to my side, and opened the door.

I peered up at him as I unbuckled my seat belt. "What is this—chivalry?"

He grinned and put out a hand to help me out of the car. As I stepped onto the street, my bag fell to the ground, and my wallet and keys scattered over the concrete. Laughing, I bent down to gather them. "I'm totally sober, for your information," I told him. "I'm just clumsy."

Ruiz looked over at the house. "You staying with your mom?"

I shook my head and waved a hand at the garage. "No, that's me over there." A narrow set of stairs led up from the driveway to the garage apartment—although *apartment* was a generous word for the tiny room with a kitchenette and adjoining bathroom.

Ruiz sized up the stairs. "Okay, well, I'm at least going to make sure you get up those safely."

"I told you, I'm totally fine."

"Mm-hmm." He followed me as I walked up the driveway and started up the stairs. Behind me, he gave the railing an experimental shake, and the whole structure wobbled.

"Stop!" I said, laughing.

"This whole thing needs to be replaced," he observed. "The wood is rotting."

"Well, take it up with my landlord."

When we reached the top of the stairs, he waited patiently as I struggled to get the key to turn in the lock.

"Stop smirking," I said. "This lock always jams."

"Sure."

"It does!" Finally, I got the key to turn, and the door swung open. When I turned, we suddenly seemed to be standing very close together.

"Well," he said, shoving his hands in his back pockets. "There you go."

I waited for him to take a step back, to gather up his polite formality, as he always did when we said goodbye. *Well, take care, Natasha.*

But he didn't move, didn't say anything. The light from the driveway highlighted the planes of his face. There were just a few inches between us. I stood very still, knowing that any small shift could turn the moment one way or another. Then, suddenly, I stepped closer to him, until our faces were just millimeters apart. Maybe it was the beers I'd had, or the thought, *What would Allie do?* that flitted through my mind. But from somewhere, I found the courage to lean forward and kiss him.

Ruiz went completely still, and for a moment I was sure I'd read things wrong. Just as I began to pull away, though, Ruiz's arms slid around my back and tightened, pulling me close.

CHAPTER 30

When we reach San Diego, Ruiz exits the freeway and takes a winding route through a coastal neighborhood. I shift in my seat, feeling my heart rate spike. According to the GPS, we'll be at Macnamara's place in less than five minutes. I pull down the car's sun visor and take a moment to check my hair, making sure the strands lie smoothly around my face. Then I catch sight of my expression in the mirror and push the visor up with a snap. What does it matter what I look like? The only thing that matters is what Macnamara can tell us about Allie.

When Ruiz pulls up to the curb, we stare up at the large, modern apartment complex. It has a boxy design, big windows that glitter in the sun. There are high walls around the complex and a guarded gate out front.

"I guess he likes the security," Ruiz says.

That figures. Macnamara's probably had his fill of reporters tracking him down. If PI-Leo on the forums knows where he lives, other people probably do too.

"How're we going to get in?" I ask.

Ruiz doesn't say anything, just pulls the car away from the curb and drives up to the gate, rolling his window down.

"What apartment?" asks the guard, barely looking up from his phone.

Ruiz reaches into his jacket pocket and flashes his badge at the guy. "Hey, man. Mind if I take a look around?"

The guard suddenly focuses, half rising from his seat as he looks at Ruiz's badge. "Oh, sure, sure." He's already hit the button to lift the gate when he says, "Anything I should be concerned about?"

"No, no," Ruiz reassures him, tucking his badge away before the guard can get too close a look at it. "Just a routine check." Then he's driving through the entrance, steering the car through the series of parking lots that surround the building. "What?" he says, when he catches me looking at him.

"Nothing," I say. "Only . . . what would happen, if the department knew you were down here?"

He doesn't answer. Instead, he concentrates on pulling the Jeep into a parking space in front of Macnamara's building. Then he unbuckles his seat belt with a snap. "Let's just stay focused on what we came here to do, okay? You remember what we talked about?"

Last night at Gina's, we'd talked through a plan. I have to go into Macnamara's place alone; that's the only way this will work. But Ruiz will be listening in.

I nod.

"Okay, go ahead, then."

I take out my phone and dial his number. He answers the call, then sets his phone on the dashboard of the Jeep. Next, he takes my phone and, after making sure the volume is turned down all the way, tucks it in the chest pocket of my jacket. He arranges the pocket flap over it, then leans back and assesses my silhouette.

"Okay, that'll work. Just don't fiddle with it, and don't look down at it, or you might draw attention to it." He grabs his own phone off the dashboard. "Keep the line open while you're in his apartment. I'll be right outside. And if anything starts to seem off, just pretend you have an incoming call. That'll be my cue to come get you."

"Okay."

He's all business now, his speech clipped. The sudden change in his demeanor makes me nervous.

"All right, let's test out the audio. Step out of the car for a sec?"

I unbuckle my seat belt and get out of the Jeep.

"Now shut the door and say something," Ruiz says.

I close the car door and take a few steps back, then start talking, waiting for Ruiz's thumbs-up, which signals he can hear me. Then he gets out of the car.

"We could record it, couldn't we?" I say as he walks toward me. "The conversation."

He shakes his head, pulling me to the entrance of the building, where we're out of the sightline of the apartment windows. "No, that's illegal. And we're in dicey enough territory as it is. Let's remember what the goal is here. We just want him talking."

"I know."

"So don't push him. Don't try to get him to admit anything. Just see if you can eventually lead him around to the essay." He adjusts the baseball cap on his head, revealing a glimpse of rumpled hair. "I know it went pretty easy for you with Greg. But Macnamara's different. He's tricky."

"Tricky, how?"

Ruiz's eyes scan the apartment building. "Back when we were interviewing him, he was . . . slippery. We'd ask him a direct question, and he'd respond to something slightly different from what we'd asked. It was hard to pin him down." He shoves his hands in his pockets. "But of course, back then, he had his guard up. He was at the police station; he was severely stressed. With you, he might be more forthcoming—but you've got to get him to relax. Make him think you're not a threat."

"Okay," I say, a little impatiently. Now that we're here, I want to get it over with. Before my nerves get any more frayed. But Ruiz is still talking. Is it possible he's as anxious as I am?

"Don't bring up the essay right away. Take your time. And watch him carefully; see if he starts to get jumpy at any point. He's a good liar, but even good liars have tells."

At the word *liar*, I wince. He hasn't meant to, but he's pressed a sore spot, a bruise that's lingered for years.

CHAPTER 31

June 2015

In the morning, the sun pushed through the blinds and warmed the sheets around me. Ruiz slept with one arm wrapped around my waist, his breath brushing my hair. I could feel the rise and fall of his chest against my shoulder blades. While he slept, I memorized the lines of the tattoo on his forearm, the ink blue-black against his tanned skin.

I didn't move. I wanted this moment to last. This moment when he wasn't a detective and I wasn't Allie's sister.

Then a car backfired on the street, and Ruiz shifted beside me. He rolled over onto his back, and suddenly there was space between us, cold air on my back. He made a low noise in the back of his throat.

In daylight, the apartment looked cramped, messy. Quickly, I sat up, pulling the sheet around me. The intimacy of last night, I sensed, was about to vanish. I knew Ruiz well enough to know he wasn't inclined to break the rules. And sleeping with me? That would be high on the list of rules not to be broken. I wrapped my arms around my knees.

Ruiz pushed himself up onto his elbows. "Natasha."

I turned my head, but when I met his gaze, I flinched from what I saw there. He reached for my arm, but I twisted away, leaned down to pick my T-shirt up off the floor. I pulled it over my head, feeling suddenly that it was very important not to be naked.

"Listen," he said quietly. "Last night . . ."

"You don't have to say anything," I said. Where the hell was my underwear? I spotted it at the bottom of the bed and snatched it up.

"Hey," he said. "Hold on a second. Can we talk?"

I scooted to the edge of the bed and pulled on my underwear, my T-shirt. Ruiz sat up, his expression serious. I knew what he was going to say. I was a part of a case he was working on; of course we couldn't get involved. If he hadn't been so upset yesterday, it never would've happened. "I know, okay?"

"Let me talk, will you?" He tugged at my T-shirt, making me turn and face him. "Last night was . . ." He touched the side of my face, brushed a piece of hair behind my ear. Then he cleared his throat. "I'm not sorry about last night."

For a moment, we just sat like that, looking at each other. And I felt something shift in my chest, a door sliding open.

Then he broke eye contact. "But I should be. I shouldn't have crossed that line. If Golanski found out about this—" He pushed his hands through his hair, as if the implications were only just now sinking in. "It would be bad."

I blinked rapidly. It wasn't that he felt nothing for me. It was just that his job meant more. For some reason, I found myself thinking about Macnamara, how he had risked everything—his reputation, his career—for Allie. But I wasn't Allie.

"I know," I said, my voice shaky. Last night, I'd been happy. I couldn't remember the last time I'd been happy. "It's fine."

"Natasha—"

"It doesn't have to mean anything," I said quickly. "It was just sex." I didn't know why I said that. It was something Allie would've said. It made last night casual, something I could brush off.

But it had been the wrong thing to say.

Ruiz's face changed, closed off. "Well. If that's the way you feel . . ."

I combed my hands through my tangled hair, then opened my mouth to say something else, but he was already getting out of bed, picking his clothes up off the floor. "That's not—" I said.

But he was talking over me. "It's my fault. I wasn't in a good place yesterday. And I shouldn't have drawn you into that." He was pulling on his clothes. Pants, shirt.

"Ruiz—"

"Christ, I don't know what I was thinking." He couldn't seem to get the buttons of his shirt fastened properly. "It would be different if you weren't such a central part of the case. God, if it turned out that somehow you—" He broke off.

A strange sensation washed over me, like I'd stepped away from my body for a moment. "What?" I said. "If it turned out I . . . what?"

He wouldn't look me in the eye. "Shit. Nothing."

"No," I said sharply. "What were you going to say? Say it."

He shook his head. "It's just . . . if it turned out you were involved somehow, even tangentially . . ."

I became aware of a dull electrical thrum in my ears, the kind you hear when you hold a shell up to your ears. "But you know," I said. "You know I had nothing to do with it."

He paused. "Of course. C'mon, you know I'm only talking theoretically."

But his response had come just a fraction of a second too late. And that was when I realized that Ruiz wasn't sure, not 100 percent, that I wasn't involved in Allie's disappearance.

Suddenly, everything shifted, and I saw the events of the past two years through a new lens. The way Ruiz had stayed in touch with me after the case went cold, the way he never tired of talking about the week before Allie went missing. Going over the details again and again.

"You've been keeping tabs on me," I said, my voice high and unnatural. All those conversations when I thought we'd been thinking through the case together. He'd been *monitoring* me. Feeling out my story for gaps, inconsistencies.

"No," he said, stepping toward me. He'd put his shirt on wrong; the collar was bent under, and the buttons didn't line up properly. "Look, it wasn't like that."

I couldn't seem to get enough air into my lungs. "What the fuck." I got out of bed and walked into the kitchenette.

"Natasha. I don't think you'd do anything to hurt Allie."

I spun around. "But?"

He drew in a deep breath. This time he met my gaze and held it. "But I don't think you've been fully honest about what happened that week. I think you've been holding something back."

My skin went hot and then cold.

"Natasha." He was talking quietly, reasonably, in a way that made me want to slap him. "A lot of people lie when they're questioned by the police. Sometimes about stupid things. Stuff that doesn't matter. But it can make them look like they have something to hide. When, really, they don't."

I wiped at my nose, which had begun to run. "I haven't held anything back."

Ruiz walked over and grasped my shoulders, his eyes searching my face. "Are you sure? Natasha—"

I swallowed, and it was painful, like there was something lodged in my throat. Then I shook myself loose from his grip and said, "Fuck you."

He stepped back, as if I were a dog that had bitten him.

Blood pulsed in my ears. I didn't get angry often, but when I did, it hit me like a tidal wave, something outside my control. "You used me," I said. I knew that wasn't the full truth, not really, but I wanted to hurl anything I could at him. If there'd been a glass nearby, I would've thrown it at his head. "I could tell Golanski what happened last night. That this is your idea of working a case."

He held his hands up. "Natasha."

"If you come near me again, I'll report you to the department. I'll let them know what kind of person you really are. I'll tell them you daydream about killing people in alleyways."

He froze. That had been a low blow.

"Get out," I said, and in the movie of my life, I was shouting, although I never shouted. "Get out!"

For a moment, he looked at me as if he'd never met me before. Then he bent down to pick up his shoes before walking out of the apartment, closing the door quietly behind him.

CHAPTER 32

As we stand facing Macnamara's building, I push that memory down. Ruiz and I have never talked about that morning in my garage apartment. What is there to say? We both know what happened, what was said. How it can't be taken back.

I step toward the entry door but stop short when I see that a key card swipe is required to get in. I glance at Ruiz. *What do we do now?*

"Just wait a sec." He pulls me back and stands to one side, pretending to be absorbed in checking something on his phone. After a minute, a woman pushes the door open from the inside. She's struggling to maneuver her stroller through the door.

"Here," Ruiz says, looking up from his phone. He holds the door open as she walks through, and she shoots him a grateful look.

"Thanks," she says.

After she passes, Ruiz keeps the door held open, and we step inside. The foyer is all soft lighting and hardwood floors, indoor trees in big glazed pots.

Ruiz follows me into the hallway and glances at the number on the first door he sees. "He'll be just around the corner."

I'm aware of the weight of my phone in my front jacket pocket, of my heartbeat knocking against it.

"You ready?" he asks.

I nod. I feel overcaffeinated, on edge, but it's not a totally unpleasant sensation. I feel very much alive.

"Okay, then." Ruiz positions himself along one wall. He's going to wait here, out of sight of Macnamara's door, while I go up and knock. "Remember, if anything goes wrong, just act like you're answering a phone call, and I'll be right there."

I nod again, then walk to the end of the corridor and turn the corner. When I arrive at Apartment 108, I stop short. The door has a glass peephole that seems to be staring balefully at me.

Slowly, I raise my hand and rap my knuckles against the door. After a few seconds, I hear footsteps, followed by rattling as someone releases a series of locks. Then the door opens, and Macnamara is standing right in front of me.

After all this time, it's jarring to see him up close. I've associated him with the photo on the forums for so long that I've forgotten the real-life details. The slight asymmetry of his mouth. The small scar next to his right eye. His once-unruly hair has been cut short, and his face looks puffy, the way Matthew's used to back when he was drinking.

"Can I help you?" He looks me up and down, scanning for a detail to give me some context—a clipboard, or pamphlets, maybe.

I swallow. He doesn't know who I am. "Hi. Um . . . Professor Macnamara—"

Before I can finish my sentence, his body stiffens. He's recognized me. "Jesus." He takes a moment to look me up and down. "Natasha. What the hell are you doing here?"

"I just want to talk."

He leans forward, glancing into the hallway as if checking to see whether other people are around. "How the hell did you find me? What is this about?"

"I'm not here to cause any trouble . . ."

"Uh-uh," he says abruptly, holding up a hand. "Sorry. I'm not getting into—whatever this is—with you. I've worked long and hard to put that mess behind me."

That mess? I feel a sudden wave of fury. As if that's all Allie's disappearance has been to him—an inconvenience.

"Too bad," I hear myself say, and then I'm pushing past him into his apartment. It's not something I'd planned on, but I know in this moment it's the right thing to do, the only way to keep from having the door slammed in my face.

Macnamara is so startled that he makes no move to stop me. I stride into his living room and have just enough time to register stark, Danish furniture and a large window that looks out onto a patio before he follows me into the room and grabs me by the arm.

"You need to leave. Now."

His grip is painful, fingers pressing against bone.

"I don't think you want to do that," I say, my voice eerily calm. Had he grabbed Allie like this? "I might start screaming. And then what would your neighbors think?" In my words, I hear an echo of Allie, her anger, her audacity.

As if he can sense her presence in the room, Macnamara drops my arm and backs away. "What is it that you want?"

"Like I said. I just want to talk. Ten minutes."

Macnamara glances behind him at his front door. He'd like to kick me out, but he's more afraid that I'll cause a scene. "Five minutes," he counters, retreating to close the apartment door. "But that's it."

He wants to sound like he's still in control. Fine. But I know, suddenly, that I'm the one in charge here. Is this how Allie used to feel, whenever she behaved outrageously?

I take a seat on the couch, my arm throbbing where Macnamara grabbed me. He hesitates for a moment, then sits down in the chair across from me, gripping his hands together as if attending a very tense prayer meeting.

The living room is untidy. His office at LACSA had been the same way. Piles of books everywhere. Papers stacked on any spare surface.

"I don't know what you're here for," he says. "But I just want to say—I don't know what happened to your sister. I want to make that clear."

Put him at ease, Ruiz had said. Make him think you're not a threat.

"I know that," I say, trying to sound convincing. "I don't think you hurt Allie."

He raises an eyebrow. "Oh? Then why are you here?"

"There are some things I need to ask you, about the time before she went missing."

He lets out an exasperated sound. "I've been over all this with the cops. I don't understand what I could possibly—"

"They're just questions I want answered for myself," I say. "Nothing to do with the investigation." *Get him to relax.* Well, I've got my work cut out for me. He's wound tight, his heels jiggling against the carpet.

"Like what?"

"I just want to know what you remember about Allie during that time. During those last weeks."

His forehead wrinkles. "Like what?"

"I mean, back then," I say, "I felt like I hardly knew her anymore. She was acting so differently. And I think—it would just mean a lot to me if you could tell me your impressions of her at that time. How she was with you." I'm startled to find myself getting teary eyed.

There's a box of tissues beside Macnamara on a side table, and after a moment's hesitation, he passes them to me.

"Thanks," I say, pulling one out of the box and pressing it against my eyes. When I look up, he seems to have dropped his guard a little. I didn't plan the tears, but there's no doubt that they're helping.

Macnamara's expression shifts, and for the first time I see a sign of the person I knew back at LACSA. "You all right?" he asks.

I nod. "I'm sorry. I just . . . the anniversary of her disappearance is really hard for me."

He swallows. "Not just for you." He stares out the window for a minute. "Allie was a unique person. She had a . . . strong impact. On many people, I think."

"On you," I say quietly.

His smile is tinged with bitterness, self-mockery. "Yes." Then he goes silent for a while.

In this moment, we're just two people who miss Allie.

"What do you remember about her?" I ask, not wanting to break the spell.

He leans back against the couch cushions, his attention drawing inward. "When she came into my class . . . it's stupid, but I actually felt intimidated. She seemed so adult. So sophisticated. She had a reputation as a party girl, but when I spoke to her in my office hours . . ." He's lost in the past. "She'd read, a lot. Apparently her dad sent her books all the time, stuff he said would expand her horizons. She never told him that she read them. But she'd read them all, had opinions that were . . . startling for someone her age."

My throat constricts. Macnamara, it seems, knows more about Allie than I did.

Now that he's started talking, it's like he doesn't want to stop. Like he's been waiting for someone to talk to. Someone who might understand. "My first impression was that she was much older than her years. But later . . ."

"What?"

"Later, when I got to know her better, I realized that sophisticated persona—that was all an act. Underneath all that, Allie was very immature, very troubled."

He wipes a hand across his face. "I suppose that's part of what made her so fascinating. And so dangerous."

I lean forward. "Dangerous?"

His eyes are the same bright blue, but there are lines on his face that weren't there four years ago. "After a while, I began to see that her grasp on reality—well, it was a child's grasp."

I swallow down a bitter taste in my mouth. "How do you mean?"

"Like, after we'd been together a few weeks, she started wanting me to call her Mia. Not Allie. It was some name she'd gotten from a book she'd read as a kid. She said she just didn't want to be Allie anymore. And then, later on that winter, she started talking about us running away together. Overseas, maybe. She was serious. I couldn't seem to explain to her that . . . it just wasn't realistic."

I knew this side of Allie. The one who wanted you to come along on whatever wild adventure she'd just dreamed up.

He leans back in his chair, his expression thoughtful. "That dreaminess, that wildness . . . it was part of what made her so attractive. I mean, at one point, I even thought—why not? Why not leave it all behind and go start a new life?" He laughs, as if astounded by himself even now. The moment lingers, then he blinks suddenly, as if realizing he's said more than he intended to. "Anyway," he says abruptly. "That's certainly more than the five minutes you asked for."

Actually, I'd asked for ten.

"There's just one other thing," I say.

He looks frustrated. "What is it?"

Watch him carefully, Ruiz said. *See if he starts to get jumpy.*

"I've been looking for something of Allie's that she used to carry around," I say carefully. "A little flash drive that looked like a panda bear."

"Oh?" His face is blank. If the flash drive rings any bells with him, he's doing a great job of hiding it.

"A friend of mine said she might have had some of her writing on it," I say, pushing further. "An essay. Something she was working on for your class."

There. His expression doesn't change, but a muscle in his jaw flexes.

"It would be really amazing if I could find it." I chatter on as if I haven't noticed his reaction. "Something from Allie's college years, something to remember her by. I'm putting together a memorial for the four-year anniversary of her disappearance. And it would be great to share something of hers like that. Something personal."

Macnamara shifts in his chair. "I don't know what you think I can do."

"Well, I wondered if you might have a copy of the essay somewhere. Since it was for your class."

He looks up at the ceiling, as if he's thinking deeply. Then he shakes his head. "No, sorry. I tossed all my stuff from LACSA years ago."

"But you remember her essay, don't you?"

He smiles wryly. "I read a lot of student essays, Natasha. If I remembered them all, I'd have no room left in my brain."

I remember what Ruiz said about Macnamara dodging questions. He hasn't actually answered the one I asked.

"Oh. Well. That's weird," I say. Ruiz told me not to push him, but I can't help it. I want to wipe that smug expression off his face. He thinks he can lie to me and get away with it.

"Why?"

"Because," I say, "Allie told me you wanted to help her publish the essay. She talked about it, like, all the time. And if you thought it was that good—well, it seems strange that you wouldn't remember it."

He goes completely still. He hadn't expected me to know about the publication. Then his face clears, as if he's just recalled something. "I mean, now that you mention it, yes, I do remember we had a discussion once about getting her writing published. But we never talked about anything specific."

Liar.

Sweat is forming at his temples, tiny beads that glint in the sunlight.

I scoot forward on the couch, my voice low and fierce. "I know you read that essay."

He draws in a deep breath, calculating the risk of continuing his denial. The knuckles of his clasped hands are white. "Okay, yes, I remember it," he concedes. "Quite a piece of writing. Did you read it?" he asks.

I shake my head. "But I know you did. So why lie about it?"

He assesses me with a look I remember from his classroom: as if he could see the inner workings of my brain. "Yes, Allie wrote an essay." His voice is flat, impersonal. "And it was very good. Good enough that I thought she could get it published. But the essay, it could've caused problems for her."

"Problems? How?"

He stands up and walks over to the window, gazing out at the potted succulents on the patio. After a moment, he says, "She'd written about Isabel. About what it was like growing up with her." He turns. "Allie didn't pull any punches. The way she portrayed Isabel was . . . less than flattering. I didn't have an issue with that, but then Allie . . ." He grimaces. "I don't know why, but she told her mother about what she was writing. I think she threw it in her face, during an argument. That turned out to be a mistake."

I can only imagine. Allie's relationship with Isabel hadn't improved after Allie moved in with us in Palos Verdes. If anything, it got worse. Later, during college, whenever I was in a room with the two of them, I got the feeling that, at any minute, an epic argument might erupt.

"Anyway," Macnamara says. "Isabel went on the warpath. Threatened to sue Allie if she published."

"Seriously? What did Allie write?" It must've been bad for Isabel to get so worked up.

Macnamara rubs his forehead. "Just . . . details about Isabel's life she wouldn't have been happy to have go public. Her drinking. Her partying. The amount of time Allie was left alone as a child. Let's just say, it wouldn't have been good for her image."

Isabel's image. Her philanthropy. The trips to Africa. The media has always portrayed her as something close to a saint.

"After that," Macnamara says, "I got nervous. At that point, Allie was only a couple of weeks sober. Wading into a public battle with Isabel, facing a potential lawsuit . . ." He spreads his hands wide. "It could've destroyed all the progress she'd made. So, I encouraged her to hold off. Just for a while. It wasn't the right time."

"What did Allie say to that?"

He lets out a humorless laugh. "It did not go over well. She called me a coward. We argued. Finally, I gave in. I told her, 'Go ahead. Do what you want. It's your funeral.'" When he realizes his choice of words, he winces. "Or something to that effect."

"But if Allie was determined to publish," I ask, "how come she never did?"

He turns to me. His skin is pale, as if he rarely leaves the house these days. "Isabel."

"Isabel?"

"Somehow she found out, about Allie and me."

A sick feeling washes over me.

"Allie swore she never told her mother about us," he says. "But all of a sudden, I have Isabel Andersen calling my office phone at LACSA. Telling me that if I don't put an end to this essay, she'll go to my supervisors about my relationship with Allie. So, again, I tried to persuade Allie to leave the essay idea alone."

"Did you tell her why?"

He shakes his head. "God, no. I knew the minute I mentioned Isabel, Allie would go off the rails. So I tried to reason with her. What would be the harm in waiting to publish? In six months, a year, she'd be in a better position."

And in a year, Allie would have graduated. She'd no longer be Macnamara's student. Had Macnamara been concerned about Allie's position or his own?

He sighs. "But it didn't work. To Allie, the issue was black and white. Either I was with her or I was against her."

"So she broke up with you." I'm sweating, but I can't take off my jacket, not with the phone in my pocket like it is, pressing against my heart.

He nods. "It was only then, at the end, that I realized how unstable she really was."

Unstable. The word hovers in the air. "What do you mean?"

He leans back against the sliding door. "When I talked to her that last time, she went completely ballistic. Screamed. Threw things. I'd never seen her get like that. I'd never seen *anyone* get like that."

I swallow. If he was lying before, he's definitely not now. Because I know exactly what he's describing. One of Allie's rages.

CHAPTER 33

December 2008

In the backyard of the house on Via Montemar, Mom and I sat at the patio table, sipping tea as we bent over our notebooks. She was grading exams, and I was trying to focus on my chemistry homework. But I kept glancing behind me, at the house.

"What do you think they're talking about?" I asked. Isabel had come over that afternoon so that she and Giles and Allie could talk. A family meeting.

Mom scribbled a note on a student's paper, a small line appearing between her eyebrows. "Honey, it's really none of our business."

I frowned down at the pages of my notebook. I was thinking about Allie's liquor stash in the AC vent. Suppose Giles had found it. Suppose Allie was going to get sent away to that boarding school. Was there something I could do to stop it? I could claim the liquor bottles were mine. But no one would buy that, not for a second.

Mom glanced up from her grading. "It's nothing serious, Tasha. They just want to talk about how they're going to handle the holidays this year. After last year, you know, when Allie stormed out . . . they just want to make sure things go more smoothly this time."

"That requires a whole meeting?"

She tapped her pen on her stack of papers. "Well, Isabel wants Allie to go up to her house for Christmas this year."

"Oh." Allie flatly refused to spend one-on-one time with Isabel. She'd go to the Malibu house if she could drag me along with her. But going to Isabel's solo . . .

"Yeah, Allie's never going to go for that," I said.

"Well, that's not really fair," Mom said mildly. "Allie spent the last two holidays with us. And Allie can't stay angry at Isabel forever."

"Mmm." I had my doubts about that. After Allie got out of Seabrook, Isabel had made it clear that Allie couldn't move back in with her. That was when Allie got shunted over to Giles, who for most of her life she'd only seen during the holidays. Allie didn't appreciate being treated like a hot potato.

I stared out at the still surface of the pool. Mom went back to grading papers, and for a minute the only sound was the birds chirping in the trees. Then a scream ripped through the air, a sound out of a slasher movie.

I dropped my pen and leaped up before I'd fully registered that the noise was coming from the house. Mom scrambled to her feet, too, her papers scattering across the deck.

"What on earth?" she said.

"I won't!" someone shrieked. It was Allie, her voice raised to a strange, distorted pitch. "I won't! I won't!"

My heart was thumping so hard that my rib cage hurt. I moved toward the sliding glass door, but my mother grabbed me by the arm. "Wait," she said, her face pale. But when I heard Allie scream again, I jerked out of Mom's grip, pulled open the door, and stepped into the kitchen.

"Keep your voice down!" Isabel was shouting, her voice carrying into the kitchen from the living room.

"I hate you!" Allie screamed. "I *hate* you."

There was a smash, the sound of glass breaking.

Giles roared, "That's *enough*. Alastriana!"

Another crash.

I stepped closer to the living room doorway, close enough to hear Giles say in a fierce tone, "I think you'd better remember the terms you agreed to when you moved into this house."

"*Fuck* you," Allie said, her voice raw and hoarse. "You think I don't know you don't want me here? You'd get rid of me in a second, if only you could think of where to put me."

"Don't be ridicul—"

"Oh, go ahead and kick me out," Allie said. "I'm tired of waiting for it. I don't care. I don't give a *fuck*." Then she screamed again—a high, awful sound—and ran upstairs.

I turned to see my mother standing behind me, her eyes wide.

In the living room, Isabel had started sobbing. "You see what she's like," she said to Giles. "You see what I've had to put up with."

"Oh, spare me the martyr act," Giles snapped. "You're the one who let Matthew spoil her rotten while you were off on your film shoots—"

"Don't you *dare* lecture me on parenting," Isabel whispered in a terrible voice. "You, you—"

"Get out!" Allie screamed from upstairs. "Get out, get out, *get out*." There was a thud as something hit the floor above us.

Her shouts must have been carrying through the walls and out into the street. I wondered if our neighbors had called the police. I would have, if I were them.

"Are you happy now?" Giles said to Isabel. "I *told* you this was a bad idea. But do you ever listen?"

After a moment, I heard the front door slam, followed by the click of Isabel's high heels as she walked down our front path. In the kitchen, Mom and I looked at each other, unsure what to do next. When Giles walked into the kitchen, his face blotchy and red, Mom went up to him and rested a hand against his face.

"Jesus. What just happened in there?"

He jerked away. "Just . . . give me a minute." He walked to the sink and poured himself a glass of water. When he brought the glass to his mouth, his hand was shaking. It was a good thirty seconds before he seemed able to trust himself to speak. "I'm sorry you had to hear that. Isabel told me that Allie had trouble controlling her temper. But I had no idea it was this bad."

"She's lived here a year, Giles," Mom said. "And I've never seen her get like that."

"Well, we've been very lenient with her, haven't we? This is the first time I've really put my foot down. I was trying to support Isabel . . ." He set the glass down on the counter with a clank. "Unfortunately, Allie's very used to getting her own way."

Mom reached out and rubbed his shoulder. This time, he clutched at her hand, as if trying to absorb her calm. Then he pulled her close, his arms wrapping around her back. "It's just theatrics," he murmured in her ear. "Not a surprise, I guess, given who her mother is." That made both of them laugh a little.

I slipped out of the kitchen. Before today, I'd never really understood what had drawn Giles and my mom to each other, but now I finally got it, what Giles saw in my plainspoken, ordinary mom. She was the anti-Isabel. She was solid ground.

Quietly, I padded up the stairs to Allie's bedroom. But when I got to her door, I hesitated.

I reached out and touched the cool metal of the door handle. Then I heard a car door slam in the driveway. Stepping away from Allie's bedroom, I moved near the window that overlooked the front yard. Isabel's white Tesla was parked in the driveway, and she sat in the driver's seat, resting her forehead on the steering wheel and crying. From that angle, she looked so much like Allie that she could've been her twin.

I watched her for a minute or two, wondering how long she was going to stay like that. And then, suddenly, she sat up, brushing her hair back from her face, her cheeks raw. For the first time, I saw her as an ordinary person. A stressed-out mom.

She drew in a deep breath. Leaning over, she took her purse from the passenger seat and set it in her lap. Then she opened a small packet and pulled a wet wipe across her face, cleaning up the mascara that had run down her cheeks. Methodically, she began to rebuild her makeup, a process that she executed with impressive efficiency. In a few minutes, she looked as perfectly composed as she'd been when she'd arrived at our door. After looking at herself in the rearview mirror for one long moment, she rubbed her lips together, readjusted the mirror, and backed out of the driveway.

Watching Isabel left me with a strange feeling, like I'd just seen her zip her personality up around her like a second skin.

Slowly, I walked back to Allie's door and knocked softly. "Als?"

No response.

"It's me. Tash."

Still nothing. This past year, I'd thought we'd gotten closer than ever. But maybe there was a limit to how close I was allowed to get.

Still, it was unlike her to not say anything at all. Tentatively, I turned the handle and pushed the door open a few inches. "Allie?"

She was lying on the bed, curled on her side, one arm drawn up around her face. At first, I thought she was ignoring me. But then I saw the slackness of her mouth, the slow rise and fall of her chest. I stepped into the room and walked over to the bed. I crouched down and gently touched her hand, expecting her to wake up. But she didn't move. A strand of black hair was caught in the corner of her mouth, and the skin around her eyes looked red and puffy.

She had cried herself unconscious.

CHAPTER 34

From my position on the couch, I study Macnamara's face.

Over the past few years, Allie's rages had faded from memory until I'd almost convinced myself they couldn't have happened like I remembered. How many times had I seen her get that way? Only a handful, in all the years we'd known each other. Afterward, she never talked about it. She reverted seamlessly back to her usual self, and I found myself disoriented. Maybe those episodes hadn't been as big a deal as I'd thought. Maybe that was just how some people expressed themselves.

But talking to Macnamara, seeing his disquiet, I realize: Those weren't temper tantrums. Or *theatrics*, as Giles called them. They were something else, something out of Allie's control. That day at the house, when I'd heard her screaming, I'd suddenly understood Isabel's insistence that Allie not live with her anymore. Being around Allie when she was like that was terrifying.

Macnamara steps away from the sliding glass door. "Anyway, that's when things got too much for me," he says. "After that argument, I told myself Allie wasn't my responsibility—not in that way, anyhow. That's what she had a therapist for."

A dog barks outside, three short yaps.

"A therapist?" I say. After Seabrook, Allie swore off counseling, despite Isabel's constant nagging. I remember Allie sitting in her bedroom in the Via Montemar house, filing her nails and telling me: *Girl, those counselors don't have a clue. You want to hear all the diagnoses they've tried out on me? ADD, BPD, HPD . . . They're not happy unless they can sum me up in three letters.*

"Allie wasn't seeing a therapist," I tell Macnamara. "She hated therapists."

He raises his eyebrows. "Well, I don't know what to tell you. She was seeing one."

"When? For how long?" I would've noticed—wouldn't I?—Allie leaving the apartment for therapy sessions. But then I remember how often Allie had been "busy" that semester, how Greg and I frequently didn't know where she was.

"Since . . ." Macnamara thinks for a second. "I guess it was that November."

"Why? Why would she suddenly go back to therapy?"

He folds his arms over his chest. "She really didn't talk to you much, did she?"

"We talked a lot," I say, a defensive note creeping into my voice. "All the time."

"She went because she'd decided to get sober," he says.

Allie had resolved to get sober a million times before. "What was special about this time? Why did she need a therapist then?"

He shrugs. And there it is again, the evasiveness Ruiz warned me about. I have the feeling he knows more than he's willing to say. "Maybe it was the photos," he says. "In that magazine. The drama that caused with her parents."

I squint. That can't be right. I know Allie didn't stop drinking that September. Two weeks after the TMZ photos came out, I'd been holding her hair back while she threw up in our bathroom after a party at Christie's place. A week later, she bailed on Greg's annual Halloween party to go to Vegas with some friends of hers from Beverly Hills.

"She didn't tell you the reason?" I ask.

He shakes his head. "Allie had a way of avoiding subjects she didn't want to talk about. And that, I think, was one of them." He holds eye contact with me, like a man who has nothing to hide.

How much can I believe of what he's told me? I stare down at the hardwood floor, an uneasy feeling creeping over me. Macnamara knows how to blend in just enough truth with his lies that it's hard to tell one from the other.

CHAPTER 35

Ruiz and I sit in his Jeep in a parking lot on a bluff overlooking the ocean, eating the burgers we grabbed from a drive-through after we left Macnamara's. The talk with Macnamara has left me feeling drained, and I'm thankful for the sugary soda, the salty fries.

Ruiz finishes eating before I do and methodically folds up the paper bag the food came in. "So," he says.

"So."

"Apparently Isabel knew about this essay." A deep furrow has appeared between his eyebrows.

"Yeah."

Outside, the ocean ripples in the wind.

"Isabel never said a thing about an essay during the investigation. In fact, she acted like Allie's relationship with Macnamara came as a complete shock to her." He shakes his head. "Why?"

I take another sip of my soda. "I don't know."

"If what Macnamara is saying is true, that makes Isabel a pretty compelling suspect."

Suddenly, the soda tastes too sweet, too cloying. I set down the cup. "You don't think that Isabel had anything to do with . . ."

Ruiz turns to me. "Think about it. She was trying to silence Allie. Then Allie disappears. That solves her problem pretty neatly."

My jaw tightens. "But Isabel wasn't even in LA that week. She was out on Catalina." Isabel had gone to some party on a yacht anchored near the island. She hadn't gotten back to the city until Sunday.

"That only means she didn't do anything herself," Ruiz says. "It doesn't rule out her, say, hiring somebody to do something. Maybe she only meant to intimidate Allie. Scare her enough to get her to back down. But things went too far."

"That's ridiculous." But is it? Isn't that the way the rich do everything? You don't take care of things yourself. You outsource. "Isabel might've had problems with Allie, but she wouldn't have her *killed*." Intimidating her, though . . . I have to admit that I can see that possibility. I can see Isabel taking that step.

"I'm not saying that's what happened. I'm just saying it's a possibility. And the Catalina trip—it's almost too good of an alibi, isn't it? In all of this, Isabel has been the only person whose alibi has been completely airtight."

It's true. Back then, the cops had looked into everyone in Allie's family. That night, Giles was home alone at his place in Brentwood. Matthew was in Redlands at a conference, but no one had seen him there after 10:00 p.m. That left at least some doubt as to their whereabouts. But Isabel was immediately in the clear.

"You're saying she planned it that way?"

His expression darkens. "I think she's a smart lady. And a hell of an actress. She sure was selling us her shock and outrage about Allie and Macnamara's relationship."

I remember Isabel sitting on the couch with me in our living room that Christmas, tucking a piece of my hair behind my ear. How charming she could be. How hypnotic. Was everything an act with her?

"What about the therapist?" Ruiz says, switching topics. He must see how much the conversation about Isabel is unsettling me. "Did you buy what Macnamara said about that?" he asks.

I chip at the plastic top of my soda. Do I? I don't think the TMZ photos made much of a difference to Allie, although she'd been deeply annoyed by the loss of her car. Still, her having a therapist would explain a lot. It was that November when Allie stopped drinking. Started showing up for her classes. Even signing up for Macnamara's seminar. None of it made sense at the time—but when I factor in some outside influence, the pieces click into place.

"Yes," I say. "I think that part could be true."

Ruiz frowns. "Except—when we looked at Allie's finances, we never saw any payments to a therapist."

"What if she paid cash? Greg said she had a lot of it during that time."

Ruiz taps his fingers against the steering wheel. "Mm. Yeah, maybe."

In the parking lot, a pair of seagulls stand side by side, blinking slowly as the wind rumples their feathers. The silence between Ruiz and me stretches long, a persistent awkwardness that floats between us, like a low-hanging cloud.

I grip the armrest on the door, gathering my nerve. "Ruiz. About what I said, that day in my apartment . . ." I can feel blood rushing to my face. "I'm sorry."

There's a long pause; then he says, "I'm the one who should apologize." His left hand grips the steering wheel. "I hope you know, I never set out to . . . use you. In my mind, it was . . . well. It was complicated."

I keep my eyes fixed on the horizon.

"You should know," he says quietly, "that night, it wasn't about the case. That night, the case was about the furthest thing from my mind."

There are surfers in the waves below, paddling at an angle to the shore.

Then he says, cautiously, "But listen, Natasha—if we're going to find this flash drive, figure out what it means, I need to know . . . if there's anything at all you've been holding back . . . even if it doesn't seem like much." He swallows. "Now's the time. It could be important." He's being so gentle, so understanding.

Below, a huge wave sweeps the surfers into the shore like they're plastic toys.

"There's nothing," I say. And there's not. Not really. Something flickers at the back of my mind, but I push it away. Turning to Ruiz, I see the doubt in his face, and say, more firmly: "I promise." And this time, I almost convince myself.

He watches me for a long moment, as if he's considering pushing the point. Then, he looks away and says, "Okay. Okay."

As he turns the key in the ignition, the car shivers into life around us. He begins backing out of the parking lot, and I rub at my eyes. The edges of my vision are starting to blur. At first, I tell myself it's just an effect of all the bright light, staring into the sun's reflection on the water. But then my vision darkens down to a narrow tunnel, and the shadows crowd in until all I see is black.

CHAPTER 36

When I get back to my apartment, I close the door firmly behind me and lean my head against its cool surface. The episode in the car lasted only a few minutes, and Ruiz didn't notice anything was amiss—but I'd spent the remainder of the drive feeling shaky.

Two episodes in a week. Not good. The next time one hits, I might be at work. I might be crossing a street. And what will I do then?

After going into the bathroom, I pull the empty bottle of Inderal out of the medicine cabinet. Then I get out my phone, call Dr. Rajmani's office, and request an appointment. Now I'll have to talk to him, and he'll want to know why, after all this time, I suddenly need more pills. I imagine his reaction if I tell him the truth. This week, I've torn down all the careful boundaries he helped me set, to protect me from the investigation.

In the mirror, my reflection stares back at me. I've been rubbing at my face, and my makeup has smudged. Underneath the powder and concealer, the old Natasha is peeking out. Pale, freckled. Dark circles under the eyes. This is the Natasha who once sat at the bus stop opposite Roy Tucker's house for hours, watching his comings and goings, until a police officer came to escort her away.

I'm backsliding. This latest episode is proof of that. As is the way I can't seem to control my thoughts. Memories of Allie keep slithering in, fleeting moments that suddenly seem significant.

Like the day when she'd draped herself across my bed, dissecting my recent breakup with Josh Takegawa. "He really liked you, you know." She was eating straight out of a box of Honey Nut Cheerios.

I sat at my desk, trying to focus on my ethics homework. "Really," I said flatly. "Then why'd he dump me for Maggie Sheehan?"

"Because," Allie said, popping a Cheerio in her mouth, "you barely talked to him. You were a total ice queen."

"No, I wasn't," I said. "I was just quiet." Quiet was good. Quiet was safe. If I spoke too much, Josh might figure out—just like Greg and the rest of Allie's friends had—that I was decidedly uncool. I didn't listen to the right bands, take the right drugs, or talk with Allie's effortless combination of sarcasm and sincerity.

"I mean, you're really awful with guys," she mused. "It's pretty fascinating."

"Thanks a bunch."

"No, I mean, I am too," she said, sitting up in a cross-legged position. "Awful, that is. But with me, you can at least see where it comes from. Whereas you"—she pointed a finger at me—"stable home, normal mother; it just doesn't add up. You should be the most securely attached person in the world."

I gave up trying to focus on my homework and swung around in my desk chair. "I didn't realize I'd signed up for psychoanalysis."

She grinned, as if I'd paid her a compliment, then dusted some crumbs off her chest. "Dr. Allie is in the house." Then, after a moment: "You should try it."

"Try what?"

"Therapy. You could really unpack some things."

Irritated, I pushed my chair away from my desk. "I don't know why you're so enthused about therapy for me," I said. "You told me it was all bullshit."

She flopped back on the bed, gazing up at the ceiling as if she could see something there that I couldn't. "Yeah, well, I say a lot of shit." Her expression was unreadable.

"You certainly do," I said, tossing my pen at her. It hit her thigh, but it was as if she didn't even feel it.

"I talk and talk, but I never really say anything. Not really," she said softly.

I frowned. What was with her today?

She propped herself up on her side, picking at loose threads on the quilt. "I mean, what if I told you something really real? Something true. Do you think you could handle it?" Her eyes were big and black.

I felt my guard go up. Was she looking for another opportunity to critique my style, my personality, my relationships? "Well, only if you're not going to be a bitch about it," I said, aiming for the jokey-sarcastic tone she and Greg used with each other.

Her face fell.

"Als. I'm joking," I said quickly. I'd read her tone wrong. I hadn't realized she really wanted to tell me something. "Obviously. You can say whatever you want."

"Yeah, obviously," she said lightly, sitting up. But whatever that moment had been, it had vanished. She pulled her hair back into a ponytail and secured it with a band she had wrapped around her wrist. I tried to regain her attention, but just then she got a call on her phone and the moment was gone.

I never did find out what she was going to say that day.

And now I wonder: When was that, that day she'd been talking about therapy?

In my bedroom, I pull the box of photographs onto my bed and sit next to it, sorting through the prints. What I need is a timeline. That conversation with Allie about therapy—that must have happened in November of 2012. I pull out the snapshots that were taken then, trying to get a sense of what was happening at the time. That party at Greg's house where I'd taken a sip of Allie's drink and realized it was sparkling water. The Thanksgiving Allie and I spent at Mom's house.

I spread more photographs out around me on the comforter. November, December. These were the months I'd been so irritated with

Allie. She'd stopped going to Luxe on Saturdays—which was fine by me—but she'd also started canceling our Wednesday night movie plans and disappearing from the apartment for long stretches of time.

Occasionally, I'd try to convince her to drop by one of Christie's parties or crack open a bottle of wine with me on Friday after classes. But she'd say she was tired, or that she had a deadline for her costume design class. She spent a lot of time in her room with the door closed, muffled music seeping from underneath the door.

During that period, I'd felt unsettled—and hurt. Even when we did hang out like before, watching bad Hallmark movies on the couch or wandering through the Fashion District, it felt different. I could still see Allie, still talk to her, but it was like she was standing behind a glass wall. I was losing her. And I didn't know why.

I arrange the photos on the bed in chronological order. 2010: Allie and me moving into the apartment in West LA. 2011: Allie and me and Greg standing in line at Luxe, holding the fake IDs Greg had gotten for us.

I've looked at these photos a hundred times before. Some of them used to be stuck to the door of our apartment fridge. But I'm seeing them now with new eyes. I'd thought I had such a clear recollection of our college years. But today I see that the pictures don't line up with my memories.

For instance, I remember Greg and me avoiding each other whenever possible. But here we are with Allie at Café Bijou, at Luxe, in the apartment living room, laughing and talking as if we're good friends. And Allie—I remember her being at the peak of her party phase in college, having the time of her life. But in the photos, I notice shadows under her eyes, a haunted expression on her face.

The photos of me are especially startling. I usually avoid looking at photos of myself with Allie, because they all seem to fall along the same lines as that terrible photo on the forums—highlighting how far I fell short compared to her.

But in the photos from junior year, I don't see that Natasha at all. In one, I'm sitting at a table at Café Bijou wearing skinny jeans and an oversize thrift-store sweater, vintage ankle boots, and a pair of Bialucci sunglasses I'd borrowed from Allie. I look almost chic. Like someone with her own distinct personality. Had I looked like that and just not known it?

I scrabble around the bottom of the cardboard box for the last of the photos. These are the larger prints I made for Hadfield's photography class, the class I'd enrolled in that last semester at LACSA.

They're a series of black-and-white self-portraits. In some, I've zoomed in so close that you can only see my eyes—the neutral-colored eyelashes, the pale streaks in my irises. And I remember how good it had felt back then, to be in the darkroom, to maneuver around in the dim light surrounded by the smell of acrid chemicals. I'd developed these portraits one Saturday when I was alone in the photography lab. In the eerie half-light, I'd watched my features come into view under the wavery liquid and been surprised to find myself beautiful.

CHAPTER 37

December 2012

At the student exhibition for Hadfield's class, I stood in front of my framed photographs, shifting on my feet as people walked by, taking in the art. Professor Hadfield had arranged the exhibition off campus in this little gallery on Melrose. He said he wanted us to feel what it was like to be real artists.

Earlier in the evening, I'd been thrilled to see my photographs displayed on the bare white walls. But as the evening dragged on, I found myself wilting. The other students had all invited so many people to the show: boyfriends, girlfriends, mothers, uncles, grandparents. But I had only asked Allie. And at the last minute, she'd texted to say she wasn't going to make it. Stuck in 405 traffic. I'll make it up to you! she promised. But her text didn't soothe the sting in my chest. I checked her location on my iPhone. Of course, she wasn't on the 405; she wasn't anywhere near it. She was in Los Feliz, where Macnamara lived. It was so like her to lie and not remember she had location sharing on.

As the crowd thinned, I tried to keep my head up, the dwindling crowd highlighting how alone I was.

I had just turned and started to pack up my stuff when a hush fell over the gallery. Looking around, I saw everyone's heads turning toward the entrance, where Isabel Andersen stood framed in the doorway. She wore jeans and a pale silk blouse, a large leather handbag slung over her shoulder. Although she was chatting with the gallery owner, her eyes scanned the room. When she caught sight of me, she broke into a wide smile and waved. Immediately, the attention in the room swung toward me.

As she walked across the gallery, people averted their eyes and pretended to be having normal conversations with each other. But an unmistakable murmur sprang up in her wake, and a few people not so subtly held up their phones, trying to get a shot of her as she passed.

When she reached me, she kissed me on both cheeks. "Natasha! How lovely to see you."

Over her shoulder, I saw my classmates suddenly reassessing their level of interest in me.

"Isabel!" I said. "What're you doing here?" Had she somehow heard about the exhibit and misunderstood, thinking Allie was a part of it?

"Well, don't you know, Rosa—she owns this place—Rosa told me she saw your name on some of the work being put up this afternoon. And she said, 'Isn't that a dear friend of Allie's?' I said, 'Yes, of course!' And then I just happened to be passing and thought, 'Wouldn't it be nice to say hello?'"

I flushed, feeling both flattered and confused. Would Isabel really come here just to see me? When was the last time we'd seen each other? Maybe four months earlier, when she'd come over to the apartment to talk to Allie—a conversation that had not gone well. During that visit, I don't remember the two of us exchanging more than a few words.

She turned to look at my photos, her face lighting up. "And is this your work?"

"Yes," I said, tugging at the sleeves of my sweater.

A camera flashed behind her. Over Isabel's shoulder, I saw a woman quickly turn away, having gotten her snapshot. Isabel stepped closer to examine my photographs. If she was aware of the interest she'd stirred by coming here, she showed no sign. She spent a long time looking at my self-portraits, regarding them with a seriousness that I found touching. Eventually, she reached out and tapped the edge of one of the frames.

"This one," she said. It was a close-up of my face. My features filled the frame, unnervingly large, my freckles standing out on my skin like flecks of paint. "This is something special." She turned to me. "Is it for sale?"

"For sale? Um, I don't know." This was only a student exhibition. I looked around at the other students. "I don't think anyone else is selling their work."

She smiled mischievously. "But that doesn't mean *you* can't, does it? Could you make an exception for me? Please?" All of a sudden, she was very Allie-like, her expression pleading.

"Of course she could," Professor Hadfield said, placing a hand on my shoulder. He'd come up behind me, and now he leaned over to stage-whisper in my ear, "Never pass up the opportunity for a sale."

Isabel laughed. "Good advice." She turned her brilliant smile on him. "And you are?"

He held out his hand. "Abe Hadfield. Natasha's photography professor. I must say, it's an honor to have you here at our show."

She grasped his hand in both of hers, squeezing earnestly. "Oh, you're too kind. It's a pleasure to be here." Then she rummaged in her handbag and pulled out a checkbook. "Now, Abe—what would you say is a fair price for a piece like this?"

I glanced back at the photo, which was encased in a cheap frame from Target. "Isabel, I'll give it to you."

"No, no," she chided.

"Please. I'd like you to have it." The thought of Professor Hadfield naming a price for the photo made me feel a little ill. I took the frame off the wall and handed it to her. "Please."

She looked between me and Professor Hadfield, then slowly eased her checkbook back in her purse. "Well, all right. If you insist."

Professor Hadfield shook his head, amused. "Natasha, if you want to make your way in the art world, you're going to have to change that attitude."

"Ah, well," Isabel said lightly. "I'm sure she'll find that out soon enough." There was something in her voice that ever so gently conveyed the idea that Professor Hadfield was now dismissed from the conversation.

He pretended he'd caught sight of someone across the room he needed to talk to. "Oh, well, I'll leave you two to it. Isabel, it was a delight to meet you."

"Likewise!" Isabel said brightly. Then she turned her attention to the frame in her hands. "This is very kind of you, Natasha." She flipped the photo toward me so that I was staring at my own face. "Would you mind if I showed this to a photographer friend of mine? He's been looking for a new model, and I think he'd be very interested in your look."

I made a startled sound. "Seriously?"

Isabel laughed. "Don't look so surprised! I spotted you years ago, remember? Back at that Christmas dinner. You have a very striking look. These pictures confirm that. Please? Could I show this to him?"

I felt an unfamiliar warmth in my chest. "Sure," I said. "Yeah, that would be great." I lifted my head, feeling my shoulders straighten. Allie hadn't thought it was worth coming to the exhibition, but Isabel had. And, in me, she'd found something worth paying attention to.

CHAPTER 38

I pick up the eight-by-ten envelope with the PL STUDIOS stamp on it and slide out several matte prints. It's only the second time I've seen these. After the first time, I couldn't bear to look at them anymore.

In one, I'm wearing a pale sweater that comes down off my shoulders, revealing my freckled skin and the sharp angle of my collarbones. My gaze is fixed on the camera, my eyes impossibly clear and bright. In others, I'm photographed facing away from the camera, my face in profile and the lighting picking up the contours of my back.

Isabel followed through on her promise to show my photo to her photographer friend, who'd then wanted to meet me, to take a few trial photos. I didn't tell anyone about it, not even Allie.

Especially not Allie.

First of all, she'd hate the fact that I was spending time with Isabel. Second of all, she'd laugh outright at the idea of me modeling. Being in front of the camera—that was her role, not mine.

After sliding the photos out of the envelope, I place them in a line on my bedspread. In another life, the photo shoot might have been important for me. Life changing, even. But a few days later, Allie went missing, and now it all seems like a silly daydream. The girl in the photos has an openness to her face that is lost to me now.

I shove the photos back in the envelope and toss them into the cardboard box. I don't know why I'm obsessing about that particular week. What's become clear over the last few days is that the chain of events leading up to Allie's disappearance stretches back much further than that January. To November of 2012, or even further.

I need to focus. I need to get my head straight about the timeline. Going to my desk, I pull out my school notebook and open it to a blank page. Then I make myself write down every significant thing I can remember about those months.

September 2012

- The TMZ photos come out.
- Allie is put on academic probation.
- Isabel and Giles cut off Allie's allowance, take away her car.

I glance over at the photos and see one, taken that fall, of Allie sulking on our living room couch after a visit from Isabel. And I remember: the TMZ photos weren't the only thing fueling Isabel's and Giles's fury that month.

- Isabel's earrings go missing.

Isabel owned a pair of antique pearl earrings that she kept in a jewelry box in her bedroom. Apparently, they were worth thousands of dollars. In September, not long after Allie and I had gone over to the Malibu house for a visit, the earrings went missing, and Isabel was convinced that Allie had taken them.

She says I stole them to pay for drugs, Allie snorted. *I mean, c'mon.*

I knew Allie didn't need money for drugs. Greg kept her supplied for free. So I'd believed her. Or, I'd 80 percent believed her. The other 20 percent of me remembered that Christmas Eve when Allie stole Isabel's pills, just for fun. Just to mess with her head.

October 2012

- Allie bails on Greg's Halloween party to go to Vegas.

Greg had been pissed about that. He and Allie had planned the party together, were even supposed to have matching costumes, but at the last minute, she'd flaked. Some childhood friends of hers were going to Vegas, she said, and she'd decided to go with them. Greg and Allie had fought about it. And then, a few weeks later, Greg told me Allie had never been in Vegas at all. He was drunk when he told me, drunk enough to make me suspect he was just stirring up drama. *Eva and Christie were in Vegas that weekend,* he said. *With those girls Allie said invited her. And there was no fucking sign of Allie.*

I add a note to that last bullet point: *But maybe she wasn't in Vegas?* Then I keep writing.

November 2012

- Starts going to therapy?
- Starts attending classes, making better grades, stops drinking
- Signs up for Macnamara's seminar
- Starts seeing Macnamara

December 2012

- Writes essay for Macnamara's class
- Macnamara wants to help Allie publish.

January 2013

- Allie tells Isabel about the essay.

- Isabel threatens Macnamara if he doesn't stop Allie from publishing.
- Macnamara tries to get Allie to hold off on publishing the essay.

I'm scribbling faster now. I'm at the point in the timeline that connects to the last week before Allie's disappearance, the series of events I thought I knew so well.

January 9

- Allie breaks up with Macnamara.

January 10

- 2:15 pm: Allie drives to Mom's house in Reseda.

My pen hovers over the page. This detail still nags at me. I'd never known Allie to go to Mom's place on her own. We always went together. What had she been doing there?

January 11

- Sometime before 10 pm: Allie and Greg fight about Allie's money—where was it coming from? Allie takes Greg's car and cash.
- 10:40 pm: Allie comes back to our apartment.
- 11:02 pm: Allie withdraws money from ATM.
- 11:23 pm: Arrives at Barclay's
- 11:39 pm: Receives phone call and leaves Barclay's

I sit back and look over what I've written. Allie's disappearance still doesn't make sense, but I'm seeing more of the picture than I ever have before. It's clear now that something was happening with her in the months before she went missing. But I still have no idea what it was.

Help me out, Allie.

I need her to show me what I'm missing. What I can't see. But for once, I can't hear her voice in my head. Tonight, Allie—who loves to explain things to me, to be my life coach, my analyst—has nothing to say.

CHAPTER 39

In the morning, I take an Uber to Mom's house. This is a tradition now—in the first week of January, before the anniversary of Allie's disappearance, Mom makes sure that we spend quality time together. I know she means it as a supportive gesture, but these visits tend to put me on edge. During them, I can feel her watching me, looking for reassurances that I'm okay. And so I do my best to appear upbeat, resilient.

It's exhausting.

At least today, I'll have an excuse to leave early—Matthew's reception is at three, and he's sending a car to take me to Isabel's house in Malibu.

When I arrive at Mom's, I stand on the sidewalk outside her house for a minute. I need some time to gather myself. Mom asks a lot of questions, and it'll require some creativity to avoid talking about what's really been going on this week.

The morning light paints the windows of her modest bungalow a bright gold. Mom bought the place with the money from the divorce settlement, and at first I'd hated it—how small the house was, how ordinary, how far from the ocean. Now, though, I have to admit it looks cozy. Potted ferns line the patio, and a wind chime sways next to the front door.

Slowly, I walk up the front path and take the two stairs up to the patio. As soon as Mom answers the door, she pulls me into a tight hug.

"Hey, let me breathe," I joke.

She releases me with a funny little laugh. "Sorry. It's just . . . it seems like forever since I last saw you."

We spent Christmas together less than two weeks ago. But I don't remind her of that fact. Mom gets agitated around the anniversary of Allie's disappearance, as if whatever happened to Allie might somehow happen to me too.

I step into the living room, where I can see the lines her vacuum has left in the carpet.

"Can I get you some tea?" she asks, following close behind me.

"Sure, sounds great." I sling my bag onto the couch and try not to notice the way her eyes run over my body, trying to assess whether I've been eating properly.

"And a cookie?" she suggests.

"No, thanks," I say. She's hovering in a way that makes my eyelids twitch. "Just tea is great."

I follow her into the kitchen, where she fills the kettle and sets it on the stove to boil.

"How was Joshua Tree?" I ask, forestalling her inevitable questions. Yesterday, when she returned home, she'd called me, worried about the news of the body in Turnbull Canyon. How was I coping? Had I made an appointment with Dr. Rajmani?

"Oh, really good." She looks good. Tan. Happy. "Everyone had so much fun. Since I've been back, though, I've been flat out, preparing for the new semester." She teaches at a school in Granada Hills now, and the job suits her.

As I watch her tear open the tea bags, I wonder if she's seeing anyone. As far as I know, she hasn't dated anybody since Giles. But maybe she has and just hasn't told me. I suppose we both keep things from each other.

"I wish I'd stayed home, though," she says, pouring hot water into two mugs. "When I came back and heard the news . . ."

"Mmm," I say, walking into the living room and gazing out at the front yard. I didn't tell her, when we spoke yesterday, that I'd gone down to the station on Sunday to see if I could identify the belongings found on the body. I'm hoping that's information I can continue to keep under wraps.

"Sorry," she says, coming into the room and handing me a mug. "We don't have to talk about that."

"It's okay." I take a sip of the tea, wincing as it burns my tongue.

"Let's talk about something else," she says as she sits down on the couch. "Are you excited for school to start back up again?"

I settle into one of the armchairs and rest my tea precariously on its arm. "Sure." I haven't thought about school once in the past week. In this moment, I can't imagine going back, focusing on textbooks, exams.

Mom smiles, tucking her legs underneath her on the couch. "I'm so proud of you, you know. It can't be easy, going back to school after all this time off. But you're doing so well. I've been telling all my friends how great you're doing."

She means well with her encouragement—so why does it leave me feeling on edge? It's been this way ever since I can remember: her celebrating my accomplishments, then nudging me to achieve even more. I used to think that was just how she was; she didn't know any other way to be. But she wasn't like that with Allie. With Allie, she was like a whole different person.

One afternoon during our senior year, not long after Mom and Giles had separated, I'd come home from school to find Mom and Allie ensconced on the couch watching a movie. All the curtains in the living room were drawn, creating a cave-like atmosphere.

Allie glanced over her shoulder at me. "We're watching *First Wives Club*."

She was sipping a smoothie. Mom was clutching a glass of wine. My whole life, I'd never seen Mom drink more than a glass of wine over the course of an evening, but these days, there always seemed to be a fresh glass in her hand.

"Come watch with us," Allie said. She'd brought her manicure kit downstairs from her room, and it was spread out on the coffee table next to the wine bottle. "What color, Elena?" she asked, thwacking a nail polish bottle against her palm. And when Mom picked out a pale-neutral color, Allie shook her head. "Screw that. You're in postbreakup mode here. You want something that screams: 'I'm single, motherfuckers!'"

I frowned, waiting for Mom to react to Allie's language, but she only laughed.

"This is *exactly* what you need," Allie said, vigorously shaking a bottle of fuchsia polish. "It's called Kiss My Sass."

"It does look nice," Mom allowed, as Allie painted her right thumbnail.

"See, she loves it," Allie said to me, grinning as if she suddenly knew my mother better than I did.

Now, I draw my attention back to Mom, who's still rattling on about law school from her seat on the couch.

"And have you been thinking about internships? For the summer, I mean. I did a little googling last night, and it seems like it's very important to get the right one—"

"Do we have to talk about this?" I snap.

She looks startled. "Tasha. What's wrong?"

"Nothing. It's fine." I stand up, tilting my head from one side to the other, trying to work out the tension in my neck. "I just don't want to talk about internships right now."

Why did Mom always act so differently around Allie? Allie was allowed to swear, to fail classes, to talk shit about Giles behind his back. And it wasn't even the double standard that bothered me most. No, it was the way Mom would open up around Allie, telling stories about her first boyfriend, the time she'd gotten suspended her senior year of high school—stories she'd never told me. Around Allie, my mom seemed more comfortable. More real.

Stupidly, I feel myself getting teary eyed.

It wasn't fair. Allie did all the wrong things, and people still loved her. And I did all the right things, and it never seemed to count.

I press my hands over my eyes. "Just . . . I need a minute."

I walk into the hallway and make my way to the bathroom. Once inside, I close the door behind me, pull down the toilet seat lid, and sit, resting my head in my hands. What's the matter with me? I'm supposed to be convincing Mom I'm fine.

After a while, I make myself stand up and go to the sink, where I splash some water on my face. Allie was right, all those years ago. *The trick, which you have not figured out yet, is to keep expectations low.* She'd tried to tell me: You didn't win anything by trying to be perfect. And now I know she was right.

I don't even want to go to law school, I realize suddenly. The thought is so clear and obvious that it might as well be written in capital letters on the mirror. I only applied because Mom wanted me to. Because it seemed like the thing that successful people do.

I pick up a clean towel and press it over my eyes.

When I come back into the living room, my mother turns from the window that looks out onto the back garden. "Tasha, what's the matter?"

My hands are shaking. "I want you to answer a question for me. About Allie."

She tenses. She doesn't like talking about Allie. About two years ago, she decided: We had to move on. She put Allie's things into boxes and erased her presence from the third bedroom. *It's not helping you to see this stuff all the time,* she said.

"What about Allie?" she asks.

"Why did you never get angry with her?"

"What do you mean?"

"No matter what she did, you accepted it. You never got mad." I can feel my voice starting to wobble. "Even after what she did. Even after she ruined everything."

CHAPTER 40

November 2009

Our family sat around the kitchen table, eating the only meal Mom really excelled at making: spaghetti bolognese. Giles had been away the past few weeks, promoting his newest book, and while he was gone, we'd eaten dinners he definitely would not have approved of: PB&J sandwiches, bacon and eggs, takeout from Bamboo River.

Mom passed the salad bowl to Giles. Tonight, she'd even put candles in the center of the table, between the serving dishes. "It's nice for us to all be together again, isn't it?" She waited for Giles to respond, but he seemed not to have heard her.

He was looking at a text on his phone. Finally, he glanced up and said, "Oh. Yes. Nice."

Allie and I exchanged a look. We'd noticed a definite atmosphere in the house ever since Giles got back from his trip the week before. He spent most evenings secluded in his study, talking on the phone to his agent, Zuri, or working on research for his next book. Meanwhile, Mom prowled around the house doing random chores, waiting for Giles to come out and talk to her.

Giles stabbed a spinach leaf with his fork and began eating. I waited for him to make a joke about Mom's cooking, which he always teased her about, but he didn't say anything. For a moment, the only sound in the dining room was utensils scraping against plates.

Mom poured herself more wine. I tried to make eye contact with Allie, but she was staring down at the table, using her fork to dig little holes in the tablecloth.

"So, tell us about New York," Mom said to Giles. "You haven't talked much about it since you've been back. What was it like?"

Giles wiped at the edges of his mouth with his napkin. "Those book events are all the same. There's not much to tell."

More silence.

"Well, it's good to have you home," she said brightly. "I've got that faculty dinner next Friday, and you know what a drag those are. At least you can distract me from all the teacher-talk."

Giles looked up. "Next Friday?"

"Yes." She'd put her hair up tonight and put on a bit of makeup. Mom never wore makeup at home.

"I can't go," he said abruptly. "Not Friday."

Mom's face fell. "But you said you would. It's on the calendar."

"Well, Zuri's scheduled me at a book festival in Boston," Giles said, frowning. "She has me flying out on Wednesday."

"Wednesday! But you only just got back."

Giles let out an exasperated sigh. "This is the job, Elena. I have to go where they send me, at least until the publishers are satisfied that this book is going to sell better than the last one."

Allie raised an eyebrow at me. Giles hardly ever mentioned his last book, which had been an undeniable flop. Sometimes, if Allie was in a mischievous mood, she'd work the book into the conversation just to annoy him.

Mom blinked rapidly, tears gathering on her eyelashes.

"Oh, for God's sake, Elena," he said, taking off his glasses and rubbing at the edges of his eyes. "It's just a dinner. I'll go to the next one."

"The next one isn't until next year," she said tightly.

Giles set his glasses down with a thump.

I stared at him. What was his problem? He'd been on edge this whole week. On Monday, when he'd found Allie in his office looking for a spare pen, he'd shouted at her, which had seemed over the top even for Giles.

"And you've been traveling this whole fall," Mom said. A muscle in her neck quivered. "When will you take a break?"

The air in the room felt thick. I willed Allie to say something, anything. This was her cue to crack a joke, change the subject, break the news that she was failing French again.

"I just don't see why there have to be so many of those events," Mom said. "Zuri knows you have a family—"

"Yes, and it's the money from my work that feeds this family." Giles balled up his napkin and threw it on the table.

"I'm not asking you to abandon your work. I'm just saying, there's got to be some balance . . ." She broke off. "You missed Allie's birthday last month," she said, more forcefully. "And Natasha's the month before that. I don't think it's me who's missing the point."

"I'm not one of your students, so please spare me the lecture," he snapped.

Allie gazed, unblinking, at Giles.

"This is my career," he said to Mom. "Forgive me if I happen to—"

"Oh, will you shut up already?" Allie snapped.

I drew in a sharp breath.

Giles turned to her. "Excuse me?" His eyes were dangerously bright.

"Oh, c'mon, Giles. How long are you going to let this drag out?" she said, pushing her plate away from her. "Weeks? Months?"

"Allie, honey . . . ," Mom said, reaching out to her.

Allie pulled away from her touch. "I want to know," Allie said to Giles, her voice rising. "How long are you going to wait for her to figure it out?"

He pointed a finger at Allie. "Watch yourself, young lady."

Was it my imagination, or did he look suddenly frightened?

Allie stood up. "There's no conference in Boston, okay?" she told my mother. "He's going there to meet Zuri. Because he's fucking her. They're fucking." She carefully enunciated each syllable.

"Allie!" Giles stood up too. "That's enough."

She spun toward him. "What? You're not even *trying* to hide it. Her texts are right there on your phone. I saw them when I was in your office. Lucky for you, Elena's too nice of a person to look through your stuff. Or wait—is that what you were hoping she would do?"

"Go to your room," Giles said. His voice was deathly quiet. "Right now."

She laughed. "I'm not *five*. You can't send me to my—"

"Go to your room!" he roared, leaning forward over the table.

I'd never been scared of Giles before, but I was frightened now. That temper, which he held in check most of the time, had finally erupted.

Allie stared at him for a long moment, and I wondered how she could look him straight in the face when it seemed like any minute he might lunge over the table at her. But she wasn't intimidated. She was calm, so calm.

She turned to Mom. "It's not you, you know. This is just what he does. He'll let it drag on until you find out, and then you'll save him the trouble of having to end things. It's what he does to all his girlfriends. It's what he did to Isabel."

Mom's face had frozen into an expression that I wished I could unsee. I stared down at my plate, where the marinara sauce looked gruesome against the white plate.

"Elena, listen," Giles said, changing his tone.

But it was too late. Mom pushed her chair away from the table and, without a word, walked out of the room.

CHAPTER 41

Mom sits across from me on the couch, her face pale. We don't talk about that night. In all the years since it happened, we've never once brought it up.

"Oh, honey," she says. "I never held that against Allie."

To my surprise, I find that I'm crying. "You must have. I mean—"

That night marked the end of everything. Afterward, Giles moved out, and soon after that, divorce proceedings began. At some point, he and Mom must have reached an agreement about living arrangements, because Allie and I ended up staying in the house on Via Montemar with Mom for the remainder of our senior year. To give us some sense of normalcy. But after high school, it was agreed, Giles would sell the house, Mom would get her own place, and Allie and I would go off to college. The terms of the prenup allowed Mom to get a chunk of money upon signing the divorce papers, but there would be no alimony, no ongoing support.

My mother reaches over and rubs my knee. "Tasha. Things with Giles, they were a mess long before Allie said anything about . . . that woman. The relationship wasn't working. I mean, it was all very romantic in the beginning. I was so dazzled by him, by his talent. So, it took me a while to see certain things."

"Like what?"

She lifts her hands helplessly. "Like the fact that he'd never managed to settle down with anyone. Not with Isabel, and not with any of his girlfriends after her either. That he wasn't very good with you kids. After the first year, things were rocky. He dropped out, emotionally. I felt so alone."

Mom's never talked to me this way before. The way she might've talked to Allie. I look at her sitting there, in jeans and a T-shirt she bought at the farmers' market twenty years ago.

"You seemed so happy together."

Mom leans forward, making sure I'm paying close attention. "Tasha, look. Even if Giles hadn't . . . you know . . . we wouldn't have lasted. So, no, I didn't blame Allie. If anything, I was grateful to her."

"Grateful?" I say in disbelief.

"Yes, grateful," she says. Her face is open, calm. "I wasn't happy. But I hadn't wanted to face it. Allie saved me from going on like that for . . . months. Years, maybe."

I feel disoriented, the way I do some nights when I sit up in bed and think there's an intruder in the room before I realize it's just my reflection in the closet mirror.

Mom didn't think Allie had taken anything from her. *I* was the one who felt that way.

"Poor Allie," Mom says quietly. "She felt terrible about it afterward."

"Did she?" She never seemed the least bit sorry to me. When Giles left our house, after he'd walked down the front path and deposited a suitcase in the trunk of his car, Allie stood at her bedroom window and gave him the finger as he drove away.

"She really did." Mom brushes a knuckle under her nose. "Do you know what she said to me, the day after that awful dinner? She said, 'If you want me to leave, I'll go.' She knew there was nowhere for her to go at that point, except to that terrible boarding school Giles had picked out." Mom shakes her head. "Of course I didn't want her to go. I told her that I wanted her to stay. But I'll always remember her saying that. 'If you want me to leave, I'll go.'"

I pick at the worn material of the armchair. I've never fully understood, have I, the feelings Allie had about Mom and me? It wasn't until the beginning of our freshman year at LACSA that I started to get it.

Mom had invited us up to Reseda so she could show us the new house she'd bought, the place she was preparing to move into as soon as the house on Via Montemar sold. When she led us into the living room, her face flushed with pleasure, I couldn't help feeling a twist of disappointment. The room was barely big enough for all three of us to stand in at once, and the paneling on the walls was dark and old fashioned.

"Cute," Allie said.

Cramped, I thought.

"C'mon. I'll give you the full tour," Mom said. She led us through the tiny kitchen to a door that led into a tangled backyard. She didn't seem to mind the smallness of the place or its general sense of faded disrepair. Her hair was drawn up in a ponytail, and she had paint stains on her shirt. She'd gained back the weight she'd lost during the divorce, and her jeans no longer gapped around her hips. But something else was different too. She looked comfortable here, I realized. It was only then that it hit me: how she'd never seemed quite at home in the Via Montemar house, with its vaulted ceilings and sleek leather couches.

"And in the spring, I'll put some raised beds out here," Mom was saying.

Behind her back, Allie winked at me. She'd been telling me all year: *Elena will bounce back. Just you wait.* And she'd been right.

"There's also a room above the garage that I can turn into an apartment, rent out for some extra money." She was so proud. She'd never owned her own home before.

"It's nice," Allie said, squeezing her shoulder. "Really nice." She sounded convincing.

"Now, I have one more thing to show you," Mom said. She grinned as she beckoned us into the hallway. Down the hall from the master bedroom were two very small rooms situated across the hall from each other. In each one, she'd put a double bed, a desk, and a chair.

"This one's for you, Tasha," she said, gesturing at the room with the blue curtains. "And this one's for Allie." Allie's had yellow curtains and a brightly colored quilt on the bed.

I noticed the nameplates on the doors before Allie did. Little ceramic ovals with our names inscribed in cursive. *Natasha. Allie.* I laughed and turned to catch Allie's gaze, waiting for her to roll her eyes at this last touch, which was sweet but a little cheesy.

But Allie wasn't looking at me. She had one hand pressed over her mouth, and a small, distressed sound came out of her throat. Suddenly, Mom put her arms around Allie and held her tight.

"What's going on?" I said, bewildered. "What's wrong?"

But neither of them seemed to have heard me.

"Is it really for me?" Allie asked, her voice small and muffled. "That room?" She was crying silently, her shoulders shaking.

Mom smoothed Allie's hair with her hand. "Of course it is. Of course. You know there's always going to be a place for you here."

At that, Allie started to sob.

CHAPTER 42

At three o'clock, a black car glides up to the curb outside Mom's house. I jog down the front steps as the driver gets out and walks around to open the back door for me. I look around, wondering what the neighbors will think. This kind of thing is not the norm in Reseda.

I settle into the soft leather upholstery of the back seat, noting the tinted windows, the television screen set into the console behind the driver's seat. As the driver climbs back behind the wheel, he asks me if the temperature is all right, and when I nod, he rolls up the window that divides the front of the car from the back.

And then I'm all alone with my thoughts.

Back then, in the house on Via Montemar, I'd thought our family had been happy. Watching bad movies in the living room, cooking grilled cheese sandwiches in the swanky kitchen, swimming in the pool on hot summer nights. But now I realize—all those memories are of Allie and me. Where were our parents on those evenings? I can't remember. If things between Giles and Mom had started to deteriorate, I'd been too wrapped up in my own world to notice.

That fall, I'd been deep in the fever of applying to colleges. All my life, I'd known that paying for college would be a struggle. Mom's salary as a high school teacher hardly stretched to support us; it wouldn't make a dent in the tuition to a good university. So I'd spent most of high school fighting for a valedictorian spot. I needed those scholarships. But after Giles came into the picture, everything changed.

All of a sudden, there was so much money. Enough to pay for a house with an ocean view, enough for summer vacations in Kauai. Enough for college tuition for two daughters. Which meant that, suddenly, I had options. For the first time, I could let myself really dream. And as soon as I did, I knew I wanted so much more than UC Berkeley. I wanted the East Coast. I wanted Ivy League. I wanted two-hundred-year-old brick buildings dusted with snow.

That fall, I filled out my college applications with a feeling of euphoria. Brown, Williams, Amherst, Cornell. The names alone felt like magic. A way to change my life forever.

And then: the divorce happened. To me, it seemed to have fallen right out of the sky, an asteroid crashing into the middle of our perfect life. Giles moved out, and my mother turned into someone I didn't recognize. Allie and I took over cooking dinners because Mom no longer had the energy. I spent the weekends doing laundry and studying for my AP classes.

Three months later, my acceptance letter from Williams arrived. When I showed it to Mom, she just sighed. *Oh, Tasha.* She didn't have to say anything else. There was no way we could afford it now.

By that point, the deadline to apply for financial aid had passed. So. There I was, with an acceptance letter to a first-class college I couldn't attend. And like a fool, I hadn't applied to any backup schools.

In the end, I swallowed my pride and applied to LACSA, where Allie had already gotten in. LACSA was the kind of place where a lackluster GPA was no barrier to entry. Where an application like mine, even submitted late in the spring, got some attention. They offered me a full ride, which at least meant that Mom wouldn't have to worry about tuition payments on top of everything else.

Outside the car window, the city is streaking by—tall office buildings, massive billboards. And then we're exiting the highway, heading left on Las Virgenes, and I let my head fall back against the seat.

Is it any wonder I felt cheated back then? By Giles. By Allie.

But staying on at LACSA—I had only myself to blame for that. I could have applied for a transfer after freshman year. That had been my plan all along. My first fall semester there, I spent hours drafting the essay I would submit with my transfer application. But somehow, as Allie and I fell into the rhythm of our life there, the urgency of the transfer application faded. It was so easy to be at LACSA with her. With Allie, I had a sister, a best friend, and a social life all rolled into one.

So the transfer deadline came and went. I told Mom I'd forgotten about it, which touched off one of the few real arguments we'd ever had. *That place is making you lazy,* she told me.

So what if it was? What I'd realized was: Being at LACSA was a relief. There, I didn't have to fight to be the smartest, the best. I didn't have to prove myself. And I liked that. For once, I wanted to have it easy. For once, I wanted to coast.

But the real reason I never left? When it came down to it, I couldn't leave Allie.

The night she told my mom about Zuri, I'd been furious with her. Later that night, I'd gone upstairs to her bedroom and pushed open the door. Allie was lying on her bed with her noise-canceling headphones on, her eyes closed. When she felt me sit down on the bed next to her, she opened her eyes. After a moment, she scooted up to a sitting position and settled the headphones around her neck.

I picked up her stuffed crocodile and held him against my stomach. The top of his head was worn from Allie rubbing her knuckles across the green plush. "How long have you known?"

Allie reached out and touched the alligator's snout. "I didn't know. Not for sure." She pulled her knees up to her chest. "Not until yesterday, in his office. When I saw the texts from Zuri." Suddenly, she shook her head. "Actually, that's a lie. To be honest, I knew all along."

I stared at her. "What do you mean, 'all along'? He's been with Zuri this whole time?"

She shook her head, pressing her lips together. "No. But I knew what he was like. How it would end up." Her eyes were big and dark.

"Why didn't you say anything?"

She examined her toenail polish like it was the most fascinating thing in the world. "The day I came over here—when I met you, met Elena—I liked you. I liked your place. I thought . . . What if I could be like that?"

"Like what?"

A sheet of dark hair fell across her face, hiding it from view. "Like . . . normal," she said.

But we weren't normal, I wanted to shout. A single mom and her kid, that was only half a family.

"And it seemed like he really loved her," she went on. "So I thought—" She broke off, laughing at herself. "I thought maybe he'd be different this time." She rested her chin on her knees. "It did seem that way, in the beginning. It did seem like he might."

After a minute, I reached out and held her hand, and we sat like that for a while, listening to the strains of the argument between Mom and Giles filtering up from the stairwell.

That night, without meaning to, without even thinking about it, I forgave her. For everything. But in the weeks and months that followed, as I watched our lives unravel, I couldn't help but wonder: What if she had just kept her mouth shut? What would our lives have looked like then?

CHAPTER 43

In the back seat of the car, I shift restlessly. We're winding through dry, scrubby hills on a road that descends closer and closer to the ocean. In the distance, the sun winks against the water, the glare hurting my eyes. Finally, the driver pulls up in front of Isabel's house, which sits on a bluff just above the beach. In the bright afternoon light, I have to blink several times before I can make out the details of the house: the low roofline, the large windows.

The driver opens my door for me, and I step out at the end of a long driveway crowded with expensive cars.

"Thanks," I say. Suddenly, I'm not at all sure about my decision to come here. I've taken care to dress nicely, but I know that, once I get inside, I'll feel hopelessly out of place. I adjust my bag on my shoulder and remind myself that I'm here for Matthew. That's all. I'll say my hellos and then leave after a polite length of time.

Picking my way down the driveway, I marvel at the size of the house, which stretches out long on either side of me. I've only been here three times, and on each of those occasions, I'd been with Allie. In her presence, distracted by her constant chatter, I had less time to take in the details.

Raising my hand, I knock on the front door. Instantly, a young woman opens it and welcomes me in, then offers to take my coat. She's wearing khaki pants and a light-colored shirt—apparel that marks her as part of the staff hired for the occasion. With a flush, I realize I'm wearing something very similar: camel-colored slacks, a white blouse. The look I was going for was simple elegance. Instead, I've landed on "household staff."

From the foyer, I walk down two steps into the massive living room. Above me, a ceiling with exposed beams catches the afternoon sun. To my right, a fire crackles in the fireplace—a sight that no one is currently appreciating because all the guests are gathered outside. Through the large windows that look out onto the deck, I see Matthew and Chloe on the far end of the patio, standing near the stairs that lead down to the beach. He has an arm around her shoulders, and the wind blows her hair across her face. Caterers circulate with trays of champagne and hors d'oeuvres. As I step outside, I snag a glass of champagne for myself, partly for courage and partly so I won't be mistaken for one of the staff.

As I slip past clusters of guests, I spot a few familiar faces—the lead actor from Matthew's latest film, the woman who produced *Broken Bones*. The others I don't recognize, but everyone looks comfortable here, as if they've spent many hours in this house. One woman lies on her back on one of the built-in benches that runs along the deck, balancing a baby on her stomach. And there's Sara, Chloe's daughter, running back and forth through the crowd, playing some game with one of the other kids at the party.

When Sara passes Matthew, he grabs her by the waist and pretends to be about to throw her over the edge of the balcony. Sara squeals until he sets her down and rumples her hair. Chloe is laughing, shaking her head at their antics.

I walk toward them, anticipating the relief I'll feel once I'm safely among friends. But just then, Isabel turns around from the group of people she's been talking to. "Natasha, my goodness!" she says.

She's wearing jeans and a sweater, simple clothes that somehow telegraph immense wealth. "Look at you—don't you look wonderful!" When she embraces me, I can feel her rib cage against my chest. Since Allie's disappearance, Isabel's beauty has become sharper, more fragile.

"How are you?" I ask her, but Isabel is already introducing me to her friends. "Everybody, this is Natasha."

I shake hands politely with the guests and listen to Isabel say nice things about me, until Matthew comes over to rescue me.

"Excuse me," I say to Isabel, relieved to get some distance from her. When I look at her now, all I can think of is the conversation Ruiz and I had in the Jeep. Would she really have hurt Allie, perhaps even killed her, just to maintain her reputation? I look at her razor-sharp jawline, the taut skin on her neck. In *Pale Heart*, her third movie, she'd played an assassin, and the performance had been so electric that it had garnered her an Oscar nomination.

Matthew hugs me, as does Chloe.

"Natasha, so good to see you," she says.

Chloe has always accepted my position in Matthew's life as a kind of honorary niece.

"Sara, come say hi," she calls to her daughter, but Sara is already off and running to the other side of the porch. "Sorry," Chloe says, rolling her eyes. "She's so hyper today." She nudges Matthew. "Your fault. You keep riling her up."

"She looks like she's having a great time," I say.

"Matthew," someone calls out, and I turn to see Giles approaching us. He startles when he recognizes me. "Natasha. I didn't know you'd be here." He doesn't quite know how to greet me, so he settles for giving me a dry kiss on the cheek.

The last time I saw him in person had been at the memorial service for Allie, held a year after she disappeared. He looks exactly the same. Same crisp button-down shirt, same wire-rimmed spectacles. Allie always claimed he didn't really need the glasses, that he just wore them to make himself look smarter.

"How is Elena?" he asks. "Well, I hope."

If I were Allie, I'd have a snarky reply at the ready. But all I manage to say is: "Good. She's good."

His expression is affable, relaxed. It would be easy to forget he ever looked the way he had the night he yelled at Allie across the dinner table, his face contorted with rage.

As he turns to talk to Matthew, I suddenly remember a moment the day after that terrible dinner, when I was in my bedroom, putting away my folded laundry. Giles had passed by in the hall, heading toward Allie's room.

"I hope you're happy with yourself," I heard him say as he stood in her doorway.

Silently, I stepped closer to my door, staying out of sight. I could see the edge of Giles's shirtsleeve, the fingers of his hand wrapped around the doorjamb.

"What's the matter, Pops?" Allie asked lightly.

"I think you'll find it doesn't pay to poke your nose in other people's business like that."

I held my breath, willing for Allie not to provoke him, for him not to fly into a rage.

"Imagine what else I could say," said Allie, her voice cool. "If I felt like it. I think people would find it interesting how you got the idea for *Alchemy*. How it was originally Liam's idea. How you took it, after he died."

There was a long silence. Then Giles said, "I don't know what you're—"

"What? You think Matthew doesn't talk about that? When he's drunk, he's very chatty. Very gossipy."

From where I was standing, I saw Giles move forward. He stepped into Allie's room and closed the door behind him.

Now I draw in a deep breath, filling my lungs with ocean air. I don't know what Giles and Allie talked about that day, but after that conversation, I noticed Allie didn't make any more pointed remarks about his career, his poor book sales.

Chloe and Matthew are rattling on about their house search, about how long it took them to find the right place.

"When we saw the one on Miradero, we just knew," Chloe says, leaning against Matthew, her cheek resting against his sweater.

Giles plucks a lobster toast from a caterer's tray. "So, you're selling the Venice place?"

Matthew nods. "It's time, I think."

Giles takes a bite of the toast, a fleck of lobster sticking to his lip. And I think: He doesn't have a solid alibi for the night Allie went missing. Is it possible he could've hurt Allie? If Allie had done something to anger him? To betray his secrets?

"And what about the cabin in Crestline?" Giles asks. "Will you be giving that up too?"

"What cabin?" Chloe asks, looking at Matthew.

He sips his sparkling water. "Oh, just a little place I bought back in the day. For fishing."

"And writing," Giles reminds him. "Matthew had big dreams of writing the great American novel out there. 'The Hideout,' he called that place. I believe at one time there might even have been a plaque over the door."

"Well," Matthew says with a laugh, looking a little uncomfortable. "Clearly, that was another time."

After they'd collaborated on adapting Giles's novel *Alchemy* for the screen, Matthew never wrote anything else that sold. Despite his success with directing, this remains a sore point for Matthew, one that Giles doesn't mind pressing every once in a while.

The heat lamps on the patio are attempting to fend off the chill in the air, but the wind from the ocean cuts right through their warmth.

"You still go up there?" Giles asks Matthew.

Matthew glances over his shoulder at the beach. "Haven't been in years. God knows what kind of condition it's in now. The place is more of a headache than it's worth, really."

I'm suddenly sorry that I came to the party. I have nothing to contribute to this conversation about the difficulty of owning multiple homes.

"Didn't it get broken into a couple times?" Giles said. "During that string of burglaries up there in 2012?"

Matthew sighs. "Yes. What a pain. The local police were no help, so I ended up putting in an alarm sys—"

Sara comes running over, interrupting him. "Can we go down to the beach?" she begs. She really is a beautiful kid. Dark eyes, flushed cheeks. Small, perfect teeth.

"Maybe in a little bit," he says.

"But I'm bored." She widens her eyes as if the boredom is about to kill her.

"Hey, chief," he says, crouching down to her level. "I have a mission for you. Are you ready?"

Immediately, she perks up. "Yeah."

"You see those little lobster things on the trays?"

She looks over her shoulder at the latest tray being carried around by the caterers. "Uh-huh."

"They are the only thing worth eating at this party. Get us as many of those as you can get your hands on, okay?"

Straightening her posture, she gives him a salute. "Aye, aye, sir." And then she spins around and disappears into the crowd.

Chloe touches Giles's arm. "So, tell me about this new book you're working on," she says. "Matthew tells me there's already a lot of buzz about it."

Giles is only too happy to fill her in. "Well, it's in the early stages, but it's going to center around a missing persons case. That's the part the media has really latched on to, of course. They're all taking it at the most obvious level. But of course, it's not about Allie. On a deeper level, it's a look at class and racial divides in this city . . ."

Matthew shifts so he's standing just outside Giles's line of sight, then looks at me and pretends to gag. I smother a smile as I take another sip of champagne.

Chloe, wrapped up in the conversation, doesn't notice any of this. "But how do you even *begin* to write a novel? I mean, I can't even wrap my head around it."

Matthew jerks his head to one side, and I step away to join him at the deck's edge, where we can see down to the beach below.

"Sorry, am I tearing you away from that riveting monologue?" he says.

I roll my eyes. "Hardly."

He grins.

"Is it really about a missing persons case?" The champagne I've drunk has left a sour aftertaste on my tongue. "His book?"

Matthew drains his glass. "Apparently. He has this elaborate justification for it, how it's not really about Allie, blah blah blah, but I'd bet dollars to doughnuts his new agent put the idea in his head. How do you think the press already knows about it? His agent knows a marketable idea when she sees one."

I glance over my shoulder at Giles. Even he wouldn't sink that low—would he? "I hope he's not actually going through with it."

Matthew shrugs. "Hopefully he'll realize at some point what an asshole he's being. And if he doesn't—well, I'm sure Isabel will have something to say about it. And God help him if he tries to go against her."

A gust of wind whips up from the beach, blowing my hair away from my face.

Isabel is working her way around the party, making sure to give each guest a little arm-squeeze and a snippet of conversation. When she arrives at Matthew and me, she narrows her eyes, feigning suspicion. "And what are you two conspiring about over here?"

Matthew leans back against the railing. "We're discussing your dear former husband."

"What's the problem?" Isabel teases him. "Giles doing too good a job of charming your wife?"

Matthew snorts. "In his dreams."

Isabel puts an arm around my shoulder. "Matthew, you've been holding out on me. You've neglected to tell me how *gorgeous* our Natasha has become."

She's a little drunk, I realize. The warmth in her voice is slightly overdone, the weight of her arm across my shoulder too heavy.

"I mean, look at her." She brushes a strand of hair away from my face. "It's such a shame you and Peter never ended up working together."

"Good for you," Matthew says, winking at me. "Models are an awful bunch."

"Hey!" Isabel says, slapping his shoulder playfully. "You're talking to a former model here."

"I rest my case."

The two of them remind me of Allie and Greg, needling each other for fun.

"Well," she says, snagging another glass of wine from a passing caterer. "I seem to remember you very much enjoying the company of models once. What was that girl's name? Nico?"

Matthew winces. Isabel isn't playing nice anymore.

The Nico Bissett scandal blew up not long after Matthew and Giles won their Golden Globe, after the press got ahold of some old photographs of Nico in various states of undress. A close examination revealed that the photos had been taken by Matthew—in one of the photos, his image appears in a mirror. Not big news, as far as celebrity scandals went, and the photos were over a decade old. But then someone did the math and figured out that Nico had only been seventeen at the time. Of course, Matthew hadn't known that. But still, the scandal had been an unpleasant interlude.

"I think maybe you should switch to water," Matthew murmurs to Isabel.

Isabel laughs as if this is the funniest thing she's ever heard. "It used to be me saying that to you, remember?"

"Um, excuse me—I'm going to go to the restroom," I say. I've never seen Isabel and Matthew argue, but it seems they're on the verge of it tonight. For whatever reason.

I slip back through the crowd, overwhelmed by the smell of char-grilled steak and expensive perfume. In the living room, I step close to the fireplace, where a blaze is still crackling for the benefit of no one. On the mantelpiece is a framed photo of Allie, from when she was maybe eleven or twelve. In it, she stares at the camera with a seriousness beyond her years. She's looking at me now with an expression that seems to say: *What the hell are you doing here, Tash?*

I don't know, Als. I don't want to be here anymore. I can hardly stand to be around Isabel, knowing what I now know about her. She knew about the essay, and she lied to the police about it. But that's not the only thought making my throat close up.

If Isabel hurt Allie, if she took steps after finding out about Allie and Macnamara, then I have to face the fact that I helped her.

CHAPTER 44

January 2013

A week after the photo shoot with Peter, Isabel arranged to meet me for lunch at the Terrace. She wanted us to look over Peter's prints together, to discuss which ones might be the best to include in my modeling portfolio.

When I arrived, I followed the waiter to her table, trying not to get distracted by the people we passed. Everyone was beautiful, and some seemed familiar, as if, at some point in my life, I'd seen them on my TV screen. It wasn't until I sat down at the table across from Isabel, though, that I became aware that people were staring at *me*. Wondering who I was to be dining with Isabel Andersen.

After we ordered our meal, Isabel slid the envelope of photographs across the table to me and waited while I looked through them.

"Peter's very enthusiastic," she said. "He'd like to line up a bigger shoot next time, if you're interested."

I felt a flush of excitement, followed almost immediately by a sinking feeling.

"What, don't you want to?" Isabel asked.

"It isn't that," I murmured. It was just that, now that this modeling thing was actually happening, I knew it would cause difficulties with Allie. How could I tell her I'd accepted Isabel's help? She would take it as a personal affront.

But it was unreasonable, wasn't it, for Allie to hold her grudge for so long? Sure, Isabel had sent her to live with Giles, but that wasn't the worst decision in the world. It was long past time for Allie to forgive.

But even if all that was true, I knew I couldn't keep lying to Allie. The day before, when Isabel had called to set up the lunch, I'd snatched my phone off the kitchen counter so Allie wouldn't glimpse Isabel's name on the caller ID. I hadn't liked the way that felt.

Thankfully, Isabel didn't press me for an answer right away. When our food arrived, along with two glasses of champagne, she seemed to forget about the photos, shifting easily into small talk.

"So, school's going all right?" she said. "And you're doing well?"

I stabbed at my salad. "Yeah, definitely. Allie too." I didn't know why I felt the need to add that.

Isabel brought her glass to her lips, her eyes straying around the room. "Is she? That's good to hear."

Something in her voice told me she didn't quite believe me. She had been frosty toward Allie ever since the pearl earrings had gone missing.

"Yeah," I said. "She's really been focusing on her classes." I felt a sudden urge to talk up Allie's good points.

Isabel raised her eyebrows. "Well, that certainly makes for a nice change. What's brought that on?"

I shrugged. "I'm not sure. She's really into this writing workshop she's taking."

I had her attention now. "Writing, huh? Allie mentioned something like that."

I felt a surge of hope. Maybe, if Isabel saw how hard Allie had been trying in school, things might smooth over between them. Maybe I'd feel less guilty for taking Isabel up on her offer of help with this modeling thing. I took a sip of my champagne. "I sort of recommended the class to her. The professor—he's really good."

She looked at me carefully. Then she smiled. "Well, see? That goes to show how much Allie respects you. She's not much for taking recommendations from anyone else."

I blushed. Isabel was good at making me feel as if I was something special.

After taking a few more bites of her salad, Isabel said casually, "And this professor—Allie likes him too?"

"Yeah, she really does."

"Well, that's wonderful," she said warmly. "What's he like?"

"Um. Really smart. Really good at connecting with the class. He's not a hundred years old, like some of our other professors."

Isabel glanced down, her eyelids fluttering. "Young, is he? I'll bet he's handsome too."

"Oh, well . . . I guess," I said. My ears felt hot. "I hadn't really noticed."

Isabel leaned back in her chair, smiling slightly. "Natasha, I know my daughter. In particular, I know her tendencies with men."

I chased a piece of lettuce around my plate with my fork. "I'm not sure what you mean."

She laughed, then reached out to touch my arm. "Oh, you're a good friend, aren't you? You don't want to betray her confidence."

I caught the delicate scent of her perfume in the air. How could Isabel have guessed so easily about Macnamara? Panicking, I mentally reviewed everything I'd said. Had I hinted at a relationship? Definitely not.

"But Allie can be self-destructive sometimes," Isabel continued. "Choosing men who are . . . inappropriate. You've seen it, too, I'm sure."

I bit my tongue. Yes, I knew exactly what she was talking about. Macnamara—that was a disaster waiting to happen. A mess I'd eventually have to help clean up.

"And I don't mean to get overprotective," Isabel continued. "It's just that—after everything we've been through with her in the past few years . . ." She stared into the middle distance, her lips betraying the slightest tremor. And then she waved a hand in front of her face, sitting back in her chair. "I'm sorry. I don't mean to get emotional."

"It's okay," I said.

After a visible struggle, she gathered herself and gave me a watery smile. Then she reached out and grasped my hand. All of a sudden, we felt like equals; we were people who shared a bond.

"Oh, Natasha. I would never ask you to tell tales on Allie; I hope you know that. The only thing I ask is: If you feel she's in real trouble, getting in over her head with this man, this professor, will you tell me?" She squeezed my hand gently, her skin impossibly smooth and soft against mine.

CHAPTER 45

From the photograph on the mantelpiece, Allie stares at me accusingly. I turn away, unable to hold her gaze. Yes, I'd told Isabel about Allie and Macnamara. And I hadn't been sorry about it. I knew that telling Isabel would mean the end of Macnamara and Allie's relationship. And that was a good thing, wasn't it? Afterward, I told myself I'd done it to protect Allie.

For days after the lunch, I'd found myself on edge, waiting for the bomb to drop, waiting for the moment Allie realized I'd told on her. But nothing happened.

Turning away from the fireplace, I look out onto the deck, where the guests are silhouetted against the sun. I can't see Isabel, but I know she's out there.

Her silence in the wake of that lunch has always puzzled me. Why would she ask for that information about Macnamara if she didn't intend to act on it? Now, though, I know she did—just not in the way I'd expected. She hadn't confronted Allie. She'd gone straight to Macnamara.

The whole time, I realize now, her interest wasn't in protecting Allie; it was in protecting herself. She'd already known about the essay, about Allie's intention to publish it. And in getting close to me, she was searching for a way to shut it down.

I hadn't seen, back then, how expertly Isabel had played me. The lunch at the Terrace. The modeling shoot. Even showing up at the exhibition—that couldn't have been an accident. She'd gone there on a mission. To find out what she wanted to know about Allie.

I feel chilly despite the warmth in the room. That week in January, the week Allie went missing, Isabel knew she'd successfully intimidated Macnamara. But Allie was another story. It wouldn't be so easy to get Allie to back down.

I head for the long corridor that leads to the north side of the house. The champagne I've drunk has begun to give me a headache. But right before I reach the bathroom, someone emerges from one of the bedrooms, nearly colliding with me.

"Oh!" she says.

It's Marisol, Isabel's housekeeper. She's short and compact, her hair cut in a stylish shoulder-length bob. Today, she's dressed in a button-down shirt, pink jeans, and blindingly white Keds.

"Natasha?" She seems surprised to see me.

"Hi, Marisol." I've only met her twice before, when Allie took me up to the Malibu house with her, and I've never known quite how to interact with her. Isabel always treated Marisol like the help, but Allie draped herself over Marisol like she was a favorite aunt. When the two of them were alone in a room together, they yammered away at each other in Spanish. Allie often made Marisol laugh, or—at other times—frown and swat her on the backside, telling her to shush.

"Are you here for the party?" I ask.

"Lord, no," she says. "I live here, now that my kids are grown. In the apartment above the pool house."

I can't help but notice that the bedroom she's emerging from is Allie's old room.

Marisol glances over her shoulder, clutching her hands together. "I like to sit in there sometimes. To remember my girl." She nudges the door open so I can get a better view. "Isabel keeps it just the same."

The room is a museum of Allie's fifteen-year-old self. Vintage movie posters on the wall. MAC makeup scattered all over the top of the dresser. Allie's hairbrush resting on the bedside table. Would Isabel really leave the room like this if she had been the one responsible for Allie's disappearance?

Seeing the expression on my face, Marisol asks, "Do you want to . . . ?" She steps aside to let me walk into the room.

I hesitate. Two years ago, Mom turned Allie's bedroom in the Reseda house into a home office. I'd been upset about it at the time, but I have to admit it's made it easier to go back to Mom's place. I don't know how Isabel lives with these reminders of Allie.

Marisol pats my arm, as if she understands what I'm feeling. "Take your time, *cariño*."

Then she leaves me there, standing on the threshold. After a minute, I gather up the nerve to step inside. The room smells like furniture polish and, underneath that, a scent that might be Allie's old perfume. In the mirror above the dresser, there are photos tucked around the frame. Allie at her old high school, with friends I don't recognize.

I run my hand across the surface of the dresser. It's been polished to a shine. Although none of Allie's belongings have been moved, everything in the room is sparkling clean. I wonder how much time Marisol spends in here each day.

I sit down on the edge of the bed, then idly pull open the top drawer of the bedside table. Inside, there's a bottle of blue nail polish. A pincushion in the shape of an eyeball. And a thick paperback book. I pull out the book, turning it over in my hands. This isn't something the fifteen-year-old Allie would have read. It's a college textbook: *History of Western Civilization*. I stare at the familiar cover: the Roman statue, the gold lettering.

Western civ was the class Allie had been flunking at the beginning of our junior year. After she'd been put on academic probation, she started carrying the book around with her. I'd never seen her actually open it, but the book was always there, like she might learn something from it by osmosis. If I ran into her at Café Bijou, she'd have the book out on the table in front of her, her sunglasses and phone resting on top of it as she flirted with the barista.

If this book is here, that means Allie brought it to the house sometime that fall. But I don't remember coming up here with Allie during those months. And Allie never came to the Malibu house alone.

I open the book and flip through the pages. In chapter 1, it looks like Allie made a halfhearted attempt to study. She underlined a few sentences and drew squares around some of the paragraphs. The markings devolved quickly, though, into random doodling in the margins. Half-finished clothing designs. A caricature of Greg, his ears sticking straight out from his head. A phone number, written in her spiky handwriting.

As I flip through the rest of the pages, something flutters out and falls onto the carpet. I bend down to pick it up. It's a strip of photo negatives, the perforated edges slightly warped. Squinting, I hold it up to the light. There are four images, all portraits of a group of people. Four adults and two teenagers. The reversed colors make the people look alien, and it takes me a moment to realize what I'm looking at.

Giles and Mom, Isabel and Matthew, me and Allie. Our first Christmas together in the house on Via Montemar, when Mom said, *Let's take a photo in front of the tree.*

I stare at the people in the negatives: white hair, black skin. Allie must've taken this strip with her the day she'd followed me into the high school photography classroom, the week after Christmas break was over.

She'd been bored by the amount of time I was taking looking at the film negatives I'd developed the day before and was swiveling back and forth in one of the chairs near the darkroom. "Are you done yet?"

I'd remained bent over the light pad, frowning. None of the shots were going to be usable. Allie was looking down or away in every frame. That meant, the day before, I'd wasted my time developing the roll of film, a tedious process that involved me shutting myself in a lightless closet and blindly ratcheting the film on a reel. "How can you even tell what you're looking at?" she asked, scrunching up her nose.

"You get used to it after a while. Here," I said, handing her the loupe I'd been using to inspect the negatives.

I don't remember what happened after that. Allie, I think, spent some time bent over the light pad while I gathered up my things. And at some point, she must have taken one of the strips of negatives. But why keep it, if she hadn't wanted to be in the photos in the first place?

Carefully, I tuck the negative strip back between the pages of the book. Then I hear someone walking down in the hallway. I step out into the hall in time to see Marisol headed toward Isabel's bedroom, a stack of folded towels in her arms.

"Marisol?"

She turns with a jerk. "Yes?"

"Can I ask you a question?"

"What's that?"

I hold out the Western civ book so she can see it. "I found this in Allie's room."

"Oh?" She looks puzzled.

"It's from one of her LACSA classes. Junior year. I'm just wondering when she left it here."

Marisol shifts her grip on the towels. "Oh. Well, I'm not sure about that. Maybe it was at Christmas."

"But she wasn't here that Christmas. She was with me and Mom." Marisol would know that; it's not the kind of thing she'd forget.

She draws in a deep breath, then lets it out slowly.

"Marisol?"

The sound of party chatter drifts down the hall from the living room. The guests are making their way inside. Marisol glances over her shoulder. "Come," she says, nodding toward Allie's bedroom. "Let's talk in here."

CHAPTER 46

In the bedroom, Marisol sets the towels down on Allie's bed. Then she turns to me, her face drawn.

"Allie came to the house," she says. "Not at Christmas. At Halloween. She wasn't supposed to. Not after those earrings went missing. Isabel would've been very angry if she knew Allie was there."

Halloween. The weekend Allie told Greg she was in Vegas.

"What was she doing here?"

Marisol sits down on the bed. Up close, I can see that she's older than I'd assumed. Her hair has been dyed that rich shade of brown, and I can see a few millimeters of gray glinting near the roots.

"I think she came to be alone," she says. Suddenly, she digs in her pocket for a Kleenex and then blows her nose.

"Okay . . . but why here?"

Marisol looks at me, the skin around her eyes creasing. "She never told you?"

"Told me what?"

She gestures for me to sit next to her on the bed, and when I do, she pats my hand several times, as if she's trying to comfort me. But she's the one who's upset.

"If I tell you, you can't tell Isabel, okay? Promise you won't tell."

"Okay." I feel a shiver of uncertainty. What is Marisol afraid of?

Marisol twists the Kleenex in her hands. "The house was empty that weekend. Isabel was away in New York. I had the week off. I only came back here because I'd forgotten my coat." Her voice wobbles on that last word.

She dabs under her nose with the balled-up Kleenex. "When I got here, the front door was unlocked. And the security system was off. That scared me. But then I saw Allie's shoes by the door." She shakes her head. "I thought, 'I hope that girl's not doing anything stupid.' Isabel was so mad about those earrings. And I know Allie took them. I just know. She could be so bad sometimes. I don't know why."

"Did she come here to steal something else?"

Marisol shakes her head again. Then she waves a hand at the pillows on the bed. "She was there," she says. "Lying there." It takes a second for her to collect herself and continue. "She'd taken pills. A lot of pills."

My hands feel numb. I remember the note on the hospital form Golanski showed me. *Continued suicidal ideation.*

A tear runs down Marisol's cheek, making a wobbly line in her foundation. "I found a little bag with a ribbon on it. There were still a few pills left in the bottom."

I know the kind of bag she's talking about. A little velvet jewelry pouch, the kind Greg packaged his deliveries in.

"She was hardly breathing." Marisol's mouth works for a moment. "I shook her and shook her. Eventually I got her into the bathroom and got her to throw up." She puts a hand to her chest, as if she feels a physical pain there.

Numbness spreads through me. Halloween weekend. What had happened then? What had propelled Allie to do something like that? I don't remember the weekend itself, only the aftermath. When I came back to the apartment that Sunday, Allie had been curled up in her bed, looking like hell. Hungover, I'd thought. "Greg's super pissed you skipped out on his party," I told her. She only grunted in response, then pulled the comforter over her head.

"I wanted to call 911," Marisol tells me. "To take her to the ER. But Allie begged me not to. She didn't want Isabel to know. She said telling Isabel would only make it worse. And I didn't like to admit it, but she was right. Things were so bad between the two of them already."

I can imagine Allie pleading with Marisol, grabbing for her hand. The room feels like it's tilting gently to one side.

"So I stayed with her," Marisol says. "I made her soup, made sure she ate and drank. I stayed with her until I knew she was all right." She talks as if she's trying to convince me, convince herself, that she did the right thing. "And I said, 'The only way I stay quiet about this is if you get yourself some help.' And Allie promised me, really promised, that she would."

The light in the room is growing dim as the sun begins to set.

That Halloween weekend—that's what had pushed Allie to see a therapist.

"And she kept her promise," Marisol insists. "I know she did." Suddenly, she looks very tired. "But it wasn't enough," she says. "In the end." She presses her hands to her lips. "I think about it all the time. That day. If I'd done something different, maybe I could've stopped . . ."

She starts to cry in earnest, and I put an arm around her, rubbing her shoulder.

And I realize: In Marisol's mind, what happened to Allie wasn't murder. It wasn't some terrible conspiracy. The day she went missing, Marisol thinks, Allie simply managed to successfully do what she hadn't the two times before.

Third time's a charm, Allie murmurs in my ear.

When I return to the party, the sun is simmering over the ocean, turning the sky a brilliant shade of purple. I need to say my goodbyes to Matthew and Chloe before I go. First, though, I walk into the foyer, find my bag hanging on a coat hook, and tuck the Western civ book inside. When I have more time, I want to look through all of Allie's doodles, the notes she scribbled in the margins.

When I return to the living room, the atmosphere has loosened. Several people are dancing near the fireplace, Isabel among them. Near the sofas, Matthew chats to Giles and a few other men. As I move toward him, I see him take a sip from a bottle of beer. He catches sight of me and waves, stepping aside from the group to talk to me.

"Where have you been?" he asks. "I thought you might have left."

I try not to stare at the bottle in his hand. Matthew doesn't drink, not anymore.

"I'm not feeling that great," I say. "I'm going to go home."

He looks disappointed. "Oh. I'm sorry we didn't get more time to catch up." He leans closer, studying my face. "What is it? Is everything all right?"

I pause. "You're drinking?" I ask. I can't pretend I haven't noticed.

He looks down at the drink in his hand as if surprised to realize it's there. Then he laughs. "Oh, this? It's just a beer. A *light* beer. God, look at your face! Don't worry so much, Natasha. Trust me, one beer is not going to send me back to rehab. It was the hard stuff that was my problem."

He sounds so reassuring. Is this really nothing to be concerned about? Certainly, no one here looks bothered. Now I feel like I used to around Allie and Greg—like a worrywart, a killjoy. After all, Matthew seems perfectly sober—far more sober, for instance, than Isabel, who is now dancing with a red-haired woman by the fireplace, leaning her head on the woman's shoulder.

"Hey. We good?" Matthew asks, squeezing my shoulder. He seems concerned that he's upset me.

I nod. Somewhere in the back of my mind, a memory bubbles up: Allie sitting cross-legged on my bed, holding a cluster of airline liquor bottles in her hand. *Trust me, alcohol was never my problem.*

"Good," he says, smiling. "And you should stay. Have a good time. Cut loose for once."

This, also, is something Allie would say. And it strikes me again, how similar the two of them are. In the end, Matthew had stopped drinking, stopped short of full-blown self-destruction. But Allie—maybe, despite her best efforts, she'd been unable to save herself.

CHAPTER 47

At home, I sit in bed with my back against the headboard, the Western civ book propped on my knees. I slip the strip of negatives out from the book and lay it on my bedside table, where it gleams in the lamplight. Then I leaf through the textbook pages, studying Allie's scribbled notes in the margins. Some are scraps of poetry. Others are little comments on the text that make me laugh.

Even in these little pencil marks, Allie's so alive. I try not to think of her at the house in Malibu, lying in her old bedroom, waiting to die.

After chapter 3 in the book, there are no more scribbles in the margins. That must be where Allie stopped reading. I flip through the remaining pages, then stop when I glimpse something wedged in the pages of the final chapter. Thumbing my way back, I find what's tucked between the pages. A business card. QUALITY AUTO, it says, followed by an address and two phone numbers. Then, beneath that, a name: MIA ROSSI.

I sit up straight, holding the card by its crisp edges. What the hell is this?

In the morning, Ruiz drives over before I go into work so he can collect the card from me. I'd texted him a photo of it last night and explained where I found it, what I now know about Allie's Halloween.

I jog down the front stairs of the apartment building, meet him at the curb, and climb into the passenger seat of the Jeep. Then I hand him the card.

He studies it for a long moment. "Mia. That was the name Allie wanted Macnamara to call her, wasn't it?"

I nod. "It's from this book we used to read when we were kids. Mia Rossi is the name she chose when Greg made us our fake IDs." I'm wired, running on only three hours of sleep. "I called the numbers on the card last night. The first goes to a body shop in Van Nuys. The other one is out of service."

Ruiz taps the card against his steering wheel. "Shit," he says under his breath. Then: "Give me a second." He pulls out his phone and makes a call. After a moment, he says, "Jerry, hey. Can you run an address for me?"

As he reads out the street name and number, I sip coffee from my travel mug.

"Uh-huh. Yup."

My phone buzzes, startling me. I pull it out of my pocket and look at the text alert. It's my doorbell camera. The motion sensor outside my apartment has been activated. Quickly, I tap on the link and watch the video through the app. But it's only the building manager, sticking a flyer by my door, seeming not to notice that the sheet covers the doorbell lens. The video now shows me only the back side of a white piece of paper.

I let out a slow sigh. So much for technology.

When Ruiz finally hangs up the phone, his eyes are shining. "So, guess who owns Quality Auto?" He sets the business card down on the dashboard in front of us. "Manny Ocampo."

"Ocampo? As in . . ."

"Jairo Ocampo's uncle. Apparently Jairo manages the place now." He frowns. "On the face of it, the business is legit," Ruiz says. "They repair cars, pay their taxes . . . everything's aboveboard. But in the past, Manny Ocampo's been busted for running a chop shop."

"So, Allie was involved with that somehow?"

Ruiz spreads his hands wide. "Maybe. It would explain her sudden source of income that semester. I need to talk to Jairo."

"Well, let's go," I say quickly. "We can go today." Forget work. Work doesn't matter.

Ruiz shakes his head. "No. Natasha, from here on out, it's got to be official. This card—it needs to be logged in to evidence. I need to go down to Quality Auto with my partner and talk to Jairo myself."

I feel a flash of panic. If Ruiz decides to go through official routes, that means the investigation will do what it's always done, which is plod along, hitting all the inevitable walls until it comes to a standstill. "Ruiz, you know Jairo won't say anything to you, to the cops. We're better off going there ourselves . . ."

He's shaking his head. "I'm sorry. I can't risk it. We've got to play by the rules now." He gestures to the card. "This? This is a real break in the case. A solid reason to reinterview Jairo."

I want to shout at him, but with great effort I keep my voice calm. "And he'll tell you what? The business card isn't worth anything unless we can actually get him to talk about it." I remember Jairo from Greg's parties, the way his voice used to reverberate across the room. Once he started talking, you couldn't get him to shut up. But he wouldn't say one word about his relationship with Allie to the police.

Ruiz hesitates, and I can see him struggling with his decision. There is a part of him, I think, that knows I'm right. But he only shakes his head. "I'm sorry. No. Jairo's a whole different ball game than Macnamara. If he's mixed up with his uncle now, that means he has a lot more to hide, a lot more to protect. He could be dangerous."

"Please." This could be our only shot, our one shot at finding out the truth.

Ruiz won't look me in the eye. "I'm sorry. I know how much this means to you. But you have to trust us with this now. The police have to handle it from now on. I'll keep you in the loop as much as I can."

But I know what that means. I'll be on the outside of the investigation again, getting by on scraps of information, having my phone calls transferred to Family Liaison.

I can't believe he's doing this. Not now. Not when we're so close.

"This is the best way," he says. "Believe me."

I grab the door handle and shove the door open, stepping out of the Jeep. I can't believe I'd been stupid enough to trust him with the card.

"Natasha," Ruiz calls after me.

For a moment, I feel a flash of hope. He's changed his mind. But when I turn around, he's just leaning across the passenger seat, holding my purse out to me.

"I'll be in touch as soon as we know something," he says. "I promise."

"All right." I'm trying not to show my fury.

A text comes through on his phone. "Shit," he murmurs as he checks the screen. "They need me down at the station." He glances at me. "You sure you're okay?"

Of course not. He's shown me now how it's going to be. How I'm on my own from now on. I lift my chin. "Yes. Yes. I'm fine."

CHAPTER 48

When I see his Jeep turn the corner at the end of the street, I pull my camera out of my purse and pull up the shot I took this morning. The business card. I zoom in on the name Mia Rossi and stare at it for a long time. Then I turn the camera off, put it back in my bag, and call work to tell them I can't come in today.

Trust us, Ruiz said. But the police aren't going to be able to get the information they need from Jairo. I know it.

I walk back into the apartment building and make my way through the lobby, down the corridor to the parking garage. When I push open the heavy door, I wait for the motion-sensor lights to flicker on, but nothing happens. The garage is still in shadow. Swearing under my breath, I feel along the wall until I find the switch and flip it. With a groan, the lights snap on throughout the garage, casting a sickly light over the cars. In the middle row, my old Honda Civic sits, covered in dust.

I grip my keys in my hand. I know it's risky to drive. Foolish, even. But I can't take an Uber to Jairo's auto shop. I don't know how long I'll be there or how quickly I'll need to leave.

For a moment, I chew on my lower lip. Then I pull up the route to Quality Auto on my phone. It's not far. I tell myself I'll take the side streets. I won't get on the highway. I'll be as cautious as I can.

When I click the key fob to unlock the car, the beep reverberates through the parking garage, loud and jarring, like a warning.

⁓

I park on the far end of the street from Quality Auto, where I have a clear view of the place but my car won't be noticed. The auto shop occupies the corner of a flat, unremarkable block in Van Nuys, across the street from an empty storefront and a place offering payday loans. It's a low-slung building with four garage bays. Through two of the open doors, I see a car hoisted up on a lift and two men working underneath.

My heart is still beating rapidly from the drive. A part of me felt exhilarated to drive again, to be in charge, in control. But my hands are still trembling, from the risk I've just taken and the one I'm about to take. Am I really going to go in there? This isn't like visiting Greg and Macnamara. I barely know Jairo, and I can't predict how he'll react to me dropping in on him.

I lift my face up, feeling the bright sunlight blazing through the windshield. I think of Allie in her old bedroom in Isabel's house, of how alone she must've felt that day. So alone she didn't believe she could talk to anyone. Not even me.

With a yank, I pull the key out of the ignition, open the car door, and step out onto the street.

⁓

When I enter the auto shop, the smell of motor oil washes over me. It's dark in here, and I have to blink a few times before my eyes adjust. There are three lifts in the center of the garage, and the back of the room contains shelves overflowing with auto parts. As I step forward, the two men working under the car turn to look at me, perplexed. The younger one walks over, wiping his hands on a dirty cloth pulled from the back pocket of his jeans.

"Can I help you?"

"I'm looking for Jairo Ocampo," I say, trying to sound sure of myself.

The man glances at his coworker and raises his eyebrows. "You want to talk to Jairo?"

"Yes. Jairo." Lamely, I add, "I'm an old friend."

The young man looks at the other guy, says something in Spanish, and they both laugh. I know I don't look like a friend of Jairo's.

"Jairo?" I say stubbornly. I'm starting to sweat. My phone is tucked in the outer pocket of my jacket and set to record. Whatever Jairo says to me, I want proof of it. Even if it can never be used in court.

The man waves toward a small office tucked away at the back of the building. "In there." As I walk past him, he murmurs something to his coworker that I can't quite hear.

The office is just a small square of space walled off from the rest of the building. As I step up to the door and look inside, I see a metal desk wedged into one corner. An ancient desktop computer sits on top of it, next to stacks of paperwork and an ashtray in the shape of a race car.

A dark-haired man sits at the desk, dressed in a crisp button-down shirt. A large silver watch glints on his wrist. When he hears me step into the office, without looking up from his computer, he says, "Yeah? What?" Then he looks up, and his tone changes. "Oh," he says, standing up. "What can I do for you, miss?"

It's Jairo. All the baby fat has disappeared from his face, and his upper body ripples with muscle. Without the shaved head, he looks like a different person—his curly hair is slicked back, carefully styled.

"Hi," I say. Now that I'm actually standing in front of him, my heart rate ratchets up. "I don't know if you remember me. I'm Allie's sister. Natasha."

For a moment, he doesn't say anything, just runs his eyes over my body. "Yeah, yeah," he says. "I remember you. The girl with the long legs." He sits back down in his swivel chair and chews on the end of his pen. Then he takes it out of his mouth. "Well, what you need, girl? I'm guessing you're not here about a car."

"Um, no. Is it okay if I . . . ?" I gesture to the chair on the other side of his desk.

He shrugs as if it makes no difference to him.

Carefully, I sit down in the chair and set my bag on my lap. The phone in my front pocket wobbles forward, and I hope to God it's picking up our conversation.

"So, what's up?" he asks. As if it's been only a few days since we last saw each other.

"I was hoping I could ask you a few questions about Allie."

He looks bemused. "Why?"

"It's just . . . I've been going back through some photos of her." I've thought about how I'm going to approach this conversation. And I know I can't lead with the business card. I've got to work up to that. "And I noticed there were some of you in them."

He looks mildly interested. "Oh yeah?"

"Yeah." I reach into my bag, pull out my SLR, flick it on, and, leaning forward, show him the picture of him and Allie standing in the hallway of Greg's apartment.

He studies it for a minute. "Yeah, that's me. Look at that pudge." He shakes his head in disgust. "That was before I found out about clean eating." He pats his flat stomach and grins at me. "Big difference, right?"

"Uh. Yeah."

He flexes one arm, showing off a massive bicep. "Now I'm in the best shape of my life." When he laughs, I see straight, white teeth, a gold filling near the back of his mouth. "I work out five, six days a week. Bench 240." He raises his eyebrows, waiting for my reaction.

"Wow. Impressive." That's what he wants to hear, right? I draw his attention back to the picture. "So, do you remember this night?"

He looks at the photo again. "Like, do I remember that night specifically? Hell no. You know what those parties were like."

I pull the camera back and examine the photo closely. "It's just . . . when I saw this picture, like how close you guys are talking, I just wondered—were you two ever . . . you know?"

He looks blank for a second; then he realizes what I'm asking and starts laughing like it's the funniest thing he's heard all week. "You mean, were we *together*? Fuck, no. I mean, no offense. Allie was a good-looking girl. A lot of fun. But she was never my type." He picks up a framed photo on his desk and flips it around for me to see. It's him with his arm around a petite Latina girl. She's holding a chubby baby on one hip.

"Now, *this*—this is my type," Jairo said proudly. "That's Lucy. And my Nando."

The baby grins at the camera, his gums showing. The woman who holds him has full cheeks, dimpled just like the baby's.

"So you and Allie were just friends," I say.

He carefully sets the framed photo back in its original position. "Yeah," he says. "'Course."

"But you hung out outside of Greg's parties."

This time there's a pause before he decides to answer. "Sure. She was kind of sick of that whole scene at Greg's. So a couple times, I took her up to my neighborhood, to hang out with *mi familia*. And shit if they didn't love her. My sisters loved her. My *abuela* loved her, and that's saying something, let me tell you. 'Course, they had no idea who she was, who her mom was. Allie liked that about them."

"When was this?"

He shrugs. "I dunno." He glances at the photo. "Wait. Lucy and me, we had just met, so it would've been, like, 2012, I guess."

"So that was it? You guys just hung out a couple of times?"

"Yeah." He rocks back in his chair. "Let me tell you something, girl—Allie was good people. The real deal."

"Why do you say that?"

This is the Jairo I remember from Greg's parties, the storyteller, the one who loved to be the center of attention.

"I mean, I barely know the girl, right? We'd hung out, like, a couple of times, had a couple of laughs. But one day, I tell her, some asshole landlord is threatening to evict my *abuela* unless she pays her back rent. I was just bitching, you know, blowing off steam. But the next time I see Allie, she hands me this stack of cash. Like, a *stack*. Enough to make sure my *abuela* doesn't have to worry about this dude for months." He shakes his head in disbelief. "At first, I'm like, 'I can't take this.' But then she tells me—get this—she says, 'Consider it a gift from Isabel.' She'd jacked a pair of her mom's earrings and sold them at some pawn shop. She said Isabel wouldn't even miss them."

The pearl earrings.

"Allie was a crazy girl. But she had a big heart." He's got one knee propped up against the desk, and he's holding his pen in his mouth like he wishes it were a cigarette.

"She did," I say. Then, slowly, I ask, "So . . . is that why you hired her? To work here?"

Silence. Jairo's eyebrows draw together. He's wary now. "What're you talking about?"

I reach toward him with the camera again, clicking forward to the photograph I took this morning. "I found this yesterday. In one of Allie's old books. Can you tell me what this is?"

Jairo leans forward. When he sees the photo, his expression shifts, just slightly. "You know what it is, girl. It's a business card." Suddenly, I'm aware that behind the genial smile, there's another Jairo. A Jairo who shouldn't be messed with.

"One of *your* business cards," I say.

He shrugs, sitting back in his chair. "Sure. But I don't see Allie's name anywhere on it."

"Mia Rossi—that's a name Allie used sometimes. It was the one on her fake ID."

Jairo's face settles into a stony expression. "Don't know anything about that."

"Jairo, this an official card from your business. With Allie's alias on it."

He lifts his hands up. "I don't know what to tell you. You know as much as I do." He folds his hands across his chest. Conversation done.

That's it. That's going to be his line. Jairo knows he doesn't have to tell me anything. The less he reveals, the safer he stays. I shift in my seat, feeling the weight of my phone against my chest.

I know I shouldn't push, shouldn't take any more risks than I already have. But if I stop now, I'll have come all the way up here for nothing. I'll lose out on my one chance of getting real answers. I have to think of what Allie would do. Allie wouldn't let herself get brushed off with a line like *You know as much as I do.*

"That's too bad," I say lightly, setting my camera in my lap. "Now I don't know what to do." I let my shoulders slump. "I thought maybe you could help me. But if you can't, I guess I'll have to take this to the cops. They're always asking me to get in touch if I come across any new information."

Jairo's eyes narrow. Any pretense of good humor has vanished from his face. "I don't think you want to do that."

"Why not?" I know I've just crossed a line. Made myself a threat.

"Because I don't like cops. And I don't want them here, crawling around my shop." He leans forward and rests his forearms on the desk. The veins under his skin bulge like raised wires.

My shirt is sticking to my back now, sweat collecting at the base of my spine. "And I guess they would come by, wouldn't they? If they thought this card had anything to do with Allie's disappearance." I take in a deep breath. The office seems very cramped, very close. But I force myself to look him straight in the eye. "I guess you could save yourself a lot of trouble if you just told me what the hell this card is. Why Allie had it."

He scowls, and for a moment, I think I'm in real trouble. Then, suddenly, he breaks into a gleaming smile. "I guess you really are Allie's sister, huh? Never saw the resemblance until now."

"Just tell me what she was doing with you," I say. "At this place. And I'll leave you alone, I promise. You'll never see me again."

Jairo's smile evaporates. "How about I just take that camera from you?" he says pleasantly. "And you give me that business card."

I feel a little dizzy. "You could do that," I acknowledge. "But I don't have the card with me. And the photos are in the cloud now. Taking my camera won't change that."

Jairo looks at me for a long moment, as if thinking through his options. Then he sighs and kicks his chair back a few inches from the desk. "Look—it was nothing, okay? Nothing to get worked up about. Allie needed some cash, so I got her a gig here."

"Doing what exactly?"

He rocks back in his chair. "Well, we fix up cars here, right? Nice cars, sometimes. And we sell them. But sometimes people get a little nervous about buying from my guys. Some people see my crew, see brown skin, a few tats, and start thinking, 'Maybe this sale's not on the up-and-up.'" He adjusts the watch on his wrist. "So, we needed someone who looked a little more . . . customer friendly."

"Allie."

He shrugs. "Customers took a shine to her. Didn't think twice about handing over their money. So. It was a win-win. My uncle moved more cars. Allie got a little spending cash."

I look down at my camera, at the image of the business card on the screen. The name Mia Rossi is printed next to the phone number I don't recognize. The one that was out of service when I called this morning. But once upon a time, it had worked. Once upon a time, Allie had a phone number associated with this business. I think of Allie sitting at the table in Barclay's, clutching an unfamiliar phone in her hands. "She had a separate phone," I say slowly. "A phone she used to talk to you."

Jairo doesn't say anything, just stretches and flexes his fingers a few times.

My skin prickles. "It was you. You're the one Allie was talking to that night." Jairo was the one she'd gone to meet. "What did you do?" I say, standing up. My voice echoes against the office walls, high and sharp.

Jairo stands up quickly, raising his hands, palms toward me. "Hey, hey. Calm down now. I never did anything to Allie."

I back up, my legs knocking against the chair. "She called you. Why was she calling you?"

For the first time since I arrived, Jairo looks spooked. "Look—don't—you've got the wrong idea, okay? Allie was my friend." As I make a move toward the door, he reaches for my arm, then backs off when I lurch away. "Yeah, okay, okay. Just hold up, all right?" He doesn't want me to walk out that door. "She called me that night, okay?" he says. "But that's all. She wanted a favor. And after what she'd done for me, for my grandma, I thought, 'Sure. Why not?'"

I should get out of here now. But my feet feel frozen to the floor. I slide my camera back into my bag. If I needed to run, could I get out of here without Jairo stopping me? "What did she want?"

Jairo pauses, thinking. What will it cost him to tell me? What will it cost to stay silent? "All right, I'll tell you, but you gotta promise to keep the cops out of this. You gotta promise that. I didn't kill Allie, and I'm sure as hell not going to let them pin it on me."

I swallow. When I look down, I can see my phone where it's fallen forward in my pocket, the lit-up screen glowing through the jacket material. Shit. Someone is calling me. "Okay," I say to Jairo. "No cops. I promise."

He steps closer, carefully, like I'm a wild animal that might bolt at any minute. "Look, it was simple. That night, she wanted a car. Something low key. She asks me, can she trade in Greg's Porsche for something a little less noticeable, a Toyota Corolla or something like that." He laughs. "Well, that Porsche was worth, like, ninety grand. That worked just fine for me."

"Why did she need a car?"

He shakes his head. "I didn't know, and I didn't ask. She said she was going to this place up in the mountains. Some kind of hideout. That's all she said, I swear to God. She drove up here, we exchanged cars, and then she left. That's all I know."

His face flushes. "And I tell you what—Allie really screwed me over with that deal. I thought I was going to sell off that Porsche, make a bundle. But the next thing I know, her name's all over the news, and every cop in the city is trying to find out what happened to her. And I'm sitting here with Greg Novak's Porsche in my garage. Like a fucking time bomb. I had to get rid of it. Broke my heart, breaking that beauty down into parts." He holds out his hand. "Now. I told you what you want to know." His face changes, becomes grim. "So you can give me that phone you've been recording me on."

I step backward, turning toward the door, but Jairo is too fast. He grabs my arm and pulls me toward him, yanking my phone out of my pocket. He stops the recording and deletes it, then throws my phone on the floor and stomps on it with his heavy work boot.

"Now get the fuck out of my shop," he whispers in my ear. "And I better not be hearing from the cops, you hear me? When you get home—you burn that business card and forget you ever saw it."

CHAPTER 49

I sit in my car, clutching my phone in my hands. The screen is a map of fine cracks, and there's a thumb-size chunk of plastic missing from the bottom corner. Tentatively, I press the Home button. The screen flickers once, twice, and I see at the top of the screen that the battery is almost dead. Ruiz has called me; it was his call that came through in Jairo's office. I hit the button to play his voicemail, but the screen only shivers, and then the phone goes dark.

"Shit." Heat builds in the space behind my eyes. "Shit, shit, shit."

The recording, the only thing I have linking Jairo and Allie on the night she went missing—I've lost it. And it's my fault. How could I have been stupid enough to think I could come up here and—what? Find out the truth when the police couldn't? Now, when Ruiz and his partner arrive to talk to Jairo, they'll find him prepared. And God knows what will happen when Jairo realizes I've turned the card over to them.

I let out a shaky breath. This is not good. This is very, very bad. Frustrated, I wipe at my eyes, fighting back tears. Then I lean my head against the steering wheel and let defeat wash over me. Where have all my reckless decisions gotten me? Even if I do know now who Allie was calling that night, and what happened to Greg's car, I have no way to prove it to the cops. And Jairo will deny it until the day he dies.

I run through the conversation in my head. Trying to solidify the words in my memory, a kind of mental recording that I can keep for

Ruiz. *She said she was going to this place up in the mountains. Some kind of hideout.*

Blinking, I lift my head from the steering wheel and brush my hair away from my face. *The mountains.* Which mountains? And why would Allie choose that location as an escape?

Something nags at the back of my mind, a snippet of conversation that flits away every time I try to grasp it. This place in the mountains, Jairo said. *Some kind of hideout.*

Hideout. I've heard that word before. At the party at Isabel's house, when Giles and Matthew were talking about Matthew's cabin in Crestline. *The Hideout*, Giles had called it. The cabin on Lake Gregory where a young Allie had gone fishing with Matthew.

I feel lightheaded, like I'm floating a few inches above my body. Because I know. I know now where Allie went.

CHAPTER 50

I park outside the Van Nuys library and hurry inside. With my phone dead, I need some other way to access the internet, and this was the closest place I could find. Walking over to the bank of computers on a long wooden table, I scoot a chair up to a monitor and google the San Bernadino County clerk's office. Once I'm on the site, I find the Search function and enter in Matthew's name. The address of the property in Crestline pops up on the bright-white screen. I scrounge an old receipt out of my bag and scribble the address down in its margins. Then I look up directions to the cabin. It's an hour's drive away, and I'll have to take several major highways to get there.

I pause, tapping my fingers on the worn mouse pad. I know it's stupid to take the risk, but I have to go. I have to see it for myself—the last place Allie went before she disappeared.

I tell myself: I was fine on the drive over here, wasn't I? I'll be okay as long as I stay calm.

Quickly, I jot down the directions to the cabin on the back of the receipt. Then I jog back to my car and slide into the driver's seat. After pulling out of the parking lot, I take Victory Boulevard toward the freeway entrance, and then I'm on the 170, nudging the Civic faster. The car groans as it accelerates, and I pray it's in good enough shape to get me to Crestline.

As I drive, adrenaline begins to spike in my veins. Marisol thought Allie had committed suicide. But given what I know now, that can't be true. Allie had Greg's money with her that night. She had a new car from Jairo's shop. She was headed to Matthew's place in the mountains. Clearly, she had a plan. But what happened next? Was she planning a whole new life? Or just a temporary escape? If she'd only planned to leave for a little while, was she intercepted before she could come back?

I feel my heart rate start to rise, so I take a few long, deep breaths. I have to stay calm. I can't risk having an episode.

I tell myself: No one knew where Allie was going that night. Not even Jairo.

You don't know that, Allie murmurs to me. *You don't know who else I might have told. Or who might've been following me.*

I grip the steering wheel. I can't think about those possibilities, not now.

I force myself to think about practicalities. I've never been up to Matthew's cabin. When was the last time anyone was up there? I struggle to remember the conversation at Matthew's party. I'd gotten the impression that Matthew hadn't been up there for a while. Maybe years.

I stare out the windshield at the wide highway ahead of me. This is the route Allie would've driven on her way out of the city. It would've been close to midnight, the sky speckled with stars. I wonder if she'd felt angry. Or fearful. Or free.

After a long while, the road winds into the mountains, and a chill seeps in through the car windows. I turn up the heat in the car. When I take the next curve of the highway, I see smatterings of snow on the road's shoulder. My car is struggling with the steep incline, but I keep pressing it forward, hoping to God the engine doesn't start smoking.

After about twenty minutes, I consult the directions I scribbled on the receipt, trying to decipher my cramped handwriting. Soon, I take a turn onto a narrower road that leads through the forest. I'm almost there. At this realization, I feel myself start to panic. What will I find at the cabin? Evidence that Allie was there? Or . . . what if, after all these years, her body has been up there, abandoned, decaying?

My vision flickers. When the black curtain comes down, it happens quickly, faster than it ever has before. I slam on the brakes, veering off onto the shoulder of the road, hoping my mind's eye can tell me how far to move over to get out of the path of traffic without running into the trees. I pull the car to the right until I hear the scrape of metal, the Honda's side dragging against a metal barrier on the side of the road. A horn blares in my left ear as a truck passes, so close that I can feel a rush of air against the car.

My whole body is buzzing. I fold over the steering wheel, trying to remember Dr. Rajmani's breathing exercises. I'm safe now. No one is hurt. But all I can think of is what could've happened those few seconds when I'd been driving blind. I could've been killed. I could've killed someone else. It takes a few minutes of ragged breathing before I begin to fully realize the full import of my situation. I'm out in the middle of nowhere on my own. Without a working cell phone. In a car I can no longer drive.

I sit there long enough for my vision to slowly start returning. The trees materialize, like ghosts, on either side of a dark road. And then I hear a car drive up behind me. The wheels crunch slowly along the gravel of the shoulder; then the engine shuts off and I hear the slam of a car door. I straighten, twisting my head over my shoulder to get a better look through the back window. But all I can see is a dark, heavy shape. A baseball cap pulled low over a man's forehead.

I look forward, into the forest that surrounds the car on either side. Then someone raps hard on my driver's side window, and I startle, whipping my head around.

"Natasha?" Ruiz is standing outside my car, his face flushed in the whipping wind.

CHAPTER 51

I open the car door, dazed. Ruiz seems to have materialized here as if by magic.

His eyes run over my car, the way it's nuzzled up against the metal barrier. "What the hell happened? Did you get into an accident?"

I stand up and step away from the car, my legs a little unsteady. "I just needed to pull off the road for a second."

His eyes narrow. "What the hell are you doing up here?" he asks, at the same time that I say, "How did you know I was here?"

He frowns. Then he steps past me and leans into the car, pulling out my bag from the passenger seat. He reaches into the outer pocket and pulls out a gold necklace that is not mine. It takes me a moment to recognize it. The GPS necklace he got for his grandma, the one I saw in his Jeep.

"I had a feeling, after we talked this morning, that you might do something reckless. So I slipped this in your bag."

I should be furious, but I can't find the energy for it. I'm just glad he's here. I'm glad I'm not alone.

Another gust of wind shakes the trees, and Ruiz folds his arms across his chest. "When I got to work, I checked the tracker app and saw you were in Van Nuys." He shakes his head, frustrated. "What the hell, Natasha. And then I called you about ten times but got no answer. That's when I got in my car and started following the GPS signal."

He looks around, pulling his jacket closer against his body. "Van Nuys, I could guess what that was about. You went to see Jairo, right? But what the hell is this? Where are you driving to?"

My lips are starting to feel numb in the cold. I tell Ruiz what Jairo told me—about Allie's phone call, Greg's car. Matthew's cabin. I leave out the detail about Jairo destroying my phone.

Ruiz takes a moment to digest this information. "So that's where you're going? Matthew's cabin?"

I nod.

I expect him to yell, to lecture, but instead his eyes stray to the road ahead. "How far away is it?"

"A few minutes, maybe." The adrenaline spike I felt earlier is beginning to fade, leaving me shaky and exhausted.

The sky behind Ruiz's head is turning dark gray, the air taking on that certain smell it gets before it begins to snow.

"Well," he says. His breath forms a misty cloud in front of his face. "If we're almost there . . ."

I blink. My vision has fully returned, and I can now see the details of his face, the flecks of yellow in his gray eyes.

"Better not let it wait," he says grimly. "If Jairo knows where the hideout is, he may be headed here soon, to make sure he's covered his tracks."

Why hadn't I thought of that? That Jairo might've known exactly where Allie was going. That he could have lied to me about that.

I follow Ruiz back to his Jeep. Once inside, I consult the crumpled receipt in my hand and give him the last few directions that will take us to Matthew's place. He pulls out onto the road, and after a few minutes, we approach a sharp bend. Just up ahead, to our right, is a gravel drive that curves and disappears into the trees. As Ruiz slows the car, I peer closer at the address marker, half-hidden by bushes.

"Is that it?" Ruiz asks.

"I think so."

He turns into the driveway, and the Jeep rocks from side to side as it struggles over the uneven road. The branches of the trees tangle above us, forming a kind of tunnel. It's a few minutes before the car emerges into a clearing and we reach the cabin, a small structure overlooking the lake. In the summer, there would be boats and Jet Skis out on the water, people swimming and laughing. But in the winter, the beach looks bleak and uninviting. Gray water, gray sky.

Overgrown shrubs scrape against the cabin's brown shingles. Nearby, a small carport sinks underneath the weight of a fallen tree.

Ruiz says, "Looks like this place has seen better days."

I wonder if Matthew knows how dilapidated the property has become. From what Giles said at the party, it sounded like the place meant something to Matthew at some point, but maybe he'd let it fall by the wayside after he let go of his writing dreams.

I open the car door and step out into the clearing. Instantly, the cold slips through my clothes, raising goose bumps on my skin. As I walk to the front porch, my shoes sink into the thick layer of pine needles underfoot. Behind me, the slam of Ruiz's door sends a jolt through the air. It's so quiet out here. The only noise comes from the birds that have built nests under the cabin's eaves.

We walk up the porch steps, the wood creaking beneath our feet, and peer in the front windows. It's dark inside, and I can only make out the vague shadows of furniture. Ruiz turns, surveying the landscape around us. From the cabin, a dirt trail leads down to a rocky beach, where the lake is still and glassy. On all other sides of the cabin, we're surrounded by trees.

Carefully, with his sleeve covering his hand, Ruiz tries the front door. It's locked, of course, but this is a newer door, the kind with a key code panel above the handle—an oddly modern touch for such a rustic place. This must be one of the security measures Matthew put in place after the break-ins he mentioned.

"Any chance you know the code?" Ruiz doesn't sound hopeful.

I shake my head. Then, after a moment, I say, "Hang on." Once, when Matthew had been running late for dinner, he'd given me the entry code to his Venice Beach place. His birthday and Isabel's combined: 8163. Tentatively, I step past Ruiz and punch in the code, being careful to use the edge of my sleeve to cover my fingertip. There's a sharp beep, then a whirring noise as the dead bolt slides open.

Ruiz and I look at each other.

"Shit," I whisper. I hadn't been expecting that to work. Suddenly, I feel pinned to the spot. I don't want to see what's inside.

Ruiz reaches past me and pushes the door open so we can see into the living room. The place is plain and old fashioned, nothing like Matthew's glamorous home in Venice. There's a small brick fireplace, and in front of it, a lumpy plaid couch. I step inside. The place smells of dust and old woodsmoke.

"Don't touch anything," Ruiz says quickly. "We'll just look around and see if we find anything that might indicate Allie was here."

I stand in the middle of the living room, turning in place. After a minute, I walk to the kitchen and glance through the doorway. Everything in this room is green: green linoleum, green cupboards, green curtains. There's a kitchen island in the center with a knife block on it. The room is tidy and clean, except for the thick layer of dust that coats every surface.

Turning, I walk to the other side of the living room, where another doorway leads into a small bedroom with a double bed and a bedside table. The room is bare. No personal items anywhere. I can't see any evidence of Allie's presence. Carefully, I nudge the closet door open with my elbow. It's empty except for a few wooden hangers. I get down on my hands and knees and look under the bed. Nothing there either.

When I stand up, Ruiz is watching me from the doorway. "Anything?"

I shake my head. I mean, what was I expecting? A note from Allie saying, *I was here*?

Ruiz walks the perimeter of the living room, tilting his head back to look at a rectangular cutout in the ceiling that must lead to an attic. It's cold in the house, and I hug myself, trying to keep warm. It was silly, thinking we might find something here. Even if Allie did make it out here to the cabin, that was four years ago. There's nothing here that can help the investigation now.

Ruiz walks into the kitchen, and I follow him. As he carefully opens cupboards and drawers with the edge of his hand, the clouds part outside, and a shaft of sunlight beams in through the window, lighting up the whole room. I stare down at the linoleum, which has a busy design—green flowers over a crisscross pattern—and notice that, in one place, the flooring has become pale, discolored.

"What is it?" Ruiz asks when he abandons his search of the cupboards.

"Look," I say. "There's a light patch by your feet."

He steps back, then squats down to examine the floor. The spot is an irregular oblong, maybe a foot wide. "Bleach?" he says.

That's what it looks like. Someone had done a spot-clean, but they'd neglected to dilute the bleach.

Ruiz shifts his attention to the edge of the kitchen island. The linoleum, where it butts up against the island, has warped and buckled, leaving a crack that exposes the floorboards underneath. Slowly, Ruiz reaches into his pocket and pulls out a pen, using it to draw back the edge of the warped linoleum. He peers underneath for a long moment. Then he stands up and says briskly, "Okay, let's step outside."

"What?" I say. "What's down there?" I try to move past him, but he blocks me with his body.

"Natasha. Let's go." His hands are on my shoulders, urging me backward. But I push away, breaking free of his grip, and kneel down to see what he's seen. "Don't touch anything," he says, his voice urgent.

But I don't have to touch anything to see what's there. Wood planks, stained with a dark, rust-colored substance. And there, caught in the edge of the warped linoleum, one long black hair.

Ruiz pulls me to my feet. "C'mon. We need to get out of here."

I let him lead me out onto the porch, no longer resisting. My brain feels like it's moving at half speed. The stain. The hair.

"No." I feel hot, sick. I won't believe it. Allie's not dead.

Carefully, Ruiz closes the front door of the cabin behind us.

I can't seem to draw in a full breath. "It's her blood, isn't it? Allie's blood."

He keeps his face carefully blank. "We won't know anything for certain until the scene is processed." But from the look in his eyes, I can tell he knows what we've just seen.

It happened here. Allie died here, with no one to call out to for help. Was it Jairo who did it? Or someone Isabel put on her trail?

"Natasha," Ruiz says. "Nothing is for sure, not yet. I need to call my partner, get an evidence team up here." He pulls out his phone, then holds it up in the air. "Shit. No signal." He turns to me. "Here. Sit down."

I ease myself down onto the top porch step, the splintery wood poking me through my jeans.

"I'm going to walk back toward the road, see if I can get reception there." His gray eyes search my face. "I'll only be a few minutes. Will you be okay?"

I nod. As he walks away, I draw my coat tighter around me and stare up at the skeletal branches of the trees, the crows circling in the sky. It's a black-and-white photograph come to life.

It's clear to me now. Allie came up here that night. And someone followed her. Not twelve feet from where I am sitting, someone killed her. I lean forward and rest my head on my knees, my breath coming quick and uneven in the back of my throat. I think of the stretch of woods, dark and silent, that surrounds the cabin. Is Allie's body out there somewhere? Or at the bottom of the lake?

Suddenly, I sit up straight, rubbing my hands across my face. I can't allow these morbid images to take over. I have to think logically. In my head, I try to re-create the sequence of events that night. If Allie came out here and someone followed her, there would've been two cars on the property. What had happened to her car, the one she'd traded for Greg's Porsche? Her killer would have needed to get rid of Allie's car and then return for their own. Unless there were two people involved . . . in which case, they could've driven away both cars at once.

I turn and stare up at the cabin, as if, by looking hard enough, I can make it give up its secrets. But all I see are brown shingles and a bird's nest perching at a precarious angle above the front door. There are no more answers to be found here.

Then I squint. The bird's nest—it's impossible for it to be jutting out from the house at that particular angle. It must be propped up on something. Standing, I walk closer and see that it's perched on an object mounted against the siding. I brush aside some sticks and pine needles to see what's underneath. A security camera.

I hear Ruiz's footsteps crunching through the clearing, feel the porch shaking as he climbs the steps behind me. "What is it?" Then he sees the camera. "Shit. Is that thing on?"

The camera's eye is trained on the cabin's doorstep, gazing right at me. "I don't know." The camera is the same brand as the one I just bought, the little logo on the side identical to the app installed on my phone.

"Do you know when this was put in?" Ruiz says. "Before or after Allie went missing?"

My brain should be connecting the camera to something important, but my thoughts are stalling out. "I'm not sure."

"Natasha. *Think.*"

I close my eyes. At the party, what exactly had Matthew said? I'd only been half listening. "I think Matthew said it was 2012 sometime. After a break-in. I don't know any more than that."

Ruiz blows out a breath. "Fuck." And then, as he examines the camera more closely: "*Fuck.* It's on. It's working."

I know I should understand why he's so upset, but my mind is a curious blank.

"Natasha," Ruiz says. "If Allie came up here that night and this camera was already installed . . ."

I shake my head. "No."

"It would've sent an alert to Matthew. Wherever he was, he had to have known that she was here."

That's not possible. "No. Matthew was . . . Matthew was at a conference. In Redlands."

"Redlands isn't far from here. He could've made it here, in—what? Thirty minutes? An hour?"

"Maybe he didn't get the alert. Maybe the camera was off that day." Maybe I have it all wrong, and Matthew didn't put the camera in until after Allie went missing. But as soon as the thought crosses my mind, I know that can't be true. Matthew, after Allie's disappearance, had been a complete wreck. Matthew could barely eat or sleep. He wouldn't have had the wherewithal to install new security measures at a cabin he barely used.

Ruiz pushes his baseball cap back on his forehead, rubbing at his hairline. "The morning after Allie went missing, Matthew missed his panel at the Redlands conference. The one he was supposed to speak at. The organizers were all bent out of shape about it."

I remember. Matthew told me he'd partied too hard the night before—going overboard, as he was in the habit of doing back in those days—at some gathering with lots of dull faculty members and free champagne. I never questioned his story. Nobody did. He'd been nowhere near LA that night.

I turn away from the cabin, toward the cloudy water of the lake. I think of Matthew, how he'd been after Allie's disappearance. Red eyed, sleepless. He'd gotten fired from the movie he was working on after he'd shown up to work drunk. Four years ago, I'd seen Matthew's behavior as proof of his shock, his distress over losing Allie. But what if Matthew was such a wreck not because he didn't know what had happened to her, but because he knew exactly what had?

Small flakes of white begin to spin in front of my eyes. At first, I think I'm hallucinating, and then I realize—it's beginning to snow.

CHAPTER 52

I sit in the Jeep, which Ruiz has turned on and left running so I can stay warm while he makes more phone calls outside. I'm not sure how much time passes while I sit there, but eventually a police car edges its way down the gravel driveway and parks next to the Jeep. Ruiz walks over to the cruiser and has a long conversation with the officer inside. Then, finally, he returns to talk to me.

"The San Bernadino Sheriff's Department is going to secure the cabin until we can get our evidence team up here. In the meantime, I'll drive you back to LA."

Although my body has warmed since sitting in the car, I still feel frozen.

Ruiz gets behind the wheel and buckles his seat belt. "We've got an APB out on Matthew," Ruiz says, "but if he's seen the footage from the security camera today, he may already be on the run."

On the run. What a far-fetched phrase. How many nights had Matthew cooked me dinner, poured me a glass of wine as he asked about my law school applications? This Matthew, the one Ruiz is talking about, doesn't seem real.

As Ruiz navigates the car back along the driveway, I see the sky growing dark and heavy. By the time we reach the main road, snow has begun to gather on the asphalt.

"Matthew loved Allie," I tell Ruiz. "He didn't have any reason to hurt her."

Ruiz is silent for a long time. Finally, he says, "Natasha, that Friday, at Redlands—Matthew didn't show up at the conference panel until after noon. That gives him maybe twelve hours of time when he's unaccounted for."

Time enough to drive up here, kill Allie, then return to the Redlands campus.

"But why?" There has to be another explanation for the blood on the floor. "Why would he hurt her?"

Ruiz frowns. "I don't know."

I lean my head against the cold car window. All these years, I've believed Matthew and I understood each other. It is the two of us, I've always thought, who've missed Allie the most. The two of us holding out hope when everyone else had given up.

But now, the picture shifts. This whole time, Matthew hadn't been helping me. He'd been keeping me close. In becoming my friend, he'd made sure that I looked for answers everywhere but where they were. Everywhere except right in front of my face.

CHAPTER 53

At my request, Ruiz drops me off at my mom's house in Reseda. I don't want to go back to my apartment right now. For the first time in a long time, all I want is my mother.

When he pulls up at the curb, he glances at the front windows of the house. "Is she home?"

"No," I say. She'll be at work for another hour or two, I know. "But I know where she keeps the spare key."

"You'll be okay till she gets here?"

I nod. I know he can't stay with me, not with everything that's going on, but I suddenly feel afraid to be on my own, alone with my thoughts.

"Hey." He reaches out and grabs my hand. "Don't get ahead of yourself. We'll figure out what happened. Then we'll deal with whatever we find."

"I know," I say numbly.

"Natasha. It's important that you don't do anything. Don't answer any calls from Matthew. Don't tell anyone what we found. Not even your mother. Not until we know more."

I nod. After a moment, he surprises me by pulling me close, wrapping his arms around my shoulders. For a minute, I let my head rest against his shoulder. He smells faintly of soap and coffee. A distant part of me thinks that I should cry. But I don't. I think I've forgotten how.

When he lets go, I brush my hair away from my face. "You should go," I say. I know he'll be needed up at the cabin.

"I'll call as soon as we know something," he says.

I get out of the car and walk around to Mom's backyard, where I retrieve the spare key from the ledge above the back door. After I let myself in, I find myself walking restlessly around the living room. Maybe it was a mistake to come here. The house is too quiet; it's too easy to think. Without my permission, my mind conjures up images. Matthew driving to the Crestline cabin. Matthew standing over Allie's body in the kitchen. Matthew dragging her body into the woods.

I force myself to shut out these thoughts. I can't get ahead of myself. Ruiz said he would call when he had more information. Except, I realize belatedly, I don't have a way to receive his call. I pull my phone out of my bag and examine the cracked screen. Experimentally, I press the Home button. Nothing. Then I remember the low-battery light that had flashed right before the phone shut off. Maybe, if I plug it in, I can see whether it's totally dead.

I walk into Mom's office and dig through her desk drawers for a charger. When I find one, I plug in my phone. There's a long moment when nothing happens; then, after a minute, the Apple logo appears, and I see that the phone is actually powering on, charging. I feel a rush of relief. After a minute, the Home screen appears, pixelated but functional. I leave the phone to charge and turn and examine the room, where I can still sense the old arrangement of Allie's bedroom furniture against the walls.

Ever since Mom turned this room into her office, it has felt odd to me. Too sparse. Just a desk and a bookshelf and a filing cabinet. Back when Mom packed up Allie's things, she'd taken Allie's nameplate off the door, but I can still see the faint outline of where it used to be. I walk over to the door, then press my hand against the outline and trace the letters as I remember them. A big dramatic *A* followed by smaller lowercase letters in cursive.

Then I stop, my fingers pressed against the door. That lettering. On the key chain, where Allie's name had been written—that wasn't Allie's handwriting. It was *this* script. The big dramatic *A* is exactly the same. I spin around. Whoever wrote her name on the key chain was trying to point me here. To her old bedroom.

I run my eyes over the furniture, the walls. The day before Allie went missing, she'd come here, to this house, for only fifteen minutes or so. It has never made sense to me. But what if she didn't come to the house to see Mom? What if she came here to hide the other half of the flash drive? This would be a safe place, a place she could be sure Isabel would never go.

I walk over to the desk and run my fingers across its surface. There's nothing of Allie's in the room anymore. Her belongings have all been packed in boxes, and—what? Returned to Isabel? I can't remember now. My heart sinks. If the flash drive was once hidden in this room, it's possible Mom sent it right back to the person Allie wanted to keep it from.

Frustrated, I turn in a circle, scanning the room for possible hiding places. The curtain rods? Under the carpet? Then I come to a stop, my eyes catching on the AC vent. The place where, in the house on Via Montemar, Allie used to stash her liquor, her notebook.

After dragging the desk chair over to the wall, I step onto it and run my hand over the edges of the vent cover. I'll need a screwdriver to get it off. I jump down, run to the hall closet, and pull out Mom's toolbox. Once I find the right screwdriver, I rush back to the vent and carefully work the screws loose, then pull back the cover and peer inside. I pass my hand around the inside of the opening, but my fingers only come away covered in dust.

Defeated, I step down off the chair and sit cross-legged on the floor, the screwdriver in one hand. The flash drive isn't here.

I don't know how long I sit there like that, my gaze level with the desk chair, staring at the electrical outlet on the wall under the desk. The slots for the electrical plugs stare back at me like little faces, mocking me. Two vertical lines for eyes and a circle for a mouth.

Then I crawl forward and run my hands across the outlet cover. "Shit," I say under my breath. That face. This was the symbol drawn on the flash drive, the one I'd thought was an emoji.

Fumbling with the screwdriver, I loosen the small screw that holds the outlet cover against the wall. When it falls away in my hand, I push my fingers into the small space behind it. Nothing.

But there are other outlets in the room. I check the one by the filing cabinet. The one by the door. Nothing. I twist around, scanning the rest of the room. There are no others. Then I remember: there should be one more, where Allie's bedside table used to be. It's blocked now by the bookshelf. Scrambling to my feet, I walk over to the bookshelf and wrestle it away from the wall, just a few inches, enough so that I can slide my hand behind it.

Then I'm down on my knees, snaking my hand between the shelf and the wall and working the outlet cover loose, scraping my knuckles in the process. This time, when I push my fingers into the gap, they brush up against something small. Something plastic. Carefully, I clasp the object and draw it out, knowing what it is before I set eyes on it.

The other half of Allie's key chain. The one that holds the USB drive.

CHAPTER 54

Mom's old desktop computer takes forever to boot up. I sit at her desk, fingers tapping frantically against the mouse. Finally, the screen loads, and I slide the flash drive into the USB port. A little icon pops up on the desktop, the colors bright and cheery.

"Okay," I whisper. "Okay." I click on the icon. Only one file is saved on the drive, a document titled "Final draft." I open the file, and a box pops up, prompting me to enter a password. Fuck. I sit there for a long moment, and then I try entering in the name "Mia Rossi"—in all possible variations. Capitalized, uncapitalized, one word, two words. On my fourth try, the document opens suddenly, black-and-white text filling up the screen.

I swallow, leaning forward to read.

> You think you know me. Maybe you've read about me in magazines, or maybe we've met in the back room at Luxe. Maybe we're friends, maybe we've dated, maybe you even call me family. But you don't know me. I can say that with certainty because, for most of my life, I've done everything I could to not know myself. The Allie you know: that's someone I created. The spoiled brat, the rebel, the diva, the train wreck. I'm just what you would expect from the daughter of

> Isabel Andersen. And you have to admit, I've played the role to perfection.
>
> It's a performance I'm in control of. And not in control of. Sometimes I enjoy it; sometimes I loathe it. But it turns out I'm not the actress my mother is. I can't keep the mask on forever.

I read quickly. Allie is writing about the suicide attempt in Malibu, being found by Marisol, Marisol making her promise to see a therapist. Reading her words is like hearing her voice in the room with me.

> So I did the thing I said I'd never do; I went back to therapy. But this time it wasn't like before, when I was trying to outsmart the person sitting across from me. This time there was nothing I could do but break apart. This time, the only thing I could do was tell the truth.
>
> But you don't want the truth from me. Not from Allie Andersen, the girl who has everything. And you're right. I've always been spoiled: the best schools, the best clothes, the best cars, the best vacations. Sure, my mother was never around, but I had Matthew. Matthew took care of me. He worshipped me. I wasn't so stupid that I didn't know what a special thing that was.
>
> When you get that kind of love from someone, you don't question it. You just hang on with all you've got. Especially if it's all you've got.
>
> So, I didn't care that Matthew drank. I didn't care that he spent more time with me than my friends did. And I didn't care that sometimes he crawled into my bed at night to sleep with his arms around me. That was love. That was what love was like.

> In the daytime, Matthew took me everywhere with him. He took photos of me. He made me feel like a star. And I liked being beautiful in his eyes. At night he stayed with me too. And at night, he took different photos, private ones. These ones were just between him and me, he said.

The screen swims in front of my eyes.

> By the time I was eleven or twelve, I knew what was happening wasn't right. But I couldn't make it stop. So I started drinking. And drinking was such a gift. It made things so much easier. It made living possible. Pills were better, though. Pills made living fun.
>
> My mother said I was pure trouble. She said my antics were all to get attention. And she was right. I wanted attention. Her attention. I wanted her to see. Because she did see the way Matthew was with me. In part, at least, she saw. And then she looked away.
>
> Sometimes, when Isabel was home from a film shoot, I thought: Just tell her. Just say the words out loud. But even when we were in the same room, she felt so far away.

It's too hard to read this. I move the mouse down the page, scanning the words quickly, as if that will somehow make them less painful. Allie talks about working up the nerve to tell Isabel, after years, daring to tell her the truth. And how Isabel hadn't believed a word of it.

> Instead, she packed me off to an expensive rehab where I would be someone else's problem. That was when I learned: No one was coming to rescue me. And for that I only had myself to blame. You couldn't act

> the way I'd acted and then expect to be believed. I'd lied, I'd stolen, I'd gotten expelled, just for kicks, for fun, to make myself feel something. So if Isabel didn't believe me, was that really her fault? Or was it mine?
>
> In rehab, they tried to get through to me, they tried to get me to tell them what was wrong. But I wasn't going to fall for that. I wasn't going to ask for anyone's help ever again.

Her voice is so clear, so angry and stubborn, that it seems impossible she's dead. Here, on the page, she is still alive.

> Recently, I gathered up the courage to tell someone about Matthew. Someone I loved, someone I trusted. And he believed me. He said it was important for me to tell my story. He said he'd help me be heard. But in the end, he turned out to be just like everyone else. In the end, I didn't matter as much to him as his safe little life.

There's a line under this paragraph, and then several blank spaces before the next ones, as if Allie left the essay and then came back later to add on more.

> Matthew called me today. Isabel told him I was writing this essay. She warned him. And that's how it's always been, since they were kids, the two of them against the world. Even when the world includes me.
>
> *No one will believe you,* Matthew said. *Don't do this to yourself. I'm only thinking of you.*
>
> And I realized he was right. Who would believe me—Allie Andersen—after everything I've done?

So, here's what I've learned: Words don't matter. I used to think they did, but now I know they don't. So, I'm hiding this essay somewhere safe. Somewhere they can't get to it.

But I'm not giving up. Words won't convince you, but I can give you what you've always loved: pictures. I mean, didn't you love those pictures of me coming out of Luxe, falling all over myself? Those were a big hit. So, let me give you some more. Matthew's photos, the ones he took of me, the ones he keeps hidden at the cabin.

Maybe you won't like those as much. Maybe those won't make it to the front page of a magazine. But I don't care. I don't give a shit about what you think. All I want is for you to know is that, after all this time, Allie Andersen is telling the goddamned truth.

My head is pounding. I turn away from the computer screen, blinking rapidly. Leaning forward, I press my hands against my eyes. And in the darkness, images emerge, adjusting and sharpening in my memory.

That first Christmas, Allie sitting as far away from Matthew at the dining table as she could. Allie, hating to visit Isabel's house so much that she would only go if I was with her, if I never left her side. Allie coming out of the bathroom at Luxe, her pupils dilated to a frightening size.

Finally: Allie standing in my bedroom, holding my modeling photos in her hands. The last time I saw her. The night I've tried to forget.

CHAPTER 55

January 2013

That night, I'd been alone in the apartment. Which was why I'd felt safe spreading the modeling photos out on my bedspread, so I could more carefully examine them, see myself through the photographer's eyes. At some point, though, I left the room to go to the bathroom, and during that time, Allie must've come home, because when I came back to my room, she was there, standing beside my bed.

A flash of shock ran through me. "What are you doing here?"

One of the eight-by-tens was in her hand. I stepped forward to grab it from her, but she yanked it out of my reach.

"What the fuck is this?" she asked.

"Nothing," I said.

She pointed at the logo stamped on the back of the print. "This is Peter's company. How the fuck do you know Peter? Did *Isabel* set this up?"

Quickly, I gathered up the other photos on the bed, clutching them against my chest. "So what if she did?"

"'So what if she did?'" Allie repeated. "Who the hell *are* you? How long has this been going on, you and Isabel palling around?"

She really couldn't believe it, that there was something about me she didn't know. Predictable, reliable Tash.

"We're not 'palling around.' She's helping me. She's being nice."

Allie made an explosive noise. "Don't you dare say she's nice."

"I can say what I want," I snapped. "Just because you don't like her doesn't mean the whole world has to hate her too." Suddenly, the words were spilling out of me. "I'm allowed to have my own opinions. She's actually really great."

All the color drained from Allie's face. "Oh, Tash. Don't do this."

"What do you mean, 'Don't do this'?"

"Don't tell me you're buying her bullshit. Can't you see she's just using you?"

"She's not!" I said. "God, she's not the supervillain you make her out to be. She's helping me. Supporting me. Which is more than you do." In that moment, I felt the burn of all the times Allie had let me down. Leaving me alone at parties so she could hook up with some guy. Letting Greg mock me, laughing at his jokes. Not coming to my photography show.

Allie pushed her hands through her hair. "Jesus. This is a nightmare."

"What are you talking about?" I hated the way her face looked, like she was about to cry and it was up to me to comfort her. "This isn't about you. For once, something is about me."

She laughed, a slightly hysterical sound. "Oh, come on! You really think she looks at you and sees model material? Wake up."

I felt like she'd punched me right in the chest. "You know what? Fuck you, Allie. I'm sick of your bullshit. You're so wrapped up in your own world that you never even stop to think about other people." I'd never fought with Allie before, not like this. It felt terrible. And wonderful.

She wiped at her eyes, smudging her eyeliner across her temples. "Is that what you think?"

"No, that's what I *know*. All you see is yourself. Your problems. Your feelings." Was that my voice echoing off the apartment walls?

"Is that right?" Allie said. Her voice was suddenly flat, emotionless. "Is that what I'm like?"

"Yes, it is." I was on a high. So this was what it felt like, to not hold anything back.

"What else?" she asked. She braced herself like she was asking me to hit her in the face. "Tell me. I want to know what you really think."

"You're spoiled," I said. "And selfish." I was on a roll now; nothing could stop me. "And you lie. All the time. You lied to me about Seabrook. You lied about going to Vegas. And you lied about not being able to make it to my show. And then you wonder why no one trusts you."

I waited for her to scream at me, to throw something across the room. I was ready.

But nothing happened. She just stood there. Something seemed to leave her body—a breath of air, the last bit of fight. She dropped the photo she was holding and walked past me without saying a word, her shoulder brushing against mine. As I stood in the bedroom, waiting for the argument to continue, I heard the front door close behind her.

CHAPTER 56

It takes a long while for my vision to return. I'm not sure how long exactly, but by the time I can see the desk in front of me again, the office has grown dim. It's early evening. The essay is still glowing on the computer screen. I lean forward and, with shaking hands, take the flash drive out of the computer and slide it into my pocket.

I need to give the flash drive to Ruiz. But more urgently, I need to get out of here. If Mom comes home and sees me like this, she'll know something is wrong. And I can't tell her yet, what I know. What Ruiz and I found at the cabin. What it says in the essay.

I need time to process the truth.

The Uber drops me off outside my apartment building, and I jog up the front steps, shivering in the cold. I take the elevator to the third floor, gripping the flash drive in my pocket. During the car ride over here, I'd texted Ruiz one sentence: I found the essay. I can explain more later. But not now. As soon as I tell Ruiz what's on the flash drive, it will become real. It will change everything. And I'm not quite ready for that.

When I reach my front door, I see the flyer taped beside the door, covering my doorbell camera. And I laugh at the part of me that once thought the camera was so important, that Allie had actually come to my apartment, that she was still alive. It doesn't matter now. Nothing matters now.

I twist my key in the lock, push the door open, and step inside. As I shut the door behind me, it takes me a moment to register that the lights are on. I hadn't left them on when I left this morning.

Turning, I see a figure standing near the bookcase.

"Shit!" I jerk backward, my shoulder blades slamming against the door. It's Matthew. He stands with his hands in his pockets, looking like he's just returned from a funeral. "Matthew. How did you . . ."

He holds up his hands in a *calm down* gesture. "I have a key. Don't you remember? You gave it to me."

Yes. When I first moved in, I'd locked myself out of the apartment. I gave a spare key to Matthew in case it happened again.

"What are you doing here?"

Matthew regards me solemnly. He's not going to pretend he doesn't know what's going on. "You've been to the cabin," he says.

My mouth is dry. "Yes." He looks so much like the Matthew I remember, the one who was so kind to me.

"Why?" He sounds sad, as if I've disappointed him somehow.

"I—"

"I wish you'd have come to me first, Natasha," he says. "Instead of Ruiz. We could've talked. I could've explained."

"Explained?" My voice rises. "Matthew, there's *blood* in there. In that kitchen."

"I know," he says. There are shadows under his eyes. "But it's not what you think. Please, just let me explain."

My phone is in my jacket pocket. If I reach for it, is there any way I could dial Ruiz without Matthew noticing?

"Please," he says, taking a step forward. "Sit down. It will make sense once I tell you."

I stare at his handsome face. These past four years, whenever we talked about the case, discussed the possibilities of where Allie might have gone—Matthew had known. He'd already known how that night had ended for her.

I see now why Matthew was always the one who talked to the cops, who managed the information the private investigator passed on. At the time, his actions had seemed noble, a way for him to shield Isabel from the stress of the case. But really, it was a way to maintain control. As the point person for the family, he would be the first to know about any new direction the investigation was taking.

"I could never hurt Allie," he says. "You know that. You know how much I love her."

He doesn't know I've read the essay. That I know who he really is.

He reaches a hand toward me but stops when he sees me flinch. "Please. Just hear me out," he says. "That's all I ask."

For a moment, it seems like it's actually possible: There's another explanation for what happened. I've gotten things wrong. Then I remember the flash drive in my pocket.

"Please," Matthew says.

Slowly, I step into the living room and sit down on the armchair, aware of the flash drive digging into my thigh. Allie went to such lengths to protect it, and now I've brought it right to Matthew.

He sits down on the sofa across from me, and I tamp down my panic, trying to form a plan. I need to let him think he has a chance of convincing me. Of winning me over. Because that's why he's here, isn't he? To get me on his side. And what will happen if he realizes he can't?

"I'm listening." I brush my left hand against my jacket pocket, feeling the outline of my phone.

Matthew leans forward and tentatively grasps my other hand. It's only through force of will that I manage not to yank it away.

"Natasha," he says. His skin is warm against mine. "I'm so sorry I lied to you. I lied to everyone. It's inexcusable, I know that. But I didn't kill Allie. That didn't happen. That could never happen."

He's so sincere. So convincing.

"That night, when Allie went to the cabin, I got an alert on my phone. I saw she was there. So I left the conference and drove down there." He lets go of my hand and presses his knuckles against his forehead. "You have to understand—at that point, Allie had caused so much trouble, been so reckless. I didn't know what she might be doing at the cabin, but I knew it couldn't be good."

I'm holding my breath. I have to remind myself to let it out.

"Anyway," he says. "When I got there, she'd turned the place inside out. I don't know what she was doing. Maybe looking for something to steal, to sell."

He knows exactly what she was looking for.

"And she'd been drinking," he adds.

I don't think that's true. But it's possible, isn't it? Allie cracking under the strain of everything. Opening a bottle of whiskey she'd found in his kitchen.

"We argued," Matthew says. "I told her she needed to get back into treatment. She called me a hypocrite—which, in retrospect, I was. I was telling her to get help, but I hadn't faced the facts about my own addiction." Suddenly, he looks very old. "I wish I had handled it differently, Natasha. But I didn't. The argument escalated. She hit me. She was out of control."

I sit very still. The heat clicks on in the apartment, and a hot stream of air billows out from the vent.

"When she came at me again, I pushed her away."

Matthew is wearing a blue button-down shirt. I find myself fixated on the ivory-colored buttons, the way they gleam in the light.

"She fell, and . . . she hit her head." His face twists, as if the memory hurts him. "It happened so fast . . . There was a lot of blood." For the first time, his voice wavers, and he has to take a moment before he goes on. "But she was okay, essentially. She was conscious. I got her to sit up. The cut wasn't serious, but it did need attention." He takes a deep breath. "I went to the bathroom to find some towels. I wanted to take her to a hospital, to get stitches. But first I needed to stop the bleeding."

Through his shirt, I can see his heart beating, the fabric shivering over his chest.

"But when I came out of the bathroom, she was gone. Then I heard a car start outside. By the time I got out there, she was driving away." His dark eyes are bottomless. "Natasha, when I last saw Allie, she was alive. Hurt, but very much alive."

I dig my fingernails into the palm of my hands. "Then why lie?" I ask. "Why didn't you tell anyone what had happened?"

He swallows. "It sounds so stupid now. Unbelievably stupid. But I didn't know that night would end up being . . . I didn't think anyone needed to know. I knew Allie. She was upset; she'd go somewhere for a while to work off her feelings, and then she'd come back." He looks exhausted. "Then time went on. The investigation began, and the longer I waited, the more impossible it became to speak up. How could I say, at that point, 'Oh, and I forgot to mention . . .'" He laughs. "How would that look? The blood in the cabin . . . They'd think the worst. I'd already lied about seeing her that night. Why would anyone believe my story after that?"

He must see the doubt in my face because he leans forward, saying, "That's why I threw myself into the investigation like I did. I did whatever was in my power to find her. To make things right. Tell me, Why would I do that, if I'd killed her?"

In my pocket, my phone vibrates—once, twice. That will be Ruiz, calling me.

"Natasha," he says, "you know me. You know I'm not capable of something like that. You have to help me talk to the detectives. They'll understand if you help me explain."

And there it is. The real reason he's here. He knows he's about to lose everything. His reputation, his freedom. His new family.

"You believe me, don't you?" he says. A tinge of desperation has crept into his voice.

The room is closing in. I hear shallow breathing and realize that it's mine. It's almost a relief when the blindness comes, when I can't see Matthew anymore.

"Natasha. Are you all right?"

My heart ricochets in my chest like I've run up ten flights of stairs. I lean forward, resting my head in my hands.

"Are you having an episode?" he asks. I can feel him moving closer, putting a concerned hand on my shoulder.

I close my eyes. All these years, I've relied so much on Matthew. He's been my ally. My friend.

"Shit," he says. "Where's your medication?"

"The bathroom," I mumble. Even as I say it, I remember: I've run out of pills.

"Okay. Don't move, all right?"

As soon as I hear his footsteps retreat down the hall, I fumble in my jacket pocket and pull out my phone. Ruiz. How can I get a message to him? The phone feels unfamiliar in my hands. It takes me forever to find the Home button, and once I've pressed it, I realize I'm not sure what to do next. I can't see what's on the screen. When I hear Matthew coming out of the bathroom, I shove the phone back into my pocket.

I hear noises in the kitchen, cupboards opening. Running water in the sink. Then Matthew's back in the living room, stirring the air in front of me. He pushes a cool glass into one of my hands and a small pill into the other.

"Here," he says. "Take this."

I clench the pill in my fist. It can't be an Inderal. I don't have any more of those.

"Please, Natasha. Take it. I hate seeing you like this."

"I need to . . ." I set the water glass on the floor and then stand up, pushing past him and stumbling into the hallway that leads to the bathroom.

"Where are you going?"

My hand slides along the wall, guiding my steps. "I just need a minute," I say. A minute out of his sight.

My hand touches the doorjamb, and I slip inside the bathroom, closing and locking the door behind me.

"Natasha?" Matthew says.

It sounds like he's still in the living room.

"I'm okay," I call out. "I just need to splash some water on my face."

I fumble for my phone, dropping the pill in the process. *Fuck. Fuck.* I have to focus. I have to get a call through to Ruiz. I try to remember the layout of the phone screen. If Ruiz was the last person to call me, I should be able to pull up the Recent Calls list and tap on his name. "Please, please," I mutter as I begin to press the screen in what I think are the right places. It takes a few tries, but finally, I hear a call go through.

Ruiz picks up on the first ring. "Natasha?"

I lean forward, pressing my forehead against the mirror.

"Hello?"

"Ruiz," I say softly. "Matthew's here."

"What? Where are you?"

There's a noise out in the hallway. Then I hear a knock on the bathroom door.

"Natasha?" Matthew says.

Fuck. I can't say anything else, not with Matthew standing right there.

"Natasha?" Ruiz says, his voice tinny through the phone speaker. "Are you there? Are you all right?"

"I'm fine, Matthew," I say, enunciating clearly. "I just need something from my bathroom cabinet." Will Ruiz understand what I'm saying? *I'm home, I'm here, come get me.*

"Let me help you," Matthew says.

The door handle turns and rattles.

My chest constricts. "I'm okay. Really." Matthew would never do anything to hurt me, I tell myself. He would never—

Ruiz's voice rises on the other end of the line. "I'm on my way. We're almost back to the city—"

"Are you on the phone?" Matthew says, his voice less gentle now.

Ruiz's voice is still coming from the phone, too loud. "Do you have the essay with you?" I press the phone against my chest to muffle the sound.

"Who are you talking to?" Matthew says.

The door handle rattles harder this time, and I jump. The phone slides out of my hand and lands with a smack on the floor. I get down on my hands and knees, sliding my hands along the tile, searching for it. I need Ruiz to stop talking. I need to end the call.

"Natasha," Matthew says. "I don't know what you've seen. What you've read. But you've got the wrong idea."

Finally, I locate the phone and push more buttons, finally managing to silence Ruiz's voice.

"Whatever Allie's said about me," Matthew says, "it's not true." There's a long silence. "You have to know it's not true." He's only a few feet away. The door is the only thing standing between us.

I scramble backward and sit with my back pressed against the cold tub.

"They're coming here," I say. "The police. They'll be here soon."

Suddenly, there's a bang. Matthew has thrown his full body weight against the door. A small sound escapes my mouth.

The essay. I have to find a place to hide it before he breaks down the door. As I dig in my pocket, Matthew slams against the door again, and this time I hear a crunching noise. The lock is about to give way.

Quickly, I pull the flash drive out of my pocket and lean over the side of the tub, feeling for the drain at the bottom. After prying off the metal cover, I shove the flash drive down into the drain, praying it falls down far enough that it can't be seen.

There's a thud as Matthew hits the door again, and this time I hear a metallic rattle against the floor, like a screw has come loose from the door.

Shakily, I back myself into the far corner of the bathroom. I can't seem to drag enough oxygen into my lungs. In some dark corner of my brain, I remember the protocol Dr. Rajmani taught me. Breathe for three counts in, three counts out. Then four counts in, four counts out.

But I can't. I can't. The next bang brings with it a splintering sound, and that's when my throat closes up completely.

CHAPTER 57

When I regain consciousness, I know immediately that I'm not in the bathroom anymore. I've been propped in a sitting position against something soft but solid, my knuckles resting on what feels like carpet. I'm sitting against the side of the couch, I think. I'm in the living room.

I still can't see anything.

From the dining area, I hear the sound of soft clattering. A zipper unzipping. The jingle of car keys. Matthew's searching through my bag.

I shift, feeling something off kilter around my middle. I move my hands, investigating. My shirt is twisted to one side, and the pockets of my jeans have been turned inside out. Matthew's searched me then, too, for the essay.

I hear him swear softly; then there's a pause in his movements near the dining table.

"Natasha?"

Suddenly, I feel the warmth of him in front of me, the press of his hands on my shoulders. "Natasha, you need to tell me where the essay is." His fingers grip too tightly, pinching my skin.

My whole body tenses. On the phone, Ruiz said, *We're almost back to the city.* But that could mean he's ten minutes away, or thirty. I lick my lips.

"You're not well, Natasha," Matthew is saying. "I want to get you to a doctor. But first, I need to know where that essay is."

I turn my face to the side. "Matthew—" What I need to do is buy myself time. Time for Ruiz to get here. Time to stop Matthew from searching the bathroom and finding the flash drive in the drain.

"If the cops get ahold of it," Matthew says, "they won't see it for what it is. They don't know what Allie was like. The trouble she loved to cause. That essay was like a bomb she'd rigged, to set off when it would benefit her the most." His breath hits my cheek. "She was lying, Natasha. You know that, don't you? You know what she was like."

I fight off a wave of nausea and force myself to nod. "I know." I need him to think I'm still on his side.

"Good. Good." He shifts in front of me. "Where did you put it, Natasha? We don't have much time."

I swallow. There isn't enough space to think. All I can think is that I want Matthew out of the apartment, before he searches further, before he thinks to turn the bathroom inside out. "My car," I say, improvising. He doesn't know my car is stranded on the side of the road in Crestline.

"Does anyone else know it's there?" he asks.

I shake my head.

"Where's your car?" His voice is brisk now. Less panicked.

"In the parking garage." If I can get him out of the apartment for a few minutes, maybe I'll have time to come up with a better plan. Maybe there will be time enough for my vision to return. For me to get out of here.

But Matthew is standing up and pulling me to my feet. He guides me forward, toward what I think is the front door; then I hear a scrape as he grabs something from the kitchen table. My car keys.

"Show me."

My feet drag against the carpet. In my head, I try to map the geography of the living room, but with nothing but Matthew's hand on my arm to ground me, I feel like I'm balanced on a tightrope, empty space on all sides.

"I can't. Leave me here, Matthew. I can't walk when I'm like this." The desperation in my voice is real. If I leave the apartment, Ruiz won't know where to find me when he arrives. If he arrives.

But Matthew's arm is like an iron rod against my back. I hear the doorknob turn. "No, I think it's best that you and I stay together for now." And from the grim humor in his voice, I know he hasn't bought my compliant act. He knows I'm the enemy now.

I stumble as Matthew prods me toward the elevator, his steps purposeful and far too fast. As we walk, I try to track where we are in the hallway. We're passing Abby's apartment; we're going by Mrs. Singh's doormat, which catches at the edge of my shoe. That means the elevator doors are straight ahead. Before Matthew can press the button, though, something seems to spook him. He swears and abruptly changes direction, pushing through the steel door that leads to the staircase. As the door closes behind us, a rush of cold air envelops me, and I can smell the iron railings in the stairwell, the aluminum strips at the edge of each concrete stair.

Beyond the stairwell door, the elevator makes a cheerful ding—it's stopping on my floor. Someone is arriving. Quickly, I twist away from Matthew. But as I do, my foot slides off the top stair, and I slip. My hip slams hard against the concrete step, and I cry out, but Matthew catches hold of my arms and drags me back up to the landing before I can fall farther. The pain in my hip is dazzling, and I can see its colors in my mind: scarlet, yellow, magenta.

Matthew breathes hard, his chest rising and falling against my back as he clamps one hand over my mouth. Out in the hallway, female voices chatter, loud at first and then fainter as they move down the hallway.

"That was stupid, wasn't it?" Matthew says, his voice conversational despite his uneven breathing. He hasn't pulled me back entirely to safety. Instead, he lets me balance unsteadily on the edge of the landing, my heels barely gaining purchase. His breath fills my ear. "You almost fell. Imagine if you fell again. My reflexes might not be so good the second time around."

If he lets go of me, I'll fall hard and heavy, down a long line of concrete steps. I feel his grip tighten around my shoulders and his weight shift slightly forward.

I let out a muffled cry and clutch at his shirt.

He hesitates. Then, after a long moment, he takes his hand away from my mouth and walks me back from the edge. "Well, then. No more shenanigans. Let's do this quickly. And quietly."

Carefully, he begins walking me down the stairs, giving me just enough time to feel out each step before I put my weight on it. I can smell his cologne, and his sweat, sour underneath the expensive scent.

In my mind's eye, I see Matthew hunched over his dining room table as he talked to the private investigator on the phone. Matthew at his wedding, beckoning me to come join the family photo. Matthew, bent over Allie's body in the cabin, dragging her body out on the porch, the same way he'd dragged me out of the apartment bathroom.

The stairs seem to take forever, but it's time I need. To think. Because, once we reach the parking lot, it won't take Matthew long to realize my car's not there. And then I'll have a bigger problem on my hands. If I can't deliver the essay to him, I'll be of no value at all. I'll just be a liability.

Like Allie.

Listening to our footsteps against the concrete stairs, I try to picture the bottom of the stairwell: a dim square barely large enough for two people to stand side by side. And I remember, suddenly, how in my high school photography class, the teacher had insisted we learn how to develop our film in an airless closet, a towel shoved against the bottom of the door to block out the light. In the blackness, you had to uncap a roll of film and carefully feed the strip of negatives onto a reel. The only way you could manage it was by carefully memorizing the position of the objects before you switched off the lights, by feeling for the things you couldn't see.

Matthew guides me down the last step, and from the smell of car exhaust in the air, I know we've reached the parking garage. I'm not ready. I can't recall the layout of the garage in my head. I've never had a reason to pay attention to it.

Matthew opens the door and pushes me through ahead of him. To my surprise, my brain instantly fills in an image of the space, details I didn't realize I'd noticed. We're standing at the edge of a concrete, windowless rectangle, lined with cars along the perimeter and in the center. To my right, I know, is Abby's Toyota Prius, the bumper held on with duct tape. Straight ahead is Mrs. Singh's boxy BMW. Somewhere along the far wall is an orange SUV with a surf rack.

"Where are you parked?" Matthew asks roughly. He's aware of the seconds ticking by, of how small his window of time is.

"Give me a second." I turn my head from side to side. "I need to get my bearings." But what I really need to do is remember where the light switch is. It's somewhere on the wall behind us—but how far to the left, and how many steps will it take me to get there? If I can manage to switch off the lights, I can level the playing field between Matthew and me.

I hear a clicking sound, repeated two, three times. And I realize Matthew is pressing on my key fob, waiting to hear the beep of my car unlocking.

"Natasha," he says, fury gathering his voice. "Where the hell is your car?"

Suddenly, I collapse against him, startling him enough that he loosens his grip on my arm. Then I twist and lunge for the wall, running my hands along the rough concrete until I find the metal box I'm looking for and slam the switch down.

The electric hum from the ceiling abruptly stops, and Matthew lets out a yelp. The lights are off.

Quickly, I squat low against the wall. I sense Matthew coming for me even before I hear the scrape of his feet against the floor. There's a flurry as his hands brush against my head, and I panic, running low and fast with my hand against the wall, scurrying between the wall and the line of bumper blocks on the left side of the garage. My shoes are making too much noise on the concrete, so I pause long enough to yank them off. Then I pad farther along the garage floor in my socks.

"Damn it," Matthew says. I can hear him fumbling along the wall for the light switch. It won't be long before he finds it. And then what? I hunker down between two cars, my heartbeat thumping so hard that I'm afraid Matthew will be able to hear it. I'm about to make a run across the aisle, headed for the street entrance, when there's a snapping sound, and a clicking, hissing sound spreads across the ceiling. Matthew has found the switch. The lights are back on.

"Natasha," he calls out. "You don't have anywhere to go. You might as well come out." I hear his footsteps moving slowly along the line of cars.

I crouch lower. Slowly, I'm beginning to make out shapes again. The looming shadow of the SUV on my right, the gap of light streaming past its bumper and almost touching my knees. Matthew's footsteps grow closer. I'd like to crawl underneath the SUV, but it's too low to the ground; I can't squeeze my body underneath.

Then I see Matthew's shadow cross the shaft of light that nudges up against my knees. He's facing away from me, bending down to peer between the cars in the opposite row. The cars there are parked at a slight incline, their back ends lower than their fronts. Matthew seems particularly interested in an old Camaro. He bends over to inspect the wheel. There's a scraping noise. When he straightens, I see something rectangular in his hands. A brick, which the Camaro's owner has put behind the back wheel to prevent the car from sliding downhill.

I creep backward, farther away from the light.

This is Matthew. Matthew, who I've known for years. But there are two Matthews now, the Matthew from my life and the Matthew from Allie's. And it's Allie's Matthew who's here with me now.

I slide back behind the SUV, searching for a safer hiding place, but as I do, my foot hits a piece of loose plastic, which skitters across the floor.

Matthew turns, his shoes scraping against the concrete. "Natasha?" he says softly. "Just come out, okay? Let's talk this through. There's no reason for it to be like this." He is good at sounding like a calm, rational person, like the Matthew who stood up at the press conference pleading for people to come forward with information about Allie's disappearance.

His footsteps move closer to the SUV.

The details of the garage are coalescing. Now I can see the dent in the SUV's back bumper, the scratch in the paint on the yellow convertible. I'm trapped here, Matthew standing between me and the exits. And even if I were able to make it to the street entrance, I realize, I can't open the gate without the clicker that's in my car, the car that isn't here. Matthew steps into the gap between the SUV and the car next to it.

Panic bubbles up in my chest, along with something else. Rage. Allie's, and my own. In the end, Matthew will get what he wants from both of us—our silence.

The pressure builds up in the back of my throat. And suddenly, I scream. I lean back against the garage wall, kicking the bumper of the SUV so hard that the whole vehicle sways forward. The car alarm bursts into life, the noise deafening as it echoes against the walls. Matthew flinches, raising a hand to his ear, and I take advantage of the moment, ducking down and running to the other side of the SUV. As I hear him start to move, I run to the opposite row of cars, then squat low behind a green Subaru.

Matthew steps out from behind the SUV. From my position, I can hear his footsteps moving in my direction. Quickly, I jam my body against the Subaru, bruising my shoulder but managing to set off its alarm too. It's only a matter of time before Matthew catches up with me—there's only so far I can run in this space—but that doesn't seem to matter anymore. I scramble through the parking garage, setting off alarms every few cars.

The garage has become an opera, a symphony, the concrete walls echoing with the sound of emergency. It feels good to cause this chaos—I'm Allie in one of her rages, powerful, out of control. I slip between two sedans and, breathing heavily, watch and listen for Matthew. He's disoriented by the noise, and from my position, I can see his feet moving away from me. If I'm fast enough, there's a chance I can make it to the stairwell doorway.

When I think I have an opening, I dart out from between the cars. But Matthew is closer than I'd anticipated, and he grabs me by the shirt, yanking me to the ground. My palms hit the rough concrete, and my knees register a white-hot feeling that is not yet pain. When I twist around, Matthew is impossibly tall above me, clutching the brick in his hand.

Don't let him do it, Allie murmurs in my ear. *Don't you fucking let him win.*

For a sliver of a second, Matthew hesitates, and that's enough time for me to kick viciously at his kneecap. He stumbles and falls, his head knocking against the back of a pickup truck. Then he's down on the ground, a trickle of blood leaking from his hairline.

Behind me, the door to the stairwell clicks open, and someone is yelling over the racket of car alarms, "What the hell is going on here?"

I scramble to my feet, grabbing for the brick that has fallen out of Matthew's hand. Matthew's hurt, but he's not hurt enough. He'll never be hurt enough.

"Natasha!" someone shouts as I raise the brick over my head. Then there's the sound of running, and then someone clamps their arms around me and drags me away.

CHAPTER 58

The street outside the apartment complex flickers with flashing red and blue lights. Ruiz sits by my side on the back bumper of an ambulance as the EMT examines me, shining a small flashlight into my eyes.

The EMT clicks off the light and slides it back into his breast pocket. "She looks all right, apart from a few scrapes and bruises. But she should come down to the hospital for a once-over, just to be on the safe side."

"Okay," Ruiz says, but I'm shaking my head.

"Matthew . . ."

Ruiz's thumb strokes my arm. "He's in custody. What you need now is to rest."

Someone walks out of the entrance doors—a police officer, murmuring into a walkie-talkie.

"The essay," I say, trying to stand up, but Ruiz pulls me back down.

"Just sit for a minute."

"It's in the bathtub drain. I put it there when Matthew . . ."

"It's okay," Ruiz says. "We have officers in your apartment right now. I'll tell them where to look." He goes over to talk to the police officer, who relays the information on her walkie-talkie. Then there's a brief exchange between Ruiz and the officer, their heads lowered as they talk.

The EMT wraps an emergency blanket around my shoulders. The apartment building, which I have seen a thousand times before, looks like a foreign landscape tonight. My ears are still ringing from the clamor of the alarms.

When Ruiz returns, his face is expansive with relief. "They've got it. That was good thinking, hiding it there."

A shudder runs through me. It's safe. The essay is safe.

Ruiz squeezes my hand. "You read what she wrote?"

I nod, watching the ambulance lights paint the side of the building in bright colors.

"What does it say?" he asks.

That's when I start to cry, sobs scraping against the back of my throat, and as hard as I try, I can't seem to make myself stop.

CHAPTER 59

At Gina's, the television mounted on the wall blares the local news. Ruiz and I sit with cups of cooling coffee, today's newspaper spread out between us, and watch the coverage in silence.

They're playing clips from the last week: a helicopter view of Matthew's cabin, the property crawling with police, the road beyond the driveway crammed with news vans.

A newscaster stands on the road outside the blocked entrance to the Crestline property, the wind blowing her hair around her face. "What we're seeing here, Gary, is the continuing search of director Matthew Andersen's vacation home in Crestline. Last month, almost four years to the day when Allie Andersen went missing, police recovered evidence from the property that may implicate Mr. Andersen in his niece's death. Now, police are conducting a thorough search of these woods, hoping to locate Ms. Andersen's body. So far, they have not been successful."

My jaw tightens.

On the TV, they're showing old photos of Matthew and Allie. Allie when she was young, Matthew carrying her on his shoulders. Matthew and Allie sitting on the steps of the cabin in Crestline, smiling happily at the camera.

"Hey, Diane," Ruiz says. "Could you turn this off? It's been the same thing on a loop for the past half hour."

"Sure, hon." Diane tops up our coffees and then walks to the cashier's station, where she picks up a remote control and switches off the TV.

"Hey! I was watching that," a man protests, but Diane ignores him.

"How're you holding up?" Ruiz asks. He looks rumpled, exhausted. The investigation has taken a lot out of him, and I know it hasn't been easy for him to carve out this time to meet with me.

"Fine, I guess."

"The press bothering you?"

I laugh. My phone has been ringing constantly. My email inbox is clogged with requests for interviews. "It got too intense at my apartment, so I'm staying at my mom's for a while. But they've caught on to that; now they're outside her place too."

"I'm sorry."

"It's not your fault." The diner is filled with sunlight. The cold front has passed, and people are wearing T-shirts again. "They'll be able to convict Matthew, won't they, even without her body? I mean, the blood, the DNA—you can prove that it's Allie's. Surely that's enough."

Ruiz frowns. He doesn't respond for a moment. "It's enough, in that it places her at the cabin. And Matthew admits to going to see her there, to the altercation in the kitchen. But you've heard his story. His version of what happened. Without her body, it could be difficult to get a conviction. His lawyers will work hard to get the essay suppressed as evidence. They'll question whether Allie really wrote it. They'll say we can't prove it's genuine."

A jolt runs through me. We need the essay to prove Matthew's motive. "You can't be serious."

He grimaces. "I just want you to know what we might be up against. When we interviewed Isabel, she claimed you were the source of the essay. Said the stress of the investigation had gotten to you and that you fabricated the whole thing."

I slump back in the booth. Why does it surprise me, even now, what Isabel is capable of? She's publicly condemned Matthew for keeping his altercation with Allie that night a secret. But she stands by his story: he didn't kill Allie. Not for the first time, I wonder why Isabel's loyalties fall the way they do. Is the bond between Isabel and Matthew that strong? Or has she simply calculated the impact on her reputation if she admits what Allie has written in her essay is true?

"But we can prove it, can't we, that Allie wrote it?"

He swirls the dregs of coffee in his cup, before taking a sip, wincing at the bitterness. "The creation date of a Word document, it seems, can be fabricated pretty easily. And no one was with you when you discovered the flash drive. It's going to be a challenge authenticating it. They may claim you had her flash drive all along." He leans forward, resting his arms on the table. "Look, Matthew's going to spend time in prison; there's no question about that. We'll get him on obstruction of justice, assault . . ."

"That's not enough!"

His face is drawn. "I know. And I'm sorry." He does know. He knows exactly what this is like. "But you may want to prepare yourself for the fact that Matthew may not be convicted for Allie's murder."

"So he's going to get away with it." After all this.

"We're going to do our best," Ruiz says. But he doesn't sound hopeful. The search for the body will be wrapping up soon. And without the essay as evidence, Matthew appears to have no motive; his story about what happened at the cabin might ring true to a jury.

While Diane's busy with a table in the back, a different waitress turns the television back on, and sound fills the diner again. On the screen, reporters crowd around Isabel as she leaves the police station. Her beautiful face looks haggard. Her bodyguard pushes a path to her car, and she ducks the microphones being shoved in her face and slides into the back seat of an SUV. After that, tinted windows protect her from view.

"What about Macnamara?" I say suddenly. "Surely he can verify that Allie wrote the essay?"

"He's lawyered up," Ruiz says. "Won't talk to us." The police have looked into Macnamara's finances, trying to determine his source of income for the past four years. On the surface, his income looks legit, deposits from some nonprofit he claims to have been doing contract consulting for. But Ruiz suspects the nonprofit's just a shell company, and that the payments funneled through it are coming from Isabel.

I feel a burning sensation in my chest. "He doesn't want to admit she paid him off. To keep quiet."

Ruiz nods.

I grip the edge of the table. None of these people will pay for what they did. Their money and their lawyers will protect them.

"It's a shitty situation," Ruiz says. "We might make more headway if we could locate Allie's therapist. But Allie never mentioned a name to anyone. So unless the therapist decides to step forward voluntarily, we're stuck on that front as well."

A long minute goes by, and I discover that I've lost feeling in my fingers. I let go of the edge of the table. Something has been bothering me the past few days, but I'm hesitant to voice the thought. "Ruiz, what if there isn't a body to find in the woods?"

His forehead wrinkles. "You mean if the body was moved?"

"I mean, if there's no body at all," I say. "If Matthew's telling the truth."

He raises his eyebrows. "Natasha. You can't possibly believe him."

"I don't know," I say, my voice strained. "It's just—I don't get why he would've pushed so hard for the investigation to keep going all those years, if the whole time he knew she was dead."

"It was a cover," Ruiz says. "He got to look like the hero."

"But that would be a hell of a gamble, wouldn't it? The longer people looked for Allie, the greater the chance he'd be found out. It doesn't make sense."

Ruiz shakes his head. "Maybe we can't understand how Matthew's mind works."

But I can't stop picking at the topic. "Well, then, what about the flash drive? Who left that on my doorstep? If not Allie, who?" I'm jittery from all the coffee I've drunk.

Ruiz sighs. "I don't know."

We've discussed this before. Who else would know where Allie had hidden the flash drive? Not Macnamara. Not Greg.

"But here's my question," Ruiz says. "If Allie's alive, if she's the one who left the flash drive for you, theoretically she could've done that at any time. Why wait four years to do it?"

I sigh. As always, this point is where my hopes stall out. "I don't know." Maybe Allie told someone else about the flash drive, someone who, years later, for reasons unknown, decided to make sure I found it.

We sit for a while, not saying anything. Finally, Ruiz checks his phone and says, "Look, I hate to do this, but I have to get back."

"Okay," I say. Tightness gathers in the back of my throat. There's something I've promised myself I'll do today, something I've been avoiding for the past hour. As he gathers up his jacket, I say, "Ruiz. Before you go. There's something I have to tell you."

"Yeah?"

"The night Allie left . . ."

He slows his movements, then rests his jacket across his lap.

"There's something I never told you."

CHAPTER 60

January 2013

After our argument, after Allie walked out of the apartment, I stood alone in my bedroom, seething. She couldn't just walk out like that. Not in the middle of a fight, not when I still had things to say. I looked at the eight-by-ten photo she'd dropped on the floor. There was a footprint across my face the size and shape of Allie's boot.

I walked into the kitchen, furious, still having the argument with her in my head. On the kitchen island, Allie's laptop sat open. The brand-new rose-gold laptop—she'd left it right next to an open bottle of water. So careless. Anyone could knock it over, and her computer would be ruined. And she probably wouldn't even care. She'd just go buy a new one.

I stopped my pacing and turned toward the laptop. I thought about the shitty summer job I'd worked, filing papers in some university basement, so I could afford my secondhand laptop—a black, ugly thing that Allie never failed to make fun of.

And I thought how easy Allie had it, how, all her life, she'd been given permission to fuck up and to know that it would never matter, not really. A hard little knot was forming behind my rib cage, pressing up against my heart. It was a pressure that had been solidifying ever since she'd told me about hooking up with Macnamara. Or maybe before that, long before that, in high school, when I'd read her secret notebook and realized: There was nothing Allie couldn't take from me if she decided she wanted to.

Gently, I reached out my hand and nudged the water bottle until it wobbled and then tilted. It was almost accidental, the way it happened, the bottle falling straight across the keyboard. And as the water burbled over the keys, seeping through the cracks, I thought of my photo on my bedroom floor, of Allie's careless footprint across my face.

The computer made a low buzzing sound, and then the screen went dark. For a moment, I felt the sweet satisfaction of destruction.

Then I heard a sound near the front door and spun around. Allie stood just inside the apartment entryway, watching me with a strange expression. When had she come back to the apartment? And why?

"Why did you do that?" she asked, her face pale. Her hands clutched at her shoulder bag as if she was afraid someone might tear it away from her.

The sweet feeling vanished, replaced by a flood of shame. "It was an accident," I said quickly. A stupid thing to say—it was obvious she'd seen what I'd done. But as soon as the words had left my mouth, they felt true. I was not the kind of person to do something destructive. I'd just been reaching across the counter, and the bottle had fallen.

"I didn't mean to," I said. "I'm sorry. It was an accident." I knew I was babbling.

Allie didn't say anything. She just looked at me for a long moment, as if she was finally seeing me with clear eyes. Gentle, quiet Natasha. The person she never had to worry about. The person that didn't really exist.

Suddenly, she moved forward, walked past me, and snatched her purse off the counter, her hair brushing my shoulder.

"Als . . . ," I started.

But she didn't look at me. She just turned and walked out of the apartment, and the door clicked softly shut behind her.

CHAPTER 61

I focus on the diner window, on the people walking on the sidewalk outside, so I don't have to meet Ruiz's eyes. "This is going to sound crazy," I say to him. "But sometimes I was sure it hadn't really happened that way." In my mind, I could see all the other ways it could've happened. Allie knocking the bottle over herself. Someone jostling the kitchen island and the bottle falling on its own. Those scenes seemed more real, somehow, than what actually happened.

But there were times, in the last few years, when the memory, what I really did, came back to me in a rush. And in those moments, I hated myself so powerfully that it felt like I'd fallen into a heaving darkness that wouldn't let go.

"I hoped it wouldn't make a difference," I said. "What I did to the laptop. But I know now it did. If you'd had it, you might have found the essay; you could've figured out what happened sooner." A sick feeling crawls up through my rib cage and gets a stranglehold on my throat. "It's my fault. What happened. If Allie hadn't come back to the apartment and seen me . . . do what I did, she might have stayed."

There's a long silence, and then Ruiz slides into the booth next to me. "No," he says quietly. "No, what happened to her is not your fault."

I turn to him. "It is." I remember Allie's face right before she walked out the door. Pale and tired. Defeated.

"Think about it," he says quietly. "By the time you had that argument, Allie had already hidden the flash drive. She'd taken Greg's money, his car. She was already planning to run away."

"But she might not have gone through with it . . ." If she'd known that she could trust me. If she'd known I was on her side.

He clasps my hand in his own. "What happened to Allie wasn't your fault. There's only one person who bears the responsibility for that."

I wipe at my eyes. "But if you'd had the laptop . . . ," I say. "Back then. It would've made a difference, wouldn't it?"

He doesn't have a response for that. We both know that it would have. There's nothing he can say to lift that weight from me. So he simply squeezes my hand and doesn't let go.

After Ruiz leaves, I find myself poring over the newspaper on the table. Matthew is front-page news again, but this time it's below the fold. They've used two different photos of him, a candid shot at some Hollywood party and a picture from his wedding. In the wedding photo, he looks clean cut and elegant. He has one arm around Chloe's waist, and another wrapped around Sara's shoulders.

It's hard to believe that this photograph was taken just two months ago. That, in some of the other photos in this series, I'm pictured standing beside him, smiling at the camera. It's hard to look at any picture of Matthew without getting a flash of the night in the parking garage.

But today, there's something else that's bothering me about seeing his face. Something I can't quite put my finger on. I look at the photograph, at Chloe smiling dreamily, her face tilted toward Matthew. Then I study little Sara, with her long hair and big dark eyes. It's only now that it occurs to me how similar she looks to a young Allie.

Sara, I think. I lean forward, feeling the room sway around me.

Matthew's relationship with Chloe—it always seemed so romantic; his relationship with Sara, so sweet. I'd never thought . . .

He has another Allie now, another child who worships him.

I examine the photo caption. MATTHEW ANDERSEN, CHLOE NAVARRO, AND NAVARRO'S DAUGHTER, SARA, AT WAYFARER'S CHAPEL. The wedding took place on December 14. Less than a month before the flash drive appeared in my jacket pocket.

The din of the coffee shop continues around me.

Ruiz asked, *Why?* Why would Allie leave the flash drive for me now, after all this time?

I fumble with my phone, searching online for Matthew's wedding photos, for the date the pictures came out in *People*. When I find the article, I zoom in on the date: December 24. A week after that, the flash drive appeared on my doorstep.

I stand up quickly, knocking my knee against the table. Allie's alive. She came back. After all this time, she came back, to give me the flash drive. Not for herself.

For Sara.

CHAPTER 62

In the weeks that follow, Ruiz and I talk almost daily. I show him the pictures of Sara. I share the latest article in *People*, the interview with Isabel where she paints Allie as mentally unstable. But it isn't until two weeks later, when he learns Chloe has been visiting Matthew regularly in prison, sometimes bringing Sara with her, that he meets me at Gina's and gives me what I've been asking for.

After our meeting, I drive back to Mom's house, where I retreat into my bedroom. There, I open up my laptop and scroll through my deleted emails. I've received copious messages from newspapers and magazines and bloggers and commenters on the forums. But I'm looking for one particular name: Neil Agarwal at the *LA Times*. His email sounded different from the rest: serious, measured, compassionate. He wants to write about who Allie was, beyond the headlines and the tabloid photos. When I find his email, I reread his message, then click through the links he's included, examples of other profiles he's written.

I sit for a moment, staring at the screen. Allie pointed me toward her essay, hoping I'd believe her, hoping I'd do the right thing. But she hadn't been totally sure of me; she hadn't been certain that I was on her side. After all, in those wedding photos, I'm standing right next to Matthew. One of the family. The flash drive—was it a kind of test?

Well, I'd done what she wanted. I found the essay. I gave it to the cops. But that wasn't enough. The essay will never come out in court. And Chloe—it seems she believes Matthew's version of events. If the case goes his way and he gets out of prison, she may welcome him back to their house. To their family.

I know what needs to happen now, but it takes me a while to work up the nerve. If I do this, Matthew and Isabel will come after me with everything they've got. What little privacy I have left will be stripped away. For the foreseeable future, I'll be in the media's crosshairs.

I reread Neil's email one last time, then hit the Reply button. Then I take the plain gray flash drive Ruiz gave me and insert it into my computer. Clicking on the one file the drive contains, I drag and drop it into the message.

The room is very quiet. I rest my hands on the keyboard, waiting for Allie's voice to direct me. But in these past few weeks, she's stopped speaking to me. For the first time in a long time, I only hear my own voice in my head.

Slowly, I begin to type: "Dear Neil." Those first two words are the hardest to get out. "My sister . . . ," I write. And after that, the words just flow.

CHAPTER 63

In mid-March, on a Friday morning, I drive down to El Matador Beach. It's almost an hour's drive from Reseda, but I like to come here with my camera right after dawn. I find it soothing to look through a viewfinder again, to focus on the composition, the structure of what I'm seeing.

Ever since Allie's essay was published, this has become one of my few moments of peace in the day. As expected, Matthew and Isabel have gone on the attack, threatening to sue me for defamation. And Allie's allegations have become fodder for every talk show in the nation. My name gets mentioned a lot, as does my credibility, or lack thereof. This is what it's like to be famous, I'm discovering. This is what it's like to be disbelieved.

As I sit in the sand, I lift the camera to my face and capture the rock formations as the morning light hits them. This place is restful for me. A refuge. When I'm out here, I can find a point of stillness among the chaos. The people who needed to hear Allie's words have heard them. Chloe and Sara have moved out of Matthew's house in Beverly Hills. The commenters on the forums have created a new thread on Matthew and are digging deep into his past. And Allie—wherever she is, I hope she's seen her words out there, at last.

On the beach, the waves surge up onto the sand, making a soothing hiss. It's strange: although my life has never been more uncertain, I feel more at peace now than I have in a long, long time. I haven't had any more episodes since the night I found the flash drive. This past month, I've been able, for the first time in years, to sleep through the night.

When the tide starts to creep up to my feet, I stand and walk up the rusting metal staircase back to the parking lot. I know I can't live in this limbo time forever. Last week, I dropped out of Loyola Marymount, and I don't know what I'm going to do next. At some point, I'll have to come up with a plan. But for now, all I aim to do is get through each day.

I drive home through the hills, watching hawks wheel over the canyons. When I return to Mom's house, I enter through the front door and pick up the mail scattered under the door drop. I've been getting my mail forwarded from my apartment for the past few weeks, while I try to decide whether I'm going to hold on to it or move in with Mom again. Idly, I sort through the pile of envelopes as I head toward my bedroom. Magazines, junk mail, ads. As I step into my room, about to trash it all, a postcard slides out from behind an envelope and lands at my feet. I bend down to pick it up. It's a small glossy card, showing a remote stretch of beach in some tropical location.

Frowning, I turn it over. This better not be another piece of hate mail, one of Isabel's superfans threatening me again. But there's nothing on the back. Just my address, handwritten. The small print on the bottom of the card tells me this is a stretch of coastline in Oaxaca near Santa Alma del Mar. As I examine the address again, my body goes very still. I know that handwriting. That spiky print, the assured downstrokes. Allie.

Flipping the postcard over, I look more closely at the image: a curving line of water, a flaming sunset. And big gold letters imprinted across the top: WISH YOU WERE HERE.

CHAPTER 64

Santa Alma del Mar is located near the tail end of Mexico's west coast, remote enough that few tourists make it down this far. Last week, I booked a plane ticket to Acapulco and reserved a rental car for the drive down to the small town. I didn't tell anyone where I was going. Not my mother, not Ruiz. They think I'm headed to an Airbnb in Palm Springs, that I'm taking a few days away to reassess my life.

By the time I arrive in Santa Alma del Mar, I'm hungry and road weary. I drain the last of my water bottle before stepping out of the car and surveying my surroundings. So much ocean and so much sky. Seabirds cry out overhead, and the salt air stings my eyes.

I imagine Allie arriving here, four years ago. Seeing the little houses with their shutters painted in bright colors. The dirt road that leads, in one direction, to a small town center, and, in the other direction, to the ocean. As I stand by my car, a little kid wobbles past me on a bike, a fishing rod balanced underneath one arm. A skinny dog trots behind him, its tongue hanging out.

For a moment, the mere fact of being here overwhelms me, and I have to sit down on the bumper of the rental car. This is where Allie has found safety. Leaving this place and coming back to LA in January would have been a great risk for her. She would've had to figure out a way to get across the border without being recognized. But she'd managed it somehow. She'd found a way.

The flash drive left in my jacket pocket, that had been her sign. Perhaps she'd thought about putting it through my mail slot first, then decided the coat was a clearer message. *I'm here. I'm alive.*

I sit in the sun for a while, letting it warm my face, my shoulders. A man walks past on his way to the town center, then pauses when he notices me. I'm a stranger, and I get the feeling that strangers aren't common here.

"A dónde va?" he asks. His voice is gravelly but friendly. He wears loose trousers and a button-down shirt with threadbare seams at the shoulders.

I stand up, trying to revive enough high school Spanish to tell him why I'm here. *"Estoy buscando a alguien."* I reach into my bag for the photos I've brought with me. Then I pass them to him. *"Esta mujer."*

He frowns, holding the edges of the photos with fingers that are rough and scarred. The first photo is the one of Allie standing outside the theater department smoking a cigarette. He examines it and then shakes his head, frowning. *"Lo siento."* Then he flips to the next one, a snapshot of Allie and me on the beach. In it, her head is tilted back and she's laughing. The man's face clears. *"Ah, sí. Sí!"*

"Sí? La reconoces?"

"Sí," he says. *"Es Mía."*

The name sends a shiver through me. She's here. She's really here.

"Mia?"

"Sí, Mia." Then he starts talking so fast that I can't follow his Spanish anymore. It's clear, though, that he's pleased to talk about Mia. I can make out a few words here and there. *Playa. Ropa.*

I shake my head. *"Lo siento. Solo sé un poco . . ."*

He points out to his shirt, then makes the motion of sewing. *"Sí?"*

Mia mends clothes? Makes clothes?

He starts talking again, another long string of words. Again, there's that word: *playa*. Beach. He points down the road in the direction of the ocean, smiling.

"Thank you." My heart is beating hard against my ribs. *"Gracias. Muchas gracias."*

I follow the path that winds through the trees down to a beach that feels like a well-kept secret. Waves lap over large, smooth rocks the size and shape of sea turtles. Two women stand with their feet in the water, chatting as a group of children play in the sand nearby. At first my eye is drawn to the dark-haired woman, the one with her hair in a long braid down her back. But she's too short to be Allie, and when she turns, I see a round face and crooked teeth. I feel a swift shock of disappointment. I've gotten it wrong; the man on the road had it wrong. Allie isn't here.

The other woman has short peroxide-blonde hair and wears cutoff shorts and a faded T-shirt. I don't recognize her, but when she shifts her feet in the water, I realize there's something familiar about her stance. Those are Allie's long limbs, her slender neck.

I open my mouth, but before I can call out, a child breaks away from the group playing in the sand and runs toward Allie, flinging herself at her legs. Without hesitation, Allie scoops her up in her arms, and the girl buries her face in Allie's neck. There's such familiarity between them, such warmth. But what I'm seeing doesn't truly hit home until the girl lifts her head and turns her face toward me. The stubborn pout of her lips, the freckles across her cheek. I could be looking at Allie at four years old. Except this child's gaze is a bright, clear blue.

I stand there for a few moments, watching them. Allie and her daughter. There's something different about Allie now, beyond the new hairstyle, the unfamiliar clothes. It takes me a minute to pinpoint what it is. And then I see. That way Allie used to have of holding herself, as if she knew she was being watched—that's gone. That tension has eased from her shoulders. She looks like any other young woman standing on a beach.

As a wave slides up the shore and hits her feet, she turns, shifting her daughter on her hip. That's when she catches sight of me. For a brief moment, something in her face contracts. One hand goes up to her daughter's back, as if to protect her. Then the moment passes, and slowly, she lifts her hand in greeting.

For a few seconds, I can only stand with my shoes sinking into the sand, taking in her familiar features. Then, finally, I lift my hand and wave—hesitantly, as if we're meeting for the first time.

ACKNOWLEDGMENTS

All told, it took about five years to bring this book from a one-sentence idea to the novel you're holding now. During this often-rocky journey, I've been very fortunate to have the support of many talented, kind, and inspiring people, and it's a delight to get to acknowledge them now.

Many thanks to my incredibly supportive and levelheaded agent, Julia Kenny, who has been a champion for me throughout this process.

I'm so grateful to my editors, Laura van der Veer and Shari MacDonald Strong at Thomas & Mercer, for their help in strengthening the book's plot and structure, as well as the copyediting team for catching small errors and inconsistencies in the text.

"Thank you" is not really a sufficient sentiment for my dear friend Ashleigh Pedersen, who not only provided editorial feedback on countless versions of this book but was also my writing retreat partner, wine-and-write buddy, and unflagging cheerleader throughout the writing of this manuscript. This book has flourished because of her encouragement, humor, and long-standing belief in my creative dreams.

I'm lucky enough to be part of two wonderful writing groups in Austin that have supported and uplifted me over the past few years. Many thanks to the SYNTs (Meg Halpin, Sara Hannon, Melinda Barsales, Amanda Rohlich, Becca Baughman, Lauren Slusher, Colleen Nothern, Caroline Wright, and Sara Saylor), who remind me weekly that writing is as much about making each other snort with laughter as it is about baring one's soul on the page. And so much appreciation to the Friday Night Salon (Kelley Janes, Anna Stewart, Justin Follin, Dorothy Meiburg-Weller, and Sebastian Langdell) for inspiring me with their creativity, receptivity, and gorgeous prose.

I'm very lucky to be doing my work alongside the writers in the Fresh Ink community, whose motivation and passion consistently reinforce my belief in the importance of creativity. Particular thanks to everyone who showed up for those Sunday Creative Community writing sessions to write together and provide support and solidarity as we worked on our various projects.

I'm deeply thankful for the early readers of this manuscript who provided feedback that helped me develop the story on a deeper level: Emily Bloom, Kelly Ramsey, and Jennifer March Soloway.

And many thanks to Leticia Clawson, who was kind enough to help me out with Spanish-language questions.

I'd also like to thank my father, Alex Knowles, for always expressing the belief that I could get this book published.

I'm very grateful to Dorothy and Eddie Gumbert, who provided me with a home away from home when I needed a solitary retreat for my writing.

Two wise guides helped me enormously in developing the courage to put my work out into the world: I owe a massive debt of gratitude to Leonor Diaz and Danielle LaSusa.

I'd also like to thank the many brilliant writing teachers I've had over the years, at the University of Texas creative writing program, USC School of Professional Writing, and Tulane University—in particular, Janet Fitch, Michael Parker, and Dale Edmonds.

Professor Edmonds led the very first writing workshop I ever took and offered copious guidance and support during my years at Tulane. I still have the note he scribbled on the bottom of a story I wrote for his class back in 2002: "I want a copy of your first book, suitably inscribed, so I can say, 'Look! I spotted one!'" Well, Professor Edmonds, twenty-odd years later, here it is! Thank you so much for starting me down this path.

ABOUT THE AUTHOR

Photo © 2023 Bailey Toksöz

Jaime deBlanc holds an MA in creative writing from the University of Texas at Austin. Her short fiction has been published in *Catapult*, *Post Road*, and *Meridian*, and she has been the recipient of a MacDowell Fellowship and a Lighthouse Works Fellowship. She lives in Austin, Texas, where she is currently at work on her second novel.

You can follow her on Instagram at @freshinkaustin or visit her website at www.jaimedeblanc.com.